DISEASE

Second Edition.

First published in 2021.

ISBN: 978-1-915251-36-7

Cover design: © The Pretty Little Design Co.

Editor: Lawrence Editing - www.lawrenceediting.com

Map of Beurre: BritsxBazaar

DISEASE

book two

KATIE LOWRIE

To cress,

MY LIFE IS SO MUCH BETTER WITH YOU IN IT

Author's Note

*This is the second edition of Disease and is the follow on from the
second edition of Disorder.
There are new chapters, new POVs, and some other changes inside.*

For any content warnings you may need, please head to my website.

*P.S. A quick heads up: the vocabulary, grammar, and spelling of
Disease is written in British English.*

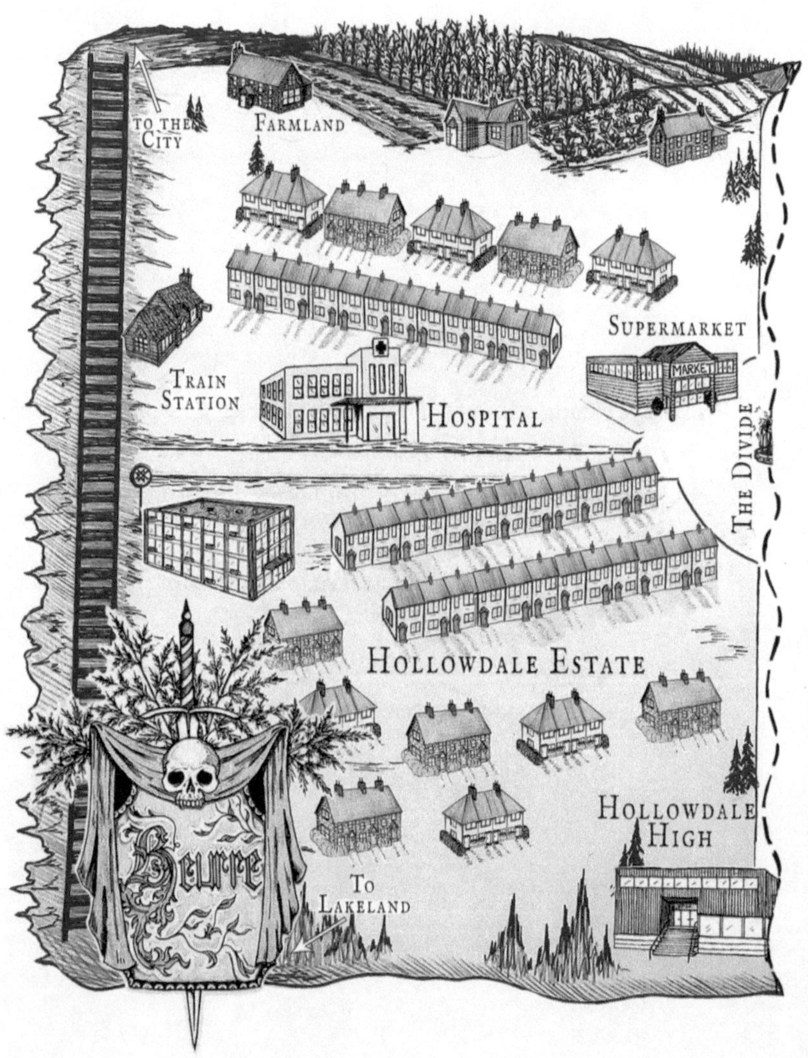

TO THE CITY
FARMLAND
TRAIN STATION
HOSPITAL
SUPERMARKET
MARKET
THE DIVIDE
HOLLOWDALE ESTATE
HOLLOWDALE HIGH
TO LAKELAND

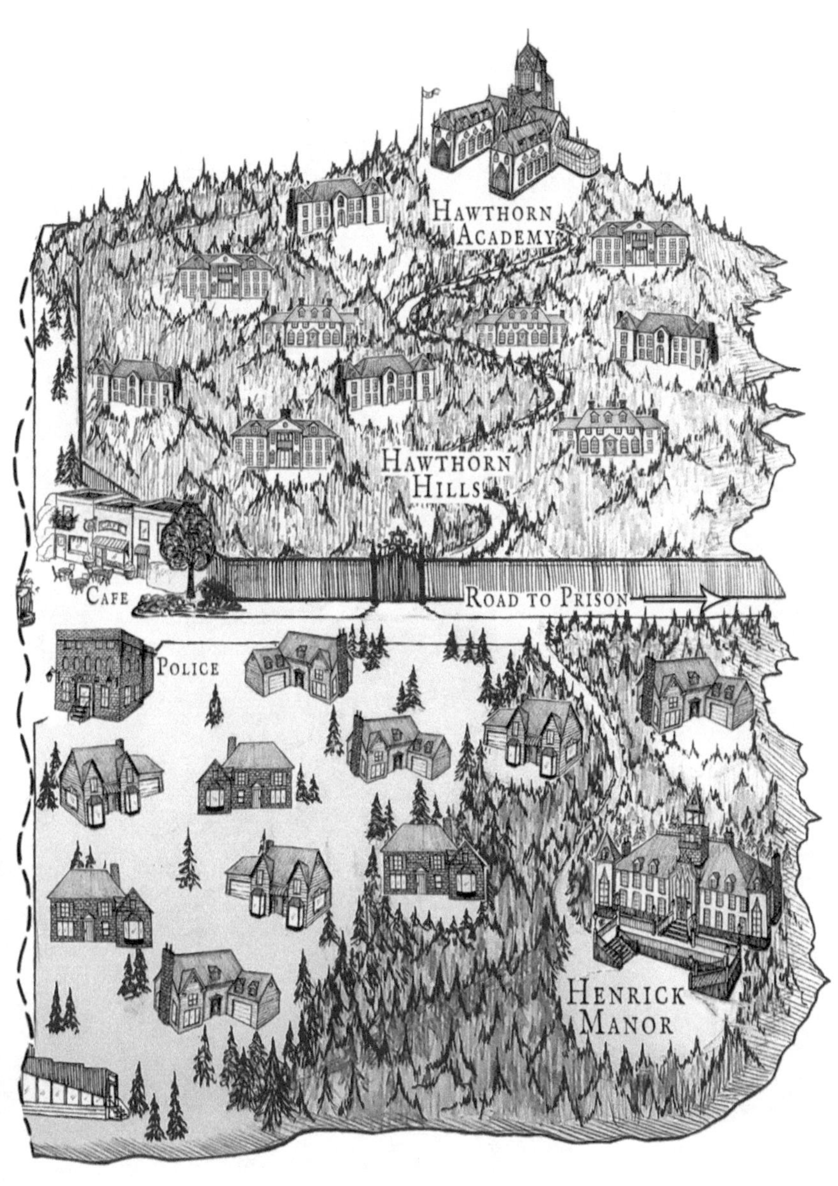

Hawthorn Academy
Hawthorn Hills
Cafe
Road to Prison
Police
Henrick Manor

DISEASE

noun -
a harmful development
something that
is considered very bad in people or society

Prologue

I LOOKED AT HIM, unable to push out the breath I'd held onto since our eyes locked, and wondered how I'd found myself in this position… again.

Something here wasn't right. I just couldn't put my finger on what it was.

He looked back at me with equal distrust in his eyes, and the showdown after the fashion show came to mind.

The image was the same, even if the setting was different. I remembered the dark indigo of his eyes, the way they'd burned in hatred, all aimed towards me; a hatred that had been there long before he'd ever met me.

'Poor little Skylar. How does it feel being the last to know?'

I broke out into all-body shivers, unable to move. Unable to breathe.

We were both standing in the middle of the hall, with nowhere to hide. Nowhere for me to run, either. All eyes were on us—the sideshow that had taken over the New Year's Gala for everybody's entertainment.

One day soon, I hoped there would be a charity function where I wasn't the main attraction.

'It w-was *you*.' My voice left me in a whisper, not wanting to put the thought in my mind out into the universe. Vocalising it would only make it worse.

'It w-was?' he asked, a glint of menace in his eyes.

'You did it.'

'I did what?'

The relaxed posture was at odds with the anger on his face as he mocked me—mocked my stutter. It was something I barely did anymore, yet he was able to bring it out of me as if it had never left in the first place.

I thought back over the previous year, ever since I was stabbed before Easter, and I could only conclude that somehow, it was all my fault. That somehow, I had brought it all upon myself with my actions and decisions.

Was I too trusting, too stupid to see the truth, to see the writing on the wall?

Or had I let my lust guide me like a stupid, naïve girl?

Part One
Revenge

One

OLLIE'S BETRAYAL sat heavy in my stomach.

Heavy in my heart.

At first, I wanted to cry. Well, at first I *did* cry. Have you ever been stabbed and then woke up to the pain of it? That shit hurts! But even after the numbness travelled through me from the copious amount of drugs the hospital gave me, I still cried for me, for him, for us. For everything I'd thought to be true but was clearly a blind bitch about.

For the first week, I couldn't understand where I'd gone so wrong, but as time went on and more memories resurfaced, I realised there were warning signs the entire time I'd known him. Clover had warned me against him from the start, and Leo and Griff—who were his best mates, so really should have been a massive indicator for me—cautioned me multiple times, but I always chose not to listen to any of them. Thinking I knew best. I told myself I *knew* him; I *understood* him. Fat load of shit that was.

It turned out I knew nothing. Nothing about Oliver, but also nothing about Griff or Leo, either, and *nothing* about their true motives. Or the fact that my dad was apparently the cause of all the turmoil. A man I'd never met, nor really wanted to, was somehow fucking me up for reasons unknown to me.

The worst part of it all? I felt stupid. Confused.

And trust me, feeling both stupid and confused were two of my biggest hates in life. Had been ever since I was a kid. I hated feeling like I wasn't in the know, like somebody else knew something I didn't. Or worse, I hated being the last to know.

Yet that was exactly what happened. The fact they were all laughing at me, and my stupidity, all year was enough to make my blood boil in my veins. Oh, how funny it must've been to laugh behind my back at how Skylar Crescent couldn't see through the falsehoods and lies spewed in her direction. Couldn't distinguish the difference between genuine affection and somebody working behind the scenes to ruin their life, ruin their dignity, and their self-worth.

The first indicator things were worse than I realised? Waking up in an actual hospital and not just the hospital wing at the academy. The second indicator? I woke up all alone. There was nobody sitting vigil in the chair by my side and I couldn't recall hearing any visitors during my recent—albeit brief—bouts of consciousness.

Things after the stabbing were all a blur, and the days that followed waking up in a hospital bed weren't much better either. The nurses were nice enough, and the doctor was too when he finally showed up.

I'd been lucky, or so he said. *He*—whoever *he* was—had stabbed me in the abdomen, and the knife hit no major organs, meaning I was going to make a full recovery. Whoever stabbed me had left the weapon in my stomach, which, according to my notes, was what saved my life. The blood loss would've been a lot worse if the knife had been removed and I may not have survived.

Thank you, my attempted murderer, for the consideration.

The police had arrived at the hospital not long after I'd regained full consciousness and told me the weapon had been tested for fingerprints already and that none were present—or so they said. I knew the people I was dealing with were rich motherfuckers, and there was no way to know just *who* they paid off to live in their back pockets for fun.

The police made it clear, though, that they found it unusual I hadn't tried to remove the knife myself, or at least touch it in my delirious state. It took a lot of restraint to refrain from asking them whether they'd ever been stabbed, and if so, did they remove their own knives?

They'd also asked me whether I had any enemies, anyone who hated me enough to literally *stab me*, but I couldn't think of anybody in particular.

My memory of the entire encounter was lost to me, and they filled in the blanks in a way that implied they thought I was lying about my lack of memory, but I wasn't going to rise to their shit. Not remembering anything that happened was so fucking cliché it hurt, but it didn't change the fact that the last I could recall was fleeing from Ollie after he'd shown his true self.

According to them, Odette Aston was found lying a short distance away from me and had suffered multiple stab wounds from the same knife. Unlike mine, her wounds were fatal. No matter what they said, I couldn't wrap my mind around the fact that Odette was dead. Yeah, she was a total bitch and yeah, she'd made my year so far pretty shit, but even a stone-cold bitch didn't deserve to be killed in a school hallway. Nobody did.

The police left after telling me about Odette and said their detectives would be along within the week to talk to me. *Yay for me.*

With nothing to do but lie in a hospital bed and heal, my thoughts turned to Ollie often and to his entire game. To the way he'd made me believe I meant something to him. Something more than friends. Something that would last a lifetime. Fuck, I'd even lost my virginity to him and fallen out with my best—and only—friend because she had known he was shady and I didn't believe her. Nope, all I did was accuse her of being jealous, which was laughable now that I had time to look back on the first half of this school year and fully dissect it.

I was still trying to grasp the fact that *so much* had happened in such a short period. God, before I started at Hawthorn, the most I had to worry about was my mum or Andy spending all of my earnings on alcohol and tobacco. A worry I'd gladly go back to. Okay, maybe not *gladly,* but still, you get my point.

I'd hoped that *maybe* Clover would come and visit me, but so far I hadn't seen hide nor hair of her. I knew we fought before all the shit happened and that she'd been right all along, but I was so desperate to make amends with her, I wouldn't even care if she came into my room and said, 'I told you so.' At least if she said that to my face, she'd be here. But no, nothing of the sort. Maybe she couldn't forgive me, or maybe we hadn't been true friends after all.

Wouldn't be the first time I was wrong about somebody's true intentions, would it?

AFTER TWO WEEKS, I felt the worst I'd ever felt in my life.

Not physically.

No, physically, I felt great. My wound had healed for the most part, and I felt more clear-headed than ever before.

No, my issue was mental. Mentally, a thick fog surrounded me constantly. A dark, red, forever swirling fog that wouldn't dissipate no matter what I did; no matter what I thought about. I was drowning in my mind and there wasn't much I could do about it.

Fuck. I wasn't even sure I *wanted* to do anything about it.

'Miss Crescent. Are you *sure* there isn't anything more you can tell us?'

I shook my head, bringing myself back into the land of the living, my mind having wandered back to the night of my stabbing. Something that happened with an alarming frequency, yet I still couldn't remember past fleeing from the pool. It was like my mind had blocked out the horror, never to reveal it again.

Detective Smith was standing at the foot of my bed, staring at me in a way that made me think he was trying to scare me and shake me into telling him the truth. If only I knew what the truth was. 'Did Odette Aston have any enemies?'

'Er...' I trailed off. The girl didn't have enemies as much as she had people who detested her and people who feared her. She ruled the school alongside the rest of *The Set* and *Sect*, and it wasn't as if people overly loved them. Not sure how I could explain all that to these two detectives, though, so I went with, 'She was a part of the mean girl group.'

'Yes, we've been told by a'—he looked down at his sheet of paper—'Miss Luck that you were being harassed by Odette and her friends. Lucky for you, your wound erases you from the suspect list.'

'Lucky for me?' I sputtered, mad he'd implied I was *lucky* to have been stabbed.

'That was poor wording,' his colleague, Detective Saunders, piped up. 'What my co-worker means is that the situation means you aren't a suspect.'

Damn straight I'm not a suspect!

'No shit,' I mumbled under my breath. I thought Saunders heard me, but he didn't ask me to clarify or repeat it, so guess I was off the hook. Lucky me.

See. That was what a real *lucky* should sound like.

'Thank you for informing me,' I said, being all extra formal, which I thought might make them suspicious, but neither of their faces changed.

And although I was no longer a suspect in Odette's death, it didn't mean I wasn't still being considered as having had something to do with Olivia's murder. I'd hoped that nearly dying myself would have excluded me, but apparently, I would have had to have been stabbed that night too to be in the clear, and I doubted my guts could've handled that.

As I watched the two detectives in front of me, I had to do my best to hold in the giggles that wanted to burst free. I'd always watched police dramas on TV and thought that certain scenarios must have been exaggerated or invented for the viewers—surely the police weren't that stupid and ridiculous in real life?

But apparently, I was wrong, because my current encounter was only proving they were indeed that ridiculous *and* stupid in real life. Even my alibi the night of the Gala wasn't enough for them not to see me as a suspect in Olivia's death. According to them, I could have snuck out that night with Ollie being none the wiser and returned before he woke. My supposed motive was the bullying I'd suffered at the hand of *The Set.*

In what could only be described as a rehearsed movement, the two of them got up out of their chairs at the same time. It was like the two of them had perfected it to intimidate people they were interrogating or questioning.

'Thank you, Miss Crescent. We'll be in touch if we need to ask you any more questions,' Detective Saunders said, and it solidified what I'd figured out during my time knowing them —he was the nice one.

I waved goodbye, the action limited by the railings of the hospital bed, and my facial expression showed my true feelings towards them, but they didn't turn around to see it.

Joy filled me, knowing they were leaving and I'd have some peace, but then it hit me. Once again, I'd be alone with my own thoughts.

Able to wallow in my self-pity.

Having time alone right now wasn't the best for my mental health. Then again, neither was spending time with Mum and Andy.

Swings and roundabouts and all that jazz.

But after ten minutes of solitude, another knock came at my door. I didn't have the strength to prop myself up on the bed to look. If it was a nurse, they'd come back later if it wasn't urgent, and they'd burst in if it was. That was the way of hospitals.

But then the knock came again—a gentle knock. One so quiet I thought I was making it up at first, but then it repeated, slightly louder, and I fought the heaviness in my neck to lift my head and look in the door's direction.

Clover was standing there, waiting for me to give her permission to enter like it hadn't been over two weeks since we last saw one another, and I almost choked on my shock. The look on her face was one of worry mixed with what could only be described as shame, and I hated to admit even to myself that it gave me a little bit of happiness to know she was feeling so wretched about it all.

'Come in,' I said, loud enough for her to hear me, then I watched as she made her way into my room tentatively, the fear clear in her small steps.

The moment she reached my bed, she burst into tears, sobs wracking her entire body, and the sight made me sad—the happiness inside dissipated as fast as it arrived. The part that worried me, though, was I couldn't tell if I was sad for her or for me. I had every right to be upset at what happened.

My frustration was climbing, and it felt like I had no outlet for it. *Eurgh.* Everything was so fucked!

'Sky,' Clo stuttered out on a sob. 'I am so, so, so very sorry.'

'What are *you* sorry for?' I snapped, a wave of anger hitting me at her apology. What exactly did *she* have to apologise for? Not like she knew what they were doing behind my back.

'For what happened to you,' she whispered, her bottom lip wobbling. 'I knew shit was going down at the show, and I know I warned you, but I should have tried harder to make you see. To get you to listen.'

'No,' I said, and her face crumpled. 'You don't need to apologise for that. I should have listened to you, but I didn't. Plus, not like you could've known that somebody was going to kill Odette and then stab me.'

I tried to smile and pass it all off as one big joke, but I wasn't sure my tone gave enough levity for the situation. Her eyes shifted, darting to look around the room instead of at me. Was that a sign of her guilt? Had she known all along they planned to stab me—whoever *they* were? Or was I just being suspicious? Seeing things in my mind that weren't really there?

The counsellor the hospital assigned me had told me I

would find it hard to trust people again. That I'd see shadows and deceit for quite some time before I felt I could open up, and seeing as I'd barely had friends before Hawthorn, and then the first ones I got tried to destroy and potentially end my life, I trusted she was right.

'True.' Clo let out a small giggle but snapped her mouth closed when it registered. 'But I could have followed you once you left the hall, instead of doing what I always do, which is act like a bitch. I just watched you run away without thinking about your safety.' A gasp bubbled up, and she began to sob once more.

I wondered if she was going to mention her kiss with Griff that the girls showed on the video, but I didn't want to push her if she wasn't ready to tell me about it. Which was bullshit really, because I'd never hidden anything from her—especially not something as huge as that.

'Anyway,' she continued with a hiccup, 'I'm sorry for our fight. I should have never stopped being your friend. You needed me to be there for you, unbiased, and I couldn't even do that right. There's so much I need to tell you, but I don't think now's the right time.'

'The police mentioned you spoke to them?'

'Yeah, just routine. You know how it is.' She shrugged her shoulders, and even though the action was cavalier, I had to admit I did in fact know how it was. I'd been questioned after Olivia's death, after all. 'I've got to ask you something, and I'm not sure I'm ready for your answer.'

'You know you can ask me anything,' I said, not a clue what she'd ask but curious nonetheless. What kind of question would put such a deep frown line across her forehead?

'Are you planning to come back to Hawthorn?' Her question was tentative, but her eyes blazed with an emotion I couldn't place. She wanted me to answer one way, that much was obvious, but I wasn't sure what answer would make her happy. I wasn't sure if *any* answer would make her happy.

So I gave her the truth. 'Of course.' To me, it was a no-brainer. There was no way I was letting them all win. 'I'll be back as soon as the hospital lets me leave. I'm already annoyed I'll miss the first couple days back.'

School started again the next day, as the Easter two-week break came to an end, and I was just glad it meant I'd missed no classes or mock exams or anything that would affect my scholarship status. I was determined to complete the year to the best of my ability, even if it killed me.

Something that had somehow become a potential outcome to consider.

'Are you sure that's a good idea?' Clo said, the look on her face telling me she quite possibly thought I'd gone mad. Maybe I had a little, but fuck, why should those rich elitist fuckers decide whether or not I obtained my A-Levels at a fancy establishment like Hawthorn?

'Nope,' I told her, knowing in my gut it was probably one of the worst ideas I'd had in a long time—though trusting Ollie had been *the* worst idea I'd had, and nothing was going to top *that* anytime soon. 'But I'm gonna do it anyway.'

'Then I'll be by your side the whole time.' Clover leaned down, grabbed my hand in hers, and squeezed it tightly. 'That fucker is going to pay for what he's done to you.'

I nodded, glad I had my partner in crime back, but then realised she wasn't going to say anything first, so I decided to be the one to bring up the subject of Griff.

'So, I haven't heard from Griff,' I said, hoping she'd take the bait. She didn't. So I continued, 'Did he know about any of it?

All of it?' I had to ask. I had to know who was involved in my torment and who had to pay.

'I think he should be the one to talk to you about it,' she said, as vague an answer as she could get away with. 'I know you must be wondering about that kiss.' She shuffled slightly, her face unsure.

'Of course I am.' It was blunt and to the point, but I didn't want to pussyfoot around with Clover anymore. She was the person I could be the most honest with, the most myself, and I didn't want something like a kiss with Griff to come between us. I added under my breath, 'Not like you've felt comfortable telling me much this year.'

'I was so upset about everything that had happened with you, Sky. It was that day I called you all those horrid names, remember? I just dropped the bomb, then ran off like a total bitch, and Griff followed me to talk me off the ledge. I promise I hadn't expected him to.

'Once we got back to the room, he said some really nice things to me. Things that made me feel better, made me feel important and wanted. It was me who kissed him first. It was my fault.' Her green eyes were staring into mine, wanting me to know how sorry she was about it all, and I wanted to believe her and forgive her straight away, but something was holding me back. 'He wanted to tell you straight away, and I begged him not to.'

'Why?'

'Because I didn't want you to be mad at him or me. I didn't want you to think badly of us. We were lying to you, and I felt like shit about it, because after that first kiss, we realised how much we liked one another and couldn't stop.'

Disgust at myself settled in my gut.

Was I really that much of a judgemental twat? Did she

genuinely believe I would've been mad at them or thought badly of them, just because they liked each other?

Why would it matter to me if they kissed, after all? Not like she'd kissed Ollie behind my back.

Yeah, it was a surprise it had been *Griff* she'd kissed and not Leo, but that was all, and the only reason it hurt me at the Fashion Show was because they had blindsided me. Plus, I'd been shocked at the whole *having cameras spying on me in my bedroom* aspect of the situation—something I hadn't forgotten and would need to correct if I was to return to Hawthorn.

'Well, I don't,' I told her, 'and I wouldn't have if you'd told me at the time either.'

'I know that *now*. Can you forgive me?' she asked, widening her green eyes, trying to look as cute as possible so I'd bend.

It totally worked.

'Yeah, of course I can, silly.' Sometimes, it was easier to just leave stuff behind and move on. Forgive but never forget.

'I'm so glad you didn't die, Sky.' A sob left Clo and a twinge of guilt wracked through me. Over the last week, I'd had a lot of terrible thoughts about her and assumed she didn't care about me at all.

Clover leaned down, putting the two of us at eye level, her eyes glittering with unshed tears. She hugged me to her, and although she was trying to avoid squeezing too tight because of my stab wound, I could sense just how much love she was putting into the hug.

'Let's not fall out again,' Clo said, and I just smiled at her.

I mean, it's all very well her saying it, but like so many things, it's easier said than done.

Two

MY RECOVERY HAD TAKEN SLIGHTLY LONGER than anticipated, and it was pissing me off. The first week of May came and went, and I still hadn't returned to Hawthorn, which made me itch, because I didn't want those fuckers thinking they'd got away with everything. They hadn't run me off, and it annoyed me they thought they'd succeeded in whatever intimidation scheme they came up with.

Classes had returned two weeks ago, and Clover—who had returned to school—told me on one of her visits that the boys had gone back to ruling the school with Ophelia and Oralie at their sides. *The Sect* were back in top form and were acting like the last seven months hadn't happened—like they'd never stopped talking to *The Set* or formed a friendship with a scholarship student.

Odette's funeral had taken place during the break, but Clover had no information about it to tell me except for some snippets she'd heard second-hand. Not like she'd attended that shit show—her words—so all we knew was that the boys went and stayed pretty silent and moody throughout the whole thing.

With Odette gone (in polite terms), Ophelia was the

natural leader replacement for their stupid tradition. She'd been as much of a bitch towards me as Odette and had given me my fair share of bruises over the last seven months, so really, she was the perfect fit. *What a bitch.*

'Are you sure you're ready?' Clover asked me, packing my pyjamas into a large duffle bag.

I watched her, trying to determine her feelings from her expression. 'To leave the hospital, or to go back to school?'

'Both, I guess.' Clo was definitely more worried about it all than I was. If anything, I was buzzing with energy at the thought of returning. The revenge boiling in my blood wasn't going to stay dormant for much longer without an explosion.

After *finally* being discharged, I was heading straight back to school. I'd already missed enough classes and fuck, wasn't like I wanted to go back to stay with my mum and Andy for even a day. *I've already suffered enough, thank you very much.*

'For the millionth time, Clo,' I growled. 'I'm more than ready! I want to do this. No, I *need* to do this for my sanity. I can't let them continue to swan around as if they didn't nearly end my life. Until they understand what they've done wrong, I won't be able to move on. Plus, I *need* Ollie to look me in the eye when he tells me everything was a lie.'

'Didn't he kinda already do that?' Clo asked in a tentative tone. I'd told her what had happened with Ollie after the show, both the mean words he'd said and the evil glint in his eye as he'd said them.

I sputtered out, 'W-well, yeah, kind of, but not fully.'

Yes, Ollie had looked me dead in the eyes when he told me I didn't belong at Hawthorn and that I never had, so his feelings on that were pretty clear, but I needed him to look me in the eye and tell me my first time was a lie. That he'd felt no ounce of affection towards me and had taken my virginity simply because he was a cruel bastard who could.

Clo's green eyes shone with sympathy for me, and I could tell she already believed I was doomed.

'If you have to, then I get it, and I'll be here to wipe away your tears.'

'No,' I said, annoyed she'd even suggested I would cry over him anymore. 'I will not shed another tear over that bastard.'

'Big words there, Sky.'

'Maybe, but not like it's a lie.' I shrugged at her, and she nodded in agreement, then continued to help me pick up all of my stuff. No more needed to be said. Not like I'd listen to her, anyway.

I took one last look around the hospital room, then I was ready to go. Clover had somehow convinced Ms Hawthorn to arrange a car for me. Pretty sure she had done it begrudgingly and wasn't too pleased about it, though. Sure, she thought I'd brought too much trouble to her academy as it was.

'Let's do this.' My voice gave off a confidence I wasn't feeling inside.

Fake it until you make it.

Hawthorn Academy still loomed at the top of the hill—of course it did; not like it had upped and moved—and the ascent towards it still gave me the same anxious feeling in the pit of my stomach as it had that first day back in September. Maybe it was even worse now that I knew the full extent of what could happen to a girl within those walls—or in the surrounding woodland.

Clover sat silently beside me the entire journey, and I knew she was as nervous as me. I could also tell she felt guilty about everything that had happened and knew in the future she'd be there at my side no matter what. She locked her hand in mine, and it was cold to the touch, like sitting next to an ice block, or like when you spent a little too long in the freezer aisle at the local supermarket.

I shivered, and I swore the cold was leaving her body and entering my bones.

'What are you nervous about?' I asked, breaking the frigid silence. 'Something major happen while I've been gone that I should know about?'

'Hm?' Her eyes shifted around the inside of the car, then stopped to take in the leather of the seats in front of us. One of the stitches was loose and I couldn't help but fixate on it while waiting for her to gather a response. 'Nope, nothing major. Why?'

Instantly, my back was up, and I was on my guard. It sounded as if she was keeping something from me, and there was no way I was letting that slide like I had earlier in the year.

'Clo. If you've got shit to say, then say it. I'm not having what happened before starting up again,' I said, nipping her reluctance in the bud straight away.

'Right.' She took a deep breath. 'I was sort of hoping we could wait to talk back at our dorm.' Her eyes flitted to the back of the driver's head. I supposed it made sense she didn't want to say much in front of him. For all we knew, he could be here as a spy for the academy—or worse, *The Sect.*

Wow, paranoid much? Which reminds me...

'Our room had a camera in it... It may even have had a microphone, too. How do we know it's gone?' I had every right to be suspicious. We'd been none the wiser, and for the last few weeks in the hospital, I'd gone over just how many conversations they may have been privy to. There were multiple times where Clo had dragged me out of the library to our room to talk in private, but all along we'd have been better off staying where we were.

'I've had our room gutted from top to bottom. There's no way a camera is hiding in there now. I forced that old witch Hawthorn to have the school pay for a bug jammer too, so if anything is planted in the future, it won't work.'

'How did you pull that off?' I asked, my scepticism rife. The woman had barely acknowledged any of the evil shit *The Set* had pulled on me last term. Fuck, she'd even had the audacity to blame *me* for the majority of what *they* did.

'Let's just say, I twisted her arm,' Clo replied vaguely. Really, did it matter how she'd managed it? Nope. As long as it was in place, I was happy.

The car pulled up to the front of the school, and straight away my body broke out into chills—chills that increased when I spotted Griff standing by the steps of the Academy, tall and imposing. He must be waiting for us.

What. The. Fuck?

'Did you tell him I was coming back today?' I asked Clover, and from her wince in response, I had my answer. For the last couple of weeks, Clo had made it seem as if she hadn't spoken to any of them since I got hurt out of solidarity.

'No, Sky, I swear I didn't.' Clo's face had gone white, draining itself of colour, and I felt a little stab of guilt for doubting her so fast.

The driver got out of the car and came around to the passenger door to open it for us both. With every step he took closer, my anxiety climbed. There were only a few moments left until I was officially back at Hawthorn Academy, and even though I'd convinced myself it was for the best while lying in my hospital room, it all felt a little different looking up at those ugly gargoyles standing watch over the main entrance, their beady eyes surveying my every move.

Clo exited the car first, but in no time at all, I too was exiting the vehicle and trying my best not to black out or lose my nerves. It was a lot easier to believe in myself and act confident when I wasn't looking into a pair of meadow-green eyes. Eyes that were glinting in the sunlight, trying to gain access to the darker recesses of my mind. Eyes that belonged to Griffin Cooper of all people.

'Hey,' Griff muttered. His hands were wringing together, and I could tell he was worried about my reaction to seeing him there. As he should be. 'How have you been?'

I reckoned it was the first time he hadn't greeted me with his carefree, cheeky grin. Even though I was pissed at him, it was odd. Like something was missing from the picture that made up Griff.

'Fine,' I replied, blunt as fuck. I couldn't look him in the eye, my anger rising simply from being in his vicinity.

He chuckled, anxious. Ever since we'd met, he'd been the confident one, and I'd been the one stuttering my way through life. I doubted he'd ever heard me be so short with him—or with anyone for that matter.

Now, I felt like I was a completely different person. Like I'd been born anew. A phoenix risen from the ashes, brushing off the dirt and debris from the previous terms. Ready to fight again.

'You look well, considering,' Griff said.

Really, Griff? I look well considering? I laughed in his face with derision. 'Considering the fact I've spent the last month in a hospital bed? Or considering the fact I was *stabbed?*'

'Yeah...' he trailed off, not sure what to say. A first for him, I was certain. 'Considering that.'

Clover looked towards him, and I saw red. I wasn't sure what made me snap, but something did. Maybe it was the expression on her face or the fact she looked torn between us both.

'Something you wanna say, Clo?' I turned on the spot to face her, and although she'd changed her expression the moment I swivelled towards her, she hadn't changed it quick enough. I saw the sheepish look she tried to cover.

'Nope,' she replied, hesitant. The two of them were pissing me off more than usual. I needed to talk to Griff alone away from Clover. Otherwise, I'd never get a real answer from him, but I wasn't ready for that yet. I wasn't sure *when* I'd be ready.

'Skylar, can we please talk?' he pleaded, causing me to freeze on the spot. He'd used my name. Not *New Girl*. Not *baby-cakes* or *babydoll*. But Skylar.

'Not today,' I told him. Even standing outside of the main entrance, those two gargoyles and their buggy eyes looking at me, was a lot harder than I thought it would be. Full disclosure? I thought I would waltz back in, taking names, all while showing them the personal brand of hell only I could deliver.

It would be so easy for my mind to enter a dark space being back and I couldn't allow myself to crumble. Because let's be honest, no matter what I did or how I acted, underneath my façade, I was still that same small, scared, stupid Skylar. The one who'd let a boy deceive her for months and never noticed a thing. Or, should I say, noticed things but chose not to believe them and ignored her best friend over indigo eyes and a chis-elled jaw.

'I understand,' Griff said after a moment, his voice pained. 'But you *will* talk to me at some point?'

'Maybe.'

'Let me just say one thing.' Griff took a step closer to us. 'I'm sorry that I've let you down and disappointed you, Sky. I'll do better, I promise. And when you're ready to talk, I'll be waiting, okay?'

I swallowed the emotion that bubbled up inside of me at his words, not wanting to dissect them out in the open.

'Come on, Sky.' Clo grabbed my arm and hooked hers with mine. 'Let's go to our room.' She nodded at Griff in goodbye, all nonchalant. I didn't pull away from her touch, but something inside of me recoiled.

This is Clover, Sky. She didn't stab you. I repeated the words in my head, hoping that if I said it enough, I might start to believe them.

Sure, she'd apologised to me, and I knew she'd meant what she said, but—and it was a big but—I didn't fully trust it.

'We'll see you later,' she told Griff, but her gaze was elsewhere, taking in everything and anything that wasn't him. Subtle, Clo.

I hadn't actually asked her much about them two, and outside of her brief explanation about their kiss, she hadn't given me much to go on either. Clover was the queen of holding shit back, even from her supposed best friend.

We made our way back to our room, luckily not bumping into anybody on our route—something I'd been scared of— but the fact we saw nobody only led to me feeling even more suspicious. If Griff had known we were coming, then there was no way the rest of them hadn't known. I'd put my very measly bank account on it.

Something wasn't right, and I was going to figure out exactly what it was.

Our room looked exactly the way I'd left it. Okay, maybe not *exactly* as I left it—my bed was made for once and there weren't any clothes lying around. I had a habit of being a bit of a mess.

Taking full advantage of the made bed, I flopped onto it with a deep sigh, my eyes searching the ceiling for some kind of sign that I was doing the right thing, but I knew there wasn't anything up there for me. There never was.

'Clo, do you believe in fate?' My eyes remained on the ceiling, and I listened as Clo shuffled around the room before she sat down on her bed and settled up against the wall.

'What d'you mean?'

'Pretty simple question, Clo,' I replied with a chuckle, but there wasn't any humour in it. 'Do you believe everything happens for a reason? That everything in life is predetermined and we're just stumbling around on whatever path that's set out for us?'

'Yes and no, I guess, but I think you've got something right with the path thing. I believe everyone is on a path and that every decision is a path. Every path has a fork in the road, and once you decide where to go, you continue on until you reach the next fork. *You* are the deciding factor and *you* decide the fork to take. For me, life is a constant make up of all these different paths and decisions. Does any of that even make sense?' She chuckled, nervous.

I nodded. It made a certain kind of sense to me now that she'd put it out there. I had been given many *forks* since joining Hawthorn, and I'd chosen my path each time, consequences be damned. Like the path where I'd chosen to believe my boyfriend over my best friend.

After a few minutes, I realised I hadn't answered her. 'Yeah, I get you.'

'What about you? What do you believe?'

'Something similar, I suppose. I believe that everything happens for a reason. Because every decision, every move I've made, has led me to now. Led me to this conversation with you.' I took a deep breath, thinking back on the last seven months. On all the small decisions I'd made, both consciously and subconsciously, to get me here. 'Do you realise how many small factors led to this moment?' I asked, really getting into the subject. 'So, so many, Clo.'

'Would you make them all again? If you were given a choice? Knowing what you know now and all that.'

'*Every* decision?' I thought about it for approximately ten seconds. 'Of course I would, Clo. 'Cause I'm here now with you. You're the family I choose for myself.'

Three

WITH EVERY NEW day that passed, I continued to ignore Griff's presence.

If he really meant what he'd said about waiting until I was ready, then he could wait a few more days for me.

A new week began, and I had to return to my classes. I'd only briefly seen Leo across campus once, and I was yet to see Oliver, which wasn't helping my nerves in the slightest. The longer it took, the more my unease grew. Dread sat low in my gut every time I thought about how our first encounter would go. I wasn't sure if it would be worse if he ignored me, or if he attempted to actually talk to me. Both scenarios gave me enough anxiety that I couldn't think of them for too long without getting green around the gills.

'Do you think he'll ask to talk to me?' I'd asked Clo my first night back. 'The way Griff seemed to want to talk to me, I mean.'

Her face was sceptical. 'I doubt it, Sky. The boy's been acting like you don't exist ever since you went to hospital.'

'You think he'll ignore me, then? Leave me alone?'

'For your sake,' she said, raising an eyebrow in my direction, 'I hope so.'

Her words hadn't filled me with much hope, but at least

she was being honest with me, which was just as important. Honesty from Clover was a new step for us and I didn't want to do anything to ruin it.

My birthday was coming up soon, and I was worried they were all waiting until then to bring me back down to earth with a bang. I knew my bullies were aware of my birthday and that they'd probably try to give me some kind of treat for it. The kind of treat only they could deliver—if destroying somebody's personal property could ever be classed as a treat.

I woke up early Monday morning, ready for my first day back in class, spending a lot longer than usual in making myself presentable. My hair was curled to perfection, and the flicks of my eyeliner were as symmetrical as I could get them. Not to mention my lips were extra plump from the lip gloss I'd applied. It stung like a bitch, though.

I was making my way across campus for the first time when it happened.

I shit you not, as I reached the front of the main building, the entire atmosphere changed. It was the only way I could explain it. There was barely anybody in my eye line, the quad seemingly deserted, but I knew *he* was nearby. Watching me. I knew it in my blood—no, deep in my soul.

A titter carried itself on the wind and into my ears—an omen, if you want. An irritating laugh that could only belong to one of two people. Well, I suppose these days it could only belong to *one* person—the other one was dead.

Without intending to, my head followed the sound's direction.

And that was when I got my first Oliver sighting. The moment I'd both dreaded and sort of looked forward to in a totally masochistic way.

Standing together by the stairs of the main building were

Ophelia, Oralie, and Oliver. A pack; united. A menacing look on each of their faces that cut into me. When I made eye contact with Ollie, a trickle of fear ran up my spine. It was the first time I'd looked at him head-on since shit went down at the end of the fashion show and I still felt just as small as I had then. Just as insignificant.

I hated how he made me feel—which was not as indifferent as I'd told myself it would be while healing up in a hospital bed. I'd managed to kid myself it would be different, that I'd worked on myself, but there was no way I was going to let my brain fool me again.

I wanted to feel nothing for him. Badly.

But fuck.

The boy looked pretty fucking fine standing there, all while doing nothing at all. And I fucking hated him for it. I fucking hated him for making me feel worthless, and he really did make me feel worthless. A sour taste filled my mouth, or maybe it was bitter, like copper?

Frozen to the spot, unable to move, I stared back at them, wondering what my next move should be. I'd stayed still too long to resume as if nothing had happened, but I also didn't want to let on just how much their appearance was affecting me.

They all made me feel like absolute dogshit. Like I'd stepped out of shit and tried to pass myself off as something else. *I don't know, okay? I'm not great at explaining it.* But you know that feeling in your gut? The one that wouldn't go anywhere. That stayed with you, festered, eating up all the good inside? That was basically how I felt when thinking about them—about *him.*

Finally, the silence was broken.

'Eurgh.' The sound came from the back of Oralie's throat,

filled with phlegm. 'This bitch again.' Her grating voice called out in my direction, but all I could do was look at her, a blank expression on my face. I would not rise to it. No matter what shit they tried.

'God, I hoped she'd get the picture,' said Ophelia, joining in, a smug smile playing on her over-glossed lips. 'Didn't you Ollie, baby?'

I almost choked on my spit. Choked on the rancid, over-perfumed air that surrounded me.

Ollie didn't even look over in my direction. He wrapped an arm around Ophelia's shoulder and pulled her close to him, managing to keep his gaze averted.

'C'mon, babe. No need to look at the trash,' he said, his tone flat. It wasn't what I'd expected as his first words, but I'd take it. Calling me trash was a given, right? An easy get out. He squeezed Ophelia's shoulder, and I saw her wince from the strength of it. Nice to know that aspect of his behaviour hadn't changed. Abusive bastard. If I'd started to doubt my resolve, seeing Ophelia wince only solidified my anger towards him.

Tears welled in my eyes, but I knew I couldn't let them fall. Not until I was somewhere private and they couldn't see me. They weren't going to see me cry over them again. But my pillow? Well, that was a different story. I hadn't grown *that* much.

'And she *is* trash,' Oralie piped up again, trying to join in, but even from where I stood I could see the girl had become a third wheel. Where the fuck was Leo and why wasn't he with them? I thought the four of them would be attached at the hip.

'She's worse than that,' Ophelia said with emphasis. 'Skylar Crescent is the biggest twat I've ever met, and honestly, we're worth so much more than her. In every. Single. Way.'

'That's because you've never met yourself.' The words left

my lips before I registered them, but I was so glad they had. It was about time I made a stand against their bullshit!

The three of them swept by me, yet Ollie still hadn't caught my eye again. Not since we locked eyes the first moment I spotted them. He'd barely glanced at me after that full stop.

I hope he feels guilty as fuck for everything he's put me through.

I felt superior. If he couldn't look at me, that had to mean something, right? In my eyes, the fact he couldn't look at me meant that maybe he wasn't as unaffected as he wanted me to believe.

And *that*? That made me feel pretty fucking fantastic.

My birthday was a pretty silent affair, which was both a surprise and a blessing.

I mean, I was only turning seventeen, so not exactly that important of an age, but I'd imagined it going differently back when I was friends with the boys. Back when I had a boyfriend.

Slight touch, though, that everybody at school ignored me, and unlike what I'd suspected, there was no extra harassment during the day. If anything, people were going out of their way to *ignore* me—averting their gazes as I made my way down the hall, or when I sat down in class.

For dinner, Clover and I decided to stay in our room and order pizza, rather than facing the dining hall. I'd risked being in public enough for one birthday. I wasn't sure how Clo had got outside food okayed by Ms Hawthorn, though, and I had my suspicions that maybe she was still in contact with Griff.

'So Ms Hawthorn let us order pizza. No strings attached?' I

asked around a bite of my extra cheesy pizza, looking at Clo's face carefully for the slightest reaction.

'Yeah, it's your birthday.' She answered as if that was answer enough, but when it came to Ms Hawthorn, I highly doubted it. First of all, Clo had managed to *have words* with her about the camera in our room, and now pizza for my birthday... I just didn't trust it.

'Did Griff ask her for you?' I asked, trying to keep my suspicions out of my voice.

'Honestly, Sky, I've barely spoken to him, seeing as you haven't spoken to him yet. And I've told you, the thing between me and Griff wasn't that serious. It was a couple of kisses. No biggie.'

'Right, you've said. But if you have feelings for him, then that's okay. I would question you, but I wouldn't be mad.'

'It doesn't matter either way,' she replied, gazing at me intently. 'I'd never do that to you.'

I chose not to tell her that *technically*, she already had. 'Okay.'

We went back to eating in silence, both of us enjoying the food too much to talk about trivial things. My phone lit up from the floor, indicating I'd received a message. Griff had already sent me a birthday text that morning, and Clo was in the room with me, so I wasn't sure who else would be messaging me.

I picked up my phone and the message that greeted me surprised me.

HAPPY BIRTHDAY, STUTTER. ENJOY YOUR PIZZA.

'Are you okay? Your face has gone white.' Clo asked, and I nodded, not wanting to tell her who'd messaged me.

'I'm fine,' I replied, putting my phone down and picking up another slice as if Leo's message hadn't rocked me to the core.

'Have you heard from your mum today?' she asked, changing the subject.

Smooth, Clover.

'Nope.' I took another big bite, ignoring the pang of sadness that disappeared as soon as it arrived.

My mum didn't deserve my sadness. She hadn't even reached out to me, and okay, I hadn't expected gifts or anything, but I had at least expected a text. Just a quick one to say happy birthday, but apparently even that was too fucking hard for her. Shit, her only daughter was stabbed and the woman barely gave a fuck—I'd seen her once since, and only heard from her twice after that.

Not surprising, but hurtful nonetheless.

Four

JUNE CAME AND WITH IT, so did our mock exams. To say that I was shitting it was an understatement. I'd stopped eating because I was so nervous about them.

Not like I didn't have a valid enough reason to be nervous. I'd missed a bit of school while in the hospital and honestly, I hadn't tried to study much since being out of there, either, because whenever I'd attempted it, I got distracted within a minute. Sometimes by something slightly important, but usually just by the colour of the ceiling and the shadows playing there.

It was also kind of hard to keep up with my studies while planning an entire group of people's demises—in my mind—while trying not to focus on the fact somebody hated me enough to stab me. To literally *stab me*. That wasn't something you did when you merely disliked a person. No, that was something you did when you despised them. Thought they were a stain on society. And there were more than enough people at Hawthorn thinking that of me.

Yeah, there was the possibility that they'd targeted me because of what I saw and not due to who I was, but I wasn't ruling anything out. Didn't even really see much of whoever it was anyway.

Okay, okay. I had just forgotten whether I'd recognised them or not.

I was pissed at myself enough as it was and every night I fell asleep hoping I'd remember *something* about the person standing in front of me that night.

But I had absolutely no recollection.

I remembered entering the hallway, gasping, and then everything went black in my mind—fat lot of good that did me.

In my nightmares, the figure in front of me had no face. You know, like how the Grim Reaper or the Ghost of Christmas Future was depicted in every version of *A Christmas Carol*.

So yeah, I could remember fuck all.

Great.

THE INDOOR SPORTS hall was converted into a makeshift exam centre, and I really hated how it felt inside. All cold and impersonal. An echo of breathing, and pens on paper, was making me feel queasy.

There wasn't much hope swimming around my head for the exam, even though it was the last. The others had gone abysmally and that wasn't even me exaggerating.

The air in the hall was hot and stifling, and I couldn't help but break out into a sweat underneath my blazer. Or maybe that was due to my nerves.

I need to keep my scholarship at all costs.

Yes, things at school weren't exactly super, but becoming a student at Hawthorn was still one of the best things to ever happen to me. The chance to study subjects I'd only dreamed of before, plus the fact I had a real chance to attend a decent university, was enough to make me want to stay—stab wounds be damned.

I removed my blazer, hoping there were no dark patches on show. Wiping the sweat off my brow, I looked down at the exam paper in front of me for the gazillionth time.

Henry VIII never seriously abandoned the Catholic faith in the years 1529 to 1547. Discuss.

No matter how many times I stared at the words on the page, they made no more sense than they had the first time I'd read them an hour before. I'd been looking at them for so long they had blurred on the page, each letter all fuzzy around the edges.

Frustrated, I made a small grunting noise, then quickly looked around me to see if anybody had heard. Nobody turned to look at me, so I guess I was in the clear. My shoulders slumped, and instead of looking back at the page, I looked at the clock.

Not that looking at the minute hand moving made me feel any better. I'd been sitting here for an hour and all I'd written was my name, exam number, and an opening statement. Actually, an opening statement might be a slight exaggeration. It was five lines at most.

What the fuck was wrong with me?

I know this shit. The Tudor era was my jam and Henry VIII my absolute fave babe. I knew the answer to the question in my heart, but my head just wasn't delivering anything of use at that moment.

A cough came from my left and I rolled my eyes without meaning to. Because I knew who had coughed, and I could just tell it was on purpose.

I'd done my best the entire exam not to look over at Ollie, and fuck me, it had been *hard*. With his surname starting with B and mine starting with C, he was sitting at the desk parallel to mine in the aisle next to me.

He looked mighty fine—as usual—and as if he had no care in the world. *Nada.* His pen was flying across the page, and I could see from my position that he'd filled one of the sixteen-page answer booklets already. What a prick. There I was, unable to even fully comprehend the question, while he had no issues whatsoever in showing me up.

Ollie's presence at Hawthorn reminded me a little of Henry VIII and his court of friends. Whatever Henry said was law, and with *The Sect* being such a big deal, it was similar, wasn't it?

I turned away from Ollie and my thoughts. Comparing him to a long-dead tyrant wasn't what I needed to be doing, so instead, I watched the invigilators walking around listlessly, up and down the aisles in between the tables, making sure that nobody talked and shared answers.

I'd always wondered whether they played *Chicken* with each other. You know, the game where they both walked down the same aisle until one of them chickened out and turned around. Right now, I hoped they would just to alleviate my boredom—and to take my mind off the fact that I was strug-gling to remember any of the events that took place between 1529 and 1547.

Stop procrastinating, Sky.

Ollie coughed again, and I saw his smug little smirk out of the corner of my eye. The bastard knew I'd written barely anything and was relishing in it.

Note to self; must talk to Clover about a revenge plan *ASAP*.

THE MOCK EXAM FINALLY FINISHED, and all I wanted to do was get out of the stifling hall as fast as humanly possible, so I could get back to my room, grab a whiteboard, and plot revenge with my best friend. It really was the simple things in life.

I was so focused on where I *wanted* to be that I wasn't anywhere near focused enough on where I actually *was*.

'Will you get out of my way!' a shrill voice pierced my eardrum at the same time a sharp pain shot through my shoulder.

'Fuck.' My voice came out in a low whisper, but I kept my head held high and stayed facing the direction I was heading in —which was the exit to the motherfucking hall. I was so close to making it out of there free. Two steps max.

But nope.

Of course I couldn't just ignore Ophelia's cry without her getting even more mad.

'Will you mind where you're going?' she said, gripping my shoulder where she'd pushed me, to make sure I couldn't keep walking and minding my own business. *Bitch.*

'What?' I growled. 'I can't exactly get out of your way if you're holding me back, can I?'

'You've already got in my way, so you may as well stop and hear what I have to say.' Ophelia's lips curled up into a grin that sent a shiver down my spine. Oralie came up beside her and stood there, blocking my path even more.

I looked around to see if we were holding anybody up, but we were the last to leave the hall. The only others in the room were Ollie and Griff, which, unlike last term when that would've filled me with a sense of safety, now filled my heart with dread.

Clover was back in our room, not having had an exam during that period, and therefore, unable to save me. Not that I needed Clover to save me. I kept reminding myself that I was perfectly capable of rescuing myself, no man or friend needed.

Griff's eye caught mine, and he seemed to sympathise with me if the look in his eyes was an indicator, but he remained silent, watching it all play out. *Coward.* Or maybe it was get back for me ignoring him still?

'And what do you have to say?' I replied, my tone dead. 'Because I can't think of anything you could say that I'd care about.'

'You're an idiot,' Oralie snapped. After the last three hours, I couldn't even deny it in good conscience. I had acted like an idiot throughout the exam, and I was also an idiot when I didn't try harder to get out of the hall before they did. I hadn't even noticed they were behind me, which was unlike me. Usually, I was aware of my surroundings at all times.

'It wasn't me who wanted to talk to you anyway.' She flicked her long hair behind her shoulder and turned away from me. Dismissing me already.

My forehead scrunched up in a frown. 'Then who did?'

'I did.'

My head snapped in Ollie's direction and I sucked in a breath of sheer hatred at his cocky tone.

'You did?' My right foot started tapping on the stone floor as I tried my hardest to keep my cool. There was a reason I'd avoided them all—the main one being I didn't want to be alone with them. I looked over at Griff, who smiled, but unlike in the past, I couldn't find much comfort in it. 'Why?'

He lifted his shoulders in a careless shrug, as if nothing mattered. 'Because.'

'Because, what?' I said through gritted teeth.

'Because I can,' he finished with a wolfish grin. And to him, it really was that simple. 'Why? Did you have somewhere more important to be?'

'Anywhere is more important than wherever you are.'

'I do love it when you show a bit of bite, Skylar.' He took a step closer. 'Makes it all a little more... exciting, don't you think?'

'I don't think about you at all, actually.' I shrugged, hoping I sounded carefree, but knowing I'd probably just made myself seem even more pathetic than they already thought I was. The lie wouldn't hold up in court. That much was for sure.

'Do you enjoy lying to yourself?' He laughed, his bright blue eyes wide and shining with amusement, the movement showing off his chiselled jawline.

'I—'

'Save the bullshit, Skylar. Not like I give a fuck. I just wanted to give you a warning.'

'A warning?' I scoffed, folding my arms across my chest. 'You, of all people, can't exactly warn me about shit.'

'I can do what I want, as you're fully aware.' He took another step closer, and the whiff of his cologne entered my nose, sending a shiver down my spine. Fuck, the boy did smell good. The smell reminded me of the times spent wrapped up in one another—times that were all a lie. 'And I want to warn you not to go home this summer.'

'Why wouldn't I go home?' I laughed, the sound brittle. 'Not like I've got anywhere else to go.'

'Go to Clo's.' His tone brooked no argument, but I couldn't bite my tongue from snapping back at him.

'No can do,' I said, a smile slowly curling my lips up. 'Clo's spending the summer at mine.'

'Skylar.' My name was a warning.

'Oliver.' His name was mocking.

'I mean it.' His hand clenched and unclenched at his side. 'Don't go home.'

'And are you going to tell me *why*? Or am I meant to just take your word for it? Because I can't exactly be safer *here* than at home. Last time I checked, I wasn't stabbed at home.'

'Please,' Griff piped up from his spot beside Ollie. 'I know you don't wanna hear it from him, but I'm asking too. Please don't go home.'

I shook my head, wanting to erase the worry on Griff's face from my mind, turning on the spot to get away from them. 'Whatever.'

'Don't walk away from me,' Ollie growled.

I didn't even dignify his bullshit with an answer. I just kept walking.

Five

LEO CAME for me a couple of days later.

Well, actually, that made it sound a lot more dramatic than it really was.

I was walking down the school hallway, making my way to my next lesson, when an arm snaked out and grabbed me, pulling me into a partially hidden alcove. One of the school's few secret, out-of-the-way spots. Somewhere you could go and make out without the entire school seeing. Something I may or may not have had first-hand experience of.

'Stutter.'

'Leo,' I bit out, knowing who it was without even having to see his face. There was only one person at Hawthorn who called me that. Plus, his scent was super distinctive. 'What do you want?'

He blinked, his lips raised in a pseudo-smile. 'I wanted to talk to you.'

'Let me guess.' I removed his hand from my upper arm and looked him in the eye. 'You don't want me to go home for the summer.'

'What makes you say that?' He put his hand in his pocket,

the slight slouch of his body giving off a casual vibe, even though his facial expression was anything but.

'Ollie and Griff have already tried,' I admitted. 'And I'll tell you what I told them—'

'Let me guess,' he mocked, cutting me off. 'You told them you wouldn't.'

'I didn't tell them anything. All I said was I didn't get stabbed at home, which I'd like to point out is a very valid f-fucking point.'

'No, you didn't get stabbed at home.' Leo's tone made me feel stupid. I hated the way he made me feel stupid all the time. It was something I'd noticed last year, and it had only grown since. 'But there's a first for everything. You'd never been stabbed at school before either, and let's be real, Stutter, your old school wasn't exactly classy.'

'Your elitism is showing.' I rolled my eyes at him. 'Hollow-dale High may not have been *classy* as you so elegantly put it, but at least I felt like I belonged there. Sure, there may have been some kids walking around with knives in their pockets, but I can tell you I never saw half as much bullshit and bullying there as I've suffered here.'

'Yeah, yeah, cry me a river.' Leo looked behind him, his eyes shifting from side-to-side. Suppose he hadn't told the others he planned to pull me aside and try to talk sense into me.

'Trouble in paradise?' I bit my bottom lip, stopping the smile fighting to break out on my face, as I assessed him.

He turned back to me. 'Paradise?'

'Between you and the boys. Don't want Ollie or Griff to see you talking to me?'

'I couldn't give a fuck if either of those pricks saw me.'

'And I'm meant to believe that when you keep looking over your shoulder?' I laughed. 'Seems to me like you're hiding us in this alcove for a reason and if it isn't to hide from them, then who exactly are we hiding from? Clover?'

'This has fuck all to do with Red,' he growled, grabbing my wrist and pulling me tighter to him so he could whisper the next sentence in my ear. 'This has everything to do with you, and me wanting to make sure you don't fucking die.'

'Leo.' My voice was a whisper, too. 'Why do you even care? We're not exactly friends.'

He inclined his head, a strand of his blond hair falling into his bright blue eye. 'I do care about you.'

'You've had a funny way of showing it.'

'That's just who I am.' He shrugged, not looking repentant in the slightest. 'But it doesn't mean I don't give a shit. Just means I don't want to let you know how I feel. Or anyone, for that matter.'

'And now you're just opening up your heart to me, huh? Bit fishy, don't you think?'

'Sky,' he hushed out, and my stomach bottomed out at his use of my name. 'I need you to tell me you won't go home for the summer. I mean it. It isn't safe.'

'Life isn't safe.'

'Sky,' he groaned. 'You're being a difficult bitch on purpose.'

'Ah, there's the Leo I know and love.'

'You love me?'

'You wish.' I poked him in the side with my free hand, a small giggle escaping. Leo was always so hot and cold, I never knew how to react to him, but for some reason, I also knew when he was playing me. Sort of. 'If I go home, there's not really much you can do about it.'

'Is that a challenge?'

'What kind of challenge would it be?'

'Stutter, I'm a relatively powerful guy. I've got money and my parents own the school. Pretty sure I could ensure you don't go home this summer.'

'And what? Come stay with you at chateau Hawthorn instead? Puh-lease. You want to spend the summer with me as much as I want to spend it with you.'

'So a lot then, yeah?'

'Ha-ha.' I shook my head, looking around us to see that a lot of students had disappeared into their classrooms. 'Neither of us wants to spend the summer together.'

'And I said nothing about spending the summer together.'

'But you said—'

'I said I could ensure you don't go home for the summer. I never said anything about coming to live with me.'

'Whatever.' I sighed. 'So what do you want from me?'

'I want you to find a way not to go home. I don't care how or what you have to do, okay? Just do it. Otherwise, I will.'

'Is that a threat?'

'Stutter, when I threaten you, you're gonna fucking know about it.'

Leo let go of my wrist and brushed himself down, probably wanting to get rid of some imaginary lint or something that would make him look unkempt. People didn't realise it, but Leo cared more about his appearance than Ollie did. Ollie just showed it more to those who didn't know him that well.

'I'll see you around, Stutter.'

He was gone and out of my eyesight so fast I didn't even have the chance to respond.

THE WARNINGS FROM LEO, Ollie, and Griff didn't stick around in my brain for long.

I had a lot of other shit on my mind, and those fuckwads weren't going to ruin my day. Or my life.

It was about time that Skylar Crescent stopped being such a walkover and started to think about her revenge.

Because I wanted revenge on them all—I just wasn't sure how the fuck to go about it.

How did one go about revenge? Without it seeming too cliché or stupid?

'Clo?'

'Yeah.' The pen in her mouth muffled the word. Clo was studying the brochure of the university she planned to go to next year and making notes of what she needed. 'What's up?'

'I was just thinking about how to get revenge on the girls and Ollie.' I put my pen down and Clo did the same, lifting her head from the paper to look me over. 'What would you do if you were in my position?'

She laughed, coarse and harsh. 'I wouldn't.'

'What do you mean you wouldn't? Thought you'd be all for it.'

'I've seen a lot since knowing these people, Sky, and I promise you, you will never be on top. They always come out of a situation looking better than you, no matter what, and that's something you need to come to terms with.'

'But why should we have to come to terms with that?' I shuffled in my chair, getting more into our conversation, the textbook open in front of me long forgotten. 'Doesn't that mean we're allowing them to get away with it, and if anything, perpetuating it further?'

'Big words for a Wednesday morning, Skylar.'

'Stop trying to distract me.' The library was super quiet,

and there was barely anybody around, so not like there was anyone who could overhear us and pass it along to *The Set* or *The Sect*. 'We could team up and go ham on their arses.'

'We could,' she admitted. 'But I don't want to. Honestly, I don't want to do anything that could jeopardise me getting out of here and leaving all this pomp and bullshit behind. Messing with them would do exactly that. They wouldn't let me get away, and that's all I really, *really* want. You can understand that, right?'

I sighed. Of course I understood, and I couldn't fault her for it either. If I were in her position, I would probably feel the same way.

'I get you. It's just hard, ya know, because I don't want to do it by myself. Fuck, I don't think there's much I could even achieve working alone. I don't know what makes them tick the way you do.'

'Look, if you're really into this whole thing, I'll see what I can do, but I'm not gonna promise anything.'

'Thank you!' I let out an excited squeal. That was surprisingly easier than I'd anticipated. Thought I'd have to wear her down over multiple conversations. 'I promise you'll still get to leave this shithole in a month's time.'

'You can't promise that.'

'Well, no. But there's nothing to hold you here, Clo. You've done your time. Two years of it.'

'Yeah...' She looked up at the ceiling, taking a deep breath. 'You're right. Thanks for understanding, Sky.'

A wide grin covered my face. 'What are best friends for?'

Six

'SKYLAR!' Clover shouted, flying towards me like the devil was on her heels. Maybe he was. 'Have you heard this shit?'

'Heard what?' I asked, wracking my brain to figure out what on earth she could be referring to. As usual, I was sitting in the library at the very back, trying to make myself invisible. I felt a great sense of comfort sitting there and I'd made—sort of but not really—friends with the librarian. She was an older lady who looked like she wouldn't hurt a fly, but she took no crap and didn't let anybody come in and give me grief. I super appreciated her. She was one of my only allies at Hawthorn, and I wouldn't be forgetting that anytime soon.

'Have you heard about my grades?'

'What about them?' I put down my pen and really looked at her. She looked wild, her face bright red—from running, or rage, I couldn't be sure. Her copper hair was flying in all directions, and I knew she had flown across campus to tell me whatever she was biting her tongue to stop herself from blurting out.

'I've failed everything!' she cried, throwing herself down heavily in the seat beside me, her arms flying up in disbelief. She wasn't the only person who didn't believe her. I didn't.

There was no way she'd failed *everything*. Sure, she didn't always pay too much attention in class, but she was smart and knuckled down when the time was right. It was her final year at Hawthorn, and unlike me, her exams weren't just mocks. They were the real deal. And the real deal didn't get results for another two months.

'You can't have failed *everything*. There'd be no way to know yet even if you had.'

'No, Skylar,' she said, her face falling into grim truth. 'I've somehow failed every fucking thing. As in, they've given me a "U" in every subject.'

I gasped, and when she shoved her phone with Hive pulled up in front of my face and I saw for myself, I knew she wasn't being overdramatic for once.

'What the actual fuck?' I muttered, staring at the pixels on the screen, thoroughly baffled at the turn of events. 'Results aren't out until August from the exam boards, and it's only July.'

'I was marked absent!' she shrilled. 'Apparently, no Clover Luck attended any of her written exams, so not like I have to wait until August to be told that.'

'For real?' Surely the reach of *The Sect* and *The Set* didn't stretch to being able to have Clo's future ruined. But then Ollie's words after the mock exam a month ago played through my head again, and all of a sudden, I wasn't quite so sure. I'd not told Clover about the exchange as I hadn't wanted her to worry, but maybe I should've done.

'Well, you know who's responsible,' she said, bitterness clear in her tone. Bending over, she hit her head on the table with a thud. 'Ouch! Is anything going to go right for me today?'

'What does this mean, though?' I asked, ignoring her melodramatics. 'Surely you can speak to Ms Hawthorn and explain what's happened and they'll rearrange for you to retake them?'

All Clover wanted was to get out of here and attend a banging university—one where nobody knew her or her past, and she could start fresh. She lifted her head and the look of despair on her face gutted me.

'It means,' she said through gritted teeth, 'that I have to return to Hawthorn next year.'

I went to speak, but she continued when she saw me take a breath.

'AND I have to attend *summer school.*' She spat the last two words, and I watched as spittle flew and landed on the table in front of us. I fixated on the spot, deep in thought.

'But why would you have to attend summer school? It doesn't make sense.'

Last time I checked, Hawthorn Academy didn't even run a summer school. Why would they? And if they did, it wouldn't be for free. Every term here cost the parents thousands of pounds, so there was no way they'd give them bed and board during the summer, alongside lessons, for zero funds. Clover, being a scholarship student, relied on the kind hearts of the school's benefactors, and I doubted they were paying extra. The fact she'd failed should be enough for them to kick her out and never offer a scholarship ever again.

A large part of me was thrilled that Clover would attend Hawthorn again next year. It would mean I wasn't alone with all the vultures. That I would have a friend, somebody who could stand by my side while I no doubt withstood more bullying and harassment. Or attempted bullying, at least.

Then it hit me. I hadn't thought to look on Hive for my own grades. To be honest, I'd totally forgotten they were being released. Plus, I was expecting them to be shocking, so I had already sort of written myself off.

I pulled up the app on my phone and navigated to the Results tab under my student profile, my stomach slowly sinking down to my toes.

What I saw didn't surprise me, but it made me sad. I'd been doing so well in my classes, my grades had only suffered when tampered with, and no matter what *The Set* had thrown at me I'd continued fighting. But apparently being stabbed was a completely different ballgame, as I was staring at a page filled with Us too.

Clover leaned over and glanced at my screen. The moment she saw the U's, she winced.

'Shit, I'm sorry, Sky. Do you think it's legit?' Her sympathy for me was radiating from her and it made me feel a tiny bit better to know she cared.

'Honestly, I don't know. I mean, I knew my test results were coming back altered over the last year, and that I'd messed up in the mock exams.' I shrugged. 'Guess I'll be attending summer school right alongside you.' I laughed, sharp and harsh, nudging her with my elbow, trying to cheer us both up.

If I was being one hundred percent honest with myself—and I would never admit to it, even with a gun to my head—I felt relieved. Relieved that I didn't have to go home and spend the summer with my mother and Andy. Relieved that I would eat well and learn more and could finally show the teachers exactly what I was capable of when other pupils didn't sabotage me.

The warning from Ollie came back, clearer than ever.

'Don't go home.'

Would he have done something to make sure I didn't go

home? Surely not. The boy didn't give that much of a fuck about me. Otherwise, he'd have tried talking to me again. Or at least wouldn't look at me like shit on his shoe every time we were in the same vicinity.

'Miss Crescent. Miss Luck.' Ms Hawthorn's voice was as no-nonsense as always, like curdled milk or something equally gross. Fuck knows when she'd arrived, or whether she'd over-heard any of our conversation, but when I looked up, I found her looming over our table, staring down her nose at us with her eyes pinched tight. 'I expect to see you both in my office on Monday morning, at nine a.m. sharp.'

She walked off straight afterwards, not giving us any time to reply, but what exactly could we say, anyway?

'Guess we're going to find out Monday morning for defi-nite,' Clo said with a resigned sigh.

'I guess so.' I reached out to rub her shoulder. 'At least no matter what happens, Clo, we're together.'

THE KNOCK CAME AT TEN. *Our* knock. The one Clover and I used to let each other know who was there.

But both Clover and I were in the room, trying to work on our schoolwork, so it wasn't either of us on the other side of our door.

Our puzzled expressions matched when I glanced over at her, and I nodded for her to go open the door. I wasn't risking my safety by opening that thing. My stomach still twinged anytime I felt even slightly unsafe.

Note to self: Get a peephole for the door like they have in hotels. Or even better, a video doorbell.

Then we'd know not to open it if it was somebody wanting to harm us. Especially so late in the evening. Okay, okay. It wasn't late, exactly, but it was pretty close to curfew and we didn't have *The Sect's* protection anymore, so the hall monitors wouldn't turn a blind eye anymore. Their loyalty lay with the others. *Bastards.*

Clo opened the door slowly to reveal Griff standing on the other side, a sheepish look on his face, his meadow-coloured eyes burning into my soul when our gazes locked. Ever since I'd returned to school, I'd avoided him. He'd tried to get me alone once he realised I wasn't coming to him anytime soon, but I wasn't having any of it. In a way, his betrayal had hurt the most. He was the one I'd have put my faith in, and he'd thrown it back in my face.

'Please, can we talk, Sky?' he asked, yet making no move to enter the room, his hands clenching and unclenching at his sides. His stance was timid and so nervous it made me uncomfortable. It was so unlike the Griff I'd grown to know and love.

Clover turned away from Griff to face me, one eyebrow raised in question. I nodded. Fuck it, I may as well listen to what the boy had to say and then send him on his way.

'Go for it,' I replied, my tone more disinterested than my mind.

He shuffled into the room, as if he was trying not to make a big deal about the fact I'd granted him entry. Or maybe he was worried I'd tell him I was kidding or something.

Griff sat down on the floor, obviously deciding that neither of our beds was an option, and it wasn't like we had the space for a sofa, or even an armchair, like the boys had in their suites.

'Skylar Crescent,' he started, looking at me in earnest. 'I am so, so sorry.'

My brain was screaming at me. I knew I should feel something at his words, but all I felt was suspicion because he'd used my full name. He *never* used my full name.

Without thinking it through, words flew out of my mouth. 'What was even real, Griff?'

'All of it, Sky.' His eyes bore into me with a sincerity that travelled into my soul. Then he ruined it by opening his big stupid mouth again. 'Okay, not *all* of it, but I've never lied in my friendship with you. We have a bond, New Girl.'

'Don't call me that,' I spat. The nickname coming from him had never given me a bad vibe. It was always something he called me that filled me with warmth, as opposed to when the girls used it and were clearly trying to make me feel less than. Griff had never made it a slur the way Odette and co. had.

'Okay, okay,' he said, his hands up in a defensive gesture. 'I get it. Lemme think of something else to call you real quick.'

'Can't you just call me Sky?'

'Boring.' He laughed, rubbing his chin with his finger, staring up at the ceiling. 'I've got it! I'll call you Clouds. That cool?'

'Clouds?' There really was no explaining the way that boy's brain worked.

'Yeah,' he said with a cheeky grin, as if the explanation made perfect sense and I was the weird one for questioning it. 'Your name is *Sky*-lar, and that's where clouds live.'

I laughed, caught off guard. 'Okay... we'll go with it.'

He didn't waste a moment. 'Look, Clouds, there's something important I wanted to talk to you about.'

'And what's that?'

'Your dad,' he blurted out. 'I didn't know that was his name until the fashion show. You've got to believe me.'

Well, my dad wasn't where I thought the conversation was going, that was for sure. I'd guessed he was going to get me to forgive him, or to give Ollie another chance, or something like that. My dad hadn't entered my mind in a while—he never really had—and learning his identity hadn't changed that for me.

'Why would I believe you?' I scoffed. 'And why does it matter that you didn't know his name?'

'It matters 'cause *your* dad is *my* uncle,' he replied with emphasis. 'My dad, Damien, was a twin. Sky, this makes us like sisters.'

'No, Griff, this makes us cousins,' I deadpanned. I'd already thought that potentially we could be related after the response from the crowd at the show, but I hadn't dug that hole yet, too scared to learn the truth. Part of me hadn't wanted to believe that yet another person who shared my blood could treat me so poorly. Especially not somebody who'd treated me the way Griff had—like somebody who mattered.

It was going to take a lot for me to decide whether I wanted to let him back in; to trust him that easily. Being family didn't instantly make it all okay.

No, it definitely made it worse.

'Being family doesn't make things between us any better,' I warned, voicing my thoughts.

'I know,' he said with a nod, his cheeky grin disappearing. 'I just want you to know I really am so very sorry and I never wanted to hurt you. Family or not.'

'So, let me get this straight...' I trailed off, slightly overwhelmed by everything, needing to ignore his apology. 'Both of your parents were twins?'

'Weird, right?' he said with a chuckle, his dimples pressed in, teeth all aglow. 'Wonder if I'll have twins.' His head gravitated in Clo's direction, and I smiled inwardly at his obvious feelings for her.

'Well, fuck, there's no hope for them,' Clover quipped.

I laughed along with her. Even the thought of one mini-Griff running around was a worry, let alone two of them born at the same time.

'You want me, Luck. Don't pretend otherwise.' His eyebrows waggled, and I noticed a faint blush rising on Clo's cheeks. Somebody hadn't been completely truthful when I'd asked if they were still crushing...

'Oh, fuck off,' Clo snapped as she threw a cushion at his head. 'What do you know about us flunking?'

The change in conversation was so abrupt it gave me whiplash.

'Huh?' he asked, confusion evident on his face. His smile vanished in a flash. 'You flunked?'

'Yep,' I replied first, 'but I'm certain mine was real.' I'd had enough time to think about it, and as much as I wanted to put the blame on Ollie and *The Set*, I knew I couldn't.

'And I'm certain that mine *wasn't*,' Clo said. 'So fess up, Griffin Cooper.'

'Babydoll, I have no idea what you're talking about,' Griff said, his tone hesitant. *Huh.* How had I never noticed how poor of a liar the boy was? He shook his head, not wanting to catch my eye. 'What's going on?'

'Ask your best friend, Leo,' Clover spat, causing me to roll my eyes. We had no proof Leo had anything to do with any of it. After my hushed conversation with Leo, my mind had wandered to him more often than it should. What would Leo even gain by flunking us both?

Clo caught me mid eye roll and snapped, 'Sorry, Skylar. Didn't realise he's your best friend now, too?'

I bit my tongue so hard to stop myself from replying to her. She was hurt and fuck, she'd been dealt a blow. The girl wasn't escaping Hawthorn the way she'd dreamt, or as fast as she'd hoped. But that was no reason to take it out on those who cared about her, like me.

'I doubt it's Leo's fault entirely, Clo,' Griff piped up. He moved to sit next to Clo on her bed, and at first I thought she was going to hit him or push him back to the floor. She did neither of those things, though, and kept herself still, not wanting to touch him. 'I'm sure Ollie and the girls have something to do with it, too.'

'How am I meant to know that you aren't bullshitting me right now?'

Griff sighed deeply. 'I've said sorry to Clouds, but maybe I need to say it to you. Clover, I'm sorry for everything, but I promise you, they've excluded me from any serious stuff. They don't tell me shit anymore.' He rubbed his chin with his forefinger, deep in thought. 'Well, turns out they'd never told me shit, anyway.'

'Likely story.' Just by looking over at Clo, I could see that she didn't believe him. Not one bit. But I could also see Griff sitting beside her, attempting to put his arm around her shoulders, and I could see the sincerity in his green eyes.

'Clo, I swear on your life.'

A small gasp left Clo's lips, as she turned to look at him for the first time since the conversation had become between the two of them, excluding me entirely. It was like they'd forgotten I was even there.

'Do you mean that?' she asked, her voice small.

'Of course I do,' he replied straight away, stroking her arm in a loving gesture. 'You know I'd never say that and not mean it.'

Suppose I should let them have some privacy.

Slowly, I stood up and made my way to the door before

opening it as quietly as I could and stepping out into the hall to leave them to it.

Did I want the two of them to become a couple? Honestly, no.

But if it sorted shit out and got them both on board with my revenge scheme—that I was yet to tell them about—then I was down with it.

All's fair in love, war, and private school drama.

Seven

ONCE OUTSIDE MY ROOM, I wasn't sure where I could head to feel safe.

Griff and Clo hadn't asked me to leave, so it wasn't that I couldn't stay in my room, but I knew they needed to talk without me there. If there were real feelings between the two of them—whether I liked it or not—it was only fair they got to discuss them without me hanging around like a bad smell.

My feet were moving superfast, in a hurry to make it across campus without being seen, even though I didn't yet have a destination in mind.

I also didn't want to be caught unawares out in the open. The area glowed a deep orange, the sun setting in the distance, and if I didn't know the truth about what really happened at Hawthorn, I'd have thought it looked beautiful and picturesque.

A deep, gravelly voice slithered its way into my ear, and I shivered. I was so immersed in my own world I hadn't spotted anybody near me.

'Fancy seeing you here, Stutter.'

I stalled, nearly tripping over, my feet having stopped before my brain could catch up with the action. And like in a slow-motion movie scene, I looked over my shoulder and locked my gaze with Leo's.

'W-what do you want?' I asked, my stutter returning because of the scare he'd given me. I was much more in control of my stutter these days, but it still crept up when I was nervous or scared. I assumed it always would.

'No need to be like that. I just want to talk.' He'd reached my side and all I could do was stare at him in silence. Hadn't we spoken not that long ago?

What more is there to say?

Leo's hand came up and pushed a piece of my hair that had fallen into my face behind my ear. The touch of his fingers grazing my skin made my cheek warm.

Snap out of it!

'Talk about w-what, exactly?' Trying to keep my anger while looking into his gorgeous blue eyes. His blond hair was wet, and I guessed he'd been at the pool. Leo spent most of his free time at the pool. Rumour had it that he was training for the Olympics, but I wasn't sure how true that was. Another rumour was that he planned to compete at university, which I could believe a little more than the Olympics thing.

'Where are you going?'

'Er...' I looked around us, hoping to see something that'd inspire me.

'Tell me,' he demanded.

Until that moment, I hadn't known where I was headed, but when he pushed me, the word came out. 'Library.'

'Of course you are,' he whispered thoughtfully and nodded at me. 'Off you go then, Stutter. Wouldn't want to bump into somebody while all alone, would you?'

With that, he turned on the spot and walked away. No

more words said. Yet I couldn't bring myself to move from the spot he had frozen me to.

Had Leo's arse always looked that good? ...*Stop drooling, Sky!*

On reaching the boys' dorm building, he stopped and looked back over his shoulder, eyebrow raised at the look he saw on my face.

He winked at me before heading inside.

What the fuck was going on?

And what had he wanted to talk to me about?

'LITTLE ONE,' a voice rasped out the moment I entered the library.

Seriously?

I headed further into the library towards the back to my favourite table, ignoring the voice trying to seduce me—and what a seductive voice it was.

Stay in control, Sky.

I quickly grabbed a book from the Classics section and threw myself into a chair, opening the book at a random page and burying my head inside.

'You hate that book,' Ollie said, taking the seat opposite mine. I refused to look up, but it was only then I registered I'd picked up *Wuthering Heights*. It irked me that he knew how much I hated it. He was the bane of my existence. All I could think was: *Don't do it, girl. Don't give in. Don't give him the power.*

I took a deep breath and continued to fake read my least

favourite "love story". If I stayed quiet, he'd go away. Wasn't that the saying?

'Are you sad, Skylar?' he asked, his tone condescending. 'Are you going to cry?'

The venom in his tone made me look up and really look at him. Had he always been such a hateful bastard? But once I looked up, and our eyes locked, I couldn't tear my gaze away. Caught in the headlights. Trapped in his stare.

'Fuck you.'

'You'd love to.' He smirked, his eyebrow raised in question.

'N-never again,' I growled.

'Sure, baby girl. Tell yourself that.'

'Why are you t-talking to me?' I asked, trying to avoid his stare, but failing miserably.

'Magnets attract. And you and me'—he pointed between us both—'we're two of the strongest.'

I dropped the book and crossed my arms across my chest, but when I saw Ollie's eyes wander downward, I realised maybe that hadn't been the right choice. Oh, well. Got to stick with it now. Also, him looking at me said a lot more about who really wanted to fuck who.

'You told me I don't belong here,' I accused, throwing his words from the pool house back at him. Of all the things he'd said to me that night, those were the ones that hit me the hardest.

'You don't.' His tone was factual. The certainty in his words told me he believed they were nothing more than the truth. 'I'm disappointed in you.'

'Disappointed? In me?' I sputtered, livid that I was allowing his words to affect me, but unable to stop myself. 'Why?'

'You returned.'

No bells. No whistles. Just a simple statement. One that caused me to visibly wince.

'I h-had no choice,' I whispered. In my heart, that was how it seemed to me. I hadn't had a choice but to return to Hawthorn. The education. The opportunity. The future. It was all too glittering for me to turn down.

'You had a choice, Little One. Everybody always has a choice. You just made the wrong one.' He laughed. 'Suppose it wouldn't be the first time.'

'What do you w-want?'

'Oh, there are many things I want, Little One. But the one that's running through my head right now? I want you to leave this place and never return. This is your last warning, Skylar. Tomorrow, the wolves will descend.'

The boy needed to make up his mind. Either I needed to leave the school and go home, or I needed to stay away from home for the summer. How could it be both? What a walking contradiction!

I chose to focus on the other part of his statement. 'Wolves?'

'Every fucking person in this school is at my command. Everywhere you turn, there will be somebody there waiting to stab you in the back.'

'Am I meant to be scared?'

'You should be,' he said darkly. His eyes were a deep indigo —soulless and dead. A blank slate, a face of indifference.

I needed to get away from him. Even being in his vicinity was making me question everything. He'd bullied me. He'd been behind everything the girls had done to me. And yet he still had the audacity to demand shit from me.

It didn't help that I'd lost my virginity to him. My brain still found it hard to separate the guy who ruined me at the end of the fashion show from the one I shared heartfelt moments with. Clover was constantly trying to convince me it had all been shady shit, but she was wrong. She chose to only see the dark. The deceit.

Unlike me. I'd seen behind the curtain. I'd seen both the wizard and the showman. And I found it hard to look at it all in such a black-and-white way.

Although, I'd also been sold a lie, so… not like I was the best judge of character when it came to him.

Fuck sticking around to listen to any more of his bullshit. Acting as if the hounds of hell were snapping at my ankles, I made my way out of the library.

Revenge. Revenge. Revenge.

Do not get sidetracked, Skylar!

Pretty eyes and killer smiles can lie and steal the very essence of who you are.

Eight

THE NEXT DAY, you bet your arse that I was terrified with every step I took. Every class I attended. Every corner I turned.

I knew Ollie hadn't been lying in the library the night before; hadn't been hiding his intent to have the other students here make my day a living nightmare.

I definitely felt as if I'd been lured into a false sense of security ever since returning. For two months I'd been back, had even attended exams, yet other than a few whispers and jeers, nothing much had happened to me.

The other shoe has to drop at some point.

Clo and Griff didn't leave my side all day. After I'd got back to our room the night before, the two of them had made up and were laughing and smiling. The joy between them evident at first glance.

I made sure to wait until Griff had gone before I opened up. Yeah, Griff had apologised to me and it had seemed genuine. Plus, he'd clearly sorted things out with Clo, but I still wasn't going to blindly trust him again. Not straight away. He needed to earn it.

When Griff left, I told Clo the full extent of my run-in with Ollie, making sure to leave out that he'd demanded I not go home for the summer. Didn't need her worrying about that.

'*Are the two of you official?*' I asked her, wanting to get the gossip. '*You looked pretty cosy when I came in.*'

She shrugged. '*I didn't want to put a label on it, so we're just keeping it casual.*'

'*And was Griff okay with that?*'

'*Why wouldn't he be?*'

'*I guess.*' I shrugged, not wanting to push her or piss her off. '*As long as you're happy, then so am I.*'

For some reason—okay, I knew why—but I'd left out the part where Leo had stopped me. Wasn't opening that can of worms if I didn't have to.

'...right, Sky?' Clo asked, her arm hooked in mine, as we made our way to the cafeteria to grab lunch to take with us to the library.

'Huh?' I shook my head, bringing myself back to my surroundings from where I was still in our room in my mind.

'I knew you weren't listening. Sometimes I wonder why I bother to talk to you. You've always got your head stuck in the clouds, girl.'

'Not always.'

'Sure you don't... I said it's odd we haven't seen Oralie or Ophelia around much.'

'They stick by Ollie's side, I think. Can't Griff answer what they've been up to?'

'Honestly, I don't think Ollie or Leo tell him much anymore. He barely knew shit last year and I think it's only grown worse. They purposefully hid things from him. He never knew who your dad was. Otherwise, he'd never have agreed to any of it.'

I was on the fence about my feelings towards Griff. A large part of me understood it. He hadn't known me at all, and his lifelong friends—not to mention cousins—had convinced him to mess with the new girl for fun. He was such a cheeky, fun-loving guy, he would go along with anything if it made him laugh.

But the other part of me thought it was wrong either way, whether he knew about our cousin link or not, it was shitty to bully me. All because I was a scholarship student trying to change my life and better myself. A scholarship student whose father had done something so heinous they bullied me because of it. Something to this day I was still unaware of.

Fuck's sake.

Every time I thought I was feeling better, something hit me and took me back into that headspace again. The headspace of a vulnerable girl who was humiliated by some rich wankers ever since entering Hawthorn's gates.

'Earth to Sky,' Clo called as we stopped outside the hall, waving her hand in front of my face.

'Tonight, make sure Griff comes to our room,' I told her, my tone serious.

'Huh?' she asked, baffled.

'If he wants to help me, and he really is on our side, then get him to come to our room tonight.'

'Okay... Are you sure? Because just the other night you weren't even sure whether you were gonna forgive him or not.'

'Positive. The boy wants to make it up to me? Well, this is a start,' I told her, nodding as if my thought process should be obvious to her without me having to go into too much detail.

'Fine. He'll be there.'

In my best imitation of a movie villain, I replied, 'Excellent.'

I PACED MY ROOM, running my fingers through my hair, going through my plan in my head. The conversation was an important one, and I needed to get it right. The way Griff and Clo responded would dictate the future.

Okay, maybe not the *future*, because that was overly dramatic even for me, but the near future at least. The rest of my time at Hawthorn minimum.

If the two of them got behind me and helped, then we could really have some fun.

Also, I was on edge. Ollie had promised last night in the library that the wolves would descend, but they never did. Nobody even looked at me differently, which made zero sense. Never before had *The Set* not taken an opportunity to harm me. Same could be said about every other pupil at school, too.

My feet stopped pacing up and down when the door handle jiggled. It opened to reveal Griff and Clo on the other side.

'Yo!' he called as he swanned into the room, his smile wide, with no care in the world. 'You called?'

'If by "called" you mean I asked you to come, then yes, I called.'

'Ah, pleasant lady. How may this knight of the realm be of assistance?' he asked, bending low into one of the deepest bows I'd ever seen. I sputtered a laugh. He could be such a fun goofball at times, it was almost easy to forget his betrayal.

'Knight of the realm?' Clo asked, entering the room behind him, a smile playing on her lips. 'What fucked-up realm is that?'

'This one,' he said, showing all of his teeth. His voice was loud and regal sounding, reminding me of a Shakespearean actor attempting to captivate an audience. 'The Hawthorn realm.'

'Even you saying the name gives me shivers.' Clo shook her body, running her hands up and down her arms.

The two of them went to sit on Clo's bed, and I started my pacing back up, thrown off track since they'd appeared. My entire planned speech left my head when they showed up and my mind was left blank.

'What is it?' Griff asked, his smile falling, sensing my distress. 'What's going on?'

'Right, so... I guess I should start with a question first. Are you on my side?' I asked, scrutinising his face for his gut reaction. Searching for lies and deceit.

'What do you mean?' he asked, his expression unchanged.

'If you had to choose between me and *The Sect*, who would you choose?' My eyes bored into his, wanting him to know just how serious the question—and his answer—would be.

'Are you making me choose?' He raised his eyebrows, his smile completely gone.

'No,' I blurted out because it wasn't an ultimatum. I'd never outright do that to him—to anybody. Maybe subliminally, but never intentionally. 'I'm just trying to decipher where your loyalties lie.' I shrugged.

'Look, I regret last year so much, Clouds. I've got your back,' he said, sincerity shining from his spring-coloured eyes. They were more green today, and they flashed with guilt as he thought of last year. Pretty sure he'd told me he had my back last year, too.

'Well then, buckle up, buttercups,' I said, addressing them both, 'as I've got a plan and I need both of you to help.'

'A plan?' Clo asked, her face blank and tone flat. Griff put his arm around her shoulders and hugged her to him, an intimate gesture they'd never done in front of me before. It was odd to see the two of them cuddling up to one another and acting so coupley.

'A revenge plan,' I replied, emphasising the word revenge. 'A wicked scheme.'

'Revenge?' Clo's tone was pissed. 'I told you I wasn't interested.'

'I remember,' I snapped. 'But I want to get my revenge on Ollie and Leo and definitely on Ophelia and Oralie.' Then I added under my breath, 'Wish I could on Odette.'

'Bit dark, Clouds. Think somebody already got their revenge on Odette, right?' Griff had a point. Somebody *had* stabbed the girl and, unlike me, she didn't survive it.

'Anyway.' I brushed off my callous thoughts. 'I've got some ideas.'

'Plot away,' Griff said, moving his arm back from around Clo to put his hands in a praying position, rippling his fingers like a movie baddie. I chuckled, seeing how similar Griff and I could be, as that was the exact motion I'd made earlier that day when talking to Clo about inviting him to our room. It was the first time I'd considered whether us being family had something to do with our similar actions.

Something for me to unpack later.

'Okay. So. What do Oralie and Ophelia love most?' I asked, even though we all knew the question was rhetorical. 'They love being all-powerful and in charge, right?'

Clover shrugged and Griff's face stayed the same. Questioning my sanity, no doubt.

'Of course they do!' I exclaimed, a little too loud for the small room.

They glanced at one another and then back at me, and I could tell they thought I was suffering mentally. As a rule, I didn't shout with enthusiasm often, so I could understand their concern.

When Clo spoke next, her tone was one I'd expect her to use with a very young child. 'Sky, do you think a revenge plan is healthy?'

'Nope,' I replied, all easy-breezy. 'But it's what I want, so here we are.'

'Okay...'

'Oh, ignore grumpy pants next to me,' Griff said with a smile, leaning back to rest on his hands. 'Continue.'

'They love the power that being a member of *The Set* gives them. They love that the rest of the school cowers when they pass and parts whenever they enter a hallway and so on. I want to stop that. I want to steal their power, and while at it, their hotness.'

'Forgive me if I'm being a little dense,' Clover started, sounding not in the least like she wanted to be forgiven. 'But *how* do you plan to steal their hotness?'

'Well, I can't steal it per se, but there are definitely things we could do to dim their shine.'

'I'm listening,' Griff said with a lopsided grin.

'It depends how petty we want to go, but we could mess with their skin cream, their hair care, their actual hair, and so on.' I'd stopped pacing and was facing them both head-on. Clover's nose wrinkled as her eyes surveyed me. 'Didn't you say when I was in the hospital that you'd be by my side?'

I felt only slightly guilty about using her words against her, but not guilty enough to *not* do it.

'Yes...' she trailed off.

'So be by my side,' I said forcefully. My vengeful heart

would do it without her, but it didn't want to do shit alone if it didn't have to.

'I'll help you with the girls.' Griff's tone was full of glee. 'Nobody messes with my cousin and gets away with it.'

'Yay!' I said, choosing not to point out that both he and his best friends messed with me last year more than the girls did. *Pick your battles wisely, Sky.*

'Fine,' Clo huffed out. 'Let me guess, we're going to go for Leo how? Making him ugly too?'

'Not quite, but I thought we could target his relationship with girls.' Then I realised something pretty disconcerting. 'Did Leo even mourn Odette?'

'By mourn...' Griff trailed off, looking around the room. 'You mean?'

'Did he give a shit?' I asked bluntly. When she died, Odette was Leo's girlfriend. Plus, I still wasn't sure who had stabbed her—or me—so I needed to be super careful. What if the guilty party was Leo?

Did I truly believe he could've murdered his girlfriend?

'Of course he didn't,' Clover spat. 'Oh, he pretended well enough at the funeral, but we all know he was only with her to... Well, you get my drift.'

I nodded, and if this had been a text conversation, it would totally be an IKYKWIM moment, which stands for, *I know you know what I mean,* and was something Clo and I used all the time.

'How d'you know that?' Griff scoffed, defensive. 'You didn't even go to the funeral.'

'I just know these things,' Clo said with a shrug.

'You don't think...' I asked, not wanting to complete the thought, even though I'd just asked myself the same thing.

Could Leo have been the figure I saw standing over Odette's lifeless body? Did he stab me?

Since returning to school and walking the halls from that night, my nightmares had given me some of my memories back, but not enough for me to see the full picture.

'No.' Griff's abrupt, hard voice made me flinch. 'He was with me during the fashion show. And after it, too.'

'The whole evening?' Clo asked, and as she spoke, I realised I'd never asked for people's whereabouts since returning. I'd tried my hardest to stay away from them all so bad, I hadn't even thought about it. The only thing I knew was that I'd left Ollie down by the pool, and it couldn't physically be possible for him to be the figure. He would've had to have teleported, and I may be living in a novel, but it wasn't a science fiction one.

It may be stupid of me, but I'd never doubted Griff, and I'd barely considered Leo before the conversation turned to Odette. Clearly, I hadn't been thinking hard enough.

Griff opened his mouth to respond but then shut it comically fast. His voice was a low mumble. 'Well, no. Not the whole evening.'

'When I left the hall, you were alone,' I told him. 'We locked eyes, remember? No Leo in sight.'

'Yeah, and after you ran out, the entire hall went into disarray. The parents were in an uproar, and Ms Hawthorn was trying to save the evening. I spent my time searching for Clo, and Leo was definitely there, too. I saw him more than once.'

'So, there's a period where Leo is unaccounted for?' Clo asked, grabbing his chin so he stopped looking around the room and looked into her mesmerising, yet rather stern, eyes instead.

Griff squirmed in Clo's grasp, not wanting to put the words out into the universe. When his response came, his tone was one of exhaustion.

'Yeah. I guess there is.' He looked so uncomfortable I felt a little sorry for him. Ultimately, Leo was another one of Griff's cousins, and they'd grown up together. Must be shit to think that maybe somebody you love could also potentially be a murderer. Not even just somebody you love, but somebody you share blood with.

'Wonderful,' I deadpanned.

'Back to your plan,' Griff said in an obvious attempt to change the conversation. A bit clumsy, but I could understand his reluctance to continue down that road.

'What about it?' I asked, grabbing the rope he'd thrown out, willing to go down with it. Its very own anchor.

'Oliver. What're you planning to do to ruin him?' Clo let go of Griff's chin, and he turned back to face me, assessing my expression.

'Swimming,' I replied matter-of-factly.

'Swimming,' Griff said, his eyes brightening. 'That could work.'

'I thought so too. He hopes for a scholarship, right?' They both nodded, and I continued, 'I want to destroy any hope he has. I want him to know it was me, and think about me every time he remembers his failures.'

The fact he even wanted to take a scholarship from somebody who needed it pissed me off. The boy was wealthy enough he never needed anything to be paid for him, or handed to him. He was only doing it to prove he could.

'Feisty. Dark.' Griff beamed at me, his dimples pressed in. 'You devious woman. I love it.'

'You do?' I asked. The confirmation felt good, like water being poured onto my head, spreading through me, and the only way I could describe it was a mixture of pure elation and euphoria. It was a long time coming, and the fact Griff didn't reject my ideas gave me a real dopamine boost.

'Yeah!' He stood up abruptly, lurched forward, and wrapped his arms around my waist. Without giving me time to process, he lifted me off the ground and spun us both around, our laughter growing louder with each rotation.

'So you'll help?' I asked him mid-spin. He nodded, still spinning us. I hit his shoulder and shouted, 'Put me down!'

I was still chuckling, but the spinning had started to make me sick. A lot of spinning in quick succession always made me nauseous. Waltzers at the fair were my least favourite ride.

My feet touched the ground, and instantly I felt better. Grounded.

'If this is what you need to heal, then yeah, I'll help,' he said.

I kissed his cheek and beamed at him. 'Thank you!'

'Yeah, yeah. I'm the best, I know,' he joked. Actually, knowing Griff the way I did, it probably wasn't a joke. He most likely believed it. *Poor, delusional boy.*

'Clo?' I asked, glancing over at her as she hadn't moved from the edge of her bed. My lips formed a pout, pushing out my bottom lip, and I gave her what I hoped were puppy-dog eyes, but were probably just really wide, scary ones.

'Fine. But we need an *actual* plan,' she said begrudgingly.

'Perfect!' I clapped in excitement.

The rest of the evening, the three of us used a whiteboard to map out our plan. I hadn't put too much thought into the actual revenge itself, but more about how to get Clo and Griff to see things my way. With them on board—and pizza—our ideas came thick and fast. Even though some of them were ridiculous and would never work, we finalised a plan of action before midnight.

Would it work? Fuck if I knew.

It would make me feel better either way. I just knew it!

Nine

MONDAY MORNING CAME, and Clover and I made our way at a snail's speed over to Ms Hawthorn's office.

'Wonder what the old bat wants to talk about,' I said to Clo as we walked arm-in-arm.

'Summer school, I suppose,' Clo replied, her tone bored. 'Our official invitation and all that crap.'

'Has the school ever run a summer school before?' Nobody had ever mentioned it, but then again, wasn't like I would've been paying attention if they had. I paid attention to teachers when it came to studies—and not much else.

'Not that I know of.' She shrugged. 'But there's a first for everything.'

'What made you even think you'd have to stick around for it, though? The meeting hasn't happened, yet you seemed pretty certain back when you flunked that you'd be staying. How come?'

Clo averted her gaze, keeping it straight ahead on the hallway in front of us. 'Just a hunch.'

I nodded, not wanting to push her or argue with her. It wasn't worth the breath. It made sense Ms Hawthorn wanted to talk to us about our exams.

Other than us flunking, there hadn't been much happening at school, and the two of us weren't in trouble for anything else.

Oh, wait. There *was* something, actually.

The swim coach's assistant was leaving at the end of the term to go work somewhere that paid more and guess who was replacing him?

Only Mister Leo "I'm-so-great-at-swimming—no, make that everything" Hawthorn.

Well, okay. Leo had never given me the impression that he thought of himself that way—that was just me being petty—but still, apparently, the boy wanted to stick around Hawthorn, and taking on the swim coach assistant position was the perfect excuse for that. I'd overheard some young sycophants talking about it, and they said Leo had put himself forward for the position rather than being roped into it by his father. So it was something he wanted. If there was one thing I knew about Leo, it was that he wouldn't get strung along by anybody. He only did things if they served him best, not the other way around.

Clo and I reached Ms Hawthorn's office door and knocked, the sound reverberating through the hallway, sending a shiver down my spine. Everything was so ominous all the time in these halls. Guess a big old gothic building had that effect on people.

'Enter,' Ms Hawthorn said from the other side, her tone razor-sharp.

From the moment we stepped over the threshold, something didn't feel right. We weren't the only two students called into the office—Ms Hawthorn had invited Griff, Ollie, and the girls, too.

This has Set/Sect bullshit written all over it.

'Take a seat, girls,' Ms Hawthorn said, gesturing to the empty spots next to Ollie and Griff. I tried to communicate with Griff through our minds, hoping he would look over at me and his face would give away what was happening here, but he didn't get the telepathic messages. Or he did and he was flat out ignoring them. Ignoring me.

We took the available seats and waited, both of us staring straight ahead, ignoring the others in the room with us. My eyes roamed the space opposite me, trying to focus on anything that wasn't Ollie, but all I could find was a chip on the corner of the desk. *Never let them see you falter. Never let them know you're bothered by them.*

'I'm sure you are all aware why you are here,' Ms Hawthorn said, taking a seat in her large, ornate chair behind her desk. It made her look regal; important. An evil queen surveying her subjects. 'All six of you have failed your exams.'

'Really?' Ollie drawled, his tone bored. Taking a quick moment to glance over at him, I saw his laid-back posture in his chair and it instantly made my blood boil. Why was he so casual and unaffected all the time? Did he already know what was happening here? Or was he genuinely not bothered by my presence the way I was with his? I hated to admit to myself that it made my heart hurt knowing I didn't affect him the way he does me.

The overthinking would make me sick if I allowed it to further seep into my psyche.

It made no sense. Well, it made sense that *I'd* failed as I barely wrote a damn word on the answer booklets, but Ollie was definitely in that History exam, and I'd watched him fill in two answer booklets, his hand whizzing across the page for the entire three hours.

Another reason I knew they couldn't have failed?

I'd looked at the boys' grades on Hive myself when they were first posted and both of them had aced every test they took. But somehow, in a mere weekend, their grades were shit, and they had flunked as well?

Yeah. Not buying it for one moment.

'Yes, Master Brandon. Somehow,' she said, her voice rising with scepticism, 'you and Master Cooper have failed everything, including Physical Education. Would you like to explain that to me?'

'Nope,' Griff said, and I knew that if I looked at him, he'd have his signature grin covering his face. You could hear the smile in his voice, and it was pretty infectious. 'Makes perfect sense to me, Ms.'

Failed Physical Education? How? The two of them were the best swimmers in the school underneath Leo, and everybody knew it.

Something shady was going on. Or maybe this was their way to ensure I didn't go home for the summer?

Fuck my life.

Pricks. Absolute pricks! They knew I wouldn't listen to them and were determined to make it happen with or without my agreement. But did they really have to ruin Clo's future to do it? I knew Ollie wasn't her biggest fan, so it made even less sense he'd want to spend another year in her presence. Plus, Griff and Clo were on the precipice of something *more* so I doubted he'd want to fuck up her future.

It just didn't make much sense.

Ophelia and Oralie looked pretty smug at the turn of events, and I wished it were acceptable to go and slap the bitches. Wonder if they were in on it, too?

Either way, I wouldn't let them win. If anything, the fact they were cooping me and Clo up here with them for the entire summer was a good thing! It gave us the perfect chance to enact some revenge while barely anybody else was on campus. Meaning: no witnesses. Nobody would get caught in the crosshairs and that could only be seen as a positive. The only downside was that it would be obvious just *who* was responsible for their misfortune. Not like we could fob it off on some year seven if there weren't any year sevens around.

Oh well. I'd cross that particular bridge when I came to it.

'...the four of you will stay on campus this summer and will attend all the classes we have scheduled for you. There will be eight members of staff on campus, including myself, and I expect you all to be on your best behaviour. This isn't how I wanted to spend my summer, so any misbehaving will be punished accordingly. I'm watching you all.' Ms Hawthorn's grey eyes narrowed, and I swore she could see through me, down to the very depths of my soul. 'Now, get out of my sight.'

'LET ME GUESS,' Clo said once the six of us had piled out of Ms Hawthorn's office. 'You had something to do with this.'

'Who? Me?' Griff asked, sweeping his hand to his heart, open-jawed. 'Would I ever?'

'Yes. Yes, you fucking would.' Clo stomped her foot, and I was lucky I stopped moving closer. Otherwise, she'd have stomped on my toes. Clo always struggled with her temper, but it was even harder for her to control it when she was faced with a cheeky-grinned, bright-eyed Griffin. 'Especially if it meant you got me all alone all summer.'

'We're not going to be alone alone,' Griff pointed out.

'Clouds will be with us. Then there's the issue of the O girls and Ollie. Not to forget Leo.'

'Leo?' I exclaimed, then coughed, hoping to cover up my dramatic reaction. 'Why would Leo be here?'

'He's one of the eight members of staff,' Ollie said, coming to stand beside Griff, as if it was his rightful place. Bastard. Why was he getting under my skin? And why was I letting it happen?

Really, I should have already made the connection myself. There was no way that Ollie and Griff would be here all summer without the pretty, blue-eyed, blond-haired Adonis that most people saw as the true leader of *The Sect*.

'Goody,' Clo deadpanned. 'Beyond thrilled for us all.'

To make matters worse, the guy in question appeared, the expression on his face telling me all I needed to know. He was enjoying every second of Clo's despair. 'No need to be like that, Red.'

'You're getting a real kick out of this, aren't you?' she spat.

'So what if I am?' Leo shrugged, his smirk firmly planted on his face. 'Needs to be some perks to being a teacher.'

'Like staying at school during the summer holidays?' I scoffed. 'Yeah, seems legit.'

'And what would you know about it?' Ollie snapped, raising an eyebrow at me. 'You're the one who failed every-thing. Maybe you should be grateful for the kindness being shown to you by the staff here.'

'Why is it that I fail to believe any of this is from kindness?' My laugh was filled with derision. 'I highly doubt you rich wankers have ever done anything out of sheer kindness.'

'You lumping me in with them, Clouds?' Griff faltered.

'If the bank account fits.' I shrugged. 'Look, I'm fed up with this bullshit, so if nobody has anything to say, I'm leaving.'

'And I'm coming with you,' Clo announced, removing herself from Griff's embrace. 'I need to clear my head.'

'But—'

'No,' I cut Griff off. 'Unlike us, Clo's actual future is being messed with. Give her space, and we'll talk to you later.'

'Promise?' The hurt in Griff's eyes wasn't lost on me, but I also couldn't help but feel like he deserved it. I should've told Clo about them asking me not to go home. If I had, then maybe we'd have seen their next move coming and could have helped prevent it somehow instead of both being blindsided.

'Promise. Now piss off.' I shoved his shoulder but gave a small laugh so he knew I wasn't being serious.

On heavy feet, the two of them left with the O girls, leaving me standing with Clover and Leo.

Clo turned to Leo and snapped, 'You can piss off, too.'

'Nice to see your friendly side, Red.'

She jabbed his shoulder with her forefinger. 'I don't have a friendly side when you're involved.'

'Whatever,' he drawled. 'I'll see you later, Stutter.'

'See you later,' I said with a small wave before reaching down to grab Clo's wrist and drag her away. 'Come on, Clo. Let's go back to our room.'

'You not gonna go to class?'

'Fuck class. We've got a whole summer of them, remember?' We began walking at a slow pace back to our room, not paying attention to anything or anyone around.

She groaned. 'Don't remind me! I'm so pissed Leo's sticking around for the summer.'

I nodded with sympathy. Nobody wanted to flaunt their new relationship in their ex's face, even if their ex was somebody as irritating as Leo Hawthorn.

'Those three are joined at the hip. Wonder if they can do anything alone?'

'Well, at least we know they have sex alone,' Clo said off the cuff, and I gasped when her words registered.

'Have you had sex with Griff?' I asked, all thoughts of Leo being here this summer gone.

'Maybe,' she said coyly. I squealed, happy for them if they were happy.

'When did it happen?' I asked, wanting the goss. I knew I was being nosey, but wasn't that what best friends did? Nose into each other's business, no matter whether they wanted to talk about it or not? Right?

'That night he came to apologise to you and you left because the two of us were arguing?' she said, but it came out like a question, as if I would have forgotten already.

Of course I remembered. Leo had accosted me on the quad, and then Ollie had cornered me in the library while the two of them were making up and getting naked. *Wonderful.*

'I remember.'

'It just sort of happened, you know.' She shrugged. 'One moment we were arguing, and then the next, he shut me up with his lips.' She smiled, and I knew she was seeing an X-rated replay of the event in her mind when her eyes glazed over.

'Cute,' I said, and it kind of was. Well, a mixture of cute and odd. The two of them gave off major best friend vibes, but what did I know? I'd lost my virginity to a bellend who was using me and lying the entire time, so not like I could use my experience to judge anybody else's relationship.

Clo's gaze narrowed. 'No need to be a bitch.'

'I actually wasn't.' I laughed, awkward. 'Not on purpose, anyway.' Tension creeped in, and even though the two of us were on uncertain footing right now, I hoped we wouldn't be for much longer. We had been for some time, never knowing the right thing to say to one another.

'Sure. You just come across as one without trying.'

I shrugged and rolled my eyes at her. Couldn't say much in my defence that wouldn't sound false, or wouldn't sound like complete and utter bullshit. Plus, I wasn't rising to the bait. Not anymore.

'Anyway,' she continued, 'I'm happy.'

'That's what matters most.'

And I meant it. That was what mattered most, even if it all seemed rather suspish.

Ten

SCHOOL ENDED, and the students all departed as soon as they could. The end-of-year assembly had been an entire hour of Ms Hawthorn talking about all that the pupils had achieved at Hawthorn over the last school year. All I could think about was what had happened to me in that time. But you know, she and I saw it differently.

There were five days between school ending and summer school starting, and even though I should be filling it with something exciting, I didn't have any money to leave campus and live it up. Griff kept telling me and Clo he'd cover the cost of whatever we wanted to do, but we kept turning him down. Neither of us wanted to feel indebted to him.

Instead, the three of us just stayed in our room and watched films. It was nice to relax together and not have to leave the room or worry about what would happen with anybody else as they all left us alone. Not sure what Griff said to them to make that happen, but whatever it was, I was super thankful.

On the penultimate night, Clo went home to see her family for the evening and didn't invite us, so it was just me and Griff. I'd known things with Griff were going to take a while to go back to normal, but the moment we were in a room alone together, it became even more apparent. After all the shit that happened last year, the two of us weren't going to just go back to how we were.

I may have forgiven, but I hadn't forgotten. I most likely never would.

He'd hurt me—maybe even more than Ollie had—and definitely more than Leo ever could. The whole thing with Leo was still odd, and I hadn't tried too much to dissect it. I felt like I'd slip down a rabbit hole if I even tried.

Griff had been the one I felt closest to on a friend level. Finding out we were related made it worse, almost. He'd been super emphatic that he hadn't known that our dads were brothers, but just because he didn't know, it didn't mean what he did to me was okay. Not on any level.

Ollie and Leo could have told him at any point throughout the year, but the bastards chose not to. Fuck, they could have told me! They'd hidden so much from both of us; denied us the chance of a family that could love each other. And why did they deny us? In order to play their piss-poor bullying games. And I'd promised myself that from the moment I'd been stabbed, I would no longer be a pawn in those games. I would not let the two of them, alongside *The Set,* walk all over me because of my relation to Jacob Cooper.

Not that I'd got to the bottom of that shit either.

'Griff,' I asked, looking over at him sitting on Clo's bed as if he lived there. 'Can I ask you about Jacob Cooper now?'

'Honestly, Sky. I'm not sure it's my place to tell you,' he said sheepishly, running his hands through his deep auburn hair. I could sense his agitation, but I couldn't place where it stemmed from.

'What do you mean?' I asked, irritated at his reluctance. 'If anyone can talk to me about him, surely it's you! He is my sperm donor after all.'

'Yeah, he is. But what he did was bad, New Girl. Like, Pompeii-bad.'

I ignored his use of the nickname New Girl because I wanted him to keep talking.

'I doubt it was like a volcanic eruption, Griff.'

'In these circles, it may as well have been.' His eyebrows rose, and he was giving me a questioning look. 'You saw the reaction to his name at the fashion show.'

'You rich people are such drama queens.' I laughed. I swear nobody in my old life was that bloody dramatic about their history.

'Yeah, maybe,' he said, shrugging. Then as if a lightning bolt had hit him, he belted out, 'Skylar!'

'What?' I smiled, as bemused by him as ever. He really was a loveable rogue.

'You're rich too!' he shouted, giddy. Infectious.

'Huh?' I asked, my gut response more of a noise than a word. 'How did you work that one out?'

'If we're related, then you're rich, too.'

'I mean, it's a strenuous link, Herc. Doesn't exactly work like that.'

'No, hear me out!' He got more comfortable on Clo's bed, shuffling closer to the edge, like we were two girlfriends sharing confidence. 'My parents left me a fortune. So your dad must have money too and there's no reason why it couldn't go to you.'

'I mean, I guess?' I asked, but it was pretty much a rhetorical question. ' No way to know really. He could've blown every penny he made. Would sort of have to know the guy. I don't even know if he knows I exist, Griff.'

'Would you want to?' he asked me, a serious expression covering his face. No sight of the cheeky grin to put me at ease.

'Want to what? Meet him?' I asked, and actually, it was the first time I'd even thought about it. Even when his name had first been told to me, I'd never considered what it would be like to meet him. Suppose I'd never thought it a possibility.

He blinked. 'Yeah. Why not?'

'Honestly, I've never thought much about it.'

'Makes sense,' he said, his smile returning. 'Not being funny, Clouds, but we'd have to wait for him to pop up, anyway. Nobody has heard from him in a *very long* time.'

'How long?'

'Years.' He scratched his chin and looked to be thinking hard. 'Must have been around the time Millie died.'

'Ollie's mum?' Ollie had told me her name last year when he was pretending to love me.

'Yeah...' he trailed off, and I nodded, mostly because I wasn't sure what else to say. He shook himself out of it in an instant. 'Oh, well. Let's watch a film.'

'You're gonna change the subject? Just like that?'

He nodded. 'Just like that.'

'You're a wanker, you know that?'

'Ah, Clouds. That's just one of the many reasons why you love me.'

I didn't give him the satisfaction of a response, because, honestly? We both knew he was speaking the truth.

GRIFF WAS MORE game than I'd expected him to be about breaking into the girls' rooms and tampering with their toiletries.

'Skylar,' Griff said, holding the key to Ophelia's room high for me to see. 'This is gonna be so much fun!'

'What's the plan?' I'd left the how up to Griff. He knew science stuff, and I definitely did not, so it made sense he chose what we put in what. I wanted to turn their skin a different shade—not burn it off. 'We just gonna break in? How do we even know the girls won't return?'

He brushed my question off. 'Clo's taking care of it.'

'How? They hate her.' I laughed at the thought of Clo trying to keep the O girls occupied. What was she gonna do? Piss them off so much they had to stick around and be so cruel to her she left crying?

'She didn't give me a play-by-play honestly,' Griff said, rubbing his temple in thought. 'We won't be long, though, will we?'

'Doubt it.' I opened the door to Ophelia's room and stepped inside. It looked exactly how I'd imagined. The walls were a pastel pink and all the furniture in the room was pink too. Even the kitchen appliances were pink. 'Whoa! Looks like a pink bomb went off in here.'

'Lia's always loved the colour pink. Says it's her thing.'

'Of course she does, the basic bitch.' I laughed. 'Trust her to have a room so hideous I actually want to leave.'

'Well, we can't leave without doing what we came here to do.' Griff tilted his head in the direction of the bathroom. 'Come on, Clouds. This won't take long.'

Griff disappeared into the en suite, but I didn't follow. 'I should stay out here as a lookout!'

'Whatever you say, mistress,' Griff replied, his voice muffled. I rolled my eyes. It wasn't long until he reappeared, looking triumphant. 'Every lotion and potion I could find has had a little extra *kick* added. It'll be gradual, but damn, it'll be fun to see the look on her face when it works.'

We left Ophelia's room as quick as we'd entered and went next door to Oralie's room.

The layout was the same as the previous one, just flipped, so instead of her bathroom being on the right, it was on the left, and so on. It also wasn't a garish pink colour either, and my eyes were thankful for that fact.

'How did Ophelia and Ollie become a couple?' I asked, knowing I should've kept the thought to myself the moment Griff turned to face me with an accusatory look on his face. He always could see more than I wanted him to.

'What do you mean?'

'Well, one second I was his girlfriend, spending every moment together, then the next, I'm in hospital after being stabbed, and when I return to school four weeks later, he's got another girl hanging all over him as if I never existed.'

'Technically,' Griff said, and I held my breath, knowing whatever came next would hurt. 'He never considered you a real girlfriend...'

'I get that, but—'

'And he knew that if you did come back, he needed to act like you meant nothing to him. Ophelia is the means.'

I could understand that, but it didn't make it easier. 'Do you think he actually likes her?'

'Couldn't tell you.' He shrugged. 'Can't say I'm on speaking terms with the guy right now.'

'You've still not spoken?' I found that hard to believe.

'Nope.' Griff took a step towards the bathroom. Then another. 'I've made it pretty clear which side I'm on and funny enough, Clouds, it isn't Ollie's.'

For the first time, it hit me that Griff had given up his

friendships—his family—for me. Ever since I'd accepted his apology, he spent all his time with me or Clover, and nobody else.

'I don't want you to end up resenting me,' I told him, meaning it. I didn't want him to look back on everything and be pissed that he'd stuck by me and disregarded Ollie and Leo because of it. I was his family, but so were they.

'I promise you, I won't.' He sent a cheeky grin my way before heading into the bathroom, calling back to me as he went. 'Keep an eye out for me!'

'I've got your back!' I called back.

Not long after he disappeared, he re-entered the room, smug as fuck with his work. 'I'm so glad I agreed to this.'

'Me too.' I smiled. 'Now let's get out of here before the girls get back. I'm sure Clo's ready to be rescued.'

'I'll text her now to meet us back in your room.'

We left the room and closed it, locking the door behind us the way we'd found it.

On the short walk back to my room, I paused, Griff stopping with me.

'What's up, Clouds?'

'I just wanted to stop and say thank you,' I said, needing Griff to know just how much I appreciated him and his support. 'I'm so glad you're my family.'

He took a step towards me and pulled me into his wide, outstretched arms. 'Give me a hug.'

I stayed still, awkward, enjoying the hug but also hoping it didn't last too long.

'I love you, Clouds. Don't ever forget that.'

My heart was nearly bursting from the happiness in his voice. 'I love you, too, Herc.'

Eleven

HEADING BACK TO MY ROOM, my head in the clouds, my eyes on the floor, I twisted around the corner and abruptly bumped into somebody.

Make that *two* somebodies.

Ollie and Ophelia were making out in the otherwise empty corridor and came apart the moment I knocked into them.

'Watch it, New Girl,' Ophelia screeched, her eyes narrowed on me. 'Are you seriously that fucking stupid that you can't see in front of your own face?'

'S-sorry,' I sputtered, stuttering without thinking. Then, as if my brain caught up with my mouth, I took it back. 'Actually, no. I'm not sorry.'

'What did you just say?' she asked, and the tone of her voice sent a chill down my spine.

Nice one, Sky. Be brave when the girl is within hitting distance.

'I'm not sorry. I didn't see you there.' I took a step back, wanting to get a little further away from them. 'And believe me, I wouldn't want to touch you on purpose. *Either* of you.'

'You expect me to believe that, bitch?' She sneered, flicking her hair over her shoulder with an accusatory glint in her eyes.

'I don't know why you're bothering talking to this nobody,

babe. She's scum,' Ollie drawled lazily, not even having the gall to look at me. 'Shame whoever stabbed her didn't aim higher.'

Did he think his words were hurting me? Because they really fucking weren't. If anything, I was trying my best to stop a laugh from slipping out. It was just all so comedic, like a bad teen movie or something. The boy gave me whiplash with the way he hated me in one breath and wanted to keep me safe in the other.

He didn't know what he wanted. That much was obvious.

'Should have killed her and left Odette,' Ophelia said, venom seeping out of her every pore.

'Well, as n-nice as this is,' I said, about to sidestep around them, but before I could, Ollie stepped into my path.

'Did I say you could leave?' he growled, and I watched as his eyes darkened. 'No, *slut*. You will stay here until I say otherwise.'

'Slut?' I questioned through gritted teeth, even though I should've ignored him and kept walking.

'You heard me'—he took a step closer, his chest touching mine as he leaned down to whisper in my ear—'slut.'

A red mist descended and covered my vision. He made me so angry, my rage coming to the forefront. It was like all of my anger at him from last year had been lying dormant since the library, but the moment he whispered that word into my ear, I remembered exactly why I'd started my revenge plan.

Involuntarily, my hand rose, and I intended to slap him across the face, but before my hand could make contact, his hand gripped my wrist, halting my motion. With every second that passed, the grip got tighter, and I knew I would have a bruise later tonight.

The grasp was threatening, dominant, and a small whimper left my lips.

'You're hurting m-me,' I whispered. Ollie's pupils dilated, and a breath shuddered out of his mouth, breezing across my skin.

'You d-deserve it,' he said. Him mocking my stutter only made me feel more helpless.

'Let her go.' A bored, yet familiar voice entered my ears, and relief travelled from my head down to my toes.

Leo had come up behind me, silently, his face indifferent as always, and I gave him a tentative smile.

He didn't reciprocate.

'This isn't over, New Girl,' Ollie spat, some of it landing on my cheek. Slowly, he let go of my wrist, and I could see his finger marks imprinted there, the entire area red and inflamed. *Bastard.*

'Come on, Ollie. Let's take this back to your room,' Ophelia whined, a smile on her face she probably saw as seductive, but really, I thought it made her look constipated.

The two of them walked away, but only after Ollie barged into me as he went. Leo didn't leave with them, so I looked at him to find his eyes fixated on my wrist.

'I'm not going to thank you,' I snapped, still furious at him for messing me around during our last couple of conversations. I crossed my arms across my chest, hiding my right wrist from his searing gaze.

'Didn't think you would,' he replied, slightly amused at my stance.

'Congratulations on b-becoming a coach,' I said, trying to stay angry but failing miserably. 'I forgot to say it when I saw you the other day.'

Congratulations on becoming a coach? What the *fuck* was wrong with me?

You hate Leo. You want him to suffer. Clearly, I needed to tell myself that a lot more than I had already.

'Cheers, Stutter.' His smile didn't reach his eyes. 'Means a lot coming from you.'

'No p-problem.'

Without waiting for him to say anything else, I stomped away down the hall, no longer looking at the floor but keeping my eyes ahead.

Moments later, I flung open my dorm room door and hurried across the threshold, then slammed the door behind me. Resting my back up against it, I slumped myself down onto the floor, my butt landing on it with a thud. Frustration—at myself, mostly—made me sick to my stomach.

A sour metallic smell hit my nostrils, and I sniffed.

Once.

Twice.

What the fuck is that smell?

It smelled like death. Death and blood.

After actually having smelt a dead body, albeit only momentarily, I worried I was about to have flashbacks. Worried I'd finally remember who had stood over Odette's lifeless body. Even though learning the truth of that night was something I wanted more than anything, I also wasn't ready for it. Not yet. I was scared of what I would see.

I had enough nightmares—I didn't need to have them in my waking hours, too.

Getting to my feet, I slowly made my way around my room, trying to locate where the smell was coming from. I checked everywhere, leaving my bed for last, and having found nothing on my perusal, I worried I was about to find something horrendous.

I pulled back my duvet, not wanting to look but knowing I needed to.

There. In my bed. A large patch of blood covered my duvet, the once cream cover now a dark red.

My nausea rose, and I fought back a gag.

What in the actual fuck is that?

I looked closer. As close as I could get without touching it.

There, in the centre of the bloody patch, lay a gutted rabbit, the innards pulled out of its tiny body, its dead eyes staring up into mine.

A whimper of shock came, and I flew to the bathroom, lifted the toilet lid and dry retched into the bowl. Although nothing came up, I didn't want to move for fear of being sick. Plus, reentering the room would mean looking at the rabbit again.

Who the fuck put it there?

Like ice, a chill trickled through me, travelling through every vein until my entire body was cold. Somebody had been in my room. Somebody had killed a defenceless animal and left its corpse in the place where I slept. A message. But for what purpose?

What were the odds that whoever did this had also stabbed me after the fashion show? Fuck. Pretty high, I would say.

Who could I text?

I grabbed my phone out of my blazer pocket and opened up my messaging app. Without even thinking twice about it, I opened up my thread with *Thorn.*

MY ROOM. NOW.

Before pressing send, I went back and added a **PLEASE.**

I hoped he would see the text as the plea it truly was and come. That he'd know I had to be really fucking desperate to message him. He'd told me last year I could message whenever I needed—I just hoped he'd meant it, and that the offer still stood.

I didn't even want to think too hard about why I hadn't messaged Clo or Griff first. Sitting by the toilet, I lied to myself, saying that I wanted to protect Clo from it all. That I didn't want to drag Griff down into my shit.

It's official. I've hit an all-time low.

'Skylar!' Leo called, knocking on my dorm door. 'Skylar, I'm coming in!'

The door barged open, and I heard Leo swear. Whether the swearing was because of breaking the door in or him finding the dead rabbit, I couldn't tell.

A figure darkened the bathroom doorway, and the energy it took to lift my head made my vision swim to the point where I saw two of him.

'Stutter,' he said, his tone confused. 'What the fuck is going on?'

I smiled tentatively and said, 'You said to text if I ever needed help.'

Neither of us mentioned that he'd said that back before shit hit the fan. Or that I'd never messaged him when I needed help before, so why was this situation any different.

'What happened?' he asked with a growl, and my stomach tingled in response.

'I don't know,' I whispered, sensing the tears shimmering in my eyes. I must look like a sorry, sore sight, hugging a toilet on the bathroom floor in my school uniform. 'I came here straight from leaving you in the hallway.'

'There's a dead rabbit on your bed,' he said, stating the

obvious, a small smile playing on his lips.

'I noticed.' I hiccupped as the tears in my eyes fell. Of course a dead rabbit was the thing that finally made the dam burst. I'd been a vegetarian since I was ten, and animals coming to any harm really hit me deep in my core. A defenceless rabbit had died because of me.

Maybe the person who did it knows that and used it to their advantage to shit me up.

'Is there a note?' he asked, and I started. The thought hadn't even crossed my mind.

'Didn't get close enough to look.' My neck ached looking up at him, but I couldn't bring myself to stand up off the floor. My voice came out in a small whisper. 'Can you go look for me, please?'

His eyes shone with an emotion I couldn't quite place. At first, it looked like pity, but Leo Hawthorn didn't pity anybody. Ever.

He walked off into my room and was back in seconds with a blood-soaked piece of paper dangling from his fingertips. He crouched down, and our eyes met once we were on the same level.

'Can you read it?' Vulnerability emanated off of me, and I did nothing to change it. After the run-in with Ollie and Ophelia, I felt drained.

Leo nodded. 'Sure.'

I watched as he read it in his head first, scrutinising every feature of his face to see if his entire act was one big lie. After all, maybe he'd placed the rabbit there. Maybe he'd known where to find the note, or that there would even be a note, because he had put it there to begin with. But if I didn't trust him even a little, then why did I message him above anyone else?

Leo nudged me with his side. 'Want to know what it says?'

I nodded, too scared to speak. Black spots were creeping in around the edges of my vision, and my breathing speed had increased to the point I was barely keeping it together.

I could really do without another anxiety attack.

'New Girl. Seems you aren't the only one to get caught in the headlights. Run, rabbit, run,' he read aloud.

Even though I knew Leo was just reading the words from the note, I still got a chill from the flat tone he was using.

'Can you g-get rid of it?' I asked, and he tilted his head in response. His blond hair was messy, brushing against his eyelashes, and I had the urge to run my fingers through it.

Where the shit did that thought come from?

'Stutter, are you okay?' He was still crouching down beside me, and his eyes were searching my face for an answer. His large hand reached out and brushed some hair away that had fallen into my eyes the way I'd thought of doing to him.

'Y-yes. Thanks.' We both knew it was a lie, but he didn't call me out on it.

The two of us fell into silence—not an uncomfortable one, but not quite a comfortable one either. I could count on one hand the amount of times Leo and I had been put in such an intimate situation.

He sat down on the bathroom floor proper and pulled me away from the toilet and into his side, the warmth of his body instantly soothing me.

We stayed like that for at least an hour.

Not talking.

Just... existing.

And fuck, it felt good.

Shit, Skylar. Snap out of it!

Twelve

IT WAS the official first day of summer school, so what better day to create a new beginning—create a new Skylar.

My revenge plan was underway, too, which excited me. Griff and I had already added dye to the girls' body lotions and their shampoos and conditioners. It wasn't exactly diabolical, but it would still piss them off. Now, we just had to wait for it to work.

My first lesson of the day was French, meaning I was about to be stuck in a room with Ophelia and Oralie for two whole hours. *Lucky me.*

It was at these times when I wondered if I'd done something wrong in a previous life—or maybe even the life I was living—because clearly somebody had it out for me. I couldn't catch a break.

As if sharing a lesson with them wasn't bad enough, we had a new teacher. Apparently, Mr Pagerson had decided a student being stabbed on campus (and two being murdered) gave him enough reason to go work elsewhere. Honestly, it killed me. Like he thought that working at a state school would be better for his health. *Bless.*

But then I remembered how I'd told Leo his elitist was

showing when he'd effectively said the same thing. Shit, was I becoming one of *them* by association?

The new teacher's name was Mr Hawkins, and from what Clover had heard whispered in the dining room before school ended, he was around twenty-five years old and rather handsome. Tall, brooding, with dark hair, the description sounded eerily similar to the one in my mind of Mr Darcy—only one of the hottest literary figures to ever exist. I hadn't seen Mr Hawkins yet to verify the claims, but I guess I'd be finding out within the hour.

After rushing to the cafeteria to grab breakfast, I made my way to the French classroom, noticing for the first time since everybody left just how eerie campus was now. The school was large enough when filled with students, so it only felt even bigger with less than twenty people pottering around. Most of the teachers kept to themselves in the staff quarters, making it even more quiet in the common areas.

The summer heat was blazing down on me, and if I stayed outside much longer, I'd be sweating through my shirt and blazer. *Yep. We still have to wear our uniform, even though it's summer.* Thank fuck I attended a private school with air conditioning. My old school used to be sweltering, the thermometers in the classroom usually showing a disgusting temperature that should have caused the school to close—although it never did—but I digress. Money may not buy class, but it did ensure some perks.

The moment I entered the building, the cool air hit me and I took a deep breath, savouring it. In through the nose, expanding the lungs, and out through the mouth. Or was it supposed to be the other way around? I could never remember. I'd never stayed chill enough to excel at yoga or meditation.

A phlegm-filled scoff came from behind me. *Oralie.* Pretty

impressive that I could tell them apart from the sound of their hatred towards me. Useful life skill that.

'You're in our way, bitch.'

'Move!' Ophelia demanded.

Instead of moving out of the way, my feet turned so I was facing the two basic bitches rather than walking away from them.

'Do you feel b-big?' I asked, and aside from the slight stutter, it came out strong. 'Does it make you feel better to make me feel like shit?'

Ophelia gave me a dirty look, her distaste for me radiating in my direction. Oralie's mouth opened in shock, and I knew I'd surprised her. Fuck, I'd surprised *myself*. Neither of them was used to me standing up to them yet; actually opening my mouth and talking back.

To be honest, they didn't scare me half as much without Odette running the show. When Odette was alive, they'd been sheep, mostly, and had instigated none of what happened to me. Just went along for the ride with whatever Odette wanted them to do. They didn't have the brains to work solo.

'You never had Ollie. You were a pity fuck. Get over yourself,' Ophelia spat, and all I could do was laugh at her. Where the fuck had that come from?

Why was she even bringing Ollie up? *Insecure much.*

'Okay?' I chuckled again.

Eventually, after realising I wouldn't be moving anytime soon, they moved around me and headed into the French classroom.

Skylar - 1, Set - 0

I chuckled to myself for a minute longer, but then I spotted the time on the large clock above the exit. *Shit.* I was late to my very first lesson of summer school. Making a bad first impression always sat wrong with me and I avoided it when I could.

I rushed into the room while talking. 'I am so sorry I'm late.'

Looking up, I locked eyes with Mr Hawkins and I instantly saw what all the fuss was about. No wonder he'd sent so many teenagers with hormones going wild into overdrive. His skin was tan, and his hair was a dark brown, and his eyes were the most gorgeous colour, like a light hazelnut. Damn, where did Ms Hawthorn find such a fine specimen? And why was she allowing him around teenagers willingly?

'Take a seat, Miss Crescent,' he said with a smile, dimples and all. I quickly brushed away the sweat forming on my upper lip with the back of my hand.

He gestured to the last free chair in front of him and I took it. He'd rearranged the room so that there were only three desks in front of the board.

As fast as I could, I pulled my pen, notebook, and laptop out of my satchel bag, not wanting to disrupt the lesson any more than I already had. Neither Ophelia nor Oralie said anything, and when I glanced over to look at them, I realised it was because they were too busy drooling over Mr Hawkins to harass me. Maybe having him as our teacher wouldn't be so bad if it meant they'd leave me alone.

'Right, girls, I don't want to be too strict. We're all here when we don't want to be, and I'm sure the four of us can come to some kind of agreement. You listen when I speak and answer when I ask a question, and if you're well-behaved, there will be a reward at the end of each week. Sound good?'

The three of us nodded, caught up in his spell. His voice was like melted honey, all oozing and trickling and—what the fuck?

Had I really just thought that? *If you want to vomit at that, then fair, because even I want to hurt myself for even thinking it.*

I shivered with revulsion at myself. Well, *half* of it was revulsion and the other half was because Mr Hawkins had just caught my eye, and I felt some tingles in places I definitely should not be feeling tingles.

'Sir,' Ophelia said, as Oralie giggled alongside her. 'Can you translate something for me?'

'Sure,' he replied, gracing her with a lopsided grin. I'd never understood why schools hired young, attractive teachers, and then were confused by the students' actions as a result. Not to be confused with me condoning any actions taken by the teacher in those situations. That shit wasn't okay in real life. Fiction life? I'd allow it.

'*Voulez-vous coucher avec moi?*' she purred.

The lack of originality really was something else. I rolled my eyes at her words, noticing how she'd left off the *ce soir* part of her sentence, making it even more suggestible. I expected him to ignore her, or to tell her he wouldn't answer her, but he didn't do either of those things. *Nope.*

'Will you sleep with me?' he drawled, one eyebrow raised.

The two of them burst into fake giggles, and I had to stop myself from groaning in disgust. Of course they found shit like that funny. The two of them barely had a brain cell to spare.

'Of course,' Ophelia said, batting her eyelashes at him, her eyes wide. Pretty sure the girl believed she looked seductive.

She did not.

To me, her eyelashes looked like spider's legs from the amount of mascara she'd coated onto them and if I were Mr Hawkins, I'd be terrified they were going to just up and walk off her face.

'Nice try, Miss Rogers. Let's start the lesson, shall we?' He winked, and I instantly warmed to him. Okay, he seemed a *little* too taken by the tweedles next to me, but he also had a sense of humour. Guessed you sort of had to when teaching teenagers at only twenty-five. Old Mr Pagerson had barely cracked a smile at anything.

'If you insist, *sir*.'

Good Lord, did the girl have no shame?

'Let's talk about drugs,' Mr Hawkins said, his voice booming throughout the classroom.

I sank into my seat, getting ready for the long haul.

THE END of the lesson didn't come as quick as I would have liked, but it didn't drag either.

Mr Hawkins had set some couple speaking tasks, and he'd picked up on the animosity between the O girls and me, so he had been my speaking partner rather than making us team up as a three.

'Miss Crescent, if you could stay behind, please,' he called out as we were packing our laptops and notebooks away. Mr Hawkins was standing beside his desk—or should I say— leaning against his desk, looking casual. A clear sign of somebody who had no cares in the world. I caught his eye and nodded. Without even looking at them, I knew Ophelia and Oralie were livid that he was asking me to stay behind and not them. Their risk earlier hadn't paid off. How sad.

With a huff, they flounced out of the room and I stood awkwardly by my desk, not wanting to get any closer unless asked.

'Can I call you Sky?' he asked, his eyes assessing my face.

Be a bit awkward to say no. 'S-sure.'

'Cool.' He rubbed his hands together. 'So, Sky, I just wanted to let you know that if anybody harasses you this summer, come and let me know and I'll sort it.'

'Thanks?' I didn't tell him I didn't think he had the power to do shit.

'No problem. Also, I wanted to talk to you about your predicted results from last term.' His brows rose, and he took up a position back in his seat. He grasped his hands together, elbows on his desk. 'Come. Sit.'

Slowly, I moved to the seat and sat down, more uncertain with every step. I couldn't put my finger on it, but there was something screaming at me to get far away. Or to at least leave the classroom. It was okay when Ophelia and Oralie were in the room, too, but once they'd left, it didn't feel quite so good anymore.

'Sky, I want you to know that I'm more than willing to give you extra tutoring sessions this summer, without Ophelia and Oralie around, if you need.'

'Huh?' I blurted.

'Ms Hawthorn has made me aware of the circumstances of last year, and I know those girls bullied you.' His eyes filled with sympathy, and I instantly wanted to wipe his pitying smile off his face. Funny enough, it was the first time anybody had ever used the word "bullied" to describe what happened to me. It seemed too tame for what they'd done.

'Right.' I fidgeted in the chair. 'Well, thank you.' I wanted to get out of there. The longer I sat opposite him, the more uncomfortable I got.

'You're welcome. I'm looking forward to our time together this summer.'

'M-me too.' I bit down the vomit threatening to rise up my

throat, with no idea why my gut reaction was that strong. He hadn't moved closer, he hadn't leered at me the way Andy used to, but he gave me the same feeling nonetheless.

'You may leave,' he said with a closed-mouth smile. I grabbed my bag from the floor and moved out of the room at a fast pace. As I reached the doorway, he added, 'Cute stutter, by the way.'

I shuddered and continued out of the room. Not once looking back.

Creepy teacher. *Just what I need.*

Thirteen

THE NEXT DAY, during my free period, I was alone in the library, and instead of warmth filling my gut, my stomach was filled with creeping spiders and wiggling worms.

I hated it. Hated that the library no longer comforted me—no longer filled me with the warm fuzzies like it had before.

Ollie had ruined that for me. Like he had ruined so much else.

And it pissed me the fuck off.

Take my trust. Take my dignity. But fuck anybody who tried to take my love of books.

The anger rippled through me, and if anybody got close enough, they'd burn from the heat emanating from me. I just wanted to be alone with my thoughts. Ollie needed to suffer and I needed to be the one who made it happen. Needed him to feel even an ounce of the pain and humiliation he'd caused me.

He'd taken my heart, blown it up to the size of the moon, and then deflated it, leaving it broken, limp, and lifeless.

There was a major part of me that believed maybe Griff was still full of shit, and that he'd meant nothing of what he said during our heart-to-heart and was still playing me. Still gaining inside information from me and passing it on to Ollie and Leo. Maybe even to Oralie and Ophelia.

Come on, Sky. Stop being such a little paranoid bitch.

I couldn't even trust my mind, and that was never a good sign.

It's said that the mind's the first to go, right?

Getting comfortable at my usual table, I pulled out my trusty paperback copy of *Pride and Prejudice* in an attempt to ignore my raging thoughts.

Jane Austen, take me away.

An hour passed, maybe even two, yet to me, it felt like mere minutes. There was something beautiful about an English literature classic, something that made me fall in love with reading even more, and *Pride and Prejudice* was my ultimate. I'd never thought of myself as much of a romantic, but there was something about this story that transformed everything in my brain.

Other than Ollie, I'd not had much experience with an actual relationship. I laughed scornfully. With Ollie, I didn't even get an experience of a "real relationship".

Really, I was a delusional cow. Or at least I was a reformed one. Knowing the problem was always the first step in resolving the problem.

I'd like to think that since the fashion show I was enlightened. The new and improved Sky. Skylar Crescent 2.0, if you will.

'What the fuck are you doing here?'

Tearing my eyes away from the page reluctantly, I looked up to find the owner of the barked words. Ollie was standing opposite me on the other side of the table, staring me down. His entire expression had my veins turning to ice. His dark indigo eyes narrowed, and his mouth was set into a deep frown.

I opened and then closed my mouth multiple times, resembling a goldfish. A mindless, pointless creature if there ever was one. I'd never wanted a goldfish as a pet because I couldn't understand their purpose.

After what felt like a long time, I stuttered out, 'W-what?'

'You heard me,' he growled, his eyes assessing me. Ollie's hate was evident, even if there was the slight glimmer of lust in his perusal of me. 'But I'll repeat myself. I know your intellect level isn't the highest. What the fuck are you doing here?'

He over enunciated each word, each syllable.

'Here as in the library?' I asked, playing dumb.

'In my eye line.'

My mind had run into a figurative brick wall, and I had no clue how to respond. *Ah, fuck it. What do I have to lose by saying the first thing that enters my mind?*

'*You* walked over to *me*. Clearly, you want me to be in your eye line.'

His face darkened further. A deep growl from his throat shocked us both, and I laughed. You know those laughs where you knew you were in shit, but you hoped that a breathy laugh would get you off the hook? Yep, it was one of those. And from the looks of him, it hadn't had the desired effect.

'Leave,' he demanded, choosing not to retaliate to what I'd said. His lips were turned down, his hand clenching and unclenching at his side, and I knew I'd rattled him. His knuckles turned white, they were clenched so tight. His other hand was in his hair, as he tried to appear nonchalant, but the twitching of his mouth, the glint of anger in his eye, gave his genuine feelings away.

And it made me feel powerful. Big.

'Make me leave,' I said, my tone hard. 'Oh, wait, you've already tried and failed.'

'You should have left this school after the fashion show and never come back.' His eyes narrowed, and his anger was close to burning me. 'I want you to leave this place and never return.'

'So you said,' I smarted, remembering him saying those exact same words in this very spot only a week ago. 'But apparently, you wanted me to stay enough to engineer me being here for the summer.'

I saw him falter a little before the shutters came back down over his disordered expression.

'I will keep telling you to leave until you listen,' he said after he came back to himself.

'You'll be saying it until the cows come home. Or at least until graduation,' I said with a small smile—I couldn't help myself from stooping down to his level.

'You *will* leave, Skylar. You're not safe here.'

If somebody else had said those words, I would have been more inclined to listen. The thing irking me? He had a valid point. Somebody had it out for me, and I wasn't safe here, but I wasn't safe at home either if he was to be believed. In either scenario, I lost.

'I'm well aware, Oliver.' I hated it when he full-named me, and I knew it pissed him off when I didn't use his nickname in return. Or at least it had, back when we had just met, but maybe that had been a façade too. Another lie. Just one more to add to the long list. 'Not like I'm safe anywhere, is it, dickhead?'

I thought he hadn't heard me until he replied. 'Do you want me to pity you?'

'No,' I uttered, my tone soft. 'But it is the truth.'

'Bullshit,' he barked. He stepped closer to me, having

moved from behind the table opposite me to almost standing beside me, his closeness having an effect on my mental capacity.

'What?' I snapped, mad that he was dismissing me, but also pissed at myself that I still let his actions affect me. Still let the actions of a dickhead take up space in my mind rent-free.

His eyebrows raised high on his forehead. 'How on earth are you safer here?'

'Well, at least here I don't have to worry about unwanted advances,' I said. An image of Mr Hawkins popped into my mind and I mumbled, 'Not yet, anyway.'

'Andy?' Ollie asked with a growl, and I nodded, confused why he sounded so angry. I could've sworn I'd told him about the events the day I came to Hawthorn. He scoffed. 'Knew I should've hit the cunt.'

No part of me minded Ollie's anger. If anything, it should have repulsed me, but it didn't. Actually, it sort of excited me a little—no, *a lot*. Watching Ollie punch Andy would be something I welcomed.

Abruptly, I stood up out of my chair and walked away from him. I couldn't be in his bubble any longer. Couldn't just sit still, breathing the same air as him, and not want to reach out and touch his face—his body. Yeah, he was a major prick, but he was a very good-looking prick.

The young adult section of the library beckoned me, the way it always did. The shelves were filled with goodies, and I wanted to grab a book I loved. A comfort read. One of my favourites was pretty old, but because I had had little money growing up, I'd relied a lot on what the local library offered me. To be honest, I was pretty sure that this particular book was old enough that it had been updated recently to change a mention of a fax to a text. *A fax.* That was the age of it. I'd been shooketh when I found it in the library here at Hawthorn; I'd expected all the books here to be dry, boring tomes.

After snatching *Diving In* by Kate Cann off the shelf, I turned and found myself faceplanting into a hard chest.

The shock caused me to drop the book, and I bent down straight away to pick it up.

'Don't move,' Ollie whispered, his voice close. He had crouched down so we were on the same level. His lips touched my ear, causing tingles to travel throughout my body, chilling me to my core. The touch of his breath doing things to my insides I didn't want to admit, even to myself.

He grabbed my arm and yanked it behind my back. I stumbled, trying to keep my balance now that he'd incapacitated me further.

'Straighten up, slowly, and face the shelves,' he growled, low and seductive.

'N-no.' My voice was barely audible above his heavy breathing.

'Do it.'

'You're hurting me,' I whimpered. The pulling on my arm was making my arm rattle in its socket, the sharp pain shooting down from my shoulder making me wince.

'Stand. Up.'

I did as he demanded, straightening and facing the shelves ladened with my favourite books. I focused on their cracked spines, studying every letter, trying to stay in the moment. Something I struggled with at the best of times.

'What are you d-doing?'

I wanted to hit myself for letting a stutter leave my lips. I'd been doing so well recently, keeping my stutter at bay and talking with confidence.

'You make me sick,' he whispered in my ear, unhinged.

'Why did you have to return? Why couldn't you have made everybody happy and stayed gone?'

He pressed up against me, pushing me closer to the shelves, turning my head to the right. My arm was still trapped behind my back, and if he pushed any more, I'd end up with a book spine imprinted on my cheek. His hard dick was pressed up against my lower back, and my nipples hardened in response. My body was betraying my brain. Betraying me.

'I-I—'

'I-I,' he mocked. 'I can see through this act, New Girl.'

'W-what act?' I whimpered again when he tightened the grip on my wrist and used his other hand to pull my other arm to put them together. He was on autopilot, his brain telling him one thing while reality battled to show the truth.

'The one where you act like you hate me.'

'I do hate you,' I whispered, hating him more than ever for putting me in such a vulnerable position. For showing my weakness around him. For not taking no as my answer.

'You only wish you hated me.' His words were poisonous; harsh. And, sadly, so fucking true.

I whimpered, like an injured animal caught by a much larger predator, but it didn't deter him. His teeth bit into my earlobe, a spot he *knew* I found sensitive, and he growled. 'You like this. You want this.'

Is he trying to convince me? Or himself?

One of Ollie's hands gripped my breast, hard, and I flinched. A sharp pain travelled through me from his touch.

His hand travelled further down, leaving a tickling sensation in its wake before breaching the top of my skirt and into my knickers. I squirmed in his hold, thinking that if I made enough movement and sound, somebody would come and find us. The librarian had to be around here somewhere. She knew I was in the back. Maybe she'd notice something was amiss.

'P-please,' I whispered, a tear running down my cheek. I didn't want this. 'No.'

'Shh, Skylar. I've got you.' Maybe he misunderstood my plea? Or maybe he chose not to understand me on purpose? Did I really mean that little to him?

Ollie's long middle finger entered me, my wetness easing the movement.

Another finger entered me, the feeling of fullness more prominent, and both of us moaned. The speed of his fingers increased, and every time he hit that spot inside me, I moaned a little louder. *Fuck.* I didn't want his touch to feel good. I didn't want to enjoy any part of what was happening. Yet I was. And it made me feel so very wrong.

'You are so fucking sexy,' he moaned in my ear, adding a third finger, and the moment he did, I saw stars. *Fuck.*

Ollie and I had been intimate enough times that he knew what to do to turn me on most, so I'd forget my name—forget my no.

I came around his fingers. My heart rate accelerated, pulsing out my orgasm with a loud moan I bit off by gritting my teeth.

'Fuck, New Girl. That was... You're... Fuck.'

'Get off me,' I stammered, wanting his hand gone. Wanting the pressure of him up against me gone. Wanting *him* gone.

When he didn't move fast enough, I shouted.

'Get off me!'

Ollie moved his hand out of my underwear and moved back in an instant. I turned around, tears filling my eyes, threatening to leak out, to look into his. I wanted him to see the despair on my face, the hurt in my heart, and know he was the one who caused it.

'Shit,' he muttered, running his hand through his hair. 'Sky, I—'

He reached for me, but I sidestepped him and continued walking. I needed to get out of here. Needed to get away from what had just happened.

I couldn't believe I'd let him finger me up against the book stacks without putting up more of a fight. Couldn't believe he hadn't listened to my pleas, listened to *me*.

Before, he had been the first person to truly hear me. To give me the time, and care, to truly listen to me.

Clearly, I was wrong earlier. I'm still *a delusional cow.*

THE DINING ROOM was so empty after everybody left for the summer. The high ceiling meant every voice echoed, and you could hear every clink of cutlery. There were only two tables occupied. One with me, Griff, and Clo. Ollie, Ophelia, Oralie, and Leo occupied the other table.

'So, what do we do first?' Clover asked our table. Ever since I'd rushed out of the library, I'd wanted to keep a low profile. I hadn't wanted Ollie to see me again so soon, but I couldn't come up with an excuse fast enough for Clo and Griff to agree to eat in our room.

The other table was completely silent, not conversing at all, although now and then, a giggle rang out and echoed off the high ceiling. I'd glanced over at Ollie once or twice when he wasn't looking, and from what I could see, he looked fucking miserable. But then again, maybe I was just projecting and seeing what I wanted to see.

'Can't exactly talk about it here,' I said through my teeth. The room was way too quiet to discuss our revenge shit; to discuss anything we didn't want to be overheard.

'I meant this weekend,' she said, looking at me like I had a screw loose.

'This weekend?' I asked, confused about how we'd got here. Had I tuned out a vital part of the conversation?

'We're allowed off campus at the weekends if we want,' Griff said, his face covered in a wide beam. 'It's still our summer, after all.'

'Exactly! So, what do we do first with our freedom?' Clo asked again.

'Hmm.' I hummed, deep in thought. I hadn't really thought about whether we'd be allowed to leave campus or not. It made sense. We were all seventeen or over now. Actually, that reminded me that Leo was turning nineteen at the weekend. 'Is Leo celebrating his birthday?' I blurted louder than I intended, and I heard Leo cough over at the other table, proving my point that there wasn't any privacy in such a large, cavernous room.

'Not like you'd be invited, bitch,' Ophelia spat, calling across to me. I rolled my eyes, not dignifying her with a response. She didn't deserve one.

My phone vibrated in my blazer pocket. Clover had a tendency to peek at my phone over my shoulder, so I had to be all covert ops about reading my messages just in case it was something I didn't want her to see, especially after that time she saw a message to me from Leo. I pulled the phone out and glanced at it under the table.

Stutter. Meet me at our place. My birthday. Midnight.

I glanced over at Leo, to see if he was looking my way, but his gaze was firmly on Ophelia, who was chatting shit about how hot she found Mr Hawkins.

Dismissing the message for now, I looked back at Griff and Clo, who were both giving me a funny, questioning look.

'Have I got something on my face?'

'Just your features,' Griff said with a smile. He went back to eating his food, and I followed suit.

Too lost in thought to even fully taste it.

Fourteen

STUTTER. MEET ME AT OUR PLACE. MY BIRTHDAY. MIDNIGHT.

I READ the message from Leo again and wondered for the umpteenth time what on earth he meant. *Where* on earth he meant?

Ever since the rabbit debacle, we'd barely spoken, choosing to ignore one another in the dining hall or if we saw each other in passing. I hadn't told Clover or Griff about any of it, not wanting to alarm them. Or have them questioning why it was Leo I went running to and not them. Even though technically it was Leo who did the running as I was stunned frozen.

Our place?

For the life of me, I couldn't think of the spot he classed as *our place.*

A list of possibilities ran through my mind. The hallway between the hospital wing and the pool house? The library? I'd never been to his room alone, so it couldn't be there. Plus, he'd moved into the staff quarters since summer started. A no-go area.

As I pondered my dilemma, Clo and Griff entered the room in the middle of a heated debate about some shit I didn't care about. It was happening more frequently since they'd become a couple—or at least a couple with no label. *Insert eye roll here.*

The two of them constantly disagreed about something, even what to call their relationship. For the most part, I ignored them, but it had started to grate on me.

'I don't understand why you can't just stop talking to them,' Clo said, looking at Griff, her eyebrows twitching.

'Luck, they're my family,' he said, his tone gentle. Placating. Like talking to a child who needed to understand the ways of the world.

'Right, but they're also total cumstains, which I'm pretty sure overrides blood.'

They must be talking about Ollie and Leo. *Again!*

At first, I'd joined in on their conversations about them, throwing in my two cents, but after it didn't go anywhere, I gave up. No use repeating myself on a daily basis to two people who weren't listening anyway.

I chose their distraction to send a quick text to Leo, having ignored his message for an entire week. When he had first sent it, I hadn't allowed myself much longer than three seconds to think about it, but since then, it hadn't left my mind. Kept telling myself I wouldn't stress myself out about whatever he meant—yeah, right.

Our spot?

'Bit rich, babe, when you stick by your parents,' Griff snapped back.

'This isn't about my parents,' Clo bit out through gritted teeth. 'This is about Leo and Ollie and the fact that you still act friendly with them when Sky and I aren't around.'

'Is it really, Red?'

'What did you just call me?' Clover seethed, spitting. Her entire face flushed tomato ketchup red, and I wished I were anywhere but in the room with them.

Griff's facial expression sank, his face paler than I'd ever seen it, and I could tell instantly that he knew he'd made a massive mistake. Red was the name Leo used for Clover. It was the name he always used in our texts—back when he was asking after her. He hadn't asked about her in a while, though.

He sputtered, 'I-I... C'mon, Clo, don't be like that.'

'Be like what?' Her entire demeanour was on the defensive, her arms crossed across her chest, her eyebrows raised.

'Like I called you that on purpose to hurt you.' He rolled his eyes, and I winced.

Wrong move, Griff.

'Well, it did,' she spat, the evil eye game strong. Nobody could give the evil eye like Clover. She was a master at it and I was lucky that she'd only directed it at me once or twice in the time I'd known her. Just one look was enough to make you shit yourself, I swear.

I had to butt in—their bullshit was tiring and pretty constant. No matter what they did, I knew the two of them weren't endgame, but they needed to figure that out for themselves. My room was no longer a sanctuary, if it ever was, and I couldn't stay silent any longer.

'Can you two per-lease give it a rest?' My voice was louder than intended, and it stopped the two of them, so they turned to face me for the first time. Griff's face was sincere and apologetic. Clo's eye was still twitching.

'Don't you mean can't *Griffin* give it a rest?' Clo had always acted petty, but she didn't need to turn on me. I wasn't her enemy here. Nobody was.

I rolled my eyes at her childish antics and pretended to

think about it for a moment, rubbing my finger on my chin. 'No, I mean both of you.'

'Oh, good lady, you wound me so,' Griff said, sweeping his arm in the air to raise his hand and place it over his heart. 'Thou doth upset me.'

'Oh, hush up!' I laughed, closing the gap between us to nudge him in the ribs.

'Oh, ha, ha. If you two find it so funny, why don't you date!'

'Maybe because that'd be hella wrong?' I laughed because if I didn't laugh I'd get pissed, and she wasn't worth it in the mood she was in. 'Family, remember?'

She turned and stormed away. Well, I say stormed away, but it was more of a flounce. Griff chuckled and then caught himself and covered it with a cough.

'Was it something I said?' he asked me, his dimples pressed in. I shook my head and smiled.

'Honestly, dude, you need to stop messing with her like that. You know Clo doesn't like it.'

He shrugged at me in response, his eyes clear. No emotion telling me either way whether he'd angered her on purpose.

'Listen, Clouds, I like her,' he told me, his expression earnest. 'But I can never decide if I'm just holding the spot, you know?'

'Holding the spot?' It was clear to me he meant Leo, but I wanted to hear it from his mouth, and not just my imagination. Assuming things had already got me into trouble more than once.

'Has Clo ever told you about the past?' he asked, more serious than his usual jolly tone. I shook my head, and he continued, 'One day, you should ask her about it.'

'Right. Like I've never tried to get into that girl's head in the past.' My response was filled with derision, but fuck, I was pissed. At all of it. These two were supposed to be my friends—fuck, they were my *only* friends—but they had secrets I didn't know. A past I couldn't touch.

He inclined his head. 'Don't judge her too harshly.'

'Whatever,' I muttered. 'I'm out.'

Griff nodded and waved at me, letting me know it was cool that I was dashing out on him.

It was only when walking down the hall that I thought to check my phone. With all the theatrics between Clo and Griff, I'd forgotten about messaging Leo.

The hallway between the hospital wing and the pool house. Don't be late, Stutter.

Confusion swirled in my brain like a fog. Surely, if he were going to pick one of those corridors, he would have picked the one between the hospital wing and the admin building where he liked to pull me into alcoves? Yet, somehow, *our* hallway was the one where I was stabbed and had found a dead body.

Love that for me.

Sunday came—Leo's birthday—and after spending the day alone, I went back to my room to find Griff and Clover were both there. They'd made up after their spat the day before, and I wasn't even going to acknowledge it. The two of them were sitting on Clo's bed, cosied up together about to watch something on TV, like nothing ever happened. Like Clo hadn't stormed out last night, acting like a five-year-old.

I nodded at them when I entered and took myself off to the

bathroom under the guise of needing a shower. Okay, so I did actually need a shower, but I also just didn't want to be with them if I didn't have to be. Their bullshit was becoming too much to handle.

If I had other friends it wouldn't be such a big deal, but because I didn't, I was stuck.

Once in the bathroom, away from their prying eyes, I pulled out my phone to text Leo. I still wasn't sure whether I was going to meet him later that night, but if I didn't go, it would always plague me. That what-if.

I hated what-ifs.

Happy birthday! Still on for midnight?

Leo was a mystery to me and he always had been. He was the moody, disinterested one of the three boys, who rarely found amusement in anything—anything that wasn't tormenting Clo, anyway—and for some unknown reason, I wanted to delve deeper and find out what made the boy tick.

The hot water soothed my skin, my soul, as I showered and washed my hair, taking my time, trying to fill every minute so that I wouldn't anxiously sit around and wait until I had to leave to meet Leo. Because of course I was going to go. I was kidding myself when I told myself I wasn't sure.

My phone was lit up with a new message when I got out, and I snatched it up as fast as I could. The movement unbalanced me, my legs jelly and my feet sliding out from beneath me, and I fell to the floor with a large thudding noise. *Shit, that hurt.*

'Sky?' There was a rustle from the room on the other side of the door, Clover's worried voice coming through it. 'Sky? Are you okay?'

'I'm fine. Don't worry!' I called back, hoping she wouldn't enter the room and find me sprawled out on the floor with my towel barely hanging on. If there was one thing I knew, it was that the position I'd landed in was *not* an attractive one.

Wonder how big the bruise on my arse will be. I'd never had much grace or rhythm, but there was nobody to blame but me. My anxiety over Leo's message was sending me into overdrive.

'You sure?' Clo asked, her voice returned to a lower volume with the panic having receded since my reply.

'Yep,' I called back. 'It's all gravy!'

'Cool beans.'

I listened, waiting to hear her shuffle away from the door before I moved again. The moment I heard her step away, I pulled myself up and rested against the sink cupboard to look at my phone. I had two messages: one from *Thorn*, the other from *Beast*.

What the fuck did he want?

SKYLAR, PLEASE MEET ME TONIGHT AT MIDNIGHT. THERE'S SOMETHING I WISH TO TALK WITH YOU ABOUT. I'LL BE WAITING AT THE TREELINE.

Ollie's text surprised me, but for all the wrong reasons.

The moment I read it, I didn't know what to think. Of course I was fucking suspicious of the fact he wanted to meet at the treeline on the exact same night and time that Leo wanted to meet. But the boy *had* said please, and that came as the biggest shock of all. He never said please. Maybe he wanted to apologise for what happened in the library...

Leo's message was easier to understand. Simple.

WE'RE STILL ON. EXCITED TO SEE YOU, STUTTER.

Goosebumps appeared all over my body, either from the chill I felt at his message or the water having dried on my skin while I read it.

'Sky, are you sure you're okay? Sounded like you fell,' Griff called through the door and I realised just how long had passed since I'd fallen.

'I'm ite, I promise. I'll be out in a moment.' In a hurry, I changed into my pyjamas. It was a habit of mine to always change out of day clothes into sleepwear as soon as I got back to my room. It was way more comfortable that way, and even though I was planning to meet Leo, I couldn't change my routine. It would alert Griff and Clo that something was up.

Shit, I may even go to meet Leo dressed in my fluffy Cookie Monster pyjamas. Really prove to him that I didn't give a fuck about what he had to say to me.

Least I'd be comfortable.

Does my carelessness sound genuine yet? Does my inner self believe the bullshit it's trying to make me believe?

Nope. I didn't think so, either.

Fifteen

THE CLOCK HIT HALF ELEVEN, and I sat bolt upright in my bed, not having got a wink of sleep. Not that I would've gone to sleep much before midnight on a normal night anyway.

Glancing over at Clo's side of the room, I could see she was fast asleep and snoring away—dead to the world around her. A good sign—and believe me, I was looking for all the signs.

You know how if you tried to creep around, quiet as a mouse, you were more likely to make a loud, crashing noise?

Well, yeah, I knew that if I crept around that would happen to me—I was clumsy as fuck—so I made sure I moved around as I always did at night time. If Clo woke up, I could be all, *Nothing different here* while lying through my teeth. Every night I was up and down anyway, having an overactive bladder, both from anxiety and in general, meaning Clo was used to my heavy footsteps while she slept.

The door closed with a soft click behind me, and I took a deep breath, excited I'd managed to escape without waking Clover up. Any questions would set me back and make me late. Plus, I just wasn't ready to answer anything she might ask. Not yet.

I made my way across campus, my feet barely touching the ground as I moved faster with each passing second. Even though there was barely anybody on campus, I still found myself looking all around me with every step. Who knew what Ophelia and Oralie got up to at night. My eyes darted into all the dark spots and my paranoia constantly told me that somebody was hiding in the shadows.

The lights in the buildings were dimmed, casting an ominous glow across the grass when I looked out the window to see if my path was clear. There was no way for me to reach the meeting spot without going outside. Maybe that was Leo's game. The dorm buildings weren't attached to any of the others, and the fact I had to go outside, in the pitch-black of night, filled me with dread. Anything could lurk out in the open, or hide in order to pounce out in front of a girl all alone out in the open.

Leo better be about to apologise to me. Otherwise, I wouldn't be impressed. Although I highly doubted he was about to apologise for how he treated me when I first came to school. I wasn't sure what I expected from our talk at all, honestly. Different topics had come and gone from my mind since his first text, but I hadn't settled on anything in particular.

Braving the outside world, knowing I needed to meet Leo for my sanity, I made my way out into the cold air. Something unusual for the time of year, but the weather was always slightly different on top of a hill. The wind was blowing so hard that you could hear it whistling through the trees surrounding the school. A whirling, gushing noise that put me on edge—fuck, everything was putting me on edge. I was living life on the edge, it would seem, and if I were an animal, my ears would be pricked and at attention for sure.

That's it. Compare yourself to a dog, Sky.

The moon shone bright in the sky, and I had to stop myself from halting and staring up at it, getting lost in its beauty. I'd always loved the moon ever since I was a little girl—I'd always felt a connection to it. My name, basically being the phrase moon sky reversed, meant I'd dreamt I was the girl who lived on the moon, who'd come down to earth as punishment, and that was why "they" (whoever "they" were) had given me to Cora. I suppose you could say I'd had an overactive imagination from a super young age and a desire to live a more exciting life than the one I'd landed.

As I came around the front of the main building, I could see the entrance to the treeline where Ollie had asked me to meet him. I thought I'd look over and see the trees and nothing else, but that wasn't the sight that greeted me. If I squinted, I *could* make out a human-shaped outline—although they were too far away for me to determine much about them. My brain assumed Ollie was standing there, but I'd been wrong about things before. Like the idea that Ollie was falling for me...

The decision to meet Leo instead of Ollie was surprisingly easier than I'd thought it would be. Leo had at least tried to talk to me since I was stabbed, and he'd come to my rescue with the rabbit, putting him in my okay books. Ollie had violated my trust and hadn't listened to me enough in the library, and that put him firmly in the not okay books.

And if he wanted to apologise for that, he could do so. Just not at night, in the dark, at the edge of the woods.

With a sigh, I opened the heavy doors of the main building, the groan echoing throughout the empty hall, and all I could think was that I hoped the sound hadn't travelled across to the shadowy figure by the trees.

My heart rate quickened in that way it does when you

know you are doing something you shouldn't be. Like the time I'd sprayed myself with my mum's perfume as a kid and had spent the rest of the day terrified she'd find out and tell me off.

Flying up the stairs and around the corner into the hallway, I could see a figure up ahead. *Fuck, that better be Leo.*

'Stutter, you came,' he said, his voice carrying down the hall, smooth and velvety. Seductive. Guess he wasn't worried about anybody hearing us.

'Yep. So, you better talk. Fast.' My tone was clipped, my displeasure radiating off of me. As I got closer to where he stood, Leo's face changed from disinterested to playful, and his lips formed into a smile. Okay, maybe not a smile. But a slight upturn of the right side of his mouth, at least.

'Somebody's testy,' he said, his grin growing wider. 'What's the matter? You in a sulk?'

'I'm not "in a sulk", you twat,' I spat, my anger rising to the surface. 'I just want to know what is so *important* you asked to talk to me in secret at midnight.'

He chuckled at my bunny fingers.

'Could've fooled me,' he drawled. 'I've got a proposition for you, Stutter.'

'Will y-you always call me that?' The fact I'd stuttered when asking my question wasn't lost on me. At first, the name had been a pisstake and a dig, something to rile me up and make me feel small, but after the events of Halloween, it had become an affectionate name of sorts. The kind of name you gave a friend where you were both in on it.

'I thought you liked it?' he asked, his eyebrow rising quizzically. His blue eyes were shining with humour, and I would have sworn that in that moment they sparkled, too.

I shrugged, trying to find the words. 'G-guess it depends on whether it's meant as a dig or not.'

'It's not,' he said, short and to the point. My nerves were still present in the shaking of my hands and the twitch I seemed to have formed in my right eye, but slowly I was easing into Leo's company. I'd have to take him at his word.

'Okay.'

'So... Stutter'—he smiled wolfishly, as I glared at him—'as I said, I've got a proposition for you.'

'And what would that be?' Scepticism was clear in my voice. What could he offer me? After all, I *was* still meant to be working on my revenge plan against *him*.

'I can help with your revenge plan.'

Huh?

'H-how do you know I've got a revenge plan?' *And did I just give away I have a revenge plan with my question?* Shit, had Griff said something to him? Surely he wouldn't betray me like that? Not if he wanted to keep his balls.

'Oh, come off it. It's what happens in those books you read.' He said it so matter-of-fact and delivered it with little thought. A smile came to my lips at the thought of Leo noticing what books I enjoyed reading. *Cute.*

'True. The books do include a lot of revenge.' I pondered his words. 'So, *how* exactly can you h-help? You're included in my revenge plan, you know?' I told him, wanting to clarify that I was just as pissed at him as I was at Ollie. Okay, maybe not as much, but still enough to want to see him pay. 'I want to see you burn too.'

'I'm sure you do, Stutter, but I've only ever had your best interests at heart.'

I coughed. 'Bullshit.'

'I think we should fake being in a relationship,' he said, as if it was the most obvious solution.

'You think we should do what?' I sputtered. *Time to get your ears tested, Skylar.* All those loud songs blasting out of my head-phones had clearly affected my hearing, because surely Leo hadn't suggested we pull off a fake relationship. What purpose would it even serve?

'You heard me. I think we should fake a relationship to make Ollie suffer.'

'How does that punish you?'

His smile was bordering on evil. 'Oh, believe me. It'll be punishment enough.'

'You dick.' I shook my head in disbelief, jabbing him in the chest with my fist. 'Not even going to try to sweet talk me?'

He ran his hand through his blond hair, and my eyes travelled to watch his hands. No. I would not let his hands distract me, of all things. *Fuck me—petty, horny Skylar needs to go away, and fast.*

He winked, catching me staring. 'You love it.'

I rolled my eyes at him and said, 'Come on then. Hit me with your master plan.'

'It isn't rocket science, *babe*. We fake date each other and make everybody believe it's real.'

'And what do you g-gain? What do *we* gain?'

'I gain the satisfaction of pissing off your two best friends,' Leo said with a smile. Well, points for the transparency.

I was surprised he had come right out with it. For the entire time I'd known him, Leo had acted as if Clover was shit on his shoe or somebody to tease, and when she and Griff had become somewhat official, he had once again acted completely unaffected. He'd never given the impression that their rela-tionship bothered him, and if he was a good actor in front of them, then I knew he'd be a great actor in our fake couple too.

'And what do I g-gain?'

'You gain the satisfaction of pissing Ollie off. Stutter, you know this will get right under his skin. Fucking up his swimming will hurt him, sure, but seeing you with *me*. That would *kill* him.'

I thought about it, and I couldn't deny that Leo had sound logic. 'I guess.'

'No guessing about it. Tell you what. I'll let you think about it. Weigh up the pros and cons as it were,' he said, his tone one of somebody who believed they were doing you the biggest favour. You know how self-entitled pricks talked down to you, as if you were nothing? Well, it was exactly like that. It was something Leo Hawthorn did a little *too* well.

'And how long do we keep it going for?' I asked, wondering how intent he was on convincing me to go ahead with this. If I was feeling devious, I could use the ploy to my advantage and have it play into my plan of revenge for him. Nobody else would date him, and if I tried hard enough, I may even make him fall a little for me and then rip out his heart.

'You've got one week,' he answered in a low whisper. Shit, Leo could be hot as fuck when he turned on the charm. *Do not fall. Do not fall.* His lips twitched, but he stopped himself from smiling. 'Don't disappoint me, Stutter.'

His threat was slightly dulled in meaning when he reached out to me, tucking a strand of my hair behind my ear. I shivered the moment his skin made contact with mine. Standing with him in an empty, dimly lit hallway at midnight felt illicit. Naughty. And, ultimately, wrong. Yet so very right.

'Happy birthday,' I said, dazed by his proximity, forgetting I'd already wished him a happy birthday earlier in the day.

'Thanks, Stutter,' Leo said as he leaned forward, his lips grazing my ear. His breath touching me made me shiver as it mixed with the cold of the hallway and made goosebumps rise up on my arms. His next sentence was a low whisper. 'We'll talk soon.'

The moment he'd entered my bubble, he left it again, leaving me confused. Confused about why his closeness had affected me so much. Confused about whether I should go through with his crazy scheme or not. Lastly, I was confused why Leo wanted to do it. *Really* wanted to do it, and not the reason he gave me. There had to be a little more to it.

By the time I came to, and by that I meant got my head out of the clouds, Leo was walking away from me in the direction of the pool house stairs. Before turning out of sight, he paused, turned, and winked at me.

Smooth wanker.

Then my irritation at him grew. He could have at least walked me back to my dorm!

Maybe only fake girlfriends got that level of attentiveness.

I crept back across campus, glancing at the treeline when I exited the main building. There was no longer a silhouette at the treeline, and I moved on as quickly as I could.

Clover was still fast asleep when I entered my room, and once I got back in my bed and snuggled under the covers, I lay awake for hours, thinking about my dilemma.

Fuck. What should I do?

At least I had a week to decide, but realistically, it was a case of Sophie's choice.

Sixteen

LEO'S WORDS played on a loop in my mind that entire night, leaving me restless for the week ahead.

Summer school started back up, and nothing out of the ordinary had happened in the last couple of days. The O girls clearly hadn't used the products Griff and I had tampered with yet, so it was a bit of a waiting game. Trust me, we'd know when they had.

Ever since Sunday night, Leo had ignored me in public like he always had, except for sending a wink in my direction anytime he saw me—while nobody else was looking, of course. The world was weird, and I was somehow living in it.

'Skylar,' Ollie growled, coming up behind me in the cafeteria as I grabbed breakfast on Wednesday morning.

I hadn't seen him without my Clo and Griff armour since the library, and honestly, I didn't particularly want to see him yet. No part of me was ready to hash it out, but if he wanted to apologise, I'd be all ears.

'Oliver.' I acknowledged him with a tilt of my head.

I flinched as he grabbed my upper arm to halt me, squeezing slightly to make sure I didn't move away.

'Get off me,' I bit out through gritted teeth, trying to shake my arm out of his grasp. It didn't work, and his grip only tightened more.

'I want to talk to you.'

'We all want a lot of things in life, and sometimes, we just don't get them.' I stopped trying to shake out of his grasp and went completely still. Pretty sure I'd read somewhere that if you went still and played dead, the predator would leave you alone. Not sure the same principle applied to Ollie, but wishful thinking never let me down.

'Talk then,' I demanded, knowing better than to let him take me to a second location. I looked around and other than the one member of kitchen staff still on property, there was nobody else in the room. I knew that Clover and Griff didn't have lessons on a Wednesday morning, so they'd stayed over at his suite last night, giving me a rare night of peace. It was lush.

'Eat dinner with me tonight.'

It wasn't a question, but yet another demand. Ollie had always been good at those. I clenched my jaw, irritated.

'I'd rather not,' I replied. He loosened his grip, and I took the opportunity handed to me, pulled my arm away, and I stepped back.

'I'm not asking,' he drawled, his eyes sparkling. Like the many times I'd looked into his eyes before, I got lost in their depths, trying to find any emotion lying below the surface. Still couldn't find shit, though. Made me wonder if he even had any depths.

I laughed, looking him in the eye. 'And I'm not joking.'

I wanted to give myself a pat on the back at the fact that I'd got that line out without a stutter in sight.

'Last time I checked, New Girl, I'm a member of *The Sect.*'

A gasp fell from my lips at his low blow. Ollie rarely ever

mentioned *The Sect*, and he'd never mentioned it when we were in a relationship. He'd barely even acknowledged its existence.

'Okay?' Uncertainty laced my question, but then I realised what he meant. He meant the fucking rules the rest of the school had always adhered to. The rules I'd never taken into consideration.

Rule One: DO NOT approach *The Sect* or *The Set* without being summoned first.

Rule Two: DO NOT look at the above-mentioned groups unless deemed necessary.

Rule Three: DO NOT bring shame upon your family or this fine institution.

Rule Four: NEVER date someone above your class without asking for permission.

Rule Five: NEVER turn down the invitation of somebody from *The Sect* or *The Set*.

We will punish anybody failing to adhere to the above as we see fit.

He was referring to rule five. 'Is that meant to rattle me?'

'You *will* eat dinner with me tonight,' he said with a smirk, ignoring my question. 'No exceptions.'

'We'll see about that,' I replied. Taking the tray with my breakfast, I walked away from him and although I'd planned to go sit at a table, I thought better of it and went to leave the room altogether. I didn't even want to eat the food anymore, so I ditched it before I left the room.

What a waste of a good croissant.

By the time dinner came, I didn't want to sit and eat dinner with Ollie. I'd pretty much decided I wouldn't bow down to him and once I made that choice, I couldn't back down from it.

Who was he to think he could still order me around?

The last ten months, he'd had me riding a rollercoaster of emotions. Every hill, loop, acceleration, and bunny hop had led us here. Plus, I was still none the wiser why he'd done any of it. He hadn't even tried to make up an excuse. Just a, *"You don't belong here, Skylar"*.

My blood boiled and defiance ran thick through my veins.

Walking at a fast clip, I headed straight from my last class back to my room, not wanting anybody to spot me. Or more specifically, not wanting Ollie to spot me.

Griff could use his influence to get me a pizza delivered or something. It was summer, so surely outside food was allowed without a reason being given? One thing I knew: I would not eat dinner in the dining hall. No way, no how!

Oliver needed to know that he didn't control me, that he couldn't just say *"jump"* and have me reply with *"how high"* like a little sycophantic follower.

I wasn't Ophelia or Oralie, and I never wanted to be. Even thinking that sentence gave me full-body chills.

Once back at my room, I darted inside just in case Ollie was waiting around a corner to block me in or something drastic.

The moment I entered, my eyes fixated straight on my bed. I didn't want a repeat of the evening I found the rabbit and I never wanted to feel fear alone in my own room. Ever since, I'd tried not to focus on how scared I truly was about it all, because if I gave it too much thought, I would never leave the dorm.

It was almost as if I had replaced my worrying about the unknown person who wanted to harm me by hating Ollie instead. By wanting to make Ophelia and Oralie feel even a fraction as small as they'd made me feel for nearly an entire year now—even if I hadn't done much to exact revenge on them.

'Shit, Sky,' I muttered under my breath, obviously having cracked as I was talking to myself. Ah, fuck it. I was better company than most of the people on campus at that moment.

The dash to my room had distracted me from thinking about too much, but being back in my room, I felt a little lost. I knew I couldn't go to the cafeteria for dinner and that I couldn't give in to Ollie's whims and demands, but it meant that, if Clo or Griff didn't come here tonight, I'd be alone, hungry, and trying to prove a point.

HERC, CAN YOU ORDER ME A PIZZA, PRETTY PLEASE?

I texted Griff, knowing he'd get back to me as soon as he saw it. Griff was one of those people who always replied as fast as they could. He never left a message on read and tried his utmost to be an instant communicator. It pissed Clo off, as she said that it wasn't just my messages he replied to straight away. He found it difficult to ignore somebody, and to be honest, I got it. I'd never needed to text anybody before coming to Hawthorn, having had nobody to text, so once that changed, I tried to be pretty prompt about my replies. Well, as prompt as somebody could be when they kept their phone on silent at all times. The anxiety, plus the sound of the vibration of a phone not on silent, was too much for me.

SURE THING, BABYDOLL. FOUR CHEESE?

YOU KNOW ME SO WELL.

It still surprised me every time Griff showed me he listened to me, showed me he cared about me, and that even though our start had been rocky, things had changed for him. Our relationship meant something to him, and I believed him when he said he hadn't known who I was. Who my dad was.

Jacob Cooper.

The only mention of him came in the conversation with Griff where I'd asked about him, but other than that, nobody had said a peep about him. As if they thought they could drop a bomb at the fashion show, then ignore it when it suited them. The whims of the rich and spoiled.

I'd tried to fish, tried to get Griff to open up a bit, but so far he hadn't taken the bait. Apparently, he could be serious and tight-lipped when he wanted to be. *Go figure.*

A knock came from the door, and I pulled myself out of my thoughts and went to open it a tiny crack. But only a crack wide enough for me to look out and determine whether an axe murderer was waiting for me or not.

Standing on the other side was a confused-looking pizza delivery guy. Bless his soul. Probably thought he was delivering to somebody unhinged, what with the building being empty and it being a school during the summer. I opened the door wider, smiling sheepishly at him.

'Sorry. Didn't know who it was.' For some reason, I felt the need to explain myself, yet the only response I got was a small nod before he thrust the pizza box into my hands, turned around, and walked away without anything else.

Oh, well. Pizza time.

Thank you, Griffin!

Seventeen

I WOKE up feeling refreshed and got ready for the day, then hotfooted it down to my first class. When I realised French with Ophelia and Oralie was my first lesson, my refreshed feeling didn't last too long.

Heading to the French classroom, I once again got lost in my thoughts about Ollie, Leo, and the choice I had to make. I was running out of time and Leo wanted an answer by the end of the week.

'Oi, bitch!' Oralie called from the end of the corridor. My head snapped up to find her storming towards me, Ophelia by her side, sick smiles on their faces.

'Where the fuck were you last night?' Ophelia asked, her bright red lips lifted in a sneer. Since taking a shine to Mr Hawkins, she'd been trying even harder with her makeup and her hair. *Pathetic.*

'In my room,' I said, pausing to look them up and down. 'Why's it matter to you?'

'Ollie told you to have dinner with him last night,' she spat.

Well, I hadn't expected them to say *that.*

In all honesty, I was surprised he'd told them, especially as Ophelia seemed to believe she was in a relationship with Ollie, even if nobody had ever confirmed it. I *had* expected him to show up at my room, though, and when he hadn't, I'd breathed a sigh of relief and gone to sleep feeling pretty smug with myself. Like a winner.

'And *you* didn't show up,' Oralie continued. She'd decided to re-enact a famous music video by putting her blonde hair into pigtail braids with fluffy pom-pom hair ties—it looked extremely classy, as you can imagine—and the uniform she wore completely offset the entire ensemble.

'And there was me thinking you didn't have a brain,' I snarked back, pissed that the two of them were trying to make me feel bad for choosing me over their leader. Why would I choose to have dinner with Oliver?

'Oh, ha-ha, slut. You really should have shown up,' she said, taking a step closer to me. 'If you had, like you were told, we wouldn't have to do this.'

In the blink of an eye, Ophelia launched herself at me, while Oralie did the same and gripped my arm, holding me down. Her grip was tight enough to stop me from running away and from getting free. I winced in pain, struggling in her grasp.

Pain split my face in two. *Shit.*

Ophelia had obviously watched closely last year when Odette punched me on the nose, because she'd just delivered a punch that rivalled it. Maybe even one that had more impact.

Blood trickled onto my top lip, and I licked it off, the taste of copper coating my tongue. My nose throbbed, pain radiating outwards into my cheeks.

'You do not'—hit—'get to'—kick—'disrespect us'—punch —'like that.'

With every word she bit out through gritted teeth, the pain

in my face worsened. Punching my stomach, pulling my hair, doing anything in her power to cause me harm.

I struggled in her grip, yet Oralie continued to keep me in place, not letting me move an inch. After more minutes than I could count, the attack still wasn't letting up, and if she wasn't holding me, I would've fallen to the floor. Curled up into the foetal position and whimpered to myself until somebody found me.

But unfortunately for me, I wasn't given the much-needed reprieve.

The hits kept coming. My eyes filled with tears, and it was my sheer willpower that stopped them from leaking out. Black floaters spotted my vision and the outer edges of my vision darkened with a dark circle travelling inwards, making it hard for me to see an inch in front of my face.

'Ms Rogers! Ms Jones!' Mr Hawkins roared. 'I suggest you take a step away from Ms Crescent. Now!'

Treating me as if I weighed the same as a bag of bricks, Oralie let go of my arm, and without her support, I crumpled to the floor, clutching at my bruised ribs.

'Stay where you are!'

I didn't look—couldn't look—but I assumed the girls were trying to flee the scene. Not like they'd get very far on a campus with six students.

'Ms Crescent, stay still and I'll call for help. You two, come with me.'

I didn't respond to him, focusing more on breathing than saying anything. It hurt to breathe—every inhale and exhale rattled through me—and now that I'd been left alone, silent tears fell down my cheeks.

The hallway was empty, and I'd never felt more alone.

After what felt a lot longer than it was, Griff and Clover arrived.

'Shit, Sky. What the fuck happened?' Clo asked, or more like growled. The girl was pissed.

'O girls,' I replied, keeping my sentence short as my breathing was still painful and laboured.

'Bitches,' Griff spat. 'For what reason?'

'Ollie,' I grunted out, wincing as I moved into a seated position now that my help had arrived. 'Dinner.' I looked up at both of them and added, 'Last night.'

'All this 'cause you didn't eat with him?' Clo asked, incredulous. 'To be honest, I'm not surprised. Not after what happened to—'

Griff cut her off with a sharp jab to her ribs. The two of them crouched down, and if I could, I would have laughed at how in sync the two of them had become.

'You're gonna have a nice shiner, Clouds.' With slow movements, Griff reached out and grazed my face with his fingertips. I winced, even the lightest of touches causing a sharp shooting pain through my cheek.

He's right. This is gonna bruise like a bitch.

'Wonderful.' I attempted a smile, but the slight grimace hurt too much. I'd thought I'd known pain after they beat me in the toilets last year, or the time in the woods, but nope. Fuck, getting stabbed was fucking painful, but there was nothing like having your entire body used as a punching bag. The two of them had done worse damage than when there were four. If I wasn't about to spit out blood, I'd probably be impressed with their improvement.

'That fucking cunt,' Clover said, looking at Griff. 'Are you seriously going to let him get away with that?'

'Huh?' Griff asked, his eyebrow quirking up. 'How is this my fault?'

'You're a part of *The Sect*, right?'

'Yes...' he said, trailing off, and I watched as his face clocked the point Clover was about to make. 'But—'

'So, you could have stopped this. A long time ago.' She raised her eyebrow at him, waiting for his answer.

'I-I,' he sputtered. 'It's not that simple, babe.'

'Hm,' she said, turning her nose up at him. 'Seems pretty simple to me.'

'Can we not?' he asked, exasperated. 'This isn't the time. Let's just help our girl here.'

I nodded, not wanting the two of them to fall into an argument. Fucking hell, if they got into it right now, I wouldn't be moving off the hallway floor for at least another hour—and that wasn't gonna fly with me.

Griff stood, brushing his hands on his trousers, and then reached out to grip his hand in mine. Slowly, he pulled me up, and I stumbled like a baby foal. Eventually, I could stand straight, landing on his arms.

'Ow!' I could feel the full extent of my injuries now that I was upright. 'I want to go back to my room, please.'

'Course. Come on, we'll go now.' Clo linked her arm with mine and we made our way out of the classroom building, our pace slow. Lucky for me, the French classroom was on the ground floor, so we didn't need to go down any stairs. Pretty sure if that were the case, I would have asked Griff to carry me down them like some princess or a bride crossing the threshold.

If I hadn't wanted to hurt Ophelia and Oralie before—and I had—I definitely did as I slowly walked away. I'd acted like a pussy when it came to my revenge plan, but I was no longer going to play ball. I wanted to hurt them in any way I could.

Down with the bitches.

Off with their heads.

HISTORY CLASS during summer school was even fucking worse than it was during normal term time.

Why?

Because it was just me and Ollie in the room.

No other students there to distract or potentially sit with.

It was even worse to share a classroom with only him after the girls had beat me up, all because I wouldn't eat dinner with him. Seriously, how unhinged was that?

An hour had passed, but that hadn't changed the deep anger sitting in my gut. If anything, it had only fuelled it further. I'd spent the last hour in my room icing my eye, but I wasn't going to let them stop me from passing my exams a second time, which meant I had to emerge and head to History even when it was the last thing I wanted.

My eye was in the first stage of the healing process, meaning it was an angry red, but not yet bruised, and my nose still felt tender. I'd definitely looked better, but then after what they did to me last year, I'd definitely looked *worse* too.

I was the first to enter the room, so I took my seat at one of the only tables in the front and began to set up my laptop, ready for the lesson.

A body flopped in the seat beside me, and it took all my power to keep my head facing the board. When he spoke, I had to work twice as hard to stay focused. 'How are you feeling today?'

How am I feeling today? I wanted to scream. Shout in his face. Hit him. Anything to show him how fucking stupid his question was. Of course I wasn't feeling okay!

'Skylar,' he growled, reaching out to tilt my head in his direction. 'I'm talking to you.'

'I gathered that,' I bit out. 'I was ignoring you.'

He rolled his eyes. 'And why are you ignoring me?'

'Are you really that obtuse?' I spat, pissed he was making me talk even after I'd said I didn't want to talk to him. 'Why the fuck would I want to talk to you? You set your dogs on me.'

'I did what?' His eyes widened when he looked at me, as if he was only just noticing the state of my face. 'What the heck happened to you?'

'As if you don't know.'

'Why would I waste my breath asking if I already knew?'

Did I believe him? Not really, but the look on his face was endearing enough that I felt compelled to answer. 'You've wasted your breath a lot in the past. Like all those times you told me you liked me or cared about me.'

Okay, so that wasn't what I'd intended to say, but it had slipped out. And with it out there, a weight lifted from my shoulders. To snap at him, to say how I felt, helped me to feel better.

'Skylar—'

I cut whatever bullshit he was about to spout off. 'No. You don't get to say my name like you give a shit. I'm not having it. The girls beat me up because I didn't have dinner with you. Is that the kind of thing you enjoy? You get off on siccing other girls on me and swooping in afterward to play the hero?'

My anger was rising, the hatred bubbling thick.

'You think I did that?'

'I *know* you did that.' It had never crossed my mind that he hadn't. Of course it was him. How else would Ophelia and Oralie know I didn't eat dinner with him after he'd asked me to? Ophelia was his girlfriend, so the girl must be truly blinded by lust or love or something else to go along with whatever Ollie wanted from her. All of it was so fucked up.

'I didn't,' he said plainly, trying to communicate something through his gaze that I chose not to understand or interpret. If he had something to say, he could use his words. If not, he could go to hell for all I cared. 'I would never.'

'With your track record, Oliver, that's a little hard to believe.'

'Believe what you want, Sky, but I promise you, I never want to hurt you again.'

Our teacher entered the classroom at that moment—thank fuck—and Ollie had to stop paying attention to me. He turned to face the board, as did I, and neither of us spoke for the rest of the hour.

And when he tried to hold me back from leaving once the lesson finished, I pulled out of his grip before he could bruise me further. Walking away without once looking back, my heart broke into even smaller pieces than before. I hadn't even known it was possible for it to split further, but like most things with Ollie, they always surprised me.

Eighteen

THE NEXT MORNING, my entire body ached. My skin had started to bruise, and my eye had acquired a shiner overnight. I should have stayed in bed, but the whole reason I was at school during the summer was because I'd failed my exams and I needed to pass my retakes in September. Otherwise, I'd lose my scholarship—and my chance of a better life.

At the last moment, I made the decision to go through the admin building before my lesson, to grab some breakfast en route, even though it was nearly lunchtime. *Sue me.*

Wandering through the corridor, I minded my business and kept my head down, not wanting to bump into Ophelia or Oralie—or Ollie, for that matter. Griff had offered to walk me everywhere, but I didn't want to look scared of them; didn't want to give them even more power.

I still couldn't believe yesterday had happened. Okay, I *could* believe it had happened, but I found the reasoning behind it bullshit. I didn't eat dinner with a member of their self-appointed royalty. Big fucking deal. They'd never implemented the rules on me before.

'Get in here,' a voice growled in my ear, as hands covered my eyes so I couldn't see anything. Warm palms touched the bottom of my back and pushed me forward, and I stumbled a little at a ridge on the floor. *Shit*, they were taking me to a second location.

It smelled of cleaning supplies and the powerful scent of bleach irritated my nose, making me lightheaded. Although my nerves were also playing a part in that feeling.

'Stay still,' the recognisable voice demanded.

I didn't dare to move or open my eyes. Even though the hands were no longer on my face, I didn't want to see where I was—or who I was with. Seeing would only make it real. Plus, it still hurt to move into certain positions, and I didn't want to injure myself further.

The hands removed from my eyes and a piece of material covered them, then they moved to cover my mouth as I tried to let out a muffled scream.

'Don't, Little One.'

Fuck. I'd known it was Ollie. The tobacco and vanilla scent he carried with him everywhere surrounded us, reaching through the potent smell of bleach and solvent. Once I knew it was him for certain, I stopped fighting, even though I knew I should make whatever Ollie had planned harder for him. I shouldn't just give in, let him have his way here.

But I knew I would.

What a mess.

'Stay quiet and we won't have an issue here,' he drawled in my ear. As much as I didn't want to feel anything towards him, especially after the events of the day before, his actions turned me on. My nipples were sharp points and I could feel myself getting wetter with each second—Ollie always had that effect on me. Goosebumps erupted all over my arms, and I gasped.

His mouth trailed tender kisses up and down my neck, interspersed with little bites, and I shivered from the excitement overwhelming me. Ollie had been the only person who ever made me feel this way.

Like he knew just what I needed, he pressed himself flush against my back and put his arms around me, cupping my breasts with his large palms, roughly squeezing them, causing a tiny moan to escape my parted lips.

'You like that?' he whispered, taunting me. It was the most intimate the two of us had been in a long time, yet it didn't feel wrong. Or right.

Shit, I was meant to still be mad at him. *Think of your revenge, Skylar.*

But then Ollie pinched my nipples, hard, and I was a goner. Fuck it. My revenge could wait until after... whatever this was.

Even though he'd blindfolded me, I could sense the room around us; could sense where Ollie was. His hard dick was pressing into my back, and I wanted nothing more than to grab it and place my hand around its warmth. It was like all of my sexual feelings towards him were no longer repressed, and they wanted to come out and play.

I leaned my head back, opening my neck up for him to bite, making it easier for him to kiss, lick, and bite from my shoulder to my earlobe.

'We don't have long, Little One,' he told me, his tone conspiring—the two of us sharing a secret. An illicit meeting.

His hands moved from my front and I heard his zip, the shuffling of his clothing, the heaviness of his breathing.

My mouth opened, my brain telling me to ask what I should do with my skirt, but I stopped myself before I made a sound. He'd told me not to speak and there was something sexy as fuck about not talking. Powerful.

I didn't have to think about it for long, as he pushed my skirt up above my hips in one violent motion, baring me to the cold air. He moved my underwear to the side, and before I could get used to the feeling, he thrust his finger inside me, my wetness acting as a lubricant, making it easy for him to add another digit—then a third. *Fuck.*

One of us should stop whatever was happening, but I really, *really* didn't want to, and I hoped he didn't want to either.

I moaned, loud, and in a flash, his hand was once again covering my mouth.

'Don't ruin this,' he threatened.

Caught up in the moment, I stilled. And even though he hadn't listened to me in the library, something in the air felt different. The whole situation was different. I hadn't said no, because in my heart, I still wanted him.

I nodded—or attempted to, anyway. The position he had trapped me in made it difficult for me to move much. And fuck, was it hot.

His fingers disappeared, and in a moment, his dick replaced them, hard and ready to invade my tight walls. In one violent movement, he fully seated himself inside of me, and I gasped at the sensation. From the position he'd trapped me in, he felt bigger than normal. It had been a while since we'd last had sex and I'd forgotten how amazing he felt.

With a grunt, he began to thrust, his cock filling me slowly and completely. Even after all of the times I'd had sex with him, it was still amazing to feel every inch of him slide into me like this, as if I were being taken for the first time all over again.

Fuck. I'd missed the feeling of him. I could be a big girl and admit that to myself.

I panted, sweat pooling in the centre of my chest, the speed of my breathing increasing with each thrust.

The way he stretched me, the way he moved, was everything I liked about having sex with Ollie. My body writhed beneath his, eager and willing. It was a raw act of possession, and I could feel the passion rising in me, like the hottest fire, clouding my thoughts and causing me to see stars.

The waves of pleasure hit a crescendo, and the two of us went over the edge at the same time, his hot cum filling me as we both groaned.

'Don't say a word, Little One,' he growled in my ear. 'And *don't turn around.*'

I stayed still, doing as he asked, while he righted his clothing. The door opened, and taking the warmth with him, Ollie left the closet, leaving me alone.

Alone, used, and sore, but smiling.

Geez, Sky. Get some self-respect.

THE EVENTS of the day raced through my brain in a constant loop. A snapshot of every moment, of every touch.

Shit. I'd let Ollie fuck me in the caretaker's closet and had put up zero resistance. It was the same place we'd hooked up on the night I lost my virginity and the memories had come rushing back. The feeling I had when I was around him was unlike any I'd experienced around another person, and it was hard to remember he'd played me when my heart was beating in such a fast rhythm around him.

I'd let him touch me, even though just the day before I'd accused him of having the girls attack me. Sure, the girls may have decided to attack me without his consent, but he must have known that by telling them I'd defied him, they would retaliate.

Like a bullet to the gut, ripping me from the inside out, I realised Ollie's game.

He intended to use the rules to make me do his bidding. To make me eat dinner with him, talk with him—spend time with him.

The sadness I experienced at the realisation overwhelmed me. Could I never break free of his hold?

Shit.

I couldn't continue to defy him and then have two basic bitches beat me up as my "punishment", and then sleep with him in a closet! I needed to fight back; I needed to knock them down a peg. Or five.

If I were being honest with myself, something I rarely liked to do but found myself doing anyway, I'd expected to hear from Leo at some point during the day. Had expected him to use such an unfortunate scenario as a way to convince me further to join him in his fake relationship scheme. It probably would've worked, too. I was so mad at myself, at Ollie, at the O girls, that I'd have agreed to anything.

He wanted an answer in twenty-four hours, and it had become pretty obvious what my answer *should* be, but what my answer *would* be was still unknown.

Yeah, yeah. I know. You're a dumb bitch, Skylar.

I felt conflicted. You know when your head and your heart were battling it out, and even though you knew the winner, you still wanted to root for the underdog? Yep. That was basically my mental space.

'Clo,' I called out to her, hoping she hadn't fallen asleep yet. For the last hour, she'd not said a word, so I wasn't sure if she'd answer me.

'Yeah,' she replied, her voice tired and a little muffled.

'What do you do when your head and your heart are telling

you two different things?' I blurted out. When I'd called out her name, I wasn't sure what I was actually going to say when she answered, so the words left my lips without much thought behind them.

'Honestly,' she said, a deep sigh accompanying the word, her voice sounding even more tired with the weight of it. 'I'm probably not the best person to ask.'

Her exhausted sounding words echoed in our small room.

'What d'you mean?'

'Well, last time my heart and my head disagreed, I just ran away from it all. It was easier to give it all up than actually make a choice.' She sounded so resigned and fed up, and I knew I should let her come to me when she was ready, but fuck, the girl never gave me anything and I had no idea when I'd get another chance to delve into it.

'Why?' I asked, hoping I didn't sound too eager. Didn't want to scare her off straight away.

'Loyalty, mostly. To my family,' she muttered, and I had to strain to hear her, as she was so quiet.

I wondered if the dilemma she was talking about had anything to do with what happened between her and Leo.

'Makes sense,' I said, even though I was bullshitting. None of it made sense to me, but I'd never felt loyalty to my mum in that way, so I couldn't relate.

'No, it doesn't,' she said with a low, dark chuckle. 'Why are you asking, anyway?'

I rolled over, getting comfortable on my left side so I could face her across the room, and I heard her shuffle to do the same. Our room was too dark to see each other, and Clo resembled a dark, lumpy shadow, but it felt better to be facing one another while we opened up to each other the way I'd always hoped we would.

'Ollie,' was all I said in response. I didn't need to give any more details. A best friend just knew and Clo didn't disappoint.

'Yeah,' she said with a sigh that echoed throughout the dark, and otherwise silent, room.

'I should listen to my head, right?' Did my voice go up at the end like I wasn't sure? Well, if it did, I'd deny it until I was blue in the face.

'That's what I did,' Clo said, distracted and deep in thought. 'Hurts less.'

'I guess.'

I'd agreed with her, but my mind was saying: really, did it? Clo may be happy with Griff, but I found it hard to believe that her shit with Leo hurt less just because she'd run away from it. It wouldn't surprise me if she hadn't come to terms with it. The way she acted around him spoke volumes about her true feelings, and the fact Leo was asking me to be his fake girl-friend to piss her off also said a lot.

'Don't let him get away with his shit, Sky,' Clo said. The rustling of covers told me she'd moved to lie on her back once again, our moment over.

'I won't,' I whispered, the lie loud.

Nineteen

TONIGHT WAS the night Leo wanted my definitive answer, and after I'd sort of but not really come to terms with how I felt about the whole sex in the closet situation with Ollie, I felt pretty sure of the option I was going to pick, but I hadn't fully committed yet.

I was in my room, contemplating my options again, pacing up and down the small floor space as I was prone to do when stressed, when Griff and Clo bustled into the room mid-conversation, making a racket. It was like the two of them could never enter the room without being in the middle of some heated debate of sorts.

'Babe, I can't help it if I'm a stud muffin,' Griff said, an overlarge smile planted on his face. Clover, who was looking at him, rolled her eyes affectionately.

'A stud muffin?' We both laughed. It wasn't that Griff couldn't be classed as a stud muffin, because he definitely could, but it sort of defeated the object when you announced it yourself.

'Would you prefer I refer to myself as a major hunk?' he asked, his white teeth beaming.

'No. No, I would not. I'd prefer you not refer to yourself as anything at all,' Clo said, laughing at him in earnest, wrinkles forming around her eyes.

It was conversations like the one I was witnessing that made me think the two of them were sweet together, and they did have some chemistry, but I felt no heat emanating from them. Saw nothing that made me believe there was more than a deep friendship there. It certainly wasn't love. Not real, I'd kill for you, love. But then again, who was I to talk about love? Not like I'd had much experience with the real deal.

I'd been weighing up my pros and cons for agreeing to Leo's scheme, and Clover's strained relationship with Leo was a major con. Top of the list kind of con. I wasn't sure if she'd forgive me if I went through with it, and I knew I *could* just tell her it was all fake, but then I wouldn't be keeping up my end of the bargain with Leo and he'd call it all off.

The real question: did I care more about pissing off Ollie than I did about Clover's feelings?

And why wasn't the answer easy?

Why did it all have to be so complicated?

'What do you have planned tonight, Sky?' Clo asked me once the two of them had settled on her bed and got comfortable. I scoffed—a response in itself. It was rare I had plans in the evening.

'Oh, you know me. Always off out and about gallivanting.' I wondered if I'd layered enough sarcasm into that one sentence... Whoever said sarcasm was the lowest form of wit could fuck off.

'Ha-ha, Clouds,' Griff said with a chuckle. 'Want to watch a film with us?'

'Of course!' I answered enthusiastically—and falsely. The enthusiasm was feigned, and I'd actually hoped that the two of them were planning to spend the evening in Griff's room so I could continue to pace and worry without an audience. I'd told the two of them they didn't need to constantly check on me and keep me company, but they thought I was covering up my genuine feelings. Or that I was too afraid to reach out and ask for help. If anything, it was the opposite. I'd been trying not to hurt *their* feelings.

'Before we watch the film, I wanted to talk to you both about something,' Griff announced, wringing his hands together in his lap, a faint blush blooming into his freckled cheeks.

'Shoot,' I said back, wanting him to get on with it so I could pretend to watch the film while my brain was thinking about anything else.

'How intent are you on this revenge plan of yours?'

'Very intent,' Clo snapped, nudging him in the side like they'd discussed it before between the two of them and had chosen not to speak to me about it.

'What makes you ask?' I asked.

'Well…' he trailed off, looking around the room, becoming very distracted with our photo collage on the wall. The collage was something Clo and I had worked on since the start of rooming together and it was a cluttered mess of pictures—but I loved it. Hadn't loved removing the pictures of me and Ollie that were on there, but you live and you learn. 'I just don't know if it's a good idea.'

'A good idea?' Clo asked, her perfectly shaped eyebrows downturned.

'Come on, Griff. Spit it out,' I said. I wanted Griff to clarify what he meant and not pussyfoot around it. Clo and I had spoken at the same time, meaning that neither of our questions was distinctive.

Clover repeated herself first. 'A good idea how?'

'Well, don't you think they'll have something in place to retaliate? They've left you alone since you returned, Sky. Do you want to risk disrupting the balance?'

I nodded at him, letting him know I'd heard him and had thought the same thing myself. I'd even considered that Leo's plan was really a ruse to have me let my guard down so they could make my life worse.

'So, what? Sky's meant to just act like last year didn't happen?' Clo snapped.

'I don't mean that, babe.' Griff glanced at me, his eyes pleading for some form of backup if things went south. 'I mean that nobody has harassed Sky in at least a couple of days, and we haven't exactly achieved much, anyway.'

'A couple of days! Are you telling me we should back off because they haven't hurt her in *a couple of days?*' Clo said with derision. 'The past week is nothing compared to the thirty-plus weeks they hurt her.'

'But maybe they've learned their lesson?' Griff was trying, I could see that much, but he also wasn't getting the hint that maybe it wasn't the right time to talk about it—and maybe he should stay silent before Clover bit his head off.

'Are you fucking serious?' Her mouth was moments from foaming.

'What now?' he asked in that way boys did when they didn't realise that the words leaving their mouths were going to get them into a whole world of trouble.

'What'—Clo's eye twitched, and I feared for Griff's well-being—'now?'

'Oh, come off it, babe. You know I didn't mean it like that.'

'Maybe it's best if you leave,' she said, scooting over on her bed and putting distance between them. The moment she moved, Griff's face fell and turned into a mixture of sad and mad.

'Is that what you want?' he asked her.

She huffed and I got the impression that a lot more was resting on her shoulders than Griff questioning our revenge plan and motives.

'Yes,' she said sullenly, her arms crossed in front of her chest.

I gave Griff a sympathetic look from across the room, hoping Clo didn't catch it. Being the third wheel was starting to affect me. The three of us were a unit, but the moment those two started arguing, it disrupted the dynamics. Girl code also dictated that I had to be on Clover's side—she'd been my friend first, after all. Even if she hadn't quite followed the code in the past with me.

'Okay,' he whispered, his bottom lip trembling. 'I'll go then.'

He got to his feet and made his way to the door, and by his slow pace, I knew he was just waiting for Clo to call him back, not thinking he'd ever make it to the door.

'Bye,' she said, choosing to lie down and turn to face the wall so she wasn't looking at him anymore.

So petty.

'See you later, Clouds,' Griff said, his hand hovering above the door handle.

'See you later,' I replied, returning his tentative smile with a slight smile and a wave.

He left, making as little noise as he could, and the moment the door had closed behind him, I threw my pillow at the back of Clo's head.

'Ouch!'

'What the fuck did you do that for?' I pointed towards the

door. 'Why are you being so ridiculous about this? That boy would do anything to make you smile, and there you are, kicking him out over something silly.'

'It isn't *silly*, Skylar. He was completely disregarding the way those bastards have treated you. The way he *helped* them treat you!'

'Right, but he was disregarding how they've treated *me*. Why does it upset *you* so much?'

At my words, Clo manoeuvred herself so she was sitting up and looking over at me.

'I don't like it when people walk all over the people I care about,' she replied, looking me in the eye. Tears glistened in hers, the light catching a tear trail as it streaked down her cheek.

'I get you.' My response was simple, and maybe it lacked empathy, but I had no real clue how to answer her. 'And I appreciate you, Clo. Accept that fact fast, 'cause I'm not sure when I'll repeat it.'

'I feel the same about you. I know that sometimes you think I'm just trying to be difficult or make things harder than they need to be, but I am always coming from a place of love.'

'I know. And after last year, I've learnt my lesson.' I exhaled, feeling heavy.

'Thank fuck for that,' she said, relieved.

THE CLOCK STRUCK MIDNIGHT.

And unlike Cinderella, who at that hour was running away from her Prince Charming, I was walking towards—well, not my Prince Charming, that was for sure.

I got to our meeting spot before Leo because maybe I'd rushed to get there before him, but that was neither here nor there, right?

Waiting in the dim hallway for him to show up, I observed my surroundings. Mostly I walked down it, taking nothing in; usually because I had Clover talking my ears off, or we were bumping into Leo with some girl wrapped around him, and that became all I could see, but standing there alone, I noticed how old the building was. Hawthorn was old, and I knew that, but I'd never appreciated it anywhere but the library.

Footsteps echoed down the empty hallway, and I turned to see Leo sauntering towards me, no care in the world. A thought hit my mind, an unbidden one at that, and I knew my cheeks flushed as a result, because all I could think about was how fucking hot he looked walking towards me.

His blond hair was long on top and swept over to the left, and the way he raked his fingers through it should be a crime. So effortless and casual, making him ten times more attractive.

Fuck. It wouldn't do me any good going into our conversation with *those* types of thoughts plaguing my mind.

'Hello, Stutter. Fancy seeing you here,' Leo said with a smirk. 'Nice shiner.'

'Hey...' My words ran off, unsure what else to say. We both knew my eye looked like shit. Self-consciously, I touched it and even though it no longer hurt, last time I'd looked in the mirror, the bruise looked brutal.

I wanted him to just come out with it. To ask me what my answer was so we could be done with it and move on, but like everything with Leo, it wasn't that easy.

'How are the two lovebirds?' he asked, surprising me with the direction of his thoughts.

Must remember, Leo never does the things I think he will.

'Clover and Griff?' I asked to clarify, although it was unlikely he meant anybody else. The only other couple on campus was Ollie and Ophelia, and I knew that was a load of bullshit as Ollie had seduced me twice already since summer started, so he didn't care much about her if that was how he acted.

'Of course,' he bit out through gritted teeth. Maybe it hurt to admit it. His blue eyes were dark, angry and intense. Very intense. Mesmerised, I couldn't look away.

'They're...' I struggled to think of another word, switching my weight from foot to foot, fidgeting. 'They're okay, I guess.'

'You guess?' he echoed back at me. 'Well, well, well. That won't do.'

'No?' I raised my eyebrows, certain that my forehead had wrinkles from the force of the expression. *I do not need wrinkles before the age of forty.*

'Of course not,' Leo said, ice attaching itself to every syllable. 'So what say you, Skylar Crescent?'

'Promise me something first,' I said, trying to sound strong and in control. Trying to sound like somebody who knew what they wanted.

'And what would that be?' His eyes glinted with menace, and I shuddered.

'I want you to promise me that we end this when I say so.'

'Is that all?' he asked. I could tell he expected me to say more.

'I also don't want to hurt Clo,' I said as Leo nodded at me, deep in thought. 'And lastly, I—'

Leo cut me off before I could finish my sentence; not that I'd had a sentence in mind, anyway. 'How about we keep the rules to a minimum for now? We can always adjust accordingly,' he said, and I giggled. His wording was so unlike him, yet it fit the moment.

'O-okay,' I stuttered out. 'I'll do it.'

'You will?' he asked, shock lacing his voice, which he attempted to cover with a cough.

'I will. I need Ollie to suffer.' I shrugged. 'And you're my best chance of making that happen.'

Leo's smile turned wolfish. Good thing my nickname wasn't "Red". Otherwise, I'd be waiting for him to eat me whole.

His bright blue eyes, no longer anger filled, were taking me in and sweeping over my face, and I felt as if I were under a microscope. His upper lip curled, a demonic smile that made me think of the devil.

'Perfect. Let the games begin.'

Twenty

THE PLAN: I was going to invite Leo to my movie night with Griff and Clo, and the two of us would flirt, or something like that. We hadn't gone into specifics.

Even just thinking about it gave me crazy anxiety, and, unsurprisingly, I was absolutely bricking telling Clo that Leo and I "liked each other" enough that we'd decided to date.

It was the only way I could think to introduce Clover to the idea of it without outright crushing her. Not that I thought it would crush her. Actually, I just thought it would make her pissed as all get-out.

We were in Griff's suite, a much more spacious room than mine and Clo's small place, and we'd ordered takeaway for dinner. The two of them had ordered Chinese, but ever since having a dodgy one back in the day, I didn't touch the stuff anymore. I'd ordered cheesy chips and mozzarella sticks—my favourite treat. Well, alongside pizza, of course.

'What kind of film are we fancying then, lads?' Clo asked, while we waited for our food to arrive. 'Horror?'

'No!' I shouted, my gut reaction showing, but then I backed down. *Oh, wait.* A scary film would be perfect for me to have an excuse to snuggle up with Leo. 'I take it back. Let's watch that one with the creepy doll.'

'*Annabelle*?' Griff asked, a sinister grin on his normally charming face.

'Nope, no way. I mean that one about the creepy ventriloquist dummy,' I told him. I'd seen it online while browsing, and any film about a ventriloquist dummy was bound to be terrifying in my opinion. Those little fuckers had such creepy faces, and ever since I'd read *Goosebumps* as a kid, they shook me the fuck up.

'Okay...' Griff looked at Clo, and the two of them exchanged a look. One of those secret couple looks they'd made more often recently, highlighting how much of a third wheel I truly was.

'I've got something to tell you,' I said, ready to tell them about Leo coming, but then a knock came and Griff jumped up from the bed and I knew I'd lost my chance to give them a heads-up.

Ah, shit. I'd meant for him to arrive after I'd told them he was coming.

'Food. Food. I love food,' Griff sang as he made his way to open the door. When he opened it, though, it wasn't the delivery person, but Leo.

'You all right?' Griff asked, his tone uncertain. I recalled what Griff had said about holding a space, and I realised he'd probably jumped to a different conclusion about Leo's presence. Oops. Definitely should've given them a heads-up! Bad Skylar.

'Yep,' Leo said, his tone bored. Damn, he really could act like the perfect villain. 'My girl said I could join you.'

I rolled my eyes at his statement. Guess the boy wanted to

throw our entire plan out of the window and cause havoc while he was at it.

'Your girl?' Griff growled, his cheeks fire extinguisher red.

'*My girl*. Right, Sky?' he asked, looking over Griff's shoulder and locking his gaze with mine. He wiggled his eyebrows in a very un-Leo-like manner and I snorted.

I smiled at him tentatively, hoping to look coy and flirtatious. Inside, I was a bundle of nerves and felt so guilty I doubted I'd be able to go along with the lie for longer than an hour tops.

My reply came out with a tittering laugh that sounded so false I cringed at myself in my mind. 'Always.'

Griff looked at me, his brow raised in question, and I knew that if I moved my head in Clo's direction, I'd see her glaring at me, sceptical.

'Since when?' Clo bit out, her arms crossed in front of her chest.

'S-since last night?' Shit. Why did my stutter always crop up at the wrong time? It wanted to give my lies away.

'Right,' Leo said, making his way over to sit down on the sofa beside me. He slung an arm around my shoulder and I froze, a statue of my own making. Griff returned to his bed to sit beside Clo and the room was silent for two minutes.

It was Clover who broke the quiet. 'What happened last night?'

I found the courage to look at her, and I could see the accusation in her gaze.

'We...' I started, looking at Leo for help. All he did was wink. Great, thanks for the help, dickhead. 'The two of us bumped into each other in the hallway, and Leo invited me back to his room to watch a film.'

'What time was that? 'Cause I'm pretty sure you spent the evening with me in our room.' Clo had a valid point. She'd gone to sleep around eleven, so of course she wouldn't know about me leaving.

'Well, y-yes. But after you went to sleep, I went out for some fresh air.'

'You cannot be serious, Skylar,' Clo spat.

'What?' I asked, sounding braver than I felt.

'You cannot be about to date this prick?' she asked. 'Surely you learned your lesson last year?'

Ouch, Clo. *Low blow much.*

'Clouds, what about the plan?' Griff asked, his face blank.

Within a moment, it was us versus them. Couple versus couple—each couple as fake as the other—but for two very different reasons.

'The plan you wanted to forgo?' I retorted, feeling bad that I was calling him out, but also I found it funny how quick he'd changed his tune.

'Er, yeah. That one.' He grinned, his dimples appearing, and I laughed back at him. We both shrugged our shoulders, and he called out, 'Cousin jinx.'

I rolled my eyes, the same way I did every time he said it. It was Griff, so of course he said it a lot, but like so many other quirks of his, it was endearing, and every time, it reminded me I had family in the world. Family that wanted me and loved me.

If you listened to Griff, the fact that we both fell asleep to ASMR and loved watching the same films over and over again was because of our shared DNA. Nothing to do with our own personalities, but everything to do with the Cooper blood flowing through our veins.

I hadn't heard from Mum or Andy since before summer school started. Actually, I'd only heard from them once since I returned to Hawthorn, and that was only because they had been short on their rent and hoped I still had my rich boyfriend to help bail them out!

'Is this what you want?' Griff asked, warming up to the idea once it became clear Leo wasn't trying to win over Clover, and that I was okay with the situation.

'Of course,' I replied. Leo's hand squeezed my shoulder in support—or at least I assumed it was in support and not a warning nudge.

'Well, as long as this is what you want, girlfriend, then I'm happy for you.' Griff calling me girlfriend caused me to laugh so hard I couldn't form words. The boy was like a seesaw. One second he was on the ground, miserable and surly, then the next he was sky-high, happy and giddy, totally forgetting about the low he'd experienced mere seconds before. He was exhausting.

'Thanks, man,' Leo said, a smirk playing on his lips, both teasing and playful, happy the plan was working.

Clo's tone made her displeasure clear. 'This is bullshit.'

'Do you want us to leave?' Leo asked the room, yet literally no syllable sounded genuine. There was no way we'd be leaving, even if I wanted to—and, as awkward as it was, I found myself not wanting to.

'Course not,' Griff said with a chuckle. 'Now, let's watch the film.'

'Anything exciting?' Leo asked, placing a kiss on my temple.

'*Dead Silence*,' I told him. 'A scary movie, so you better be ready to hold me.'

Gosh, I'm a fucking fraud.

My aim for flirtatiousness missed the mark and I was pretty sure it came across as cringe instead. Lucky for me, Leo took the bait and smiled, leaning into me and kissing me once more. My cheeks warmed, and I gulped. *Cute, Sky. A guy loves it when you resemble a goldfish. Or any animal, for that matter.*

'Of course, babe,' he responded, getting a kick out of the entire scenario we'd found ourselves in. Or should I say, put ourselves in? Because we were the only reason any of it was happening.

A knock on the door stopped us from talking more. Food time, baby!

Griff rushed to the door, and on opening it, took the take-away bags from the delivery guy so fast that the guy at the door flinched at the speed.

'Thanks, dude!' Griff told him as he closed the door on the guy's open-mouthed face before he distributed the food. 'Let's dig in.'

'Such a shame we didn't get you anything,' Clo said, looking anything but sad about it—she appeared smug as fuck, and I laughed at the bite in her voice.

'Actually,' Leo said, looking even more smug than Clover—something I didn't know was possible. 'You got me food, right, babe?'

'Yep,' I answered, handing him over the food I'd got for him. I wasn't getting involved in *that*.

'You are perfect!' He kissed me for the third time—THIRD—before getting comfortable with his food.

Inside, I was feeling pretty crappy. When she thought nobody was watching, Clover's face had fallen, her eyes turning so sad that all I wanted to do was reach out—maybe even let her hug me—anything to put a smile back on her face.

But then her green eyes locked with mine and narrowed, and I thought maybe it was for the best I was nowhere near her reach.

THE MOVIE WASN'T SCARY, more creepy than anything, but I still held on to Leo throughout. His body warmth, pleasant against mine, caused me to feel flushed and halfway through, I removed my jumper. I was sweating balls! Clo's eyes scrutinised me every few minutes, and I was certain that her eyes had been on us more than they'd been on the movie. She hadn't even gasped, squirmed, or flinched at the big reveal and trust me, the movie was fucked and went places I totally hadn't expected it to. The sign of a great plot twist.

'Well, that was summin' else!' Griff said once the credits finished rolling.

The rest of us were all still sitting in silence, unsure of what to say. Summin' else was putting it lightly!

'Now that the movie's over, shall we go back to my room, babe?' Leo squeezed me tight to him, a gesture that took me by surprise, as I hadn't expected him to go full-hog so early into our ruse. I thought he'd ease me into it, but apparently, that wasn't the case. Maybe he was hoping it would look like we'd liked each other for a while but only just got the guts to admit it? Fuck if I knew.

'Y-yeah. Sure,' I replied, hoping I sounded unaffected by the raging thoughts plaguing my mind. Pissing off Ollie was worth it, yeah, but I didn't enjoy lying to Clo and Griff, and so far, Ollie knew nothing about any of what we were doing.

'You two offskies then?' Griff asked, his cheeky grin becoming a whole lot less wholesome.

'Yeah.' I nodded and smiled at him and Clover, who were still sitting together on his bed. I'd glanced over at them once or twice during the film and seen Clo's head resting on his shoulder and their hands entwined.

Yeah, of course they looked cute as fuck together, but once again, cute did not a relationship make. There was no heat— no spice. No chemistry.

'Will I see you in our room later? Or do you plan to stay out?' Clo asked, her tone clipped. I wished I could say the bitter note in her voice surprised me, but it didn't. I'd known everything about me and Leo would annoy her, yet I'd gone through with it, anyway.

'We started dating last night,' I told the room and said no more. I wouldn't dignify her petty dig with more of an explanation. Fuck that. So what if I stayed out? Not that I planned to, but still. The relationship was new, fake or not, and I hated Clo's assumption.

'C'mon, Stutter. We don't need to be somewhere we're not wanted,' Leo said.

His words amused me because even though he'd said the right thing, I knew he didn't mean any of it. We all knew he wanted to stay right there, unwanted and a nuisance. But slow and steady wins the race and all that good shit.

The two of us left the room hand in hand, but the moment the door closed behind us, I let go and put some distance between us.

'You did good.' His lips twitched, and I thought maybe they'd form a smile, but of course the moment went without a smile happening. *Go figure.*

'I d-did?' I asked, feeling more uncertain than I should, but the guilt and worry was close to eating me alive. I needed my friends to believe it, so I could convince Ollie and *The Set* that it was real. That the two of us were an actual couple that wanted to be with one another and not just a big joke.

'We riled her up, and they believed it. That's good in my book,' he drawled. 'So, are you coming to my room?'

'Do you think I sh-should?' I assumed Clo would stay with Griff for a while longer, but with the mood we'd put her in, she may decide to go back to our room and sulk once she heard us leave the corridor. Meaning I couldn't be there as she'd see through the lie too early.

Guess that answers that.

Leo's voice held a rasp of excitement. 'Stutter?'

I nodded. 'Let's go.'

'Positive?' he asked, as he shuffled his weight from leg to leg. Nervous energy that he needed an outlet for. I was rinsing my hands together as an outlet for mine.

'Yep. Let's go before I change my mind—and before Clo leaves in a huff.'

'Reckon we've ruined their night that much?' he asked, his face hopeful. Leo's bored expression always disappeared the moment he knew he'd got under Clover's skin.

'For sure. I'm going to get an earful the next time I'm alone with her, so may as well make it worth my while!'

'Perfect. If she does, I'll make an even better plan to irritate Ollie. How about that?'

'Yes!' I blurted out, the word leaving my lips on impulse. Irritating Ollie was the only reason I'd agreed to this hare-brained plan in the first place. Yes, I felt guilty pissing off Clo, but not enough to stop the train. It had already left the station and was full steam ahead and every other train metaphor or cliché you could think of.

'Excellent.'

Honestly, from the look on Leo's face and the mischief shining out of his bright, azure blue eyes, if I were Clo or Ollie, I'd be scared.

Shit. I'm scared.

Twenty-One

OLLIE

I STAYED in Leo's suite until midnight.

The two of us chilled and played old-school video games to pass the time, and then like a perfect gentleman he walked me back to my room.

Before I could make it across the threshold, he grabbed my arm, pulled me close to him, and kissed me on the lips as a goodbye—a goodbye that was witnessed by none other than Clover Luck because I'd already opened the door when he grabbed me.

Why else would he do it?

The moment his lips touched mine, I doubted the overall plan a little. Lying and pretending to be a couple was so different from actually kissing, groping, and all the other escalations I could see unfolding in my mind.

'Bye,' I whispered when the kiss ended, a little shell-shocked and unsure how to proceed.

'Bye, Stutter.' The last expression on his face was one of pure amusement. I smiled at him and gave a little wave.

'Did you have fun?' Clo asked once I'd shut the door on

Leo's smirking face. Walking the short distance from the door to my bed, I honestly felt as if I were doing the walk of shame, and Clover's disgusted face implied I was.

'I did, thanks,' I answered as politely as I could. I wouldn't be rising to her pettiness. Not yet, anyway.

'I waited up,' she said, and all I could think was, *Do you want a medal?*

'Thanks.' It came out muffled as I changed out of my clothes into my pyjamas. I'd got my top caught on something, and for a little minute, it trapped me inside my clothing. I stumbled around for a bit, but Clo didn't come to my rescue, and after what felt like *way too long*, I found the opening of my top and sorted myself out.

Once I was changed and no longer being held hostage by my fleece jumper, I got under my covers and instantly moved around to get comfy. The duvet was fluffy and warm and I felt safe. Content.

'What did the two of you do?' she asked, and when I glanced over at her face, I realised how much the question pained her to ask. Yet she'd asked it anyway, even not wanting to hear the answer.

'Played *Spyro* and *Crash Bandicoot*,' I told her, a smile, unbidden, playing on my lips. Even though I'd never been alone with Leo in an intimate setting, I'd had a good time. He was nowhere near as uptight and boring as I'd thought he was. He was charming, funny, and surprisingly, a good sport. Also helped that the boy was pleasing to the eye. 'What did you and Griff get up to?'

'I left not long after you did,' she told me, her voice flat.

I knew it.

'Oh, why's that?' I asked, pretending to be genuine even though I was pretty sure I already knew the actual answer. Yes,

I realised how much of a shitty human I had become in the short span of one night, but there was something so thrilling in the whole thing that sparked electricity through my veins. A drug of sorts.

'Just wasn't feeling it.' She shrugged. 'Wanted to come chill here, get some homework done.'

I nodded, all while wondering if the girl believed her own shit—my opinion varied depending on the day. Clover was as much of a mystery to me still as she was the first day I met her. She never gave much away and certainly didn't divulge any secrets, to the point where it was hard to know if I meant as much to her as she did to me. Were we only friends because she'd needed an ally, and I happened to be the other scholarship student at the school *and* we shared a room?

My pillow rustled as I plugged my phone into the speaker within it and set up my videos for the night. The pillow had to be hands down one of my favourite possessions because I could listen to ASMR all night long and not have Clo complain about it.

Pulling my eye mask over my eyes to block out the world, the sound of Clo fidgeting, followed by the click of the bedroom light switch, reached my ears. Just as I was about to turn to face the wall and up the volume on my phone, Clo cleared her throat.

'Yes?' I called out, knowing she wanted my attention but was too afraid to outright come out with whatever bullshit question was stirring within her.

She coughed again.

'Sky, do you really like him?' Her voice was so low I almost missed it.

Trapped, a true rabbit in the headlights, I was glad my eye mask was covering my deceit.

Man, I'm a terrible person.

'I don't know if I'd use the word *really*,' I replied, trying to be honest with her. May as well be, seeing as I was lying about everything else. 'But yeah, I do like him.'

Clo stayed silent and her silence gave me a moment to think over my reply. Then it hit me. It wasn't a total lie!

I *did* like him.

Leo was attractive, kind of mysterious, and a total C-bomb most of the time, but also, he intrigued me. Sometimes he made me laugh, and even though he'd known a lot more than he told me last year, he did also message me and check I was okay. It never came across as if he didn't care about me at all.

Note to self: Ask Leo to explain his role in what happened to me last year.

'I thought so,' Clo mumbled. 'I didn't think you'd do this to me otherwise.'

I opened my mouth but closed it again. The guilt gnawed at my insides. My stomach a tornado of emotions.

'If you're happy, then I suppose I can learn to be, too. Night, Sky.'

'Night, Clo.'

And in that exact moment in time, I felt like the worst human being. Scum of the earth.

The plan better be worth it and it better make Ollie mad. Otherwise, I'd lose a friend for no real gain.

Nice one, Skylar. Great life choices, as usual.

THE NEXT MORNING, neither Clo nor I said any more about the fact I was dating Leo. In order to maintain our friendship, that was probably for the best.

Summer school, lucky for me, started later than regular school. The fact there were only a few members of staff on campus meant they also wanted to sleep in, and there were fewer classes to fit into each day. I hated getting up early, and I'd never understood those early birds who liked to watch the sunrise. If I watched a sunrise, it was because I hadn't been to sleep yet, not because I'd just woken up.

'Want to grab lunch together?' Clo asked from her bed, where she was staring up at the ceiling.

'I was going to eat with Leo,' I told her, already feeling crappy about my life choices. The way her eyes narrowed and her lips pursed only made me feel even worse.

'Oh, right,' she mumbled.

'Sorry,' I said, and I meant it, but that didn't stop it from tasting wrong on my tongue. My stomach was a pit of butter-flies being eaten by insects and other horrible, creepy things I hated.

'That's okay.' She was putting a brave face on it, and I appreciated it on a deeper level. She may not be happy, but she wasn't going to let me see it. 'Might see if Griff wants to eat in his room together.' She sat bolt upright, a little more pep in her step, and I glimpsed the briefest smile on her face at the mention of her red-haired beau.

I saw my opening, and fuck me, I ran with it. 'How are things going with him?'

'Good.' Her teeth showed with the beaming smile she sent in my direction. 'Really good, actually.'

'Really?' I asked, trying not to sound too sceptical, but c'mon, I couldn't help it.

'No need to sound so surprised,' she grumbled.

'I just...' I went to say more, but then realised I couldn't tell her I thought she was better suited to my new "boyfriend". Mostly for the obvious, but also because I wasn't sure if I genuinely thought that either. If you'd asked me last year, my feelings on the subject would have differed completely, but things were so different then.

'You just what?'

'Nothing,' I muttered, breaking our eye contact by getting up and heading to the bathroom to get ready for the day. Before I closed the door behind me, Clo sighed—one of those deep sighs from the heart—and I halted my action, hand paused on the door, waiting for whatever words she needed to say.

'This won't come between us, right? You and Leo being a thing and me and him being an ex-thing?' she asked, the courage it had taken her to push those words out clear in her overly bright eyes. I didn't want to walk on eggshells around her, and I knew she didn't want to avoid me. After all, it wasn't me she had a problem with.

'Not if we don't let it,' I said with a laugh. 'And can I just point out this is only like the second time you've even hinted that you were an ex-thing?'

'Eurgh,' she said, the sound coming from the back of her throat. 'Don't remind me about it.'

Her green eyes sparkled back at me, and I knew we were going to be okay. She was my girl and, being honest, we'd come a long way since the start of our friendship. She'd forgiven me for not listening to her about Ollie's true intentions, with only a couple of *I told you sos*. Really, I'd expected more, so I'd taken it as a win.

'So we're good?'

'We're good. You're my best friend, Sky. Leo Hawthorn doesn't mean shit compared to that,' she replied, her smile wide.

'Did a bit of vomit just rise in your throat?' I asked, chuckling, feeling like the moment had got *way too emotional* for me. Anything too emotional made me feel uncomfortable. As a kid, I'd thought everybody felt like that, but apparently, nope. That wasn't the norm at all.

'Yeah, a bit,' Clo said, holding her thumb and forefinger out close together in front of her face. 'Maybe we should get ready now.'

'Yep,' I said and entered the bathroom in a flash, leaving Clo chuckling behind me.

Twenty-Two

'SO, you actually prefer goat cheese on pizza to blue cheese?' I asked, feeling a little ill. A *lot* ill.

'I mean, if I had to choose,' Leo said with an amused smile. 'But people don't feel as strongly about pizza as you do.'

'Valid point.' I chuckled and reached out to touch his hair, acting every inch the doting star-struck girlfriend. The two of us were standing in front of the classroom buildings, passing the time by talking about something and nothing. Nothing deep, but if you were to glance at us from a distance, it would look a lot more important than it was. 'Is anybody around?'

If they were, I'd continue acting all touchy-feely, but if nobody was around, I wouldn't lay it on quite as thick. Best to save the good shit for an audience.

'If I'm correct, and I usually am, Ollie and Ophelia are about to leave the admin building and come over here.'

'You sound very sure,' I said, smiling up at him. Even though we were closer now—both physically and personally— the boy was still a big mystery to me. His true motives were unknown, and that made him dangerous. Yeah, he said he wanted to be my fake boyfriend to piss Clo off and I believed that was a large portion of it, but I also believed there had to be something more, something else driving him. Something *big*.

'They do the same shit every day,' he replied, entertained. Recently, he acted less bored, which made a pleasant change. Especially if I had to act like we were doing a hell of a lot more in private than playing video games.

'Makes sense. They're boring as fuck.'

Leo looked over my head, and his eyes lit up. 'Showtime.'

His tone was darkly gleeful. The two of us moved, so we were standing closer together, his arms draped over my shoulders, his hands grasped behind my neck, as we stood chest to chest. Or, well, make that chest to face. Leo was at least eight inches taller than me and I needed to crane my neck in order to look up at him. He leaned down, putting his lips level with my ear. 'When I finish this whisper, giggle. Give me flirtatious eyes. Anything to make that douche jealous. Anything to make him believe this is real and hate us both.'

I gave him the tiniest nod to tell him I understood, and the moment he straightened up, I giggled on cue. Batting my eyelashes in what I hoped was a coquettish fashion, I gripped his bicep and smiled.

Fuck, I may as well go for it.

I stood on my tiptoes and planted multiple small kisses on his lips. Ones that from afar would make an onlooker believe I couldn't get enough, that I needed one more kiss, one more touch.

'Good girl,' Leo said in a low murmur, and warmth shot straight... *there*. Shit, was I about to uncover some kind of praise kink? Because of Leo Hawthorn? Damn, I'd stooped lower than I'd realised. 'They're coming over here. Ollie's face looks even more pissed off than normal.'

'Score,' I said, speaking with a wide smile I thought might look flirty. Flirting didn't come easy to me—it wasn't in my nature.

Ollie and Ophelia descended the steps, the two of them looking like a picture-perfect couple. It was only when you knew them you saw the true rot on the inside leaking out. Ophelia's long flowing blonde hair was model straight and always styled to perfection, and Ollie's attractive features meant he could be a model too. Plus, I knew what he hid beneath his clothes. I mean, so did everybody else, seeing as he was a part of the school swim team and liked to show off at all opportunities, but still, I'd like to think I was special and had seen a whole lot more than others.

My stomach sank.

Of course you're not special, Sky. He'd had sexual partners before me. I was just the last on a long list. Or maybe not even the last. God, I had to stop thinking. In general. Full stop. Could I survive the summer with shit for brains?

'You look like somebody killed your rabbit,' Leo said, his tone bored. My face must have shown my shock at his reference as he backtracked. 'Figure of speech, Stutter.'

'Pretty sure that's a dog or cat, dickweed.'

He smirked, but it disappeared when my hand squeezed his bicep extra hard, hoping to hurt him even the tiniest fraction.

'What the fuck do you two think you're doing?' Ollie growled. They stopped next to us, and Leo and I made a big deal out of having to break apart, shifty eyeballs and all, to stand side by side.

Leo, holding my hand in his, lifted it like a trophy of sorts. 'Kissing my girl.'

'*Your* girl?' Ollie spat, taking a step towards Leo. His eye twitched, and his top lip formed a snarl. Watching the colour form in his cheeks brought me joy. Literal joy. I bit my cheek, so I didn't look too happy about it.

'Last time I checked,' Leo said with a shrug, tugging at my hand so he could manoeuvre us into a different position. He put his arm around my back and rested his hand on my bum, tucking me closer to his body.

Ollie's eyes darted between the two of us.

'Since when?' he roared, his anger growing with every second. Ophelia, still standing beside him, all but forgotten.

'Since my birthday,' Leo lied. 'Well, that was the night I told her how I felt, and lucky for me, Sky felt the same way back.'

I smiled, loving how he'd twisted the truth to fit our purpose. Technically, it was only a little white lie. We *had* discussed his plan on the night of his birthday.

'Is that why you didn't meet me that night?' Ollie asked, looking at me for the first time since they'd come over to us.

'Yep,' I said, popping my P to irritate him further. I shrugged. 'Meeting Leo was more important.'

Ollie's fists clenched tightly at his sides. Every action, every sign of how pissed off he was, only fuelled me more. It made the fire inside of me burst into actual flames. Ones that wanted to continue burning for a long time.

Fuck him. And not that kind of fuck. No, I wanted him to suffer the way I had when he crushed my heart in his palm.

I needed to stay strong. Stay focused.

Determination is key.

'I find that hard to believe,' Ophelia said with a titter. 'Everybody knows Leo isn't interested in anybody but—'

Leo cut her off, ensuring she didn't finish her sentence. 'I'm interested in Stutter. No need to twist shit.'

To further sell the lie, Leo kissed the top of my head, and I smiled wide enough for the two arseholes in front of us to notice the shit-eating grin covering my face.

'No need to justify it to these dicks,' I said aloud, and even though I was looking at Leo, everybody knew I meant my words for them. Standing next to Leo, a unified front, I felt invincible. Or at least like I could speak to Ollie and Ophelia without any hint of a stutter.

'Come on, babe. Let's go back to my room,' Leo said, using his bored tone once again, our purpose achieved.

'Let's. Sorry we can't stick around and chat,' I said to Ollie and Ophelia, feeling smug as fuck.

The two of us didn't wait for either of them to respond and walked away with our arms still awkwardly around each other's waists. 'Do you think they believed it?' I whispered, not wanting my voice to somehow carry back to them on the wind. Not like that actually happened outside of fiction and animated movies, but you could never be too careful.

'For now,' Leo murmured back, 'but that was only the beginning. We've got a long way to go, Stutter.'

'We've got this,' I said, slightly louder when we reached the building that housed the staff rooms.

'You better hope so.'

I rolled my eyes. *Ominous much?*

LATER THAT SAME DAY, I was leaving my room when I bumped into none other than a furious Ollie.

He pushed me back into my room, closing the door behind him, and pressed his back up against the door to block my way around him. I stepped back so there was a safe distance between us.

Clover had classes all day, so she wasn't around. It wouldn't surprise me if he'd known Clo's schedule and that was why he'd chosen now to strike.

'What d-do you want?' I asked, all my bravado from earlier having disappeared once I no longer had Leo standing at my side. He'd needed to go do something, so we'd split up and planned to meet up again for dinner.

'Just wanted to talk,' he said, one eyebrow raised. 'Are you scared of me?'

I could tell by the dark expression on his face that he got a kick out of that thought. A short, sharp thrill at the thought of intimidating me.

'N-no.' Pretty sure neither of us bought it.

'Want to tell me what's going on?' he asked, taking a tiny step towards me. I took the same tiny-sized step back, keeping the distance between us the same.

'What d-do you mean?' I took another step back, knowing there wasn't much more space behind me to move into. My room was only so big, and soon, I'd be landing arse first on my bed.

'I m-mean, how come you and Leo are suddenly an item?'

'An item?' I asked with a scoff to throw him off by mocking his word choice, while trying to ignore him mocking my stutter. 'Maybe because we like each other.'

'Likely story.'

'Sorry?' I brushed my hair behind my ear, feigning ignorance.

'You expect me to believe you?' He looked me up and down. 'Sure it isn't just a way to get back at me?'

'Why would it be?' I clenched my hands into a tight fist, and I knew I was going to have moon-shaped indents in my palms later. *Do not punch him. Do not punch him.* 'The world doesn't revolve around you, Oliver.'

'Because you still want me. We both know it.'

Do not punch him!

'We do?' Clearly, there were two delusional people in the room living in denial. 'I do?'

'Yes. You do,' he bit out through gritted teeth, almost like he wanted me to believe it as much as he wanted to. 'You don't want *Leo.*'

'You sure about that?' I raised my eyebrows and crossed my arms across my chest, realising too late that my action was bound to catch his eye and draw his eyes to my boobs.

His eyes did exactly that. *Predictable bastard.*

'I am.' His salacious grin chilled me. 'You felt something towards me in the library.'

'You're delusional,' I blurted out, too surprised for my stutter to rear its irritating head.

'Oh, I am, am I?' he asked, taking another step towards me. His eyes held a sinister glint, and he had pushed me into a corner. Or, more like, pushed me to the edge of my bed. 'Swear on my life that you're not doing this to get at me.'

I faltered. Why the fuck did he have to bring out the *swear on my life* card?

I'd mentioned to him once that to me, it was a very serious thing. That I wouldn't swear on his life if I didn't mean my words. Initially, I'd introduced it to establish trust in our relationship.

Turns out, he'd never taken it seriously, because he'd never taken our relationship seriously.

His words had trapped me.

Of course, I could swear on his life and be a liar and annihilate my own principles in the process, or I could *not*, and have him know the truth. I went for an in-between reply.

'I swear,' I whispered. 'Genuinely, I like Leo.'

It felt like a dirty secret. But the thing was, I wasn't lying when I'd told Clover and I wasn't lying to Ollie, either. I *did* like Leo.

'Well, he could never like you,' he spat, maliciousness clear to me in each syllable. 'You don't belong with him. He'll never see you as anything more than a pawn in his game with Clover.'

'Then who do I belong with?' I asked, wondering how he was going to respond. The fact he believed I belonged with anyone made me laugh—internally, anyway.

Ollie opened his mouth and then shut it again.

Did I want him to say it was him I belonged with?

And how would I react if he did?

Not like it fucking mattered.

I looked deep into his bright blue eyes, hoping to see something lying beneath the surface. 'That's what I thought.'

A small laugh left my lips and it triggered something in Ollie. His lips turned up at the edges—not quite a smile, but no longer angry either. Once again, he stepped closer to me, but this time I didn't feel threatened. His anger had dissipated, and I couldn't quite figure out the emotion left in its place.

'Sky,' he said and reached out to touch my cheek. I shivered at his touch, the warmth of his fingers warming my insides even though I didn't want them to. 'One day you'll see.'

'See what?' I asked, wondering what on earth he could mean.

'The truth,' he said, his tone low. 'But just know this, Skylar. Not everything between us was a lie, and one day, I'll get to prove that to you. I'll see myself out.'

And with that, he was gone, and I was left feeling alone and confused.

Twenty-Three

SUMMER WAS MOVING FASTER than I'd expected.

We were already over halfway through the break, and yet nothing much of note had happened since Ollie cornered me in my bedroom. Nope. He'd gone straight back to ignoring my existence—well, as much as he could—and pretending me and Leo weren't a thing.

So much for proving shit.

Leo and I were spending every spare moment with each other, except for when I was in class, and it shocked me, but we hadn't argued or become bored of one another yet. It turned out the two of us were good at being friends and getting along, and on the odd occasion, kissing and hugging.

Trust me, I'm as surprised as you are.

Clover and Griff were still making whatever the thing between them was work, and I for one wasn't going to tell them my true opinions without provocation.

Ophelia was still simping over Ollie, and Oralie was the third wheel at all times.

When I learned I'd be stuck at Hawthorn for the summer holidays, I would've never imagined things to be so boring and routine. Other than their one attempt, the girls hadn't even tried to punch me or anything. Seemed like a wasted chance to me.

Then there was the learning itself.

Mr Hawkins hadn't been joking when he told me we were to embark on private French lessons. The schedule had changed, and I was expected to stay longer than Ophelia and Oralie to continue learning French one-on-one. Ever since that first lesson, the man gave off a creepy vibe, but I couldn't place my finger on the reason. It wasn't like he'd made a move on me or said anything else to make me wary.

When I told Leo about the ick he gave me, he was surprisingly caring about it.

'If he keeps making you feel weird, let me know, Stutter. No teacher should give you the creeps. Especially not in a place like this that kids pay a fuck ton to attend. My words from last year still stand.'

When he'd finished talking, I nodded and gave him a quick peck on the cheek to show my gratitude. If we weren't in a fake relationship to piss others off, I'd worry a little about my heart.

The heart that thawed a little more with every hour we spent together.

I arrived at my French class in a rush, having just left Leo's suite minutes before.

'Ms Crescent,' Mr Hawkins said when I entered the classroom, brushing my hands through my hair to make it more presentable. 'For a change, you're the first one to arrive.'

'I am?' I looked around the room, confused. The O girls always showed before I did in hopes some of their flirting was going to rub off on Mr Hawkins. Ever since summer started, the two of them flirted with Mr Hawkins like it was their job.

They were hoping he'd bite, eventually, but so far they'd got nowhere. 'How unusual.'

He was looking at me, his stare never leaving my face, and I shuffled on the spot, wanting to go to my seat but also not wanting to get any closer to him.

'*En français*,' he said with a smile, and I glanced at the door, hoping the girls would fly through it and derail our conversation. The man gave me the creeps. It was as simple as that.

Dreams did come true, as at that moment, Ophelia flew through the door, nearly taking me out as she did so.

'YOU BITCH!' The anger in Ophelia's voice took me by surprise, and the moment I took in her appearance as she stood in front of the board, I burst into laughter. Real stomach-hurting chortles. The girl looked crazed: her skin a dark shade of purple and her ice-blonde hair no longer ice-blonde, but the brightest orange.

Ah, so she'd used the products Griff and I had tampered with. *Finally!*

Oralie appeared behind her, her skin a similar hue, but her hair was a bright green, and I lost it with laughter once again. There was no way I could take either of them seriously looking like *that*.

'You did this to us!' Oralie shouted, throwing herself in my direction, gearing her arm back, and I expected her fist to make contact with my face, but Mr Hawkins stood in between us and took her punch in his stomach instead.

'Girls,' he said, placating, breathing normally, like he hadn't just been punched. 'Calm down. There's no way of knowing whether Ms Crescent did this to you.'

'Yes, there is!' Ophelia spat. 'There's nobody else on campus who would want to embarrass us and make us ugly!'

'And are you hurt?' he asked, looking them both over from top to toe.

'Well, n-no,' sputtered Oralie. 'But she *wanted* to hurt us.'

'Yes, Ms Jones, but if I recall, you planned to punch Ms Crescent just now?'

Oralie stayed silent.

'Plus, I found the two of you punching Ms Crescent a week ago, so if she had something to do with this, then I can't blame her.'

Ophelia and Oralie dropped their jaws in disbelief.

'Our parents will hear about this!' Ophelia shrieked and Oralie nodded profusely behind her.

'I'm sure they will. I'm also sure Ms Hawthorn will hear about this, too. Now sit down. We've got a lesson to get to.'

I still hadn't stopped laughing, and seeing the shock on their faces just made me laugh more. As revenge plans go, it had been a little simplistic and childish, but man, what fun!

Ophelia leaned over in her chair and whispered, 'Sleep with one eye open, bitch.'

THE EVENING after the girls had showed up looking... different... Ollie had sat down in the chair next to me at the dining table while I waited for Leo, Griff, and Clo to show up.

'Excuse me?' I said the moment he sat down. 'Can I help you?'

'Knock it off, will you?' His mouth took on an unpleasant twist.

'Knock what off?' I pretended I had no idea what he was

talking about, but it made sense he was talking about Ophelia and Oralie.

'I've seen what you did to the girls and it isn't on.'

'Isn't on? Ha! Are you having me on right now?' I laughed. 'There's no way to prove it was me, anyway.'

'I don't have to prove anything. You're the only person on campus who would bother with something so petty.'

'You have to admit it was pretty amusing.'

His face didn't even twitch.

'Even if it was me, which I'm not saying it was, why would I stop? Not like they've ever stopped their crap with me.'

'They will from now on. After they hurt you for not having dinner with me, I made it clear if they touched you again, they'd regret it.'

'And you think you wield that much power over them?' I rolled my eyes at his optimism. He may think he ruled the school—and the O girls—but I knew better. They did what they wanted, when they wanted. Their whole lives, they'd been told they could do anything and their money and power would mean they never suffered because of it. 'Those girls would drop you if it suited them.'

'Ophelia's my girlfriend, so I highly doubt that.' His words shocked me. I hadn't expected him to come out and say it. 'And Lee and I have known each other since we were two. She wouldn't turn on me. Neither of them would.'

'Whatever you say.' I looked towards the dining room door, hoping to see Leo walk through, or even Griff and Clo, but it was empty. Trust me to come to dinner early and alone. 'I don't really care either way.'

'You can lie to yourself all you want, Skylar, but you can't lie to me. I see right through you and always have. I see *you*.' He leaned forward, putting himself in my bubble. 'I don't want us to fight anymore.'

'I didn't realise we were fighting,' I said with a pout. 'I thought you'd decided I was scum of the earth and I'd decided you weren't worth my time. Or something to that effect anyway. Ollie, get up and go bother somebody else.'

'There's nobody in here but you to bother.'

'Then leave the room for all I care.' I huffed, getting bored with him being near me. At first I was having fun with it, but he'd overstayed his welcome by at least five minutes. 'I'm waiting for my boyfriend.'

'Want to remind me how the two of you became a thing?'

'Not particularly.' And not just because I didn't actually know the version of events we were meant to stick to...

'If you'd met me that night, maybe things would be different.' Ollie's eyes bored into mine, and I had to look away from the intensity in them. '*We* would be different.'

I shrugged. 'Maybe, but I guess we'll never know.'

'I could tell you now,' he said, and I frowned. He could tell me what? My blank stare clued him in to my confusion. 'What I wanted to say to you that night.'

'How about you tell both of us,' Leo said, taking his rightful place in the other seat next to me. He pulled me in, placed a kiss on my head, and held me close while staring Ollie down. There was something awfully sexy about a territorial Leo. 'I'm sure we'd both love to hear it.'

'I'd rather tell only Skylar,' Ollie said, not missing a beat. 'If you ever want to talk, Sky, you know where to find me. Or you can text me. I assume you still have my number.'

Of course I still had his number, but it didn't mean I'd use it.

'I'm okay. Thanks,' I said, leaning back into Leo's embrace.

The epitome of a happy couple. The happiest. 'It wouldn't have changed anything.'

'Sure it wouldn't,' Ollie drawled. 'I'll leave you two to your evening.'

'Don't fancy joining us, mate?' Leo laughed, not meaning a word, and I worried Ollie knew that and would jump on the invitation. Lucky for me, Ollie shook his head, his eyes dark.

'I've got a girlfriend to go see.'

Leo shrugged. 'Suit yourself.'

Ollie finally stood from the chair and left the room, leaving me and Leo alone together. 'Thanks for the rescue.'

'You didn't need rescuing, Stutter. Not this time.' I turned to face him and was blinded by the rare wide smile covering the bottom half of his face. 'I heard you when I came in. You were holding your own.'

'He doesn't hold the power over me anymore.'

'Good.' Leo squeezed my hand, then turned to read the menu on the table. 'I'm proud of you and how far you've come.'

'Thanks.' I opened the menu and glanced at it, but I wasn't seeing the words written on the page, my mind filled with happiness from Leo's praise. 'You're not so bad yourself.'

Leo's eyes really were beautiful when they shone like that. Carefree. Happy. So different from the eyes I looked into last year and only saw boredom in. But which one was the façade? The bored guy who gave a shit about nothing, or the one with open eyes who gave a shit about me?

'...having pizza tonight.'

'Huh?' I shook my head, looking at his lips as if the first half of his sentence would appear there.

'There's stonebaked margherita on the menu tonight.' He pointed at my menu on the table in front of me. 'Guess we both know what you're having.'

I laughed. 'Yep. You know me so well.'

'Anyone who's seen your eating habits would know what meal you'd pick.'

'True,' I agreed. 'And let me guess'—I perused the menu, trying to correctly guess Leo's choice—'you'll be having the steak, rare.'

'Looks like you know me just as well,' he said with a wolfish smile. 'Aren't we the lucky ones?'

'Aren't we just!' I tried not to dwell on the unsaid part of my sentence. *Wonder when it'll end?*

Twenty-Four

LEO

AT SOME POINT in the last month, I'd fucked up.

Everything had seemed so simple at first. Ask Stutter to be my fake girlfriend, make Clover jealous, and piss Ollie off all in one fell swoop with zero effort on my part. Stutter was a pretty girl, and I liked her as a person when she wasn't miserable about the way Ollie treated her, so it seemed like a win-win to me. It was a brilliant plan.

It was also something I'd done without being told to.

I'd gone rogue, so to speak.

'You think we can complete this tonight?' Stutter asked, pausing the game and moving her gaze from the TV to face me. The two of us were in my room, sitting on the bed playing *Spyro*, after another day of faking everything in front of those fuckers I called my friends.

Actually, I was watching her play while I did fuck all but admire her. She was trying her hardest to make that little purple fucker fly the wrong way. She'd seen a hack online, or something like that, and she was adamant she could crack the game faster if she could just fly through the cliff.

'Don't see why not?' I replied, blinking at her. 'If you can figure out how to do it.'

'Hm, true,' she said with a smile, then turned back to the game, even more determined than before to make it work. That was something I'd noticed about Skylar—she loved to win and had quite the competitive streak. If you doubted her, she'd do her best to prove you wrong, no matter how long it took.

Her lips always looked best when smiling. All full, plump, and they made me think of things I shouldn't be thinking of— like what it would be like to bite her lip as I thrust inside her. Or how her glossy lips would look wrapped around my cock.

I had to adjust myself, hoping she was as unobservant as she'd always been around us all.

Stutter had the tendency to be oblivious.

Somehow she'd believed Ollie last year, when it was pretty obvious to everybody else that he was playing her. Even Red fucking noticed, and she wasn't always the sharpest tool. She also happened to be a backstabbing fucking bitch and the whole reason I was sitting here hard for her best friend in the first place.

'Leo?'

'Yeah,' I replied, the thought of Red causing my dick to die down. She was an instant libido killer.

'Has Ollie said anything to you?' she asked, her tone uncertain, telling me she didn't want to know the answer but had asked, regardless. Sky was a curious thing and she couldn't leave questions unasked, even if the answer was going to make her day worse.

'About?' I drawled, wanting her to work for it.

'About us? About me?'

'Not gonna lie, Stutter, not like I talk to the boy much these days. Not since my birthday, at least. Wonder why that is.' I laughed, but it held little humour in it.

And I wasn't lying. I barely spoke to him outside of the times we were all together, or when I needed to for *Sect* stuff. The prick deserved to be excluded from what I was doing. He didn't get to call the shots around here and not have any repercussions for his shitty actions.

'You don't?' she asked, pausing the game once again and putting the controller down to give me her full attention. It was nice to have her attention, her bright eyes taking in every part of my face as she tried to figure something out. I hadn't yet figured out what it was she was searching for.

The two of us were lying on top of the duvet, and she moved onto her side to face me. I stayed where I was, not wanting to make the situation even more intimate. I didn't need more on my plate.

'When do I have the time?' I shrugged. 'I'm mostly with you.'

'Yeah, true.' She blinked, her eyes a blue I wanted to look at longer. 'What about during swim practice?'

I chuckled, once again reminded how little Stutter knew about the swim team and what happened at practice. The girl was totally oblivious—Stutter never noticed things unless they were in front of her face and sometimes even then they went over her head.

'He swims,' I replied.

She nudged me in the side. 'Hey! You make me sound stupid.'

'Do I?' I asked, raising my eyebrow at her. 'Or do you do that all by yourself?'

'I am not stupid!' she said and then laughed. 'No, I totally can be stupid.'

'Glad you realise it.'

I turned and looked at her, once again feeling my dick twitch when she turned her full beam smile in my direction. No wonder Ollie became whipped—even if the prick couldn't admit it to himself. He'd rather dig himself a hole with Ophelia than admit he fucked up and lost a good thing.

'I wonder what Griff and Clo are up to right now.'

'No, you don't,' I said, knowing that *I* definitely didn't want to know, but not for the reason I usually didn't want to know. To be honest, I'd reached a point where I just didn't give a shit about them. Or about anybody that wasn't in the room.

Shit.

Things were definitely getting twisted.

I'd started to actually *like* Stutter. And not just in that friendship way we'd had before. Or in a protective way I'd felt last year when... well, when shit went down.

'Kiss me,' I blurted, no thought behind the statement, and once it had made its way into the atmosphere, I'd look like a right wanker trying to take it back. I tried to stay casual and act cavalier, as if I was in full control of my faculties.

'Huh?' she asked as her eyes looked at my face, taking in every part, until her eyes locked with mine.

'Kiss. Me.'

'W-why?' she stuttered, and my dick responded. Damn, that stutter really did something to me. Like Ollie last year, *I* was wondering what it sounded like with *my* dick deep inside her.

'Don't you want to?' I asked, turning it around on her. If she said no, I'd leave it at that, no harm done. The ball, as always, was in Stutter's court.

'I...' She took a deep breath. 'Is that what you want?'

Neither a yes nor a no. Helpful. 'We should probably practise, right? Make sure that when we kiss in public, it looks natural. Like we do it in private.'

'To keep up the lie?'

I nodded. If my agreement was what she needed to hear to believe it—to justify it in her head—then I'd agree.

'Okay,' she whispered.

I turned onto my side, so our foreheads touched, and our lips inched closer together. Gently putting her chin in my hold, I tilted her head so I could look into the depth of colour swimming in her irises and the doubt that lingered under the surface.

'Are you s-sure?'

Responding with words seemed cheap, and even though she was a scholarship student, Skylar was anything but cheap. My lips touched hers, urgent and exploratory. Stutter gasped slightly and parted her lips. My tongue explored, and then, like a switch turning on, she ripped herself out of my hold.

'That's enough practice for now,' she said in a hushed voice, her eyes wide.

I nodded and lay back to face the ceiling again, breathing deep to stop myself from claiming her. We both needed to cool down. 'Sure, Stutter. Don't want you to like kissing me *too* much, do we?'

My question was meant to sound casual and offhand, but it came out strained.

Fuck.

Maybe it wasn't just my dick that wanted a piece of Stutter.

THE REST of summer passed the way the first month did—odd spurts of excitement, mixed with long, tedious bouts of boredom.

Ollie was barely talking to me. Griff spoke to me but only if Stutter was present.

'What's the plan?' I leaned forward and murmured in Sky's ear, the two of us standing close together, chests touching while we waited in an alcove outside the hall for Griff and Clo to join us for lunch. I'd arranged for us to go off campus and get lunch at her favourite café down the hill in town, and although Stutter didn't know about it yet, I knew she'd love it.

'Tonight?' she asked, tilting her head up to look into my eyes. I nodded. 'Same as usual, I guess.'

Hawthorn Academy was a place I hated and loved in equal measure. For most of my life, I'd spent all my summer and winter breaks on campus at the family estate, and when it wasn't school time, the place was peaceful and somewhere I could be and think without having to put on an act.

I never thought I'd be ready for other students to arrive, but fuck, I was. Having only six students on campus meant there wasn't enough going on, and my plan with Stutter didn't have as much clout as it would when the rest of the student body was watching it unfold. The real revenge was having Ollie seen as less than by the Hawthorn population, and even though he was my cousin and therefore family, I still wanted to knock the wanker down a bit.

'I had an idea of what we could do Friday night,' I said. Sky raised her eyebrow, waiting for me to continue.

'Yeah?' she asked when I didn't say anything.

'Yeah,' I said with a nod. 'But it's a surprise.'

'You know I hate surprises.'

'You'll probably hate this one, too,' I said, a dark smile playing on my lips. *Probably* was an understatement. She'd *definitely* hate it. Maybe not as much as she'd hate me if she knew the truth about everything I was doing...

'Great. I'm thrilled,' she deadpanned, and I gave a low chuckle.

I lifted one hand from where it was resting on Sky's arse to tuck her hair behind my ear. 'Promise, Stutter, it'll be fun. I wouldn't drag you into something you'd hate.'

'I find that hard to believe,' she whispered. The kiss I gave her in reply was involuntary. She was making me feel things I knew I shouldn't feel, yet I couldn't help myself. I was enjoying our deception too much. I was enjoying her company just as much. Why shouldn't I get something out of it? Something as fun as pissing off Clover.

And pissing off Clover was a fuck ton of fun. Every time she was around us, she pretended not to care, but when she thought we weren't looking, her eyes didn't leave the area where Sky's and my bodies touched.

'Ready for lunch, bitches?' Griff's voice brought me back to the moment, the thought of Clover forgotten, even though she was heading towards us from the end of the hall. Sky laughed, stepping back from my embrace to face them.

'Ready for what, exactly?' Clover asked. 'Crappy school food?'

'No way! We're leaving campus. The car's waiting outside.' Griff beamed at us, and for the tiniest second, a twinge of guilt ran through me. I wanted Clo to hurt, sure, but Griff was my cousin. Family. I hated that he was getting caught in every crosshair, but there was nothing to be done about it. I had to let the chips fall and pick up the pieces after the fact.

'Come on, Stutter. Let's get the fuck out of dodge.'

Sky instantly moved into my outstretched arm, and I pulled her close once more before standing beside her and holding her hand. Her responding squeeze made me smile.

Sky's enthusiasm was one of the many endearing things about her. 'Let's do this shit!'

Twenty-Five

EVERY SLASHER HORROR movie included an end of summer camp out, right?

Yep, that's what I thought.

But apparently, I wanted to be the new dead girl in a remake of *Friday the 13th* because here I was, getting ready to go camp out in the woods with the boys. From what Leo had told me, Ollie and *The Set* were going to be there, but all I had to do was make Ollie jealous and ignore them otherwise.

Easier said than done.

'You wearing that?' Leo asked, looking me up and down, his eyes appraising.

I looked down to remind myself of my outfit, wondering why Leo was asking. Did he mean it in a good way, or like *you're wearing garbage, Sky, go change?*

My black dress showed major cleavage, and the skirt flowed out at my waist, showing off my hourglass curves. The dress itself was pretty plain, but we were camping out, not going to the Ritz.

'I was going to?'

'You look hot,' he said. My lips twitched upwards, an involuntary movement, and my insides warmed. Leo could deliver the simplest of lines but make me feel fantastic about myself. Things between us were heating up and I wasn't sure if it was all a game to him.

'Thanks. You look pretty good, too.'

The smile Leo graced me with could only be described as wolfish and seductive. Spending more time with him had changed my perception of him—for the better—and a small part of me wished we were spending the night together without the others.

'So, we're sharing a tent?' he asked, his eyebrow raised. I took back my praise of him. He could be such a prick. He knew the answer already, but he just wanted to embarrass me and make me say it out loud.

'Y-yes.' My cheeks flushed, and my chest turned a dark shade of red with nerves.

'How far are you willing to go to sell this, Stutter?'

'I...' *Shit, how far was I willing to go?* 'I don't know,' I replied. 'Why?'

'We're all going to be in close proximity. And any light inside a tent shows what is going on inside. Plus, our tent is small.'

'How small is small?' My eyebrows furrowed, praying he wasn't about to tell me it was one of those two-man pop-up things. The boy had enough money to at least upgrade our tent to a four-man, surely!

'Think we've got ourselves a pop-up,' he replied with a grin, almost as if he knew the thoughts going through my head. He was getting a kick out of all of it and fair play to him. He knew what would grate on Clo the most, and the two of us being in a two-man tent with barely any space to move? Yeah, that'd send her over the edge.

'Yay,' I cheered.

'It'll be fine, Stutter. We won't do anything you don't want to do.' His blue eyes looked earnest, and the sincerity shone out at me. I released a breath, knowing Leo meant his words. He wasn't Ollie, who still hadn't apologised—or even mentioned —the closet since.

'I mean, we can kiss.' He nodded, and I added, 'And hug, act touchy-feely. Stuff we've already done.'

'Define touchy-feely?'

'I don't know... ' My cheeks warmed. You'd have thought a virgin was standing before him, but really, it was just little, old, inexperienced me.

His words were playing on a loop in my mind. *How far are you willing to go to sell this?*

'Sky, what do you mean?' he asked, and the fact that he used my name set my racing heart at ease. 'I don't want you to be uncomfortable.'

'You can grope my bum?' I asked, then burst out into laughter. He'd already done that before, so it wasn't like I was saying something we hadn't already agreed to. 'Touch me up, I guess?' His eyes locked with mine. 'Stop looking at me like that! The fact you're making me say shit is causing me to break out into a rash.'

'Calm down, Stutter. I can make it work,' he said, and the look in his eye made me move closer to him. Close enough that I could wrap my arms around him and grope *his* bum. His large hands warmed my waist as he rested them there, and the intimacy for once didn't feel forced. Trying to get my mind away from that avenue, I searched for something else to wonder about. God forbid my mind be blank without thought for once.

A thought hit me and I muttered, 'Poor Oralie. She'll be seventh wheeling it tonight.'

How awkward. If I were her, I wouldn't show up, but there

was no way in hell that girl would do that. The FOMO was real. If I were her, I'd rather stay in my room alone, watching films or reading an excellent book, than go spend a creepy night in the woods with three couples.

Fuck, I'd rather do that and I was a part of one of the "couples". Honestly, all three pairings were as fake as the next, just for different reasons.

'That's the goal, right? Making the O girls suffer alongside Ollie?' he asked. 'Feeling sympathy for the twat, Stutter?'

I scoffed, trying to cover up the fact that my heart was feeling bad for the girl who'd tormented me last year with no remorse. *Get your head in the game.*

'Eurgh, I sort of hate myself.' I chuckled.

'Why?'

'I should want her to feel awkward, should want her to suffer, and trust me, this will definitely cause her ego to suffer. She believes she should be your girlfriend.'

'Probably.' He shrugged, and my body moved with his motion. 'But she's not.'

'True. I am, 'cause we're both dickheads.'

He laughed at that, and I joined him. We broke apart, and I continued getting ready for an evening I already knew I wouldn't enjoy.

'Come on, grumps. I'll make sure you have a good time,' he said.

I wasn't even going to question how he knew my mind. 'Promise?'

'Promise. And if not, we can just get trashed.'

'Sounds like a plan, Batman.'

I took a deep breath, gearing myself up to put a jacket on and leave Leo's suite with him.

'Breathe, Stutter. We've got this,' he drawled and took my

hand in his. His hand heated my own, and he squeezed to reassure me.

Camp Hawthorn, here we come.

So, this had to be the worst camp out I'd ever attended in my life.

I mean, it was the *only* camp out I'd ever attended in my life, but semantics.

In the middle of the clearing, a large fire raged, and around it there were camp chairs in a semicircle. The flames were the only light in the area and caused everything to have an orange, sinister glow. Clover and Griff were sitting next to each other, heads close together, talking animatedly about something. In their own bubble, ignoring the rest of us.

Ophelia and Ollie were standing together, swaying along to some ballad Oralie was playing out of the Bluetooth speaker she'd hooked up to her phone. The entire view made me cringe. Knowing what I knew of my fake relationship, it had become glaringly obvious to me over the last couple of weeks just how much Ollie was lying with Ophelia. No bone in his body wanted to be near her. I'd even witnessed him flinching when she sank her talons into his arm to grab his attention.

Then there was Leo and me, hands gripped together, standing off to the side, talking in hushed tones about our plan of action. To the outside looking in, I felt certain we looked like a genuine couple talking about private matters.

'Right, we need to liven up this shit,' he whispered, his breath skating across my face and causing me to shiver.

'What do you suggest?' I pressed up onto my tiptoes to

whisper into his ear. My skin tingled as if it could sense Ollie's boring stare in our direction, and I knew how intimate this would look to him. 'I'm coming up blank.'

'We need to get everyone to play a game.'

'All right, Jigsaw.' I lowered my feet, knowing that my intention had hit its mark. Leo followed my lead and leant down to whisper in my ear. His lips brushed my ear, and I giggled at the tickling sensation.

'Oh, ha-ha. Help me think of a game.'

'I have never?' I asked, but then thought better of it. 'Truth or dare?'

'Of course,' he said and then warned me. 'Be careful. Those girls will be out for blood.'

'I could say the same to you, but it isn't the girls who would like to see you bleed.'

He chuckled, sending chills down my spine, and kissed my cheek, making a big show of the action, and moved to stand beside me. It burned where his lips had been, and I knew I had turned the colour of a tomato. To me, in that moment, it felt like we were two outsiders looking over the kingdom they intended to overthrow. *Listen to me.* I'd been watching one too many television programmes about the Tudor court.

Swinging his arm around my shoulder, I leaned into him. I hoped we looked as real as we were selling it to be.

'Let's play a game,' I called out. An ominous statement if ever there was one. Instantly, five pairs of eyes were on us and every single pair was sceptical.

'What game are you thinking, Clouds?' Griff called back, his cheeky grin plastered on his face. If there was anybody I trusted and could always rely on, it was him.

'Truth or dare,' Leo said at his normal level. One thing that impressed me about Leo was that no matter what, he made it clear he was above all the petty bullshit. Not going to lie, it made me the slightest bit turned on when he was so himself. He never acted in a way that didn't feel genuine to him, if that made sense? His self-assuredness was extremely hot to me; super appealing.

'I'm down,' Griff said, and as soon as he agreed, the spell was cast over the other people in the clearing.

'Sounds fun,' Ollie drawled, his eyes that dark indigo they turned when he was acting his most devious. *Side note: must not take a dare from Oliver.*

'We're in,' Oralie and Ophelia said in unison. *Creepy.*

'Looks like we're doing this,' Clo said in a sour tone. Couldn't blame her. If the game hadn't been my idea, I would have been running for the edge of the hill the school sat upon.

The seven of us all took our seats around the campfire, the flames flickering on everybody's faces causing every facial expression to alter to something darker. I trusted nobody. My hand was still gripped in Leo's—I was using him as an anchor of sorts. Something tangible and real that would keep me sane; keep me grounded. Somebody there to ensure I didn't throw caution to the wind and forget about my revenge plot.

'Who wants to start?' I asked, and surprise, surprise, nobody jumped up to go first. I looked at Griff sitting opposite me and tried to use our cousin's telepathy to get him to pipe up. The boy loved to hear his own voice every day of the week, so I could do with his gung-ho attitude.

Lucky for me, the communication waves must have opened between us as he smiled and nodded.

'I'll go,' he said. Shit you not, his dimples looked even cuter in the dim fire lighting.

'Truth or dare?' I asked, not knowing what I would do for either of his responses. I was full-blown winging it.

'Dare, of course,' Griff replied as if it were a given. And I suppose it was.

'Err… I dare you to…' I looked around, hoping for inspiration. 'I dare you to climb that tree.' I pointed over to a large hawthorn tree that looked like it could take his weight. He may be tall, but his body was made up of pure muscle, his broad shoulders made even more powerful through the many hours of swim training he put himself through.

'Easy-peasy,' he said, so cocksure that a small part of me hoped he'd fail. That would at least make him think twice before being so confident all the time.

Griff stood and sauntered over to the tree. Sizing it up, I could see his brain working a mile a minute, trying to figure out how to tackle the task. A second later, the boy was off, climbing the tree as if it were nothing at all. He didn't even pause to take a deep breath or to think of his next move.

'No fair!' I realised the boy had some kind of rock climbing skill I hadn't been privy to.

Griff got to the highest branch he could, then laughed and shouted something corny that I couldn't quite make out. Although if I *had* to guess, I'd say he quoted Jack from *Titanic*. Yes, *that* scene. The boy was nothing if not predictable.

He climbed back down as quick as he'd scaled up and jumped the last couple of feet with triumph blazing in his eyes. 'Nice one, Clouds. That's a point for me.'

'There aren't points in truth or dare, Griff,' Clo said with a roll of her eyes, although I could tell she found him amusing all the same.

'There should be,' he grumbled.

'Then there will be,' Ollie piped up. 'The team to reach ten points first, wins. And for every point you forfeit, you drink.'

Everybody met his words with an agreement. Everybody

but me. Leo nudged me in the side. A reminder. So I did what was expected of me and said, 'Deal.'

Let the games begin.

HONESTLY, who the fuck would ever believe that a stupid, simple game of truth or dare could go on for three hours?

Apparently, with seven players, each round took an age to complete. Plus, at first there had been a lot of arguing about whether we could give points to answers given to a 'Truth' as there was no way of proving the person was in fact telling the truth.

Fuck me. This had actually seemed like a fun idea when I suggested it. *Oh, how naïve young Skylar of three hours ago was.*

'Truth or dare?' Ophelia slurred, and she wasn't the only one slurring, repeating the words Leo had just said to Clover.

'Truth,' Clo responded lightning fast. The alcohol had made her brave. For the past few rounds, she'd opted for a dare and had failed miserably, so was now rather drunk on the energy drink and vodka she was consuming like it would run out. I'd been trying to drink as little as I could in order to keep my faculties intact, but it seemed nobody else in the circle was doing the same.

Leo chuckled next to me, the glimmer of the flames matching the glint of evil in his eyes. 'Are you jealous of Stutter?'

Clover bristled, her dislike of Leo clear to everybody. Griff's face darkened too.

'Nope,' she replied, scoffing. 'If anything, I feel sorry for her.'

I flinched at her venom. *Gee, Clo, ta muchly.*

'Sorry for her?' Leo asked sardonically. 'Expect us to believe that, Red?'

'Expect you to believe the truth? Yes.' Her statement came out pretty clear, except for the slight slur at the end that changed the meaning.

'You need to drink!' Oralie called out, giddy, watching the events unfold like a tennis match. Her ice-blonde hair had got stuck to her lip gloss, and it had taken a lot of willpower not to stand up and yank it off for her. It was irritating me so much, but I wasn't going to save her from the embarrassment. Both she and Ophelia had blatantly decided the only way they could get through the evening was by getting wasted. *Fair.*

Alongside Leo and me, Ollie was the only other person who hadn't touched their drink much, or at least I hadn't seen him drink loads. Not that I was watching him—often. Of course he wouldn't be drinking. He needed control at all times. Power was more effective when sober.

'Why?' Clo snapped. 'I didn't lie.'

Oralie hiccupped and said in a snooty tone, '*Duh*. I meant Leo needs to drink.'

'Oh.' Clover looked thoroughly schooled and I couldn't help but laugh. The entire scenario I'd found myself in killed me a little inside. What even was life?

'Truth or dare?' Clo asked me, her eyes narrowed. Her venom wasn't unfounded, but I couldn't be arsed to deal with it.

'Truth,' I replied, feeling pretty confident that Clo wouldn't come for me too hard. Although I had just laughed at her, maybe I shouldn't be quite so cocky.

'How do you really feel about Leo?' she asked, triumphant. In my peripheral, I saw Ollie sit up a little straighter, interested in my answer. The whole circle was interested in my answer, including the guy in question sitting next to me, rubbing his hand along my leg. I didn't even have to think twice about it.

'I like him,' I said with a shrug. Everybody knew that to pass a lie detector you had to answer as close to the truth as you could. 'And let's be honest, the boy's fucking hot.'

I'd meant for my last sentence to be kept in the dark, in the back recesses of my brain, but clearly, I had drunk just enough for it to be let loose.

'Tell us how you *really* feel,' Griff said with a chuckle, breaking the tension in that way only he could.

'You think I'm hot, Stutter?' Leo's voice rumbled in his chest and vibrated down my back. His front was pressed up against my back and I was sitting on his lap, the epitome of a couple that couldn't stay away from one another. His arms were wrapped around me, engulfing me and making me feel small, yet warm and somewhat safe.

'You know you are,' I murmured. 'Truth or dare?' My question was aimed in Ollie's direction, wanting to ignore Leo's amused chuckle from behind me. What better way to do that than to ask my ex a question I didn't want an answer to.

'Truth,' he replied, his blue eyes drawing me in, daring me. Ah shit, I hadn't been expecting that! Whenever it had been his turn, he'd gone for a dare.

'Right,' I said, adjusting in Leo's lap so I could nudge him somehow to help me. His breath tickled my ear as he whispered a question I could ask and I squirmed at the way it made me feel. His dick hardened, and we both ignored it, choosing not to blur the line, especially as everyone's eyes were on us. 'Why d-did you lie to me last year?' My stutter reared its ugly head, as it always did when I felt nervous. Man, I'd really begun to hate that part of myself.

'When?' he asked, his eyebrow raised with amusement. The smirk covering his lips made my skin crawl. Who the fuck did this twat think he was? ''Cause there are a few instances you could be referring to.'

Wanker. I racked my brain for a specific time to ask about. A lot of our time together played on my mind in a constant loop, especially when I'd been stuck in my hospital bed, but recently I'd sort of tried to fixate less. An unhealthy fixation wasn't good for my mental state. Plus, Leo was a damn good distraction.

Finally, a memory flashed in my mind. 'Valentine's Day. When you made me believe.'

I couldn't take my eyes away from his face, waiting to spot any changes, any flicker of emotion or remorse he might try to hide deep down, but all I saw was confusion he quickly masked with distaste.

'Made you believe what, New Girl?' He sneered and took a large swig of his drink. 'That I could actually like you?'

Leo's arms squeezed me, giving me the support I needed not to stand up and go deck him. I'd love to rearrange his face with my fists. Okay, maybe I wouldn't. He may be a bastard, but damn, his face was pretty.

'Doesn't answer my q-question.'

'Why did I lie?' he asked, getting a thrill from repeating the words. 'Because you were so fucking gullible. The whole time, we were *all* laughing at you. Including your boy Griff and your *boyfriend* Leo. Everybody was in on it but you. How does it feel to learn you're the butt of a joke and you're the only one oblivious to the punchline?'

Tears filled my eyes, threatening to spill out, but I couldn't let them. Fuck him! Fuck him for trying to make me feel small and worthless, *again.* He'd succeeded after the charity fashion show, but I wouldn't take it any longer. Three months had passed and in that time, my confidence had grown. My self-worth and dignity alongside it.

'Fuck you,' I spat, the only response I could muster up the energy for. He didn't deserve anything more. Leo pulled me closer and kissed me on the head, giving me strength. And if you were to ask me why I said my next sentence, I'd say it was because Leo's kiss had given me the idea. 'Shall we call it a night and go to our tent?'

I turned around and spontaneously gave Leo a lingering kiss full on the lips. The small amount of alcohol running through my system had bolstered me to act with more confidence than usual and I was revelling in it.

'Thought you'd never ask. I'd love to, baby,' Leo replied in a tone low enough to pretend it was for my ears only, but loud enough that everybody heard it.

The fire had died down earlier on in the game and the only sound remaining was a low crackling.

'Let's go then.' I stood, reaching out my hand so that Leo could put his in mine. He didn't disappoint.

Once he was standing too, he pulled me along behind him towards our tent, while I giggled like a giddy girl in lust.

Sometimes, it surprised me how good of an actress I could be.

And the award goes to...

Twenty-Six

MY HANGOVER, luckily for me, was basically non-existent. Probably due to the fact that I'd consumed little alcohol, knowing that a sloppy Skylar would not have been good for the revenge plan. The revenge plan that was starting to seem a little redundant.

The opposite of non-existent? The feelings that were stirring in my stomach for Leo, but maybe that had to do with the fact he was pressed up against my back, having slept with his arm draped over my stomach, holding me close like I'd disappear if he didn't.

The summer heat blazed outside, and the tent lining was covered in tiny drops of condensation that were clinging to the material. I'd never been more glad that I slept wearing an eye mask, as the way the sun shone through the bright green tent was making me feel ill already. The inside of a tent looked so different in the light of day.

In the middle of the night, Leo had shed his T-shirt, and I'd had to remove my leggings. Our body heat, alongside the sleeping bag, had been overwhelming. The air was stuffy, and even after removing my leggings, a slight sheen of sweat still covered me when I awoke.

'Morning, babe,' Leo muttered, his voice thick with sleep. His eyes were still closed, and as much as I wanted to see his bright blues, his long eyelashes looked so pretty when his eyes were closed. Peaceful.

'Morning,' I whispered back, awkward for the first time since we'd started this thing. 'Do you think we did good last night?'

'I think Ollie and Clo both went to their tents miserable as fuck because of us,' he said with a low chuckle. '*You* did good.' His emphasis made my heart flutter. I swear, praise was like a drug to me.

'Thanks.' I blushed, glancing away from him so that he wouldn't notice me staring if he opened his eyes. 'Those noises last night...' I started but didn't want to complete the sentence. Poor Oralie. Grunts and groans could be heard for at least an hour after we went to our tent, and it reminded me of those scenes in films where couples competed to be the loudest. *Which, yeah, how fucked is that?*

'Ha,' Leo scoffed. 'None of that was real.'

'It wasn't?' I asked, unsure. Sure sounded real to me.

'Nope. None of them sound like that when they're fucking —or at least not when they're enjoying it.'

The casual way he said it caught me so off guard I choked on my own spit. I sat bolt upright, my hand flailing around on the floor, trying to locate a bottle of water.

Once my coughing died down, I gasped. 'What do you even mean?' I grabbed the water and gulped it down, trying to soothe my throat.

'Well, I'm telling the truth.' He opened his eyes, a glimmer of mischief shining from them.

'And you know that how?'

'Don't be so dense, Stutter.' To soften the blow of his

words, he sat up and kissed my cheek. Already the lines between us were blurred. We spent so much time together it was hard not to fall into the roles we were playacting. He looked me dead in the eye, his face bored once again. 'Remember, if anybody asks, our night went well.'

I nodded, knowing what he wanted me to imply, and I had already thought of a couple of coy sentences I could feed Clo to make it believable.

'Make him suffer,' he whispered. 'And I doubt he did what you're thinking he did.'

'What? Fuck Ophelia?'

'That,' he replied. 'He's pissed at himself, at you. At a lot of things. But I know him and even if he believes himself capable, he isn't.'

'Are you sticking up for him?'

'Nope, just giving you some background.'

'Okay. Well, maybe keep his background in the background for the time being.' My brows rose, causing my forehead to wrinkle, as I waited for Leo to nod. He did, and I rewarded him with an open-mouthed smile—a rare occurrence.

'As you wish, Stutter.'

'Oh, come on, dickhead'—I chucked my pillow at his head, which he ducked away from fast—'let's get this shit over with.'

THE GROUP PACKED up the tents in silence—well, everybody but Griff. The entire morning, the boy had been singing at the top of his lungs. I'd been attempting to tune him out, but the last time I listened, he had moved on to singing Adele. Or rather, butchering Adele.

Clover's eyes were bloodshot, and the dark circles under her eyes looked pretty rough. Her hangover had hit her hard, I'd say. Energy drinks and vodka were not for the weak.

Ophelia and Oralie had emerged from their tents wearing large circular sunglasses that covered not just their eyes but the majority of their faces too. A major improvement if you asked me.

Ollie had been glaring at me the entire morning and was using any opportunity he could to enter my personal bubble to make me shiver. Then if Leo was already in my bubble, and he couldn't get close enough, he went to Ophelia and attempted to make me uncomfortable that way. It was all a bit predictable, but a pain in the arse regardless.

The difference between Sky of last year and the Sky of this year: she could see through his bullshit. Knowing how fake Leo and I were at our core, I was no longer blind to just how fake Ollie and Ophelia acted together. Well, how fake Ollie acted. Pretty sure Ophelia believed it was real—bless her heart.

'I'm hungry,' Ophelia whined, stomping her foot for good measure. I looked at Leo and rolled my eyes at her antics. His lip twitched in response, which I took as a win.

'Me too,' Oralie whined even louder. Fuck, it wasn't a competition.

'Come eat with us, Skylar.' Ophelia turned to me, and even though I couldn't see her eyes through her dark lenses, I knew they weren't full of human kindness. Nope. They probably had daggers in them.

'I...' I looked around for anybody to save me, but Clo clearly still harboured ill will toward me, and Griff was so busy trying to keep her happy that he wasn't about to come to my aid. Ollie's wolfish grin told me that shit had been his idea. Leo just shrugged, his hands in his pockets, the epitome of casual. *Wonderful.*

'Girls have to eat, right?' Oralie joined in, in cahoots with her best friend—her only friend—totally ignoring the fact they weren't inviting Clover, who was also a girl. Whatever. 'And we totally forgive you for the whole hair thing.'

Ophelia nodded in agreement. 'Yep. Totally forgotten.' She barked a brittle laugh. 'And I've totally forgiven you for dying my skin, too.'

'Totally,' Oralie said. 'Even if we had to scrub our skin for hours.'

Their words were only making me more suspicious of their true intentions, but nobody was saving me, and fuck it, I could look after myself.

'Right.' I looked at Leo, hoping for a knight in shining armour, but all I saw was a knight in shit-covered armour, a bemused expression on his face. Through gritted teeth, I asked, 'Do you mind?'

'Nope,' he replied, popping the P in a way that he knew irritated me. Oh, he was going to pay for that.

'Super!' Ophelia cooed, clapping her hands together while Oralie shimmied her body next to her. What the actual fuck?

'Super,' I deadpanned, still waiting for somebody to announce it was all a big joke.

They didn't.

The three of us walked through the trees in a line, heading back towards the school, the only sound the birds calling to one another. Glad they could keep up a conversation when all I wanted was for the ground to swallow me whole.

'So, New Girl,' Ophelia piped up after we'd been walking for ten very long, very quiet, minutes. 'How did you and Leo become a thing?'

Her question caught me off guard. She wanted the gossip, apparently. Girls baffled me. I'd never understood how you could beat somebody up one moment, then try to befriend them the next.

'Errr...' I took in a deep breath, stalling for time, trying to think of something I could say that sounded genuine. Not like I could say, *Oh well, you know. He texted me for a midnight rendezvous where we plotted like Burke and Hare.* I mean, I could say that, as I was pretty sure that my historical reference would fly over the top of their bleached blonde heads.

'Tell us,' Oralie tittered. 'I've always had a bit of a soft spot for Leo, but I never thought I had a chance. Not until Cl—'

Ophelia elbowed her in the ribs, cutting her off, and from the grunt she let out, it must have been a hard jab.

Eurgh, if you can't beat them, join them.

'I guess I've always had a soft spot for him too,' I told them, throwing in a giggle, trying to convince them I was letting them in on a big secret. That we were in one another's confidence. I needed to know what they wanted from me, and the only way I could think of going about that was by lulling them into a false sense of security.

We would never be friends, and I would never forget what they'd done to me, but I could definitely ride the conversation out and see where they were taking me.

'And you pulled him, you lucky bitch.' Ophelia's eyes were alight with humour, and Oralie giggled. Fuck me, her laugh was the furthest thing from pleasant. It grated, and if I had to listen to it for much longer, my ears would probably start to leak blood.

Finally, the three of us walked out of the trees and made our way to the grand entrance of the school. Those beady-eyed gargoyles watching our approach in silence, and I knew if we were in a cartoon, they'd be gossiping about the worrying sight before them.

Ascending the stairs and entering the large dark wood doors, the three of us must have looked as mismatched as anything. I didn't fit. The two of them were wearing pink, short, skimpy pyjamas and there was me, wearing one of Leo's T-shirts and some old, colour-faded leggings.

Outside of the hall, the two of them stopped, and I did too, worried I'd been taken here just so the two of them could beat me up again. Fool me twice and all that crap.

'Skylar,' Oralie started, and hearing her say my name in such a sickly sweet tone set my teeth on edge. 'We have something we want to say.'

'Yeah, we do,' Ophelia said, her tone equally sickening. 'This may come as a complete shock to you, but the two of us just wanted to tell you how sorry we are for everything.'

'What?' I blurted out, fully having expected bullshit to come out of their mouth, but not *that* kind of bullshit.

'We're sorry, Skylar. Truly,' Ophelia said, while Oralie nodded like a nodding-head dog toy behind her.

'You are?' I hated the uncertainty in my tone, but of course I was sceptical. They'd beat me up a month ago and now wanted me to believe they were sorry for that. Yeah, something didn't add up.

If it looked like shit.

Sounded like shit.

It probably was, in fact, shit.

'We are. Honestly, we don't know what came over us.' The two of them lifted up their sunglasses and rested them on top of their heads, and underneath they were both giving me a wide-eyed, extremely bloodshot stare, their huge eyes caked in last night's dried makeup.

'On what occasion?' I blurted, knowing I shouldn't needle them, to just take it all at face value like they clearly wanted me to, but that wasn't very *me*.

'Don't be like that,' Ophelia snapped, her eyes narrowed, the hint of the mean girl surfacing. 'We mean it.'

Oralie, who was definitely the more subservient of the two, just nodded to agree with her leader.

'Fine,' I said in what I hoped was a placating tone. Shit, I didn't need another black eye. 'Thanks.'

'No problem, New Girl. So, tell us some real tea! Have you fucked Leo?' Ophelia sounded like a gossipy friend. Even the way she'd said New Girl was ten times friendlier than I'd ever heard it before.

What's the catch?

'Wouldn't you like to know?' Was all I said, knowing that my refusal to answer outright would only excite them more. Would have the two of them speculating for days to come.

Both of them broke out into a chorus of, 'Oohh.'

Breakfast was going to be a lot longer than usual.

But it was a start.

Part Two
Progress

Twenty-Seven

THE FIRST WEEK of September finally arrived and along with it came a lot of students and school starting back up—for real and not just summer stuff.

I'd never believed I would be excited for school to start again, but I was more than ready for it. Maybe spending an entire six weeks on campus more than expected had something to do with it?

Summer school had been nowhere near as bad as it could have been, but shitting hell, I needed to be around more people. A wider selection of arseholes, y'know. Variety was the spice of life.

The first day of term, I could sense the tension in the air. Everywhere I went, students either stared or pointed and laughed. Whispering amongst themselves. Waiting for a showdown that wasn't going to come. They'd missed it by leaving.

It became obvious after the first period that a lot of the whispers were about me, about what they'd heard during the summer and speculation about what had happened on campus while they were all at home. However, the whispers that weren't about me were the ones I was more interested in, because they all revolved around *The Set* and how the position was most likely cursed. Nobody wanted to become the third and fourth members, even though every other year, people were vying for the chance. Or at least that was what Griff had whispered to me when we overheard some year eights talking about it.

Even if the two of them hadn't died, both Odette and Olivia would have graduated anyway, so technically the two positions up for grabs would've existed with or without murder. In previous years, *The Sect* and *The Set* got to choose their new members, but Leo had already told me that Griff and Ollie were refusing to add anyone else. Plus, the fact Leo was still on campus meant he could be a member if he wanted.

A thought flashed into my mind and I needed to get it out pronto. 'Leo?'

'Stutter?'

'Do we need to keep our relationship on the DL once school starts back up?' I moved onto my side to face him, and he did the same. 'Now that you're a member of staff and that?'

'Haven't really thought about it,' he said with a half-arsed shrug. 'Not like I'd listen even if Winifred did tell me to stop.'

'What about the parents of the kids who go here? Could they not intervene?'

'Why would they? They pay a lot of money for their kids to be looked after here, sure, but they also pay a lot of money so they're not bothered by the petty stuff. We're pretty much the same age, and you don't swim. Stop worrying.'

'Okay,' I said but knew I wouldn't stop worrying just because Leo told me to. Believe it or not, that wasn't how anxiety worked. Otherwise, we'd all just tell ourselves to get the fuck over it. 'Are you leaving The Sect*?'*

'Yet another thing I haven't thought about,' he said with a

laugh, reaching out to brush my hair from in front of my eyes. 'You do the thinking for us.'

I laughed, but there was a tense edge to it. 'Doesn't it go against tradition? You not leaving, I mean.'

'Probably, but fuck it.' His eyes burned with an intensity that was new to me. 'I'm a Hawthorn. People won't say shit.'

From the talk I'd heard all day, Leo was right, people wouldn't say shit against him on either count.

Breathe. Only eight more months and I'd be free. Hopefully, with a great university to go to. That was the dream—the whole reason I'd returned.

Making my way to my second lesson of the day, I braced myself for the next two hours.

You guessed it, the next lesson was History with Oliver—my favourite—and yeah, okay, we'd no longer be the only two in the classroom like we were in summer, thank fuck, but I was pretty certain he'd still try and sit near me. If he hated me as much as he tried to let on, or wanted me to leave the school, you'd think he'd be on me at all times, make me miserable enough to quit, but he wasn't doing that. He was leaving me to do my thing.

Taking a seat at the back of the classroom, I ignored the attention from the other students. Back before summer, most of the other kids left me alone for the most part. Getting stabbed caused people to give you a wide berth. It seemed in their eyes, I'd had sufficient time to get the fuck over it, and the harassment could once again begin.

'Did you hear?' one girl whispered to her friend, loud enough for me to hear. 'That *trash* is with Leo now.'

'What an upgrade!' the friend replied, fanning herself with her hand. 'Leo has that whole mysterious vibe going on. So much hotter than Ollie.'

'Really? I've always preferred Ollie. He's got that whole chiselled jaw thing going on.' Both girls nodded at one another before turning their piercing gazes in my direction.

I rolled my eyes at them and they quickly snapped their heads back to the front of the room. They stopped talking when Ollie entered, and they weren't the only ones. The whole classroom fell into a silence so quiet you could've heard a pin drop.

I smothered a groan, watching as if in slow motion as he sauntered into the room without a care in the world. *Dickhead.*

As expected, he pulled out the seat at the desk next to me and casually sat down. He knew all eyes were on him, and *I* knew he loved every second of it, even if his face tried to say otherwise. His expression was a mask of stone.

'New Girl,' he said in greeting, as if the entire summer hadn't happened. Like he hadn't ignored my arse since the camp out.

My gaze stayed on the board up ahead.

'No need to be like that,' he said with deceptive calm. I bit my tongue, refraining from stooping to his level. Honestly, the boy acted like he had two personalities and I had to just go along with whatever he did, but it was hard, never knowing what side of him would present itself. 'I'm sure your boyfriend won't mind you talking to me.'

The classroom broke out into titters.

'And I'm sure your girlfriend *will*,' I snapped. As far as I was aware, he was still in a relationship—of sorts—with Ophelia. Sure, the girl had apologised to me, but I wasn't taking that at face value. I wondered how long he'd keep up the charade with Ophelia with school back in session. The students would bow down to her and *The Set* even more than before with Ollie's backing.

Thank fuck I have Leo in my corner.

EVER SINCE THE GIRLS' apology, I'd stayed wary of them.

With the school year started, the two of them had avoided my gaze whenever I saw them, but they also hadn't done anything to make me think they still had it out for me. That couldn't be said for the two new members of *The Set*, though.

Celia and Cordelia.

Even their names made me want to barf. Once again, we had two girls with names beginning with the same letter and ending in *ia*. It made me wonder whether their parents had got together and planned it. It wouldn't surprise me—rich people did weird things. Celia and Cordelia were both brunettes, so at least they didn't all *look* the same.

They acted the way the O girls had when I first started at Hawthorn. They had the brattiness of youth—well, the brattiness of a wealthy youth—and the cocksuredness of people who were never penalised for their actions.

'Do you think that now that you've bagged another member of Hawthorn royalty you're something, bitch?' Celia sneered in the hallway one morning as she passed with Cordelia on her heels. Ignoring them, I pulled my French textbook out of my locker, hoping if I said nothing, they'd continue on their merry way.

Wishful thinking and all that shit.

Nope.

'Did you not hear what she just said?' Cordelia called, barging into my shoulder from the side. 'Don't disrespect us, slut.'

'Oh, I heard her,' I replied, 'but I didn't give a shit. Not sure if you've noticed, but I'm no longer a target.'

'Do not fucking speak to me like that,' Cordelia said, shoving me into the lockers with a hard push. The lockers at Hawthorn were made of solid wood, so being pushed into them was like being shoved into a door. *Ouch.*

My head took the full force of the impact, and my vision swam, blurred and spotty.

Oh no, they fucking didn't.

The pain—and the shock—took my breath away, but I wasn't going to let them get away with it. I was going to fight back and show these little pricks a lesson.

Skylar Crescent wasn't going down again without a fight.

I'd never noticed these little bitches last year. Clearly, they were insignificant before joining *The Set* and were making up for it.

Righting myself, I swung for Cordelia's face, landing a backhander on her cheek with a smack. 'Do not touch me ever again!'

'Skylar!' a voice boomed down the hall. I turned to see Leo storming towards us, a face full of thunder, his eyes blazing with fire, and if I were the girls, I'd be terrified. My punch would mean shit compared to the dressing-down Leo Hawthorn could give them in such a public setting.

Leo's anger had caused a tingling sensation to sit low in my stomach, and my heart jolted. Him going all caveman was super attractive.

'What's up, Leo?' Celia said, her tone simpering. She either couldn't read the look on his face, or maybe she hadn't heard how serious our relationship was these days.

'That's Mr Hawthorn to you,' he growled, not returning her smile. 'And I just saw you provoke Skylar here.'

Cordelia was rubbing her face where my hand had slapped her and I couldn't hide the smile from my face. It felt good to stand up for myself, and I wished I'd done it earlier.

Another person joined our small group.

'Celia. Cordelia.' Ollie accompanied each name with a tilt of the head. 'Skylar, are you okay?'

'I'm fine,' I replied, still smiling wide. 'But maybe Cordelia needs to have her cheek looked at.'

'Why?' Ollie raised an eyebrow, suspicious of the joy on my face, no doubt. It was rare I looked so happy in any of the girls' presence. 'What's happening here?'

'Skylar hit me—' Cordelia started.

'Because you shoved me into a locker!' I cut her off. Leo pulled me close, and I leaned into his warmth. 'Twice!'

'Let me get one thing clear,' Ollie said, looking at the girls, his nostrils flaring. 'Touch Skylar again and Skylar hitting you will be the last thing you have to worry about. Skylar is off-limits. Touch her again and you die.' A group of students had stopped to pay attention when Celia and Cordelia first came over to me, and the group had only got bigger the longer we all stood there. Ollie raised his voice, addressing the entire hallway. 'And that goes for all of you! Skylar is protected by *The Sect* and anybody who goes against that will pay!'

Whispers broke out across the hall.

'But—' Celia stuttered.

'Shut up,' Ollie growled, 'and get out of my sight.'

They didn't need to be told twice. Within seconds, the two of them were a blur in the distance, having moved faster than I knew possible. Maybe they truly were witches.

'Thanks for that,' I said, looking into Ollie's eyes. 'I appreciate it.'

'No need to thank me, Skylar,' he said, his eyes turning

away as he rubbed his jaw. Something I knew he did when deep in thought. 'It's because of me they think they can do it in the first place.' He shrugged. 'I'll see you both later.'

'What was that about?' I whispered, turning my head in Leo's direction.

He shook his head, his eyes following Ollie's back. 'Guilt, Stutter. He feels bad.'

'So he should.' And even though it was me who said the words, I wasn't sure I believed them anymore. Well, not entirely. Of course the boy should feel bad for the shit he put me through, but all he needed to do was apologise. Although making it clear to the school I was off-limits was a step in the right direction, and I couldn't overlook that. I gathered my things and shut my locker door. Leo wrapped his arm around my shoulder, and we walked away from the group of kids still hanging around, waiting for whatever happened next.

'If you were having a problem with them, you should've told me,' he chided me, and I felt like a scolded child. The graze of his fingertips on the back of my neck caught me off guard but also instantly calmed me.

'Literally, that's the first time they've spoken to me,' I told him, telling the truth, leaning into his oh-so-welcome touch. 'Think they just wanted to assert their power, make it clear they're big fish here.'

'Well, they're not and like with most people, the power is in their mind only.' On reaching an alcove, he pulled me close, hiding us away from the onlookers in the hallway. It was odd to be standing here with him, in a position I'd been in with Ollie more than once last school year. 'What lesson have you got next?'

'I have a free now, but French after that.' Looking at Leo, I realised how attractive I found him. Okay, that was bullshit. I already knew how devilishly handsome he was, but with him no longer in uniform, he seemed even more alluring.

As the assistant swim coach, he wore casual clothes; grey joggers and a white fitted T-shirt. No idea why, but I fucking adored a guy in grey. Especially *this* guy. His muscles rippled underneath as he reached out to stroke my arms, and my pulse quickened.

'You're free now?' A cheeky glint flashed in his electric blue eyes. 'How should we spend it?'

I blinked, a thrill running through me at the seduction in his tone. 'You don't need to be anywhere?'

'Only wherever you are.'

I blushed, not knowing whether he was acting up for the students still filtering through the hallway, or whether he genuinely meant it.

'Oh, shut up!' I scoffed, and a small chuckle escaped my lips. I beamed at him, happy in that moment, the two of us holding one another close. 'Let's go to your room.'

'That's one of the best ideas you've had, Stutter.'

If I could have paused the moment, I would have.

But sadly, we rarely get what we wish for in life.

Twenty-Eight

MR HAWKINS.

There was something terribly fucking off about that man.

Attractive? Yes.

Creepy? *Fuck yes.*

Ever since the end of summer, I'd hoped he wouldn't want to continue our private tutoring sessions. Hoped his schedule would make him too busy, or that I'd improved enough to not need them, but he'd told me we should wait until after my next mock exam to know for definite. If he were anybody else, I'd agree. It made sense for the lessons to continue—didn't mean I had to like it.

I watched as he prowled in front of the board, answering a question from some girl in the front row who hadn't stopped batting her eyelashes at him since he entered. It was sickening to watch, but I couldn't draw my eyes away from it.

When the lesson came to an end, and the rest of the students were filing out of the classroom, making loads of noise as they did, I threw my notebook into my bag, hoping to get out as quickly as I could. Then I heard him. 'Ms Crescent, I'd like you to stay behind to discuss our tutoring schedule.'

I looked over to where he was standing, and his eyes were

alight with an emotion I couldn't place. My stomach dropped, and I inhaled a deep breath before responding. 'Sure.'

He waited until everybody else had vacated the classroom before he spoke again.

'Sky,' he said, dropping my surname the moment everyone was out of earshot. 'I've arranged a schedule for us to work on your français.' He gave a small chortle, as if he'd told a funny joke.

He hadn't.

'Cool beans,' I said, itching to get out of here and head to lunch, shuffling from foot to foot, wondering if he was going to say any more. After a pause, one in which he'd said nothing, I went to walk away, but a movement in my peripheral stopped me.

Mr Hawkins had moved around his desk, so he was standing on my side of it—the pungent scent of his cologne entered my nostrils, a spicy, overwhelming smell, but expensive. It burned.

'I thought we could have a session now,' he asked, and with every word, he took a small step closer to the door. 'You're free, yeah?'

'It's lunchtime,' I told him. My stomach rumbled to make a point, and all I wanted was to go meet Clo. We'd agreed that because it was the first day back, we'd eat lunch together, just us two, no Griff or Leo allowed.

'It is,' he said, unbothered. 'But you need to pass your exam, don't you?'

The bolt of the door being pushed across brought me out of the funk I'd slipped into. His light brown eyes were no longer light, but the deepest black. His entire face twisted into an expression that struck fear in me. Gone was the nice guy. The handsome teacher all the girls wanted the attention of.

'We both know you want to pass. So, let's practise now.' His tone was ominous, his demeanour twisted, and the enormity of the situation registered in my brain.

Without even making a conscious decision, I moved a step back even though I had nowhere to go. I was a big enough girl to admit I was scared.

Terrified, actually.

He may be tall and thin, but that didn't mean he wasn't strong. He could overpower me if he wanted to, and if the gleam in his eyes was any indication, he wanted to. The bulge in his slacks told me all I needed to know. The power he wielded excited him and trapping me gave him a sick thrill.

I wondered how long he'd been planning to get me alone, or whether he had seen the opportunity and run with it. All summer we were alone in the room, just us two, yet he'd made no move. Now the campus was crawling with people, so why would he choose a time when he could get caught?

Stumbling back, the backs of my legs hit the edge of his desk and my mind reverted back to my bedroom at home on the day I first came to Hawthorn. Like Andy, Mr Hawkins had given me the creeps for some time, but I'd never thought either of them would act upon their sick fantasies.

Glancing around the room, I looked for anything I could use as a shield or a weapon of sorts. With my focus elsewhere, Mr Hawkins bounded across the short distance between us and pushed me up against the desk, leaving me with no room to get free.

His hardness pressed into my stomach and disgust filled me.

'Scared, Skylar?' His face transformed from his sneer, and it was so close to mine, I could see the stubble on his chin. Before, I'd found that sort of unkempt look exciting, attractive, but I knew from that moment on it would forever repulse me. *He* repulsed me.

'N-no,' I said, attempting to sound strong.

My thoughts kept repeating the same thing: *please, please don't do this.*

The door handle rattled, and my wishful thinking went into overdrive. Please let whoever it was on the other side of the door be Leo or Griff, or fuck, I'd even accept it being Ollie. I hoped Clo had raised the alarm when I wasn't waiting for her in the dining hall.

His large hand slowly pushed my chest down until I was lying flat out on the desk. I dug my fingers into his forearms, hoping I could hurt him enough to stop his movement, stop his strength from pushing me down, but it was useless. *I* was useless. I'd never been very strong, and my nails barely left a dent.

'Ever since I laid eyes on you, I knew I had to have you. Had to get you alone. And I tried so hard to fight the urge, but I can't fight it anymore. I want you underneath me, squirming under my touch.' His foul breath covered my face, and it felt like a mask, like clay blocking my skin. 'You are perfect.'

'Somebody will f-find out,' I whispered, showing my fear. I knew I shouldn't, knew it would only arouse him further, but my fear won out.

'You won't say a word,' he growled, pressing me further into the table. 'Not like anybody will believe you.'

'Leo will.' The second the words left my mouth, I doubted them. I hated the way Mr Hawkins was making me doubt Leo of all people. Hated how he'd spouted his poison into my ear and was changing the way I thought.

'Will he really?' he asked, then chuckled sardonically, raising one dark, bushy eyebrow.

'Y-yes.'

He stood up and looked down at me, perusing me from head to toe. With his weight lifted off me, I wondered if I could fight him. Would I have enough strength to beat him?

I moved my hands to my side, to support my weight as I lifted myself up.

'Oh no, you don't,' he said, pushing me back down with one palm with little effort, then undid his tie, opening his top button.

My body wasn't cooperating. My limbs were heavy, like stone blocks weighing me down. There was no way I could try to get free again without him overpowering me. He'd already done it once with ease.

The sound of his zipper echoed in the otherwise silent classroom, and I gulped. Mr Hawkins took advantage of my brief second gasp and shoved his balled-up tie inside my mouth.

'Be quiet, bitch,' he hissed, repositioning himself.

The ripping of my tights disturbed me, and then my fight or flight kicked in. Fuck him. Fuck the power he was trying to exert over me!

No man, no teacher, nobody in a position of power, should get away with something so heinous. So wrong. So fucking wrong. He wasn't going to get away with it. I wouldn't let him.

Tears filled my eyes as I struggled to breathe through the gag in my mouth. I thrashed around, but I was struggling under his domineering grip. I'd always found it hard to breathe through my nose, and I was fighting to keep my gag reflex under control, the rolled-up fabric filling my mouth completely.

I needed to feel in control of some small fragment of my life.

Breathe in. Breathe out. I stopped fighting and attempted to calm down. A level head may help, may help me see a way out that I hadn't found yet, and I had to try.

'That's it. Stop fighting this. It's inevitable,' he said, his soft voice entering my ear and trickling through me like syrup. Thick, sickly sweet syrup that wouldn't come away no matter how hard I tried to mentally scrub it gone.

With dark intention, he moved my underwear to the side. Air touched my bare skin. A large, thick finger entered me, and I had to swallow to prevent the scream threatening to tear from my throat.

The lack of lubrication meant that his finger was met with obstruction. Not that he cared. My lack of lubrication was only making him want me more. His eyes were wide, bloodshot, and slightly crazed.

'That's it, pretty baby. Open for me.'

I gagged.

Another finger entered me, stretching me too far, and I cried out in pain from behind the tie. The tears still not leaving my eyes, stubborn and strong, blurring my vision.

A thudding noise came from the door, and all I wanted was for somebody to enter and get him away from me. Get his vile fingers out of me.

Please. I'll do anything.

Did I somehow deserve it? Was it somehow my fault? Had I given him the wrong impression? Laughed too loud at any of his jokes? Smiled too much?

My mind was spiralling.

He was still moving, but I could no longer feel it.

Numb.

Empty.

Alone.

The door burst open, almost flying off its hinges, and I looked towards it, hoping to see somebody who cared about me. Somebody who would rescue me, no questions asked.

'Sky!' Ollie called, flying through the door. I didn't know how he'd got in. All I knew was how thankful I was that he had. Nothing else mattered.

Ollie grabbed Mr Hawkins by the shoulders and pulled him off of me, turned him around, and punched him so hard his face swung out to the side from the power. Ollie's face had turned red, and I knew he was lost to me. He kept punching, even after Mr Hawkins had hit the ground and had fallen unconscious.

Punch. Punch. Punch.

'Ollie!' I screamed, scared of the rage on his face. Scared he was going to kill him. 'Stop!'

He looked at me, blood spattered on his face, his electric blues now darker than ever before. Black, to the point you couldn't tell the pupil from the iris.

'Come back,' I whispered, my tears leaving my eyes and slowly travelling down my cheeks. His eyes softened and creased at the sides. Moving towards me tentatively, so I wouldn't flinch or move away.

'Are you okay?' he asked, glancing back at the unconscious man on the floor when he let out a groan.

'I.' I faltered. 'I d-don't know.'

He wrapped me into a hug, being careful to treat me as if I were a porcelain doll. 'Let me take you to my suite.' He pulled back to look me in the eyes. 'I promise no funny business. I just want to make sure you're okay.'

More tears leaked out at his words. Ollie and I had a chequered past, but in that moment, I knew he meant every word—he wouldn't cause me harm, and he cared enough about me to want to make sure I was okay. No strings attached.

'What will happen to him?' I asked, my voice wobbling. I tried not to let my gaze go to where *he* was lying, but it was very hard not to look. So instead, I looked down at myself. My uniform was disrupted and ripped, and it made me feel so fucking dirty.

'I'll make a call,' was all Ollie said.

Ollie wrapped a supportive arm around my shoulders, and slowly the two of us made our way out of the classroom, neither of us looking back.

Twenty-Nine

OLLIE

THE MOMENT we made it back to my room, Sky ran to the bathroom without a word and hurled up the contents of her stomach. In an instant, I was at her side, rubbing her back, trying to soothe her with one hand and keep her hair from her face with the other.

The tears were flowing and I crouched there feeling lost. What was I meant to do? I wasn't equipped to help her. I shouldn't be the one helping her. That job fell to Leo these days, and I was fighting the bitterness within. Sky's relationship status wasn't important.

Helping and caring for her was.

After a time, Sky stopped vomiting, flushed the toilet, and propped herself up against it, staring ahead but not seeing anything.

Knowing she wasn't about to bolt or vomit again, I pulled my phone out and messaged Leo.

I'M WITH SKY. I FOUND HER IN HAWKINS' CLASSROOM, HIS FILTHY HANDS ALL OVER HER. HE NEEDS TO GO. MEET ME TOMORROW.

I didn't check my phone again to see if he replied, instead putting all of my focus on Sky once more. I wanted her to know I was there for her, even if things between us weren't good—that I cared and hated seeing her so miserable and lost.

'Come on, bub,' I said, crouching down to put us at eye level. 'Want to come get comfortable and watch a film?'

She nodded, wiping her tears with the back of her hands. 'O-okay.'

I helped her to stand, and the two of us hobbled over to my bed. It wasn't lost on me that I'd never expected to see Skylar on my bed again—or in my room. The hatred I'd burned with towards her for too long had thawed, but something was holding me back from talking to her and telling her the truth about why we did what we did. She'd forgiven Griff and Leo, yet was still giving me the cold shoulder.

Not like it mattered at that moment. Even if she was happy with Leo, I would support her whenever she needed.

Sky lay down on the bed, and I scooted in behind her, acting as her big spoon and pulling her close. Was I crossing a line? The last time we'd spoken was in History and I'd acted like a prick to give the other kids a show. *The Sect* needed to show dominance, and I couldn't let anybody know I was bummed about Skylar choosing Leo, or that I cared about her when I'd made it clear the year before she was shit on my shoe.

After an hour of lying together, breathing in her scent, I broke the silence.

Tentatively, I whispered, 'Baby, I think you should have a bath.' Sky was still in the foetal position and my arms were covering her to keep her safe. I didn't want to startle her.

When she didn't respond, I tried again, giving her a gentle squeeze to coax her to open up. To tell me to shut up. Anything. As long as she was talking to me.

'I can help,' I added, hating myself for the words as they left my lips. It wasn't right for me to help. Yes, I'd seen her naked, but under completely different circumstances. She had every right to hate me. To ask me to take her to Leo and tell me to fuck off. Scream at me. Shout. Whisper how she felt. It didn't matter. I just wanted to hear her say *something*.

'Not yet,' she whispered, a crack in her voice.

'Whatever you need,' I assured her. Then I had an idea I thought she might go for. 'Want me to put on *Pride and Prejudice?*'

It was her favourite, and she never turned down the chance to watch Mr Darcy's hand flex.

'Please,' she said, wiping away new tears from underneath her eyes. I couldn't tell what had set her off, but I didn't pry. She'd tell me if she wanted to.

I went about setting up the TV and putting the film on, as Sky chuckled darkly from the bed.

'Everything okay?' I tried not to sound worried, but it was hard. The laugh was like one of those evil villains in a cartoon and it sounded out of place coming from Sky's lips. The springs in the mattress bounced as I got back on the bed, wrapping my arms around her once more.

She shuffled and turned in my arms, putting the two of us chest to chest. She inhaled deeply, looking into my eyes. 'I don't want to cry anymore.'

'What do you want?'

'I don't know,' she murmured, her small button nose wrinkling as she thought about it. My hand reached out to her, to stroke her face, to touch her cute nose. The flinch she gave when my finger made contact with her skin set my blood on fire. The beating I'd given that wanker wasn't enough damage. Touching Skylar was a big mistake.

I caught a tear as it ran down her cheek and all I wanted was to distract her.

'I've watched this film a lot recently,' I confessed.

'You have?' She looked up at me, her nose wrinkling even more than before, and I smiled softly at her. She was so damn beautiful.

'Yeah.' My hand gravitated towards her hip, and I drew patterns there, taking pleasure when she shivered from my touch.

'Why?' Her eyes searched mine, seeking an answer I was reluctant to give, even though I'd started the line of conversation in the first place. My confession, although small, was a big deal for multiple reasons. It could change the vibe, and the tenderness of the last hours could shatter.

'Reminds me of you,' I whispered, glancing at the screen as the opening montage began. Eliza Bennet appeared on screen, and I smiled, for some reason always reminded of my mum and her sister. Guess it was because of Aunt Eliza sharing the name rather than any attributes or actions, but still. Although it felt silly to admit it, the film comforted me in more ways than one.

'In a good way?' she asked, more interested in me than the screen.

I laughed under my breath and admitted, 'Depends.'

'On?'

'On what day it is.'

Her bright blue eyes were staring into mine, searching for a soul I was only just beginning to notice myself. Growing up, I always thought I was soulless. My mum dying only confirmed it. Of course I was. My mother wouldn't have chosen to leave me if I had a soul worth saving.

'Oh well, that explains it,' she joked, showing a hint of the Sky I knew. 'Feel like I know exactly what you mean now.'

'On whether I've spent time around you, or you and Leo, that day,' I admitted, squirming at my truth, but with the start out in the open, it made sense to follow it through. 'On those days, I put this on to remind myself of how much I hate you.'

And that I hate my mum for leaving me the way she did.

'Not gonna lie, but that's pretty fucked up,' she said, chuckling.

'You're telling me,' I said, blunt but soft.

'So, you do hate me?' She bit her bottom lip, and I wished I could bite it. But she wasn't mine. I couldn't do that to her. My hand gripped her hip, pushing in my fingers, feeling her solid beneath me. 'That isn't something you made up to piss me off?'

'I want to hate you,' I admitted. And I meant every word. I wanted to hate her so fucking bad. And for so long I *did* hate her, but that was back before I knew her. Before I heard her laugh, saw her smile, felt her lips pressed against mine. Everything had got so twisted so fast, and I'd had no choice but to continue with the plan even when my mind was battling my heart.

'I wish I hated you, too,' she admitted. 'Would make things a hell of a lot easier.'

Our eyes locked. I gravitated towards her at the same time she gravitated towards me. Like a magnet was pulling our bodies together without our say so, our lips clashed in a mix of lips and tongues, a different kind of passion. It was real. A kiss we both wanted. That wasn't a part of a scheme or some kind of humiliation plot.

A kiss with genuine affection.

Sky moaned into my mouth, and I hardened in my trousers, wanting so badly to do all the things to her I fantasised about at night. She pushed her body closer, hooking her leg over my hip, placing her heat where I wanted her most.

'We should stop,' I whispered in between kisses. 'You're with Leo.'

'No,' she said, trying with all her strength—which wasn't a lot—to pull my head back down to hers to place my lips on hers again.

'Yes,' I growled, using my strength to resist her. I knew it was wrong, but I also knew I wouldn't stop if she told me not to. After the day Sky had, I was letting her lead it wherever she wanted it to go. Never again would I ignore her, or assume she wanted something just because of our past. I'd learned my lesson after the library, and it didn't sit well with me that not too long ago, I'd done a similar thing to what happened in that classroom with Mr Hawkins.

With mental clarity, I moved her leg away and moved back a little to create some space—both mentally and physically —between us.

'Why?' she whispered. Her bottom lip wobbled as tears filled her eyes. *Shit.* I didn't want her to think I was rejecting her. Far from it. I just wanted to make sure she wasn't going to regret any decision she made.

'Because of what happened earlier,' I said, making it clear that was the main reason for my hesitation, but I also didn't want to lie and pretend the library never took place. 'And what happened in the library between us. I was a prick and I didn't listen to you.'

'Please don't remind me,' she pleaded, covering her ears with her hands when she saw me open my mouth to say more. Blocking it out wouldn't work in the long run, but I couldn't bring myself to bring up that blackness again. 'And you're not listening to me now either.'

'Sky...'

'No, Oliver,' she growled, baring her teeth, but then her face softened, and her large blue eyes blinked at me. Wiping the tears away. 'Make me forget.'

'What?'

'You heard me.' She blinked again, her eyes clear and bright and sure. 'Make me forget what happened.'

'Sky...' I repeated. Fuck, I wanted to. I really did, but I also didn't want her to hate me for anything afterwards. Not when we were so at odds all the time. Every thought about her clouded my head. My time with Sky was a rollercoaster—due to my own actions—and now we were parked in the station, deciding whether to have another ride or get out of the vehicle and leave.

'Please.'

'What about Leo?' I asked, hoping I didn't sound bitter. Not like I'd done anything to show I deserved her or to be her boyfriend. Fuck, she probably didn't even know I'd want that. Or maybe she thought Ophelia and I were real.

'He never has to know,' she whispered, closing the gap between us.

Shit. She was going to make saying no hard for me—not that she hadn't already. But my actions would change everything if I let her go through with it.

Fuck it.

You only live once, right? And Skylar Crescent was destined to be mine, Leo be damned. She just didn't see it yet.

With no more thought, my hand grabbed her hip and pulled her close to me, closing the distance.

I swore and captured her lips with mine. Sky's moans ensured all bets were off. She moved on top of me, and I let her. Gave over that control she was so desperately seeking.

Sky moved against me, bucking her hips so that her centre rubbed up against my hard dick, causing the most delicious friction. Roaming her body, my hands explored until they settled on her hips to help guide her, increasing the motion.

We weren't naked, but there was something just as intimate about what was happening between us. Just as fucking powerful and meaningful. Our foreheads pressed together to the point of pain, and the air around us was as intense as the emotions within us. Her blue eyes locked with mine, and I had to blink away the strong wave of lust and love that hit me in the face.

With a grunt, I came in my boxers like a horny virgin teenage boy, and Sky came too, her face exquisite as the pleasure hit her. The strong, overwhelming sense of possessiveness came full force and knocked the breath from my body.

'Fuck, Skylar,' I whispered, my lips grazing the side of her face softly. 'You're it for me. Endgame.'

And I was fucking screwed.

Thirty

I LEFT Ollie asleep in his bed.

I didn't leave a note, and I didn't say goodbye.

Already, I was questioning my actions. Doubting myself and whether I'd done the right thing. Oh, who the fuck was I kidding? Of course I hadn't done the right thing.

Ollie had acted like a completely different person—all sweet and caring—and it had melted the ice wall I erected around myself anytime I was in his presence. He'd learned from the library, too, and had asked me multiple times whether I truly wanted him. Had asked about Leo, even. And then there I was, acting like the biggest piece of trash on the planet, telling him Leo didn't have to know.

Of course the whole thing with Leo was fake, Leo and I both knew it, but recently things were twisting and it hadn't seemed quite so false.

I hung my head in shame, creeping towards Leo's room, hoping not to alert anybody in the building to my presence. The events of the day washed over me, covering me from head to toe, and I wanted to scrub my skin with a sponge until I was left red and raw.

Leo deserved to know all of it, and I intended to leave nothing out.

Not because I owed him shit, but because I *wanted* to. I wanted to talk to him; felt a compelling need to be honest with him.

The knock on his door echoed in the empty, dark hallway and I shivered, the cold air of the evening seeping its way into my bones.

Leo opened the door, and the minute I saw his face, saw his azure eyes looking at me, I burst into tears. All the emotions and feelings of the day were catching up with me, and I was drained.

'Come in, Stutter.' Leo pulled the door open and moved aside so I could enter. The moment he closed the door behind him, I threw myself into his arms, not giving him a moment to second-guess his reaction. 'Who do I need to beat up?'

'Mr H-Hawkins,' I managed to say through my sobs. 'He a-attacked me. Then Ollie c-came in. And then I... I went to his room and...'

I knew I wasn't making much sense, my tears over-whelming me, my words running into one another.

'Come on,' he said, slowly manoeuvring me to the edge of his bed. We sat down, our hands gripped tightly together—you'd have had to break my fingers to get my hand out of his. I needed his warmth. His safety. 'Take a deep breath, Stutter.'

'I'm so sorry,' I said in a whisper. What kind of shit human came and laid their crap at somebody else's door? Me, that was who. Maybe I was as low as the O girls always told me I was.

'What for?' he asked, frowning. 'Skylar, you've got nothing to apologise for.'

Hearing him use my name had me cracking further. 'Mr Hawkins cornered me in his classroom after the lesson. He tried to'—I swallowed, knowing I couldn't say the word without vomit rising up from my stomach—'you know.'

My voice was barely audible. I worried Leo would make me repeat myself, but he didn't. He just pulled me to him, awkward as fuck with my hands still trapped in his.

I'd always wondered if your heart could fall for two people at the same time. Was it possible to love two people, but in two completely different ways?

My heart fluttered when one of his hands unlatched from mine, and he reached out to touch my cheek to wipe my tears away, a soft smile making his features look kind and approachable and as if he cared. Maybe he did a little? With Leo, it was so hard to know for definite what he was thinking.

'He's gone, Skylar. Nobody touches you and gets away with it.' His calm response was so at odds with Ollie's, but it meant the same to me. A quiet calm could be just as deadly as a raging storm.

'You promise?' I asked. Even though Ollie had said the same thing, I didn't know if he held the power to make it happen. If either of them did. But then I remembered Leo's dad owned the school, so I suppose they had more sway than others.

'Of course,' he said, his words reassuring. He rested his hand on my shoulder, and I shivered. 'How dare he touch you? The fucker's lucky if we leave him alive.'

I smiled for the first time in hours.

Leo had that effect on me.

'There's something else I need to tell you,' I whispered, not wanting the words out in the universe but knowing I couldn't rest until they were out.

'What's up?'

I just needed to blurt it out. 'I made out with Ollie.' I swallowed, my face flushing. 'Actually, I think I sort of—no, not sort of but actually—dry humped him.'

Leo's top lip twitched, and if he started laughing at me, I swear I'd break out into tears again. He could judge me for it, sure, but if he laughed at me, I wasn't sure I'd live it down.

'Stutter,' Leo said, a smile on his lips for real. 'I'm not going to judge you. You had a horrible day and he showed a side he rarely shows anybody. I get it.'

'You don't think I'm a stupid cow?'

'Do you think you're a stupid cow?' His voice was low and smooth and I wanted to drown in it.

'Maybe.' I shrugged. 'I'm meant to be getting revenge on Ollie, not kissing him and making him come.'

'That's enough on the info there, Stutter,' Leo said, but his smile remained, so I knew he wasn't mad at me. 'Emotions can be a bitch, and I don't know a lot in this life, but one thing I do know? You're not a stupid cow. You're the furthest from it.'

'Promise?'

'I promise.' He leaned forward and placed a kiss on my temple. 'Are you staying? Or do you want me to walk you back to your room?'

'Can I stay? I'd rather not face Clover or Griff right now.'

'Oh, so it has nothing to do with my winning company?' he teased.

'Well, I couldn't be so blatant,' I replied with a laugh. 'Can't have you knowing, can I?'

His resulting chuckle sent shockwaves through me. 'There's a spare key for my suite I want you to have. You can come here whenever you need rescuing.'

'Thanks,' I said, surprised and overwhelmed by the gesture.

And for the rest of the evening, he took my mind off of

everything. Well, mostly everything. But by the end of the night, I'd forgotten what happened with Ollie, what happened with Mr Hawkins, and most importantly, he made me realise none of it was my fault.

The only thing he couldn't take my mind off was how I felt towards him. How I felt towards Ollie. About Ollie calling us endgame.

And those thoughts were the loudest.

Even as I lay in bed next to Leo, sleeping next to him for the first time since the tent, and the first time in an actual bed, my mind was caught between him and Ollie.

'Sleep, Stutter. Turn your brain off,' he whispered in my ear, squeezing my waist and pulling me closer. 'Sure we can worry more when we wake.'

I smiled to myself, the way I always did when Leo let on just how well he knew me.

Really knew me.

Thirty-One

'HOW ARE THINGS GOING WITH LEO?' Clo asked, looking at me, her gaze intense, the question out of the blue.

Recently, the two of us had had little time to shoot the shit together. Most of the time, Clo was with Griff, even spending most nights with him, and if she was spending the night with him, I spent the night with Leo to keep up the charade. What better way to seem like a real couple than to be joined at the hip?

At first, he had slept in my bed and I'd slept in Clo's, but since the night in his room, we'd become more comfortable around one another and began to share a bed. Snuggles were nice, and I enjoyed being the big spoon. Not that I'd ever tell anybody that. Reckon even if I did, people wouldn't believe that Leo loved being the little spoon.

'Honest?' I asked, and she nodded. 'They're going pretty bloody fantastic.'

It hit me: I was telling the truth. Things *were* great. We got along; we didn't fight much as shit wasn't real. Really, we had all the perks of a real relationship—except the sexual aspect, of course. The thought of a friends-with-benefits arrangement had entered my mind once or twice, but it would complicate and confuse things that were already confused. Also, a small part of me worried it was all in my head and he'd reject me if I even suggested it.

'I'm glad,' she said, while her face looked anything but. Her beautiful green eyes didn't have any sparkle to them, and her lips had turned down at the edges.

'How are things going with Griff?' I asked, wanting to know. Not being funny, but my thoughts on their relationship hadn't changed. It still rang false to me.

'Yeah,' she said, the features of her face unwavering. No joy visible. 'They're okay.'

'Just okay?'

Look, I didn't want to rub it in—not completely—*but* I wanted her to be honest with me. We were best friends. Ride or die. And I hated how she felt like she couldn't open up to me anymore because of Leo. Or at least I assumed it was due to me being with Leo, but maybe the fact I shared blood with Griff didn't help my cause either.

'Yeah, I mean...' She looked around the room, no longer staring at me. 'We're fine.'

'You can tell me anything. You know that, right?'

She barked out a sharp laugh. 'No, Skylar, I don't know that.'

'Clo, if you're not happy, only you can change it,' I said, trying a different tactic. 'You don't have to be with him if you don't want to, you know?'

'I know that. Thank you, Captain Obvious,' she spat, sarcasm thick.

'Okay,' I said, attempting to placate her, my hands up in a *whoa* kind of gesture.

'No need to act like I'm going to bite your head off,' she

grumbled, her gaze once again on me. I shuffled around my bed and perched my bum on the edge. Maybe if I sat down, I wouldn't look as threatening.

'I wasn't. I just want you to be happy.' I shrugged, at a loss to know what she wanted to hear. 'And, I don't know, I guess I've always wondered whether you're truly happy. That butterflies overtaking your stomach, can't eat or sleep kind of love.'

'What even is love?' she asked, frustrated.

It was my turn to bark out a laugh. 'Not like I'm the person to know, but I get it. Either way, I want you to have that kind of love. I want it for Griff, too.' I took a deep breath. 'And I don't think the two of you have that together.'

'You telling me you have that kind of love with Leo?' she spat, her eyebrows rising so high, they were about to disappear into her hairline.

'No,' I replied, taken off guard. I should have realised she'd turn the tables on me. It was one of Clo's defence mechanisms, after all. To fight fire with fire. When feeling threatened, she went out of her way to make others feel worse, to take the heat off herself, with no thought of how the other person felt.

'That's what I thought,' she said with an eye roll.

'I just don't want either you or Griff to get hurt,' I added, knowing I should have just shut my mouth and left it the hell alone. *Dig that hole, Skylar.*

'Thanks for your concern, Sky, but I think you should evaluate your own life first, don't you?'

'Right.' My cheeks warmed, and it was taking a lot for me to keep my anger in check. I knew she was hitting low on purpose, and fuck, it was working.

'Everybody knows you're with Leo out of desperation.'

'Sorry,' I sputtered, 'but what the *fuck* does that even mean?'

'I—' she faltered, the regret swimming in her eyes. But for once, I wasn't going to let her off easily.

'Maybe, Clover, evaluate your life before you judge me about mine. Me and my desperate arse are out of here.' I turned around, grabbed my phone and bag, and without thinking it through, walked to the door and left, slamming it behind me.

Shit, me leaving my room after an argument was becoming a bit of a pattern. It wouldn't surprise me if cracks appeared in the ceiling from the amount of times someone had slammed our door.

I took a deep breath, blinking away the frustrated tears blurring my vision. I had to remember I'd been lying to Clo for quite a while, and there was stuff she didn't know.

There *were* genuine times between Leo and me. Like that time he sat with me in silence and disposed of a dead rabbit for me. I'd never told her about it, because I hadn't wanted her to feel unsafe in our room because of me—again.

One day, Clover and I would go an entire month without disagreeing about stupid shit.

Right?

I looked down the empty corridor, kind of at a loss for where to head. Leo was at the pool with the team, and I didn't want to be around all three of them. I hadn't spoken to Ollie since that day after... after everything, and not like I could seek out Griff for comfort as I was certain Clo would've already messaged him about our spat.

Then I remembered the conversation I'd had with Leo the other night.

There's a spare key for my suite I want you to have. You can come here whenever you need rescuing.

When he'd walked me back to my dorm the morning after, he'd slipped the key into my back pocket during our goodbye hug. Grabbing my bag, I riffled through its contents, trying to locate it.

My fingers found it in moments and I pulled it out in triumph, thankful I hadn't put it elsewhere in my room. How embarrassing would that have been? Having to go back and tell Clo I was getting the key to Leo's suite. No, thank you.

At the fastest pace known to man—okay, the fastest pace known to *me*—I made my way to the staff building. Since becoming the assistant swim coach, Leo had moved out of the boys' dorm building and had been upgraded to the biggest suite of them all.

Leo wasn't due back for at least another hour, so I knew I'd have time to work on my homework without interruption.

The moment I got comfortable on his bed, I sent him a quick text with a selfie. Even though he'd made it clear I could come to his room whenever I needed, I still wanted him to know I was there just in case.

HEY YOU. I'M IN YOUR ROOM. HAD A FIGHT WITH CLO. SEE YOU LATER, TATER.

Within seconds, my phone lit up with his response. I smiled at my screen, hoping he wouldn't be mad because I'd used the key he'd given me. That would be embarrassing. The lines of our fake relationship had blurred and I wasn't sure how to act. I'd expected it to finish once school started back up, but Leo hadn't even hinted at it.

HEY YOURSELF. DON'T GET TOO LONELY WITHOUT ME. IN A WHILE, CROCODILE.

I squealed at his cute response and then stopped myself.

Shit, bollocks, balls. I wasn't meant to be getting giddy about a text from Leo Hawthorn of all people, especially one that referenced a silly kids' nursery rhyme, right?

While I pondered my newfound dilemma, a knock reverberated throughout the suite and I froze. Did I answer it? Or just ignore it and hope whoever was on the other side would leave? Not like it was my place to open the door.

It could be a teacher.

At least I didn't have to worry about Mr Hawkins anymore. Leo was true to his word, and the very next day he was off the premises, escorted by police—something to do with drugs being found in his suite. I assumed Leo and Ollie had framed him, as they'd known I wouldn't have wanted to press charges and regurgitate what happened. I'd not asked for any more details, not wanting to have to think of that repulsive man more than my nightmares already did.

My breathing sped up, my anxiety climbing. The room spotted black, swirling in at the edges, creeping into the centre.

Another knock. *Shit.*

'Little One, it's me,' Ollie's voice called, reaching me and causing the black in my vision to recede as quickly as it had appeared. Instantly, my heart sped up for a different reason. Shouldn't he be at practise with Leo?

'Are you going to open up? Or do I have to force it?' he asked through the door, and even though there was a dark, wooden slab between us, I knew he had a smirking smile on his face.

'O-okay,' I called back, my feet moving of their own accord.

Ollie came into my view, and I couldn't help but form a small smile. His hair was wet, and his blue eyes were sparkling with mischief. He looked fucking delicious, the bastard.

'W-what are you doing here?'

'Leo said I'd find you here,' he drawled, amused. 'You going to let me in?'

'He did?' I stepped back, creating a small gap for him to enter through. He took it, brushing against me as he made his way past, and I shivered at the electricity that travelled between us. I'd said it before, and I'd say it again, but I would have sworn our bodies were drawn to one another. Our magnetism was as strong as ever, never fading.

Clearly, while I'd been in Leo's room thinking of him like a lovesick twat, he'd been telling my enemy where to find me. Okay, enemy was a strong word. We weren't enemies anymore. We'd become people who kissed sometimes and never spoke about it afterwards. Which, yeah? I *was* aware of how fucked up that was.

'How have you been?' he asked, standing in front of me, his heat entering my bubble. All I could do in response was make a noise that I thought may have been a *huh* but could also have just been nonsense. 'We don't talk enough.'

I scoffed at that. *No, Oliver, we don't talk a lot. We just kiss and avoid any feelings that aren't taking place in our underwear.*

I gave him a quizzical look. Or that was my intention, anyway. Pretty sure that instead of looking quizzical, I just looked like somebody with constipation. *Smooth.*

'And I wonder why that is,' I snapped. My anger simmered to the surface, and honestly, before that moment, I hadn't even realised the anger I was still harbouring against him. I'd tried to act cool. Act like I didn't mind that he gave me orgasms in closets and then ignored me afterwards. Act like it didn't bother me that he fingered me in the library, but then made sure I saw his make-out session with Ophelia the very next day. Act like he hadn't walked in and saved me from that fucker and made me feel better afterwards.

'Whoa.' He gestured with his hands, palms forward, as if worried I was a bomb about to explode. Maybe I was. The glint in his eyes caught my glare, and I melted a little. Damn. Ollie's eyes were one of his best features. The chiselled jaw was hot, and his full lips were pretty great to kiss, but those eyes made me see stars.

'What?' I muttered, irritated that his eyes had such an effect on me and my anger.

'You look crazy fucking beautiful when you're mad. Have I told you that?'

'Yeah, once or twice,' I grumbled.

'Interesting.'

I rolled my eyes. 'Seriously, Ollie. Why are you here?'

'I wanted to see you. Talk to you. Apologise to you,' he said, as if that were the most obvious answer. Like I should have known all along he had sought me out to apologise. You know, because he was such an apologetic person.

'I thought you were at swim practise?' I brushed my hair behind my ear, trying to keep my hands—and my mind —busy.

'I left early. I told Leo I wanted to talk to you.' He shrugged.

'I told Leo about what happened between us,' I said, wanting to make it clear I hadn't hidden it from him. Ollie didn't know my relationship wasn't real, and I wanted it to stay that way. I didn't need a repeat. 'After...'

He nodded, his eyes swimming with anger. 'Oh.'

My patience with him breathing the same air as me was wearing thin. 'You want to talk, Oliver, then talk.'

'We're back to Oliver, are we?' He was amused at my frustration. My cheeks were flushed, and I could sense a rash forming on my chest. I hated when that happened, but it always seemed to happen in times of stress or aggravation. An ugly, angry, blotchy rash. Eurgh. 'I thought we were over that.'

'We're not friends,' I told him.

'What are we then?' He laughed at me, a low, deep chuckle that caused the hairs on my arms to stand on end.

'We're nothing,' I said with a sigh, my shoulders rising and dropping as if the weight of the world weighed them down. 'Just people who never really knew one another.'

'What makes you think you never knew me?'

'Are you fucking serious?' How could he even stand there and ask me that question with a straight face? Seriously, how did this boy sleep easy at night?

'Come off it, Sky. Not everything between us was fake.'

'Explain,' I demanded, my throat scratchy at how low those words had been uttered. 'Then maybe I'll believe you.'

'All in good time,' he whispered, leaning down to talk into my ear. 'I see you shiver in... anticipation.'

My resulting smile was involuntary. I loved that movie, but —huh? Odd. Last time I'd begged to watch it, back when we were "dating", Ollie had refused. Said it was *too confusing* and *too camp*.

Of course it's camp!

'I thought you hated *Rocky Horror*?'

'Yep,' he drawled, 'but you don't.'

He was right. I didn't hate it. I pulled my head back to look into his eyes, to search them, see if there was any falsehood there. Any lies simmering under the surface. But I couldn't see any. Not that I'd ever known what to look for.

'Right,' I muttered, a bit pissed he knew me better than I knew him. But it made sense. *I've never lied about who I am.*

'Little One, you do know me. The *real* me.'

'P-please, just go.' I shoved him towards the door, wanting

him out of my space. Breathing the same air as him was torture most of the time, but in Leo's room, it was too intimate. Too much.

'Fine,' he murmured, 'but I promise we *will* sort this out.' He kissed my cheek, the slightest graze of lips that reached me deep down in my soul—well, there and somewhere else. 'Oh, and before I go. There's a party in the woods Friday night.'

I nodded at him. Of course there was. It was the beginning of school, after all, and the party in the woods I'd attended last year was where the whole *Ollie fingered me up against a tree while the girls filmed it situation* happened. How could I forget such a night?

'See you there,' he said, his tone ominous, and then he opened the door and left me standing there alone, unsure what to do next.

Thirty-Two

NOT LONG AFTER OLLIE LEFT, Leo returned, yet I couldn't get excited. It felt like he'd thrown me to the big bad wolf without a heads-up. Ollie's ominous departing words played in my head in a loop and I wondered whether I should avoid the party on Friday at all costs.

'You okay?' Leo asked, hugging me tight to him.

'You told Ollie I was here?' I asked, not answering him. I hoped hugging me was like hugging a sack of potatoes—or a corpse—cold and unmoving, no part of me reciprocating the tightness of Leo's strong, muscled arms around me. 'Why would you do that?'

One thing I'd learned in all the time I spent with Leo was that the boy could hide his genuine feelings in the bat of an eye. Sometimes, I caught him off guard and saw a glimpse of the real Leo hiding behind the boredom, but it was rare. The moment my question left my lips, his face shuttered over, the darkness creeping in, but not before he looked guilty for the tiniest moment. A blink-and-you'd-miss-it moment in time.

'Did he bother you?' he asked darkly, not denying the fact he'd told him where to find me.

'Not exactly,' I said evasively, taking in a deep breath,

preparing myself to ask a hard question, but before I could bring myself to ask it, Leo spoke.

'He told me he wanted to apologise.' He let me out of our hug, and the two of us moved to sit on the edge of his bed. 'Sorry if I fucked up.'

Leo rested his hand on my knee, moving his finger in a repetitive circular motion, causing me to shiver.

'He didn't,' I blurted out. Then to clarify, added, 'Apologise, I mean.'

'Pity,' Leo drawled. 'The boy clearly hasn't learned from his mistakes.'

'What are we doing?' I sputtered. The question plagued me anytime it entered my mind, and my reaction to his message earlier solidified that I needed to clear things up with him. The fact I'd sought solace in his room spoke volumes to me, but I wanted to know where Leo stood before I blurted anything out.

His dark eyebrows slanted into a frown. 'What do you mean?'

'I mean, what are we doing? We've been in this fake relationship for a couple of months, and we've hurt the people we intended to hurt.' I shrugged, unsure of myself. 'Or disgruntled them, at least.'

'You saying you want out?' he asked, his hand coming up to grip the bottom of my chin and move my head so we were nose to nose. His breath touched my face, our lips close enough for my mind to go elsewhere.

Stay focused, Skylar.

The two of us had kissed, yes. Multiple times. Usually, it was for show in front of other people and didn't mean much more. There were a couple of occasions where we'd kissed in private, and I always brushed those off in my mind as the two of us getting caught up in our fake moment. We spent so much time together, it was only natural to explore the chemistry that thrummed between us.

But things felt different. More real.

'N-no,' I whispered. 'Unless you do?'

'I don't,' he whispered back. Our eyes locked, his blues meeting mine, and I realised I'd never seen Leo looking so vulnerable in the entire time I'd known him.

Intimacy crept in, blurring the edges of everything we were meant to be. Of our intentions.

'W-why?' My voice was barely audible, but Leo heard me. His eyes sparkled, intense, but I saw a glimpse of uncertainty he couldn't mask.

'Because, Stutter'—he sighed—'we're not finished yet.'

I let out the breath I'd been holding. 'We're not?'

'No.' He shook his head, his gaze never leaving mine. 'Not in our plan, and not with us.' His words hit me deep in my gut. I hadn't wanted to think too much about how my feelings for him were changing—and they *definitely* were. I no longer saw the bored dickhead I'd thought he was when I looked at him. We'd spent so much time together solo, without having to hide our true selves, I knew his bored demeanour was a front. A coping mechanism of sorts he used to stop anybody getting too close.

'Okay,' I whispered.

His lips touched mine, soft at first, but then like a cable snapping, something changed. The very air around us had heated; had become stifling. The resulting kiss differed from any other we'd shared. It wasn't a passionate kiss to make Clover jealous, or to piss Ollie off; it wasn't a gentle kiss good-night, or something we'd stumbled upon while watching a romantic film.

No. It was a kiss filled with electricity. Lightning. *Deadly.*

Fuck. I moaned, at the same time Leo moved us so I was lying on my back, with him pressed up against me. My mind was racing. *Abort. Abort.*

But I couldn't bring myself to stop. Or to ask him to stop.

Our tongues were tangled together, neither of us stopping when our teeth clashed. His dick was pressing into me and I shuddered at the forbidden thoughts racing through my head. Leo growled and took my bottom lip between his teeth and bit down so hard I tasted metal.

The fucker had drawn blood.

I should be disgusted, but after that time in the closet with Ollie, I'd been a lot more open to the darker side of life. I'd gone from a timid virgin to some kind of vixen—or at least that was how I felt—and it felt fucking awesome.

One thing I knew about my fake relationship with Leo? That it had helped me grow in confidence. My anxiety still lived in me. I doubted it would ever disappear, but it rarely showed anymore. I couldn't even remember my last anxiety attack—ignoring the moment earlier in the evening when Ollie knocked. And I was totally ignoring it.

'Stutter,' Leo moaned, somehow making the nickname sound like a seductive caress, as opposed to the slur it had started out as. 'Get out of your head.'

'How'd you know I was in there?'

'Because I know you,' he replied in between placing kisses on my neck.

'Leo,' I moaned back, the weight of him causing my lungs to strain a little. Fuck, why was it so hot to hear somebody tell you they knew you? And to actually believe them only made it that much hotter.

He eased off, breaking the kiss to look at me, his eyes

searching for an answer to a question he hadn't voiced out loud, but one I could hear just as loud as if he had. *Are you sure? Is this okay?*

Without putting any thought into it, I nodded, encouraging him to continue. He needed little persuading, and instantly his lips were back on mine, his right hand cupping my breast, squeezing me roughly above my uniform.

I gasped and tightened my grip on his hips.

Leo moved and lifted himself off me, but before I could start to protest his absence, he slowly peeled my skirt and underwear down my legs in a slow, seductive way that had me clenching my thighs together.

Shit. Once I was bared to him, he paused in his perusal to kiss me, and instinctively my body arched towards his, wanting to be as close as possible. He broke our kiss and moved down my body, and all I could do was close my eyes to stop myself from feeling too self-conscious.

Leo's tongue touched my folds, and I clenched my thighs, trapping his head between them in an involuntary action. He chuckled. The moment he licked my centre, I lost all sense of what was happening and writhed under his touch.

He stopped to murmur, 'Look at me, Stutter.'

His words caused the hairs on my arms to stand on end, and I opened my eyes to look down at his. It was illicit and private; and so very intimate. A thrill of excitement shot through my veins, as Leo's tongue returned to my core, and he inserted a finger to beckon at that most inner part of me.

A knot formed in my throat, and I bit my lip to stifle my outcry of ecstasy when everything reached its peak.

'Fuck,' Leo said, his voice thick, moving to gaze up at me, and I shivered at the glimmer of possession in his eyes.

No longer able to stop myself, I lifted myself up and

grabbed his hair, bringing his head to my level, gripped the back of his neck and pulled his mouth down to mine. He growled and bit my lip again, unleashing a feral side of me. A side I never knew I possessed. I grabbed his waist and fumbled with the button on his trousers, needing to hold his dick in my hand; needing to feel his warmth and how turned on he was. A compulsion of sorts.

'Are you sure?' he asked, using his finger to tilt my chin up; to look me in the eye and see my confirmation.

'P-positive,' I said, breathless. My heart thudded away in my chest as I watched his lips turn up into a satisfied smile. 'Are you?'

'Lie down,' he commanded, and I did as he said, the obedience coming from somewhere deep within. He undid the button of his trousers and took them off, revealing his enormous dick to me. 'Are you a good girl, Stutter?'

Why was it so fucking sexy to be called a good girl? What a fucking rush. I nodded. 'I'm always a good girl.'

'Do you trust me?' he asked, and I nodded once more. I trusted him, and the fact we were about to fuck meant I'd let him in a lot more than I first realised.

His touch set my skin on fire. He grabbed my legs and hooked them over his shoulders. Slowly, he pushed inside me, letting me adjust to every inch. My walls adjusted around him, and I could feel myself clenching and unclenching the further he pushed. *Fuck.*

Once fully seated inside of me, Leo thrust, holding my hips in a tight grip so that we would stay joined together. The emotions swirling in the air spurred us on, and with each thrust, the intensity increased. Our eyes locked; neither one of us wanting to look away. I couldn't believe I was in such an intimate position with Leo. It didn't compute.

I tried to turn my brain off. To swim in the sensation of his touch. But it was hard.

I was an overthinker by nature.

'Come with me,' he whispered, coaxing me. The pad of his thumb found my clit, teasing it in slow, pressured circles and sending me into a frenzy as my body fought for release.

'Oh, fuck,' I panted, almost there.

'Now,' he bit out, and the sound of his voice, the look on his face, pushed me over the edge.

Leo increased his speed, and I knew he was as ready to finish as me. His hot cum filled me, and the sensation overwhelmed me. I groaned in pleasure and went lightheaded.

Fuck.

That was definitely *not* a part of the plan.

Thirty-Three

THE START of the school year party in the woods.

Believe it or not, I wasn't looking forward to it. I didn't have an impressive track record with school parties in the woods—or just the woods in general—and I'd hoped Leo would want to avoid it too.

'Do we have to?' I whined to nobody in particular. I got a resounding response of yes from the other occupants in the room.

Clover, Griff, Leo, and I had all crowded into Clo's and my tiny room. Still couldn't put my finger on why that was, seeing as you could fit our room in Griff's or Leo's at least twice over, but here we were.

'It'll be fun, jelly tot,' Griff said, an enormous grin on his face. He donned a tight-fitted shirt and jeans, and from the appreciative glances Clover kept throwing at him, the boy was going to have some fun tonight.

Since our argument, Clo and I hadn't talked about her relationship with Griff, or mine with Leo. It seemed easier that way. Avoidance may not be healthy, but it meant we didn't argue every time we opened our mouths, so that was a win in my books.

'Yeah, yeah,' I said. Leo came up behind me and wrapped his arms around my waist. I leaned into him and smiled. Ever since the other night in his room, the two of us were more comfortable around one another. More natural.

The line was no longer blurred. It had disappeared entirely.

'You've got this,' he whispered in my ear and I sighed. He knew I was a sucker for ASMR, and he'd been going out of his way to give me tingles. To me, it was like an egg being cracked on the top of my head, travelling down and leaving goo in its wake.

'Shall we pre-drink?' Clo asked, irritation at the two of us obvious if her scowl was any indication. It was a pretty scowl, but a scowl nonetheless.

'I'm game,' I said with a shrug. Not like I was in any rush to head into the woods. I wasn't in any damn musical.

'Fine,' Leo agreed, sounding bored, or at least that was the impression he was trying to give off. I hadn't asked him how he felt about Clo anymore. If I were being honest with myself, I didn't *want* to know the truth, even though I needed to. Maybe I'd ask him once the alcohol hit my system and I was feeling the effects of liquid courage.

'Let's get this show on the road, bitches,' Griff called, pulling a bottle of vodka out of nowhere.

'Dude, you can't call us bitches,' Clo said, chuckling.

'If I can't call us bitches, you can't call me dude,' he replied, a smug grin on his face. The boy loved having a comeback at hand, even if it wasn't his best work.

I rolled my eyes at the two of them and sat on the floor cross-legged. Leo followed suit, arranging himself behind me, never breaking our touch. Clo and Griff sat down too, keeping a bit of distance between their bodies, and Griff placed a deck of cards on the floor in a circle around an empty cup. My groan was involuntary.

'When you said pre-drink, I didn't think you meant *Ring of Fire.' Man, I hate this game.* I was never good at the waterfall part, and there was no way in fucking hell that I would drink a dirty cup if I selected the fourth King. No way, no how.

'Yes!' Griff enthusiastically arranged the cards just so. 'It's this or *Bullshit Taxi.'*

I groaned again. It was an amalgamation of *Taxi* and *Bullshit* and one of Griff's favourite games to play. He loved handing out shots to people but rarely got to, as his face gave him away. If there was one thing for certain in life, it was that Griffin Cooper should never sit down at a table and play poker.

'Fine, *Ring of Fire* it is!' I said, faking cheer, pouring myself a vodka lemonade before making Leo a strong whiskey and Coke.

'Thanks, baby,' he said when I handed him the drink.

Clo's eyes narrowed and then I watched—in shock or awe, I couldn't decide—as she grabbed Griff's face and pulled it to hers for a big, sloppy kiss. Griff looked delighted. I sighed, but Leo didn't react. Maybe his face had, and I just couldn't see it, so I turned around and found him distracted, staring at my head, twirling my hair around his finger. I smiled at him, and when his gaze moved to mine, we shared a moment without words.

'You go first,' I said, facing the others once more, feeling only the tiniest bit smug at the look on both Clo's and Griff's faces.

The game started, and with each card turned over, we played the corresponding mini game. The longer we played, the more drunk we got.

Time passed fast, and when I looked at my phone, I saw

we'd been pre-drinking for two hours and knew we needed to head to the party soon. My mood soured.

'We need to leave,' I announced to the very drunk people in the room with me. All of us were way past tipsy. 'There's a party going on.'

'You don't even want to go!' Clo pointed at me.

I laughed. 'You're not wrong there.'

'Stutter's right, though. We should go.' Leo squeezed me tight, placing a kiss on my head, sending my hormones into overdrive. The more I'd had to drink, the more I wanted a repeat of our night together. 'Do you think you'll be able to walk there?'

'Sure!' I nodded with every ounce of enthusiasm I could muster. 'I'm Superwoman.'

'Okay.' Leo gave out a low chuckle. 'Let's see your walking superpower.'

So maybe I wasn't Superwoman.

Clo and I stumbled the entire journey, falling over branches and debris, but also our own feet. Every stumble and loss of balance caused us to break out into a giggling fit.

'Stop it!' she whisper-yelled at me through laughter tears, which just made me laugh more. 'I'm going to wet myself.'

'Classy,' Griff said from in front of us. He and Leo were ahead, probably because they weren't falling all over the show.

Ha-ha. What a funny saying. All over the show.

Neither of the boys acted like they'd drunk anywhere near as much as I knew they had. Not once had they stumbled or even swayed in the breeze.

Isn't language funny? As if anybody could actually sway in the breeze.

'Oh, hush.' Clo hooked her arm tighter through mine, using me for support. 'I suppose it wouldn't be very classy of me to suck your dick later either, right?'

Her words caused me to erupt into another round of giggles. My stomach hurt just from how much I was laughing. Out of the corner of my eye, I saw Clo's face blushing a dark red. When I focused back on the treacherous path we were treading, I watched Leo elbowing Griff in that way lads do. It was always a surprise to see the guys getting on, acting the way guys their age should. At times, they seemed older and serious, but then they joked around and reminded me they were the same as everyone else.

Leo's action made me happier than I had been in some time. Would he have done that a year ago? Would he have been happy to hear that *Red* planned to suck another guy's dick? I doubted it.

Was I maybe looking too much into it? Maybe, but fucking sue me.

'Did I just say that super loud?' Clo asked, covering her face with her hands.

'Oh yeah, girl, you did.' I laughed at her expense, happy to not be the butt of the joke.

'Ground eat me whole and let the worms feast on my innards.'

'Oh, stop it. I thought it was funny.'

'You would!' she said but laughed again too, so I knew she was also seeing the funny side of it all. 'I suppose I *am* funny as fuck.'

Her tone was so serious and sure, I couldn't keep my gut reaction in.

'You *are* delusional.'

'You know it,' she muttered under her breath.

We continued walking, close to the party spot now. It had taken us *ages* because we were pissed and I was struggling to see clearly.

A shriek pierced through the air, causing goosebumps to rise on my arms in an instant.

'What the fuck was that?' Griff called out, but before any of us could answer, another ear-splitting yell reached us.

The four of us broke out into a run—*okay, I'm bullshitting*—the boys broke out into a run, and Clover and I sort of jogged behind them. Or walked at a fast pace.

The cold September air whipped at our faces, biting at us, and the two of us were too far from sober, meaning we felt sick pretty fast. We could no longer see the boys, and I couldn't get my bearings. I just hoped we hadn't run astray. Fuck knew who could be out here.

'Shit!' Griff blurted from somewhere further into the trees. Heading towards his shout, we moved as fast as we could. Whatever it was sounded serious.

Stumbling into the clearing, we found Griff and Leo standing over a very badly beaten Ophelia.

'Shit,' Clo hissed beside me.

Ophelia's lips were split, and her eyes were both bruising and swelling up. Blood covered her, and, although I couldn't see much in the darkness, it looked as if it had come from her nose, which sat oddly on her face.

Clover, looking at Ophelia more closely, moved further away and was sick up against a tree. The powerful stench of stomach acid and vodka hit my nose, and I had to hold myself together. I'd always struggled to keep my gag reflex from reacting when somebody else was sick.

'Fuck,' Leo groaned out. 'Sky, help Clo. We're going to take Lia to the hospital wing.'

I nodded, knowing they needed to help her, but also I was shit scared that whoever had hurt her was still lurking nearby. She was in no condition to talk to anybody to let them know what happened. She was trying to stay conscious, but her eyes were rolling back into her skull.

I knew I should feel avenged. Should feel happy that somebody had harmed her the way she'd helped to harm me multiple times.

But I didn't.

I'd made up a shit revenge scheme, sure. One that was pretty moot. But at no point had I wanted anybody to get hurt. I'd just wanted to knock them down a peg.

Something I didn't really care about anymore. I was happy —truly happy—with how my life was going, and holding onto the anger and resentment just seemed stupid. The girls had apologised and Ollie wasn't acting anywhere near as self-important or arsehole-ish.

I felt sick to my stomach, and it wasn't just the cheap vodka swirling around in there causing it.

Somebody had taken everything too far, and I had a gut feeling that whoever had hurt Ophelia had also tried to drown me. There was an unhinged person on campus, and we needed to figure out *who*.

Soon.

But then another emotion hit me—hard.

Disgust.

Disgust aimed at Ollie. He'd instructed *The Set* to hurt me last year. He had been the one who sent them to beat me up in the toilets, and the woods after our picnic, and all those other times he'd orchestrated my torture.

How could he look me in the eye after finding me beaten on the toilet floor?

How could he look at my bruises and my pain and still pretend to care about me? Still kiss me and court me and make me fall in love with him?

Just the sight of Ophelia had my heart twinging with sympathy for her—and I didn't even particularly like the girl!

Over the last month, I'd lost my anger towards him. Lost my fuel and my drive for revenge. And I was okay with that. I'd even let him in, let him worm his way into my heart, in a small capacity. Especially after he'd found me that day, and we'd had a conversation that wasn't filled with venom.

But I wasn't angry.

I was just sad. And, really, that was the lowest he'd ever made me feel.

Thirty-Four

OPHELIA HAD BEEN in the hospital wing for the last couple of days.

'Can I go visit her?' I asked Leo on her third day. 'I'd really like to talk to her.'

'If you want,' he said with a shrug. 'Doubt she'll tell you anything more than what she's said to us.'

'I know,' I agreed. 'But I'd like to talk to her anyway.'

After my lessons ended for the day, Leo escorted me up to the hospital wing, straight to Ophelia's bed. She looked awful, her bruising a dark purple, and her hair was scraped up into a bun high on her head. It was the least put together I'd ever seen her.

When she saw Leo, she began to brush some wisps of her hair that had escaped the bun away from her face. Then she spotted me and rolled her eyes so far back in her head she looked possessed. Nice to know that getting beat up hadn't changed her.

'What is she doing here?' she hissed.

'I promise you I come in peace,' I said, not even letting Leo give some bullshit answer on my behalf. 'I just wanted to talk.'

'So talk.'

'I was kinda hoping we could talk alone? Without Leo here.'

Ophelia's gaze narrowed, and I could tell she was suspicious of me, but I could also see she was curious enough to know what I wanted to let me stay. Which was exactly what I thought would happen.

'I'll leave you girls to it. I'll be outside, Stutter.' He left the room, leaving the two of us alone together. The moment he was out of earshot, Ophelia began talking.

'Hurry up and get on with what you want to say. I'm on some pretty good drugs right about now, so I'd use that to your advantage if I were you.'

'First off,' I started, trying to collect my thoughts and order them so they made sense. 'I wanted to apologise for my petty shit during the summer.' Ophelia opened her mouth and I kept going, not letting her butt in. 'Yes, you deserved it. Actually, you deserved a hell of a lot worse than any of the stupid shit I did to you. But still, I want to put it behind us.'

'Okay...' The suspicious look hadn't wavered. 'Thanks, I guess?'

'Second, I wanted to talk to you about the attack.'

'I've already told the guys I can't remember anything.'

'Yeah, I know.' I nodded. 'But I wasn't sure if there was something missing. Maybe something you hadn't wanted to tell the guys, or a note that had shown up? Anything like that.'

She shook her head, but her eyes were clouded. 'No, I don't think so. I was out in the woods to meet Ollie, and then the next thing I remember is waking up in here with everyone looking at me.'

Her words surprised me. 'You were meeting Ollie?'

'Yeah, he'd sent me a text to meet there rather than at the party itself.' She shrugged, her bony shoulders pointing through her thin gown. 'But I highly doubt it was him who hurt me.'

I wasn't as sure as her, but I also didn't see Ollie doing it either.

'Just frustrating that we don't know who did this to you. Do you reckon it was the same person who stabbed me? Killed Odette and Olivia?'

'Shit,' Ophelia cursed, her eyes widened in alarm. 'I hadn't even connected it, honestly. Been a bit too busy worrying whether any of this will scar or permanently damage my good looks.'

'I'm sure with your money and contacts you could always pay a surgeon to change anything you're not happy with.' The words were out of my mouth before I thought it through, and I felt like a piece of shit for just assuming that because she had money, she'd go down that route. 'But I doubt it will scar. Nothing you've done to me is visible.'

Once again I'd somehow put my foot in it, but I didn't want to take it back. I may have forgiven her and Oralie, but I would never forget the shit they put me through.

'I know I've said it before, but I really am sorry, New Girl.' She reached out and grabbed my hand in hers. 'We were bitches and honestly, there's nothing I can say to really explain it away. We got a kick out of it. It's really that simple.'

'I get it, and we're good. As long as you never touch me again. Might want to mention that to Celia and Cordelia, too, just in case they didn't get the message from Ollie and Leo last time.'

'Just in case who didn't get the message?' Ollie asked, appearing around the corner like a ghost, holding a bunch of flowers.

'Nothing, babe,' Ophelia replied, fluffing her pillow to sit a little straighter in her bed, her smile wide. 'Sky and I were just having a nice chat.'

'Really?' He raised an eyebrow and I laughed.

'Really,' I affirmed. 'Thanks for agreeing to talk to me. I hope you feel better soon!'

'Thanks.' Ophelia smiled and for once, it was genuine. It wasn't hiding knives or a lie. It was a real smile, and it was actually quite pretty when she wasn't trying so hard.

'I'll leave you two to it.' I gave a small wave before backing away from the bed. The door beckoned and I made it there as quickly as I could, no longer wanting to watch Ollie's faux-mance with Ophelia. Or maybe it wasn't a faux-mance anymore. He'd brought her flowers, after all.

'Skylar, wait up!' Ollie's voice called and I groaned. I'd hoped not to bump into him. Ever since I'd found Ophelia hurt, I couldn't get over the idea that Ollie had aided them in doing that to me. Whenever I thought about it or tried to rationalise it, sadness overwhelmed me.

'What do *you* want?' I couldn't hold in my bite.

'I just wanted to talk to—'

'Well, I don't want to talk to you,' I said, being honest, hoping it'd end the conversation faster.

It didn't.

'What's going on?'

'Ollie'—I sighed and turned to face him—'I just can't be arsed with this right now, okay? I need time.'

He looked at me with confusion. 'Time from what?'

'From being around you!' My eyes filled with tears and I looked away at the ceiling. The stone pillars calmed me, grounded me enough to remind me to keep my cool. 'Actually, I've got a question for you.'

'Okay...'

I crossed my arms across my chest, a fighting stance, and looked at him. *Really* looked at him. Took in the chiselled jaw, the defined cheekbones, and the bright blue of his wary eyes.

'There's something I've not been able to get my head around and I need you to clear it up for me.'

His tone was honest. 'Whatever you want, Sky.'

'How could you instruct people, the girls, to beat me up and then still look at me like you cared about me?' I asked, nearly choking on my words. It was hard to be so open, so vulnerable, in front of Ollie. 'Looking at Ophelia in the woods made me feel sick. Seeing the terror in her eyes, the sadness, the confusion, was like looking at myself on the bathroom floor the day *you* set your minions on me. Did you get off on my pain? Enjoy laughing about it when my back was turned?'

'Skylar,' he said, his eyes pained. 'I never told the girls to hurt you.'

My disbelief manifested itself in a loud scoff. 'Why do I find that so hard to believe?'

'I know it sounds like I'm bullshitting you, but I'm not. I would never have asked them to beat you the way they did. They went too far and believe me when I say I didn't let them get away with it in private.'

'Whatever.' I sighed. 'I can't be around you right now. I'll see you later, okay?'

'Sky, let's talk this out.' His arm reached out for me and I took a step back, not wanting his proximity to make me do something I'd no doubt regret. 'We can go back in and ask Lia. She'll tell you.'

'Tell me what? That she did what Odette told her to do?' I shrugged. 'There's nothing more for me to say right now. Can you at least respect that?'

Ollie went quiet, his protests dying on his lips.

'Thank you,' I said, surprised he'd listened to me without putting up more of a fight. Maybe he truly was listening to me more these days. 'I'll see you around.'

I didn't turn back to look at him as I walked away.

Yay for progress.

Thirty-Five

PARENTS' Day.

The bane of the required school calendar—or at least it was in my eyes. After the events of the last one, I was in no rush to have a repeat, but at least I was the one who invited Mum and Andy this time so I wouldn't be blindsided like before. If the two of them were going to show up in all of their glory, then I wanted to be aware and prepared. I hadn't seen the two of them since, well, a long time ago. I had received a text from my mum after Mr Hawkins was charged for possession, but only because she'd seen a post about it on her social feed.

From the moment I woke up in the morning, dread sat low in my stomach.

'How are you feeling?' Clo called from her bed, still lying and staring up at the ceiling. ''Cause I feel bad and I'm not the one going.'

'Gee, thanks a bunch.' My pillow somehow found its way soaring across the room, hitting Clo on the side of her face. 'Honestly? I feel uneasy as fuck. I've been worrying all night about how today is going to go. I barely slept a wink.'

'I'm aware,' she said. 'You went to the toilet at least ten times.'

'Soz,' I said. 'Didn't mean to keep you up.'

'No big,' she replied as she sat up. 'It was my fault for not staying in Griff's room.'

'Very true. You do seem to spend a lot of time there these days.'

She thought about it for a second. 'Much better company. Not to forget he's gorgeous.'

'And I'm not?'

'You're beautiful, Skylar.' She laughed. 'But you look like you could use a wash.'

'Thanks again!' I joked but got out of bed and went to the bathroom for a quick shower anyway.

When I returned to the room, Clo was already dressed in a cute floral jumpsuit and had curled her hair. She looked bubbly and adorable and not like herself at all.

'Are you feeling okay?' I asked, watching her face.

'Yep.' She looked at me just as intently. 'Why'd you ask?'

'Well, your outfit is very... cutesy.' I'd tried for tact, but who knew if I'd hit the mark. These days, Clo got offended pretty easily, and I felt a bit like I was walking on eggshells.

'You like it?' she asked, giving me a twirl so I could see all angles.

'I do! Didn't think you would, though?'

'Maybe I'm feeling better in myself.' She shrugged, and if a visible weight had been on her shoulders, it would have dropped to the ground with a thud. 'And ready to show my true self.'

'If that's the case, I'm happy about it,' I told her, meaning it. Even if I doubted it.

'Thanks.' She smiled at me. 'So, you reckon you'll spend the day with Leo and his rents?'

'I think so, and if Mum and Andy weren't coming, I'd be totally fine with it. Lottie's always been nice to me, and I don't know enough about Edward to have an opinion,' I said, my thoughts running away with my mouth, forgetting the person I was talking to. Clover didn't have many agreeable things to say about the Hawthorns. I changed the subject. 'You and Griff are coming, right?'

'I mean, we don't have a choice, but at least we're both going to be without parents together.'

'So yours definitely aren't coming?' I asked for maybe the twentieth time. It was like I had word diarrhoea. I just couldn't help it!

'Nope,' she said, glancing away. 'They wouldn't come even if I asked them.'

'That's a shame.' I gave her a tentative smile, but she just rolled her eyes in response.

'No, it's not.'

'Well then. Yay, I guess,' I said with a small chuckle, trying to ease the tension lurking. Clover's parents were still as mysterious to me as they were when I first met her over a year ago, and in all that time, I'd learned nothing new.

'Indeed.' She gave me a taut smile, her lips a thin line. 'Let's get this show on the road.'

'Let's,' I said, gearing myself up for a train wreck of a day.

I MET Leo outside the main entrance, having decided it was best to meet my mum and Andy before they could enter the school. Didn't need a repeat of Mum calling across the hall to me, did I? An entire year had passed and I still wasn't past the embarrassment of that moment. A blush started at my hairline just thinking about it.

From the moment I spotted the black car making its way up the hill, the feeling in my gut just got worse and worse. My hand and Leo's larger one were entwined, and he gave me a quick, reassuring squeeze, as he knew how apprehensive I was about the day.

I'd wondered how everything would be seeing as Odette had outed my father's name in front of everybody at the fashion show. It helped me put Henry Brandon's questions during last year's New Year's Gala into perspective. The way he'd asked meant he'd known the truth or at least had an inkling of my parentage.

'Just breathe, Stutter,' Leo reminded me, his tone low as the car stopped at the bottom of the academy steps. 'We get through dinner and we ditch. I'll even let you choose the movie we watch.'

I nodded, my tongue lying heavy in my mouth, making words too hard to muster. Slowly, I took a breath in through my nose and pushed it out of my mouth. I'd used Google to determine the right order after the last time I'd questioned myself.

The car door opened, and in the exact way I'd assumed she would, my mum stepped out with a big flourish of her arms. The moment our eyes locked, her face became one of pure joy and I knew once she opened her mouth, shit would fall out of it.

'Oh, my darling daughter Skylar. Oh, let Mummy hold you!'

Yep. Pure and utter dog shit.

She flew at me, her arms wide, and the speed of her ascent up the stairs startled me. The heels she wore were so high I worried she'd trip and break her ankle. I gripped Leo's hand harder than before, so that even when she threw her arms around me, he was still anchoring me.

'My beautiful baby girl, I've been so worried about you. That mean man should never have touched one of mine.'

God, I nearly vommed on the spot. *She always knows how to lay it on thick when other people are present.*

'I'm fine, Mum,' I told her, trying to get myself out from in between her arms. Was the mean man the guy who stabbed me? Couldn't be her husband, could it, because that would mean she wasn't completely obtuse about the world around her.

Today, her outfit had to be one of the worst things she owned—maybe. I mean, the woman owned a *lot* of shit, loud clothing. Her top was made from a flimsy, chiffon-esque material and I hoped she wasn't planning on standing under any bright lights today. Otherwise, everybody here would see the underwear she was sporting underneath. The top's print was a snake one in grey—you know, the colour you see on real snakes all the time—and it buttoned up in the front, with god-awful ruffles hiding the buttons. Ruffles that went downward, resembling a certain part of a woman's anatomy. *Urgh.*

She'd teamed the top with white denim jeans and black stiletto heels. Honestly, if I hadn't been in her bedroom—or her house—I would think there were no mirrors to be found.

While Mum embraced me, my face squished up against her bosom, Andy joined us. He looked his usual ratty self, grey tracksuit bottoms matched with a black leather jacket, and his hair unbrushed, reaching his shoulders. *What a delight.*

'Skylar,' he slurred, his arms outstretched. He leaned in, and I dodged him, dragging Leo with me. Leo's face was one of pure horror and if I wasn't trying so hard to get away from the situation, I'd have pissed myself laughing.

'Oh, we are so glad to see you,' Mum said, but instead of looking at me, her eyes were glued to Leo. She looked him up and down, assessing him, and I realised the last time Mum was here, Ollie had been my boyfriend. 'What are you doing on my baby's arm?'

'Leo's my boyfriend now, Mum,' I said, hoping to ward off any tension or awkwardness by coming out with it.

'I'm impressed,' she said, pride shining in her eyes. 'I told you last year this boy is a fine specimen.'

'So you did,' I replied, stifling a laugh.

'Ditched that other one then, did ya?' Andy asked, all while chewing gum and smacking it.

'And so she should have!' Mum's voice was loud as ever, and luckily we were still outside the school building, so nobody inside could hear her—yet. 'That boy has some nerve.'

I rolled my eyes at her theatrics. If a complete stranger were to overhear her, they'd see a caring mother, but I knew better. So did Leo, who just gave my hand a quick squeeze to show he understood. Or maybe to calm me down so I didn't lose my cool and punch her. One or the other.

'Mum, he wasn't the one who stabbed me.' I'd told her this more than once, but it never seemed to make its way through all the hairspray vapours into her ears. Today, her brassy blonde hair was shorter than the last time I saw her, and it was as wide and high as it was long.

'You can't remember who stabbed you. That's what the police officers told me,' she said, nodding vigorously. I tried to focus on her words, but all I could focus on was the fact that her hair didn't move *at all*.

'It wasn't Ollie, Cora,' Leo said, his tone reassuring. He took his hand out of mine and moved his arms to point towards the large doors. 'Shall we head inside?'

'Let's! Oh, I hope they've put on a decent spread again.' Mum came closer to me, looping her arm into mine so that we could walk into the school together. 'One of the true perks of you coming here is the freebies!'

'Mum, it's a sit-down meal, remember?' I asked, already exasperated, and the woman hadn't even been here for a whole ten minutes!

'Yes, yes,' she said, patting my hand with the arm not looped in mine. 'Suppose we may as well head to the bar while we wait.'

'I thought we could meet up with Clover and Griff,' I told her, and then added, 'Lottie will arrive soon, too.'

Pretty certain my mum believed she and Lottie were besties. I was also certain Lottie was a lovely woman who was simply humouring Mum. She wouldn't be the first—or the last.

'Wonderful! Clover's a darling, isn't she?' Mum elongated the word darling, and I cringed internally. Part of me hated how strongly I felt about Mum and how badly she embarrassed me. I hated how strongly I wanted to pretend my mother was more like Lottie Hawthorn.

'That she is,' I said, trying to steer Mum towards the subject tables set out and not the bar at the far end of the room.

Andy had roped poor Leo into a conversation behind me. I'd briefly heard the words *tyres* and *paint job* and honestly, I didn't want to know what the fuck he was boring him about. Cars, I assumed.

Clover and Griff were standing together in the hall, and Mum waved wildly the moment they spotted her. 'Hello!' she called, dropping my arm like a hot potato and continuing to wave, using both arms like one of those car dealership balloon men. 'Cooey!'

The two of them looked at her, amusement lacing both of their features at Cora's lack of, well, everything. Griff's cheeky chappy grin covered his face as he waved back to her, and Clo was trying hard to disguise a grimace but was doing a pretty shit job of it. Couldn't blame her.

'Wonderful to see you again, Cora,' Griff said, sucking up and acting like a charming, flattering bastard. 'You look fabulous today!'

'Oh, you are such a darling,' Mum tittered, fanning her face with her hand. She moved her gaze to Clo. 'You're a very lucky girlie snagging this one!'

'Something like that,' Clo said, her smile fake as fuck. 'Lovely to see you, Cora.'

'You remember Andy, of course,' Mum said, sweeping her hand out to gesture at her husband. Somehow, the smiles on both Griff's and Clo's faces became even more false with each passing second.

'Of course. Nice to see you,' Clo said through gritted teeth that were still in a smile. Quite impressive if you asked me.

'You look beautiful, you stunner,' Andy said, his eyes leering at Clo, taking her in from top to toe. His pupils dilated when they travelled across her breasts. *Gross.*

'Thanks.' Clo turned to Griff, disgust clear in her features. 'Shall we go get a drink, babe?'

'How wonderful! That's where I want to head. Come with me, dear!' Mum grabbed Clo's arm, hooking it in with hers and almost dragging her away.

Too mortified to laugh, I stayed silent.

Apparently, Griff didn't feel the same way. Well, not until

Andy wrapped his arm around his shoulders and said, 'Let's go join our sexy women, shall we?'

Like Clover before him, Griff was dragged in the direction of the bar.

'What the fuck just happened?' I asked Leo, who had stayed by my side silent throughout the whole encounter.

'Honestly, baby, I have no clue.' He chuckled, and I swear the sound of it made my nipples harden.

Down, Skylar. Calm down.

I'D CONCLUDED that the powers that be hated me.

The formal dinner portion of the day finally arrived, and once again, we were placed at a table with the Hawthorns and Henry Brandon, meaning Ollie was sitting with us, too. *You couldn't make this shit up, could you?*

So far, Mum had said nothing, but I knew she was gagging at the bit to talk to Ollie, or rather tell him off, for whatever slight she thought he'd made towards me. On the other side of the table, I could sense that Henry wanted to talk about the elephant in the room—my biological father.

The meal had barely begun, and I was certain that over the six-course meal, somebody would open their big mouth. The question was: who would bite first?

'Well, Oliver,' Mum spat out over the starters. 'I hope you're happy with yourself.'

Here we go.

Ollie sank a little in his seat, not making eye contact with anybody at the table. If I was feeling kinder, I would tell him that nothing would stop Mum once she'd started, so he may as well grin and bear it, but I wasn't feeling overly generous towards him since finding Ophelia in the woods and our conversation afterward.

Griff opened his mouth to join the fray, but a booming voice stopped him. 'Cora, don't you think we should let boys be boys?' The smarmy look on Henry's face made me sick. That statement was one of the many things wrong with the world—a tiny thing in comparison, but still.

'And what exactly do you mean by that, Henry?' Lottie piped up after taking a dainty sip of her cocktail.

'Oh, you know…' he trailed off, and Lottie raised her thin eyebrow, waiting for him to continue.

'No, we *don't* know. Anything to say, young man?' Mum looked surprisingly fierce—and slightly like a circus clown. Her bright blue eyeshadow reached her too-black filled-in eyebrows, and her coral shade of lipstick caused her lips to blend into her rouged cheeks. Basically, my mum looked a right state.

Ollie coughed, realising he was trapped, and said, 'I'm sorry, Cora.' His expression was uncertain; unsure whether he should apologise to Mum or to me. He made the right choice when he turned to me and said, 'I'm sorry, Skylar.'

'Sorry for what?' Mum slurred, pointing the stem of her wineglass in his direction. Under the table, Leo squeezed my thigh in support and I shuddered. The warmth from his hand travelled through me, and I smiled, glad to have him by my side.

'For everything,' Ollie said, and his tone sounded earnest. I'd taken a sip of my drink at the wrong time and choked, surprised as fuck that he sounded sincere. He'd had so many chances to apologise to me, yet he'd chosen a time when we were in public and I couldn't reply honestly without seeming like a bitch. The only reason he'd said anything was because a drunk woman had pushed him to!

'Although,' Mum continued. 'I heard you saved my baby from that awful, perverted man and for that I thank you.' Mum sounded sincere, and it was the first time in a very long time that my heart felt a bit of love towards her.

The table fell silent at the mention of Mr Hawkins. I hadn't even known Mum knew about what happened. I turned an accusing gaze to each of the boys, wanting to see a crack in their armour, wanting to figure out which one had told her. None of them looked me in the eyes.

The silence was only broken when the servers arrived and placed dishes in front of us that smelled divine. One thing I could agree with Cora on was the fact that Hawthorn definitely knew how to put on a spread in style. I caught Mum's eye, and we shared a conspiratorial look. It was the first time, in a *very* long time, where I felt like the two of us were on the same wavelength. *Minor miracles.*

The meal passed, and after the last of the plates were cleared away, Ms Hawthorn took to the stage, microphone in hand.

'Welcome, parents and students.' Standing in the centre of the stage, she looked as important as she probably believed she was. The stage—the school—was her domain; her forte. Where she felt most at home and in her element. 'Once again, we welcome you to our fine establishment.'

She surveyed the room, her grey eyes narrowed and filled with judgement when they landed on Mum and Andy.

'After the events of last year,' she said pointedly, looking at the table where Ophelia and Oralie were sitting with their parents, 'we do not have an informational video to show you, but we have a band instead. So enjoy the music, and I will be at the back of the hall to answer any and all of your questions.'

As quick as she started talking, she left the stage. I watched her walk off, her gait slightly unbalanced because of a small limp I hadn't noticed when she stepped onto the stage.

'Short and sweet, thank fuck,' Andy blurted out, rubbing his bulbous nose that was red from drink. He disgusted me, and I was thankful summer school had meant I didn't have to return home and be cornered by him again, even if I disagreed with how the boys had made that possible. 'That woman is a witch.'

I coughed as Leo chuckled beside me.

'That *witch* is my sister,' Edward said, a twitch in his eye, as Lottie patted his arm in a soothing gesture. I caught Lottie's eye, and she winked at me in a conspiratorial manner.

'Doesn't make her any less of a witch, mate.' Andy looked at each person sitting at the table, hoping somebody would pipe up and agree with him. Nobody did. The only noise was Edward's grunts of displeasure.

'Well, as fun as this has been,' Griff announced. 'Clover and I have plans to speak with her parents on video call.'

'How come your parents couldn't make it, dear?' Lottie asked, a smile on her face. If Lottie hated Clo's parents, then why did she always seem so genuine when they were brought up in conversation? None of it added up.

'Business,' Clo mumbled, avoiding Lottie's eyeline. 'Lovely to see you all, as always.'

'Let your mum know I'd love to hear from her,' Lottie said.

'Sure,' Clo replied, but I knew she wouldn't. Her face told me as much.

'Bye, darling,' Mum said, her bloodshot eyes struggling to

focus on Clo and Griff as they stood to leave. 'Make sure you keep this one happy! He's a keeper.'

Griff winked at Mum, then the two of them left, and I glanced at Leo, who was watching them with a smirk on his face. One day, I expected him to tell me what the fuck had happened between them all.

'It's probably time I head out too, Son,' Henry announced. I'd forgotten that Henry Brandon and Ollie were still with us, my mind having been occupied by Mum, Andy, and the Hawthorn drama.

'Are you not staying over at the house for the swim meet tomorrow?' he asked, looking like a lost little boy seeking their parents' approval. 'I thought you'd want to stick around and watch.'

'No can do. Places to go, people to see, and all that. You understand, don't you, Son?' Henry asked, not really wanting an answer. He'd already made it clear he was getting out of dodge at the earliest opportunity.

'Sure.' Ollie's face darkened. 'If you'll excuse me.'

With that, he stood and walked out of the hall, not looking back once. A pang of sympathy went through me. I hated it when something happened to make me see him as a proper person. One with actual feelings and emotions.

'He's always so touchy.' Henry chortled. To give my mum and Andy credit, they stayed silent.

I was pulled out of my thoughts by my mum clapping her hands together to get everybody's attention. 'So, who's for another round of drinks then?'

Thirty-Six

THE FIRST SWIM meet of the season—and the first since Leo had been assisting with coaching the team—was upon us, and everybody had high hopes for the results.

Griff had been pumped up all morning, telling Clo and me that he was ready to *slay the competition* and I hoped he was going to live up to his own hype. I didn't want to be around him later if he didn't. A surly Griff didn't happen often, but when it did, you hid and waited for him to snap out of his funk.

'You ready to head over to the pool?' Clo asked, grabbing her bag and phone as she prepared to leave our room.

'Yep,' I said, checking that I had everything I needed on me. 'You not pumped up?'

'Pumped up? Who the fuck are you?'

I laughed and shook my head at myself. Pretty certain I'd never used that phrase before in my entire life. 'Honestly, Clo, I don't know where that came from. I think Griff's rubbing off on me.'

'You sounded like an idiot.'

'I'd have to be an idiot to be friends with you,' I replied, laughing harder. She giggled too, and then it became infectious, even though it wasn't that funny. The two of us started laughing to the point of tears. Full-blown, stomach-hurting laughter. I wrapped my arms around myself and clutched my hands on my ribs, bent over to stop the hurt. Clo was doing the same thing, and I watched as a streak of mascara travelled down her cheek. Infectious laughter soothed the soul as much as it hurt the stomach.

'Fuck sake, Sky.' She tried to give me an evil look, but that just made me laugh more. It was a vicious cycle. 'I'm gonna have to touch up my makeup now!'

Eventually, the two of us got ourselves under control and, after touching up our makeup, we were ready to leave.

'Shit, we're gonna be late,' I said, looking at the time on my phone. We'd been laughing for longer than I thought.

'I'm sure they won't even notice,' Clo said, although her pace picked up.

'Leo will,' I said under my breath. 'He always does.'

'Of course he does. You're his girl, remember?' She sounded both jealous and bothered, and a dagger buried between my ribs. I shouldn't be shocked. The reason Leo wanted to be with me in the first place was to hurt Clover, but things had changed enough that I'd forgotten that was the original goal in his eyes. I wondered if it still was.

'And you're Griff's,' I said, emphasising his name—and my point. Griff was my family, and even though Clo was my best friend, I wouldn't let her ruin him.

'Right,' she muttered, the laughter of a few minutes ago gone, leaving only tension in its wake.

When did shit get so complicated?

We moved fast enough that we didn't reach the pool house too late. We'd also done ourselves a favour. We'd missed the earlier races of the younger years and only had to wait a little while for Griff to compete. *Small mercies.*

We sat down, and the second Griff spotted us, he waved enthusiastically. He looked so funny standing in his skimpy speedos with a swim cap on, waving and smiling widely.

Clo sighed and said, 'He is such a massive dork, isn't he?'

'Yeah, he really is. But an endearing one, y'know?'

'Most of the time...' she trailed off. 'Sometimes I wonder if I feel as much for him as he does for me.'

I didn't say I'd thought about it for a while myself. 'And did you come up with an answer?'

'Most of the time I think I feel the same, but then that tiny doubt creeps in. Do you get what I mean?'

'I do,' I replied absentmindedly, looking over at Ollie, who was preparing for his race, and then over at Leo, who smiled when our gazes locked. I smiled back and gave him a tiny wave. *Fuck, now I'm the dork.* 'Boys are confusing.'

'Proper.'

'You think they find us just as baffling?' I asked, curious.

'Oh, yeah, for sure. Griff looks at me sometimes and it's like I can see the cogs turning.'

I laughed at that, imagining the *exact* face she was referring to.

I wished I could give a blow-by-blow account of what happened next. How the races went. How the boys looked— other than fit as fuck—but I couldn't. The events were a blur. All I knew was that Griff and Ollie won their respective races.

Seconds after they awarded the last medal, a shout rang throughout the room, echoing off of the high ceiling. Another loud shout, followed by somebody barging into the room, caused a commotion and every eye was drawn to them.

'Help! Help!' A large, burly-looking man entered, hollering to anybody who could hear him. 'It's Ms Hawthorn. Somebody's attacked her!'

Gasps and whispers started up across the room, and I looked at Clo in shock. I didn't know what to do. I was frozen to the spot, and I sought out Leo across the room. His face was pale, and he looked worried—unnaturally so. Ollie and Griff looked perplexed, and then in sync, the three of them headed in the direction the man had come from.

A few rows in front of us, Edward's head came into my eye line as he stood up and hurried after the boys. It had surprised me the night before when Edward and Lottie announced they were staying, seeing as Leo wasn't competing anymore, but it also highlighted how different they were as parents compared to Henry. No matter what Clo's issues with them were, you couldn't deny that they were supportive parents who loved their only child.

'What the eff is going on here at Hawthorn?' Clo asked, her voice as shocked as I felt. Ms Hawthorn always seemed so untouchable, and the thought of somebody hurting her in her own domain seemed so surreal.

'Who would attack her?' I asked back, having no answers yet plenty of questions. 'Reckon it was the same person who attacked Ophelia? Or me?'

'No way to know for sure,' Clo said, uncertain. 'But I suppose it'd make sense.'

'None of this makes sense.' My brain was drawing a blank. 'It rules out the boys, though.' The three of them had been in our eyesight the whole time, meaning they couldn't have done it.

'Always seeing a bright side, aren't you?' she said with a slight smile.

'I mean,' I replied with a shrug. 'Kind of got to at this school.'

'Should we go follow them or...?' Clo asked, as the two of us watched the other spectators follow Edward and *The Sect*.

'Honestly, it's probably not our place?' Even as I said it, I knew we wouldn't be staying where we were. Too many people had left, and fuck it, we may as well join them. Sort of looked suspicious if we didn't go see—like we had something to hide.

'You're totally right...' Clo said, and then added, 'Let's go.'

The two of us hotfooted it down the stairs, trying to avoid colliding with everybody who was doing the same. Eventually, we got to the door and barged our way through the forming crowd. Breaking free, we stumbled upon Leo, Ollie, and Edward hovering over Ms Hawthorn on the floor. I couldn't see Griff anywhere, and that boy's height meant he could rarely hide. Maybe he'd gone for some help.

Ms Hawthorn was cowering on the floor, holding her limp wrist with her other hand. Her sallow face had already bruised, one of her eyes swollen shut, and it looked to me that there were unshed tears in her open eye.

Leo surveyed the area, and when his eyes landed on me, he beckoned me forward with his hand. I tiptoed forward, making my way to him in silence, not wanting to draw much attention to myself even though everybody was staring at us.

'I don't want you going anywhere alone,' he whispered in my ear, as he pulled me into a hug when I got close enough. 'Stay close to me at all times.'

I tilted my head up to meet his eyes, and after seeing the worry and fear in them, I bobbed my head in agreement. Knowing he wanted to keep me safe was enough for me to agree. Leo's face regained its colour the moment I nodded, but the worry surrounded him like a dark cloud.

'I need you to say it, Stutter.' He placed a kiss on my cheek and then a soft one on my lips. 'I just want you safe.'

'I promise,' I mumbled, wanting to reassure him and not be the person who added to his problems. To lighten the mood between us, I added, 'Not like I'm going to complain about having you at my side at all times.'

'At your beck and call?' he joked.

'Of course,' I replied with a chuckle, but then I remembered what was happening around us, and I sobered. 'What happened to her?'

'Same thing that happened to Ophelia. An unknown person attacked her from behind and she didn't see who it was. Or at least she won't say even if she did. Ol' Aunt Winnie doesn't like to be seen as weak.'

I believed that. The woman gave off those vibes, and I could understand why. She was a female running an elite establishment, ruling in circles that were traditionally male-dominated.

'Where's Griff?' I asked. Clo was still standing at the edge of the crowd, looking lost and alone.

'Gone with Mum to the hospital wing to get the place prepared. That's if Dad can convince Winnie to go there. She's too tough for her own good.'

'Makes sense. She's not the type to allow others to wait on her.' I stepped out of Leo's embrace and gestured over at Clo, feeling she should be a part of this conversation. She and Ollie both came to stand by us at the same time.

'We need to talk,' he whispered. 'Come to my room tonight at seven, all of you.'

'Why should we trust you?' Clover harshly whispered back, but at the same time Leo spoke, overriding Clover's question.

'Sure,' Leo replied, bored. 'We'll be there.'

Curiosity got the better of me—a habit of mine I needed to break, or at least evaluate—but we move.

I gave him my sweetest smile.

'We'll be there.'

Thirty-Seven

LATER THAT EVENING, the four of us headed to Ollie's suite together deciding there was safety in numbers. Plus, Leo had asked me so nicely not to leave his side, it made me want to be even closer to him at all times. My hormones were working hard, and every little thing Leo did was only making me want him more.

After Edward begged her, Ms Hawthorn had finally agreed to be taken to the hospital wing, and once she'd left, there was no reason for everybody to stick around, so ever since, Leo and I had chilled out in my room with Clo and Griff, just waiting until the time Ollie said to meet.

'Wonder what he wants to tell us,' Clo said, looking back over her shoulder at me and Leo. She and Griff were a few paces in front, swinging their joined hands between them like two kids on a school playground. It was cute.

'No clue,' I said, perplexed. The thought had plagued me all afternoon, and I was still none the wiser about what he wanted from us. It had nothing to do with our relationship or what happened between us, because he'd invited the others too. I looked at Leo, who had been pretty silent all day. 'Any ideas?'

'None,' he said, blunt. *Don't take his mood personally,* I told myself. All day he'd acted odd and until we were alone, I wouldn't find out why. Twice, I'd caught him deep in thought, and I'd had to repeat myself before he heard me. Something had hit him, *hard.*

Ollie's black door beckoned at the end of the hall, calling to me, and I picked up my speed. I tried to tell myself it was because I wanted to know what Ollie wanted—and only that—but I wasn't fooling myself.

Griff pounded on the door with both fists and I wouldn't have been shocked if Ollie opened it and decked him square in the face. Griff's grin was wide. He was doing it to be an annoying bastard on purpose. I laughed a little at his antics and I watched as Clo rolled her eyes at him, her expression amused.

The door creaked open to reveal Ollie on the other side, an eyebrow raised in annoyance. I knew that arsehole's facial expressions, and *he* wasn't amused. 'Get in here, dickhead,' he growled, his lips slightly upturned, showing he wasn't *that* irritated at his cousin.

He stepped back, creating enough room for us to enter, and when I moved past him, his fingers grazed my arm, like he wanted to stop me but had chosen at the last second not to.

From behind me, Leo's hand gripped my arm in the same spot Ollie's fingers had grazed, and I shivered. Being around the two of them at the same time was going to be harder than I'd like. It was the first time with them both in the same place at the same time since my kiss with Ollie and my night with Leo.

Griff and Clo had taken a seat on the sofa, so Leo and I went and joined them. It was a little snug, but it was that or the floor, and even though I was one of those strange people who enjoyed lying on the floor, it didn't feel right in Ollie's room. *I promise you, some of the best thinking takes place on the floor.*

Once we'd settled, and I was leaning into Leo's side, Ollie started pacing in front of us all. We all watched him, staying silent as he did so, waiting for him to get to the point of why he asked us all to his room.

Leo's scent filled my nose, and I checked out a little. Where Ollie smelled of tobacco and vanilla, Leo was a mix of leather and ginger—a real aphrodisiac.

I shook my head, focusing my eyes back on Ollie, who had finally stopped pacing and was staring at the part of my body touching Leo's. He shook his head, his eyes hooded.

'I found this,' he announced, holding out a crumpled piece of paper.

'Where?' Griff asked.

'On the floor besides Winifred.' Ollie held it out to Leo, who leaned forwards to take it out of his hand.

'What is it?' Clo asked.

'A note,' Leo said, and the two of us read it in silence.

We have warned you.
Breaking the sacred bonds of *The Sanctum* results in death.
Audentes fortuna iuvat. Dulce periculum.

If I thought I was confused earlier, the note only made it ten times worse. The only part that made sense to me was the school motto. *Fortune favours the bold. Danger is sweet.* Underneath, there was a name and signature I didn't recognise, but then again, I'd grown up poor and in a different world to them, so of course I didn't recognise the name. Had the note been intended for Ms Hawthorn?

I took it from Leo and passed it to Clover on my right.

'What the hell is *The Sanctum*?' Griff asked, handing the paper back to Ollie. Griff sounded as befuddled as I felt, and when I looked around the room, I could see that everybody was feeling the same way. Confused.

'I've never heard of them,' Ollie said, pacing once more. It was something I had in common with him. 'But it's linked to the school. The note says as much.'

We all made noises, agreeing with him—all of us except for Leo.

'Should we look into it?' I asked, not knowing what else to say. 'Where would we even start?'

'Do you mean should we research the school's history?' Ollie asked, and I nodded. 'We could, and the best place to start is the library.'

'Sounds like a plan!' Griff piped up, fidgeting in his spot on the sofa. 'Library time, Skylar, your favourite.'

'That is very true,' I said, pondering the situation. Before I agreed, I wanted Leo's opinion. 'What do you think, babe?'

'If you want,' he said, his eyes dark. His mood hadn't improved, so I chose to ignore it for the time being. No point arguing and giving Clover fuel. Or Ollie. Pretty sure he still believed our relationship was fake deep down but doubted himself.

'I'm in,' Clo said.

'I *am* interested in history...' I pretended to think for a moment longer, but I wasn't fooling anybody. 'I'm in.'

'Excellent,' Ollie drawled.

My arms were covered in goosebumps, and a chill crept in. Not because I found Ollie attractive. Nope. Not one bit.

Yeah, I don't believe myself either.

AT THE EARLIEST OPPORTUNITY, I went to the library to start my research.

My love of the library served me well when it came to delving into the school's history and trying to find any old yearbooks or articles that would tell us more about what had happened in the school's past.

The librarian, an older kind lady who was hard of hearing, wanted to aid me in any way she could. I thanked her but said I was okay for the time being, that I'd ask for help if I needed it.

We didn't need anybody knowing what we were doing. Especially not somebody on the payroll.

I found it hard to believe that the boys had never looked into the past, or *The Sect* or *The Set* in general. Apparently, it was just something they knew.

I turned to Griff, who was sitting beside me at our usual table at the back of the library. 'Tell me again how you found out about *The Sect*?'

'Uncle Edward told us stories when we were younger, and it was just always a given we would one day rule the school. None of us questioned it.'

'You just accepted it as fact?' I asked to clarify.

'Yeah. He always told us how our parents were members, and so were their parents before them, and so on.' He shrugged, his eyes looking a little lost. 'I never thought to question it, to be honest, Clouds.'

It made sense. The boys had wealth and power—they had all their lives—and they didn't know any different. Didn't know just how fucking weird the whole concept was.

I assumed Ophelia and Oralie had also grown up being told the same thing, and knowing that you could punish anybody that stepped a toe out of line with no repercussions must be pretty heady.

It also made sense to me why Ms Hawthorn had never looked into any of the attacks on me. Had never included the authorities in anything that happened at the school, and had been pissed when the police had briefly investigated the murders of Odette and Olivia.

Because that was what they were. *Murders.*

I'd asked Leo about the investigations when we started our fake relationship, wondering if the police were any closer to finding out who'd stabbed me.

'So did the police find out anything new?'

'Not that I know,' he said, taking a glance at me before returning to the video game we were playing. 'A lot of money changed hands to make them go away fast.'

'Who paid?'

'Dad, I assume.' He shrugged. 'Maybe Winnie. Either way, Stutter, it's best for you that they're no longer digging around. From the last update we got, you were their biggest suspect for what happened to Olivia.'

'But what about Odette? And the person who stabbed me?'

'They've got no idea. Told them to keep us updated.'

'And if you hear anything, you'll let me know. Right?' I asked, knowing he would but wanting that reassurance anyway.

'Of course.' He paused the game to turn and give me a smile. 'I've got your back.'

I pulled myself back to my conversation with Griff. 'So your parents were both members?'

'Yep,' he said with a nod. 'Your dad was a member, too.'

'My d-dad?' I stopped looking through the yearbook in front of me and looked at Griff's face.

'Yeah, course,' he said, still looking down at the documents in front of him, not having noticed the shock his words had put me in. 'They all went to school here. I thought you knew.'

He looked up at me, his smile firm, but then he spotted my expression, and his face fell.

'I'm sorry,' he said, his eyes sympathetic. 'I need to think more before I speak.'

'It's fine,' I said as I looked back down to avoid his pity. *Fuck that*. 'I don't even know the dickhead.'

'Right,' he said, his tone uneasy. 'You're better off, anyway.'

'That's what my mum said.'

'And, as much as it pains me to say this, Clouds, I'm with Cora on this one.' He fake shivered and made me giggle. 'The man's a douche.'

He may be a douche, but Griff was my only link to him, and as much as it pained me to admit it, I wanted to know about him. 'Do you remember him?'

'Not much.' He shrugged. 'He went off the grid when we were pretty young. Before my parents died, otherwise I'd have gone to live with him when they died.'

'I know these are shit words, but I'm sorry they died.' I reached out and squeezed his shoulder. 'I'd have loved to meet your parents.'

'They'd have loved you, and they would never have let you have such a shit upbringing knowing you were their niece. But it's okay. I know they can see us.' His smile was wide, causing me to break out into a wide grin back at him. 'Pretty sure they're ghosts.'

The way he said it was so casual I couldn't help but laugh, spitting out the drink I'd just taken a small sip of. I put my bottle down and tried to calm the nervous giggles threatening to take over. Whenever I thought I knew what he was going to say next, he surprised me and said something left field. Being around him was never boring, that was for damn sure.

'Ghosts?' I questioned, my eyebrow raised.

'Yep,' he answered, not seeming to hear my scepticism. 'They're definitely spirits.'

'You kill me,' I said with a small laugh, picking up my bottle of water again, hoping I'd be able to take a sip again soon without spitting it out. 'I'm sure they're kind spirits.'

'Oh yeah. None of that poltergeist maliciousness.'

'That's good, I guess.' I pointed at the stack of papers Griff had been shifting through. 'Found anything in those documents?'

'Nothing we didn't already know. Just a list of past members,' he grumbled, frustrated he didn't have any better news to tell me. 'And the years they attended.'

'Eurgh,' I said, just as frustrated. 'Maybe I should search the old school newspaper?'

'The school had a newspaper?'

'Yeah, it ran from 1955 to 2000.' A thought hit me. 'Hey, what year were our parents in charge?'

Griff shuffled through the papers, finding the one he wanted. 'Well, our rents graduated in 2000.' Griff nodded, reaching the same conclusion as me. 'So, the year they left school is the year the newspaper ended?'

'Right!' I shouted enthusiastically—maybe a little too much—but fuck, it could be the break we'd been looking for. 'I wonder what the explanation is... Hey, what year did old Winnie become a faculty member?'

'She joined as an assistant the year she graduated, so'—he shuffled the paper again, and I got the impression he was enjoying it, probably thinking it made him look scholarly —'1990.'

'Bet she knows what went on.' I nodded, my thoughts running away with me. I had a suspicion, but no real clue of what or why. 'Could you grab me the yearbook from 2000?'

'You gonna dive into that rabbit hole?' he asked, but the glint in his eye told me he already knew the answer.

'You bet your arse I am,' I said, a grin on my face. Determined once again to uncover whatever it was we needed to know. Before somebody else ended up dead.

Thirty-Eight

HALLOWEEN CAME, which meant another fucking party in the woods, and not just any party.

Oliver's 18th Birthday Bash.

Or at least that was how Griff referred to it and the rest of the school whenever it was spoken about in the halls.

I was attending the party as Leo's date, and we'd come up with a pretty cool outfit idea. I couldn't wait to see how hot he looked wearing it. My outfit last year had been awesome too, so I needed to go one further.

'What do you think?' he asked, entering his room from the bathroom, dressed as a super dead, super suave, Bugsy Siegel. He was wearing a houndstooth patterned suit jacket, white shirt and tie, and grey slacks. Even his shoes were era specific black brogues. He'd even blackened his blond hair and gelled it back.

'Damn!' I whistled. 'Do you think this getup suits me?'

His eyes perused my body and lit up with lust, his tongue peeking out to slowly lick his bottom lip. My black dress was tight with a pencil skirt, and I had teamed it with a long faux fur coat and some black pumps. Virginia Hill in all her fashion- able glory.

'You look good, Stutter. Real fucking good.' He grabbed my waist and pulled me to him, then placed a bruising kiss on my temple. I shivered, goosebumps covering my arms in seconds. 'The perfect mobster's girl.'

'You look pretty hot yourself,' I said as I wrapped my arms around his waist to keep him close. The line between fake and real no longer existed between us and we were both caught in the middle. It was difficult acting so couple-y in public and then switching it off in private—to the point where we were turning it off less and less even when alone.

'You sure we have to go? We could stay here...' he said, the implication behind his words clear. My lips formed a smile on their own, but I pinched his side, anyway, even if I wanted to stay in his room and explore.

'Yep,' I replied, ignoring his suggestion. 'Course we do. Have to show off our love.'

I laughed, and his lips rose into an almost-smile. 'Very true. Got anything in mind to show off tonight or are we winging it?'

'Winging it.' My response was breezy, but my thoughts were anything but. 'I'm sure the perfect opportunity will present itself to show how obsessed with each other we are.'

'I'm sure you're right. You usually are.'

I hit him, but it didn't have much of an impact seeing as we were still standing close together, chests touching. He squeezed his arms around my shoulders in a brief hug and then took a step back.

'For once, Stutter, I wasn't taking the piss,' he drawled with a wink. 'Let's get out of dodge.'

My cheeks warmed. Hopefully, the makeup and all the fake blood would cover it from him.

He reached for my hand, and I entwined my fingers with his. The moment we left the suite, we had to be switched on.

What with the campus once again crawling with teachers and students, the act needed to be even more believable at all times.

And the entire time, I had to remind myself that none of it was real.

It could *never* be real.

THE PARTY WAS in full swing by the time we walked into the clearing, the bass of the music thumping all around, and a large crowd of people dancing in the centre.

Like the last Halloween party, witches, ghouls, and ghosts hung from the trees, and the punch bowl had fake eyeballs floating in it. I guessed they'd reused the decorations, which surprised me. I thought rich fuckers enjoyed flaunting their wealth and always used it to buy new things, even when they didn't need to.

Myth busted. Well, for teenage students throwing a Halloween party in the woods at their expensive private school at least.

'Ello, ello, ello,' called Griff, as he sauntered over with Clover on his arm. The two of them were dressed as Hercules and Megara and the effect the two of them had on those around them was clear. They looked great together and happy. Genuinely happy. Leo elbowed me in the ribs, but for once our telepathy was dried up and I had no clue why he'd elbowed me.

'Hello yourself,' I replied, smiling at Griff. Just being in the boy's presence made me feel content. 'You two look great!'

'Thanks,' Clo said, beaming at me. Then she looked at Leo

standing at my side and at our clasped hands, frowning. 'You look great too, Sky. Shame about the dead weight.'

She looked Leo up-and-down with disgust.

'He is a super dead mobster and I guess that's pretty weighty,' I said, laughing off her negative vibes. We weren't going to let Clover bring us down. Fuck that.

'Oh, don't listen to old sourpuss here,' Griff said, nudging her in the ribcage. 'Both of you look beautiful.' He batted his eyelashes at us both, causing me to giggle at him.

'So, where's the booze?' I asked, taking my hand away from Leo's and grabbing Clo's arm. The two of us made our way over to the table, laden with alcohol, leaving the boys standing together.

As soon as we were out of earshot, I hissed, 'Where is he?'

'Not here yet,' she replied, knowing without his name who I was referring to. 'He'll be here. It's his birthday party after all.'

'I know. Just thought he'd be here already.' The two of us had reached the table, and I stood surveying the area while Clo went hunting. 'I haven't spoken to him alone since... well, I can't even remember.'

'He's not yours to care about anymore, remember?' Clo said, emphasis on the end of her sentence. 'You're with Leo, and happy, so get the fuck over it.'

She was right, but something still sat unwelcome in the pit of my stomach. Hopefully, it was just gas.

'I'm sure he just wants to make an entrance,' Clo added with a shrug and I nodded, even though I thought that was bullshit. Ollie may be a dick, and he may have the shithole we called a school believing he ruled it, but I knew the truth. He hated the attention and he didn't have his crap together. If he were anybody else, I may even feel sorry for him a little. But it was Ollie, and all I felt was slight dislike—and potentially some lust.

'Here comes the birthday boy!' a voice hollered, breaking up the party.

I stand corrected. But then, when I glimpsed at who was attached to Ollie's body like a python, I knew whose idea it had been to make a late attention-seeking entrance, and it definitely wasn't Ollie.

Ophelia had come dressed as Britney, circa 2001 VMAs. You know, the performance with a snake, pre-head shave? I hated to admit it, but the girl looked fucking stunning. Her bruises had faded and she looked as if she'd never been beaten in the very woods she stood in. I scoffed, keeping up pretences, then looked at Oralie, who was standing next to the couple.

Oralie had taken the sexy memo even further and had come dressed as Britney's rival, 2002 *Dirrty* era Christina. Chaps and all. Jeez, the two of them had really pulled out all the stops to be the most talked about girls in the school.

Ollie clearly hadn't got the early 2000s mandate, as he was dressed like a vampire. I couldn't decide if he was meant to be Edward Cullen or maybe Stefan or Damon. Either way, he looked hot. Surprised they hadn't tried to convince him to double denim it up and come as JT.

Celia and Cordelia were traipsing behind them, in what I could only describe as an oversized scarf that barely covered anything. Maybe they were Romans? They must be freezing— and if they weren't, they would be in an hour or two. October on a hill in England did not make for good partying conditions at the best of times. My faux fur coat was thick and I was still shivering!

'Fucking hell,' Clover said, handing me a drink. I took a sip and spat it out again. Man, that tasted bad! Maybe I should worry that the eyeballs in the bowl were real?

'Is there anything else?' I asked. ''Cause this is vile.'

'Think there are some alcopops,' Clover said, rooting through the ice bucket by her feet. 'Oh wait.'

She straightened, and in her hand was a bottle of vanilla vodka.

'You've hit the motherload,' I replied and in a fit of excitement, kissed her on the cheek.

'Sure you haven't been hitting the hard stuff to pre-game?' she asked, her eyebrow raised in question.

'Nope.' I laughed, knowing she didn't believe me. 'Swear. We're both sober as.'

'Hm.' She mumbled under her breath something I couldn't make out while pouring us some diet cola and vanilla vodkas.

'Thanks,' I said as she handed me my fresh drink. I took a sip and sighed in relief. 'Much better.'

'I'm glad.' She looked around, and her next words were spoken out of the side of her mouth. 'Ollie incoming.'

'Wonderful,' I muttered. I'd been expecting him to seek me out, but I had hoped I'd have Leo by my side when it happened. A buffer of sorts.

'Clover,' he greeted when he was close enough to the two of us. 'Skylar.'

Neither of us spoke back. We just sort of nodded. The barest hint of an acknowledgement we could get away with without being seen as rude.

'Can I talk to you?' he asked, reaching out to touch my wrist. The moment his fingers grazed my bare skin, I felt electricity run from the spot he touched to every single inch of my body.

'S-sure,' I replied, as Clo asked me with her eyes if I was

sure. I tilted my head, thinking it over for a moment, then gave a brief nod. 'I'll see you in a bit, Clo.'

Clo walked off, back over to where Griff and Leo were still standing, without even a 'see you later'. I watched her go, knowing that if I looked at Ollie, I'd probably drool a little. No matter how hard I tried, I wasn't immune to his charms.

'You look fucking perfect,' he said, causing a blush to rise on my cheeks and on my chest, too.

'Leo mentioned, yeah,' I said, knowing it would rile him up but unable to stop my tongue. The small sip of alcohol I'd had was already making me bold.

'Bet he didn't mention you look good enough to eat.'

'I'd rather you didn't,' I said without giving it any thought. It felt nice not to lose my head in his presence. Okay, there was still a chance I would put my foot in my mouth, but fuck, couldn't a girl be happy to get out one sentence without stumbling over every word?

'Shame. I think we'd both enjoy it.' His voice oozed sex appeal, and if I had been alone, I'd have been fanning myself to cool down. 'You always did in the past.'

'I think you're delusional.'

His lips formed a small smile, and I found my gaze focused on his full lips. Knowing what it felt like to kiss those lips, have those lips exploring my body, my mind started wandering somewhere else.

'Your boyfriend is watching us,' he spat, and if I didn't know better, I'd think he was jealous. 'He can't take his eyes off you.'

'Of course,' I said. 'I am his girl, after all.'

I still wasn't the best at flirting or acting seductive, but I hoped my words were having the desired effect.

'His girl? Still?' he growled, taking a step closer to me.

Automatically, I took a step back, trying to keep the distance between us. 'Tell me how the fuck that works, Sky.'

'Exactly how you expect it to, Oliver,' I spat out, anger simmering. 'We fuck. We're together.'

I tried to maintain eye contact with his indigo blues, hoping he couldn't hear—or see—the lie I'd just put out into the universe. I'd made it sound like we were at it like rabbits.

'You've fucked him?' Once again, he stepped closer, his tone even lower, the growl darker.

I looked at Leo standing across the clearing. He looked as if he was about to come over and intervene. I shook my head, trying to convey with my eyes I was okay and that I didn't need him—yet.

'Yes,' I said, clear and unwavering. 'Often.'

A low growl left his throat. An actual growl. Like a beast. 'Tell me this. Has Leo heard your stutter with his dick deep inside you?'

I tried to keep my face from heating as I thought of the memory. 'Of course.'

'When?' he bit out, his face pained.

'We've been together since summer, so it's happened more than once.'

'Before?' he asked, his voice small.

'Before?' I repeated, not sure I understood.

'Before we...' He looked uncomfortable and brushed his hand through his hair. 'Before the last time?'

I saw a fork in the path before me. One of those decisions I'd spoken to Clover about back when I first returned to Hawthorn. How you always had forks in the path, each one leading to a different future. On one hand, I could lie to him and say I slept with Leo before the last time we hooked up, even though I hadn't. *Or* I could tell the truth. What did I actually gain by lying?

But the truth probably wasn't going to go down well, either. Was it worse to have slept with Leo before I hooked up with Ollie last, or to have hooked up with Ollie and then fallen into Leo's arms?

I went with the truth.

'No,' I replied. 'Not before.'

'Right,' he said in a whisper. He coughed and seemed to knock off whatever thought ran through his mind. 'Can we go somewhere more private to talk?'

'You want to leave your birthday party to talk to me?' I asked, then added, 'Happy birthday, Ollie.'

'Thanks.' His eyes wrinkled at the edges, a smile covering the bottom of his face. 'Can't believe I'm eighteen.'

'You're getting old,' I joked. 'You don't look it, though, so that's a good thing, right?'

He shook his head, his eyes once again glinting with malice. 'Let's go further into the trees.'

'I never said we could leave this spot.'

'You didn't have to.' He turned away from me and started walking, so cocksure I would trail behind.

'I don't want to,' I grumbled but followed him regardless. A large part of me was curious, and unlike the cat, I wasn't dead yet.

With one last glance of assurance to Leo, I followed Ollie at a fast enough pace to keep up with him, not wanting to lose sight of him.

He stopped, far enough away we could only hear the music from the party as a low hum. The bass thumped in the background, but the music itself was indecipherable.

'Sky, there is so much you don't understand.' Our gazes locked, and I wished I could see behind the façade. See the truth. *His* truth. 'So much you need to know.'

'So explain.'

'I can't,' he said, reaching out to touch my arm, lazily running his fingers up and down. 'Not right now. But I want to. Badly.'

'You wanted to talk to me,' I said, irritated that he'd taken me away from the party and my friends just to tell me pointless shit I'd already heard. 'Why ask me to talk if you're not gonna actually talk?'

'And I do. Want to, I mean. I just *can't*.'

'You can't?' My foot began tapping on the woodland floor. Patience wasn't my strong suit. 'Why?'

'If I told you that, I'd have to kill you,' he said with a sad smile. It felt strangely human for somebody so inhuman at times.

'Oh, ha-ha.'

'We can't talk here. Can you meet me tomorrow?' he asked, his other hand reaching out to me, until both of his hands were on me, my arms clammy through the faux fur from his warmth.

'Where?' I asked him, wondering what he wanted. My interest piqued. I should've flat out denied him, but one thing I'd learned about myself during my time at Hawthorn was that I struggled to deny Ollie anything.

'My room?' he asked, and I shook my head violently.

'Not happening,' I growled. 'Somewhere else.'

'Fine,' he bit out. 'The library?'

'Fine.' I smiled but turned it into a frown as soon as it registered. 'Can I go now?'

'You could stay,' he said wistfully. 'We could enjoy the party together.'

'No, I really couldn't,' I said with a sad smile and a shrug of my shoulders. I walked away before he could say any more. Before he could convince me to stay.

And I knew myself well enough to know that if he'd kissed me, all bets were off.

Welcome back, petty, horny, bitch Skylar.

Thirty-Nine

'DRINK!' I shouted, gesturing at Griff's almost empty cup.

The four of us had decided that the only way to get through the evening, without hurting anybody or starting any arguments, was to get drunk. *Really* fucking drunk.

And what better way to get drunk than to play *Ring of Fire*, followed by *Bullshit Taxi* and then to top it off, the pièce de résistance, *I Have Never*.

Yeah, I was questioning my life choices, too.

'I have never had sex with somebody playing this game,' uttered a random girl from year ten dressed as a nurse. The girls she'd joined the group with all broke out into titters, excited in the way girls got whenever something juicy was about to be said.

I took a drink, as did Leo, Griff, and Clo. I hoped Clo didn't look at me because Ollie wasn't playing, and it was obvious then who I was drinking for. But when I looked over at her, she was staring at Leo, a blush on her cheeks.

Guess that was confirmation enough that he and Clover had fucked in the past. I'd guessed at it, but having the evidence in front of me was nauseating—more than the copious amounts of alcohol swishing around in my stomach.

Drunk Skylar was crude, clearly. And thought of herself in the third person. I giggled but then remembered what I was thinking about.

Without meaning to, I got mad and a little jealous. All she needed to do now was fuck Ollie, and she'd have hit a *Sect* trifecta. I scoffed.

'You okay, Stutter?' Leo leaned in to whisper in my ear, and I shivered. He kissed my cheek, gentle and sweet. 'You've gone quiet.'

'Yep,' I replied, trying not to sound like a miserable bitch, but most likely failing miserably. Maybe I could blame it on the alcohol?

'Really?' he asked, his tone filled with teasing. 'Sure, it has nothing to do with what you just had confirmed?'

I nodded, gulping. He could see right through me—it hit me that he always had. 'Nothing at all.'

'Sky,' he whispered, and my skin set aflame. 'That was a long time ago. A time I rarely even think about.'

I took another sip of my drink to avoid talking more. I couldn't trust my tongue. Leo leaned back with a small sigh, but not before kissing my cheek again.

Still caught up in my swirling thoughts, I wasn't paying much attention to the game when a commotion came from the left-hand side of the clearing. People were shouting something unintelligible from where we were and a girl screeched. 'Has anybody seen Ollie?'

Ophelia.

She was stumbling through the clearing, but at least she was stumbling because of her inebriation, not because she'd been hurt. When nobody replied, she screeched her question again.

'Nope,' Griff called out, chuckling when she tripped over a

branch. Maybe she shouldn't have been wearing such high heels on the woodland floor. 'When'd you last see him?'

'At least half an hour ago,' she spat out as Oralie helped her stand. It was like watching a baby deer flailing around, trying to find their legs. *Cute.*

'Did he not say anything before he went?' Leo asked, a crease between his eyebrows. I wanted to reach out and smooth it out but refrained. The moment seemed too serious for affection somehow. 'Or tell you where he was headed?'

'Just that he had somewhere he needed to be,' she said with a shrug of her shivering shoulders—I knew her outfit would give her frostbite—having now drawn the attention of everybody here.

Somebody cut the music and an eerie hush descended across the area. The couples who had been dirty dancing on the makeshift dance floor looked dazed and confused, like they'd just woken up from a trance.

'Odd,' Griff said but didn't sound overly worried. Nobody else knew what to say. Ollie was an eighteen-year-old boy, who had left his own party for unknown reasons sure, but it didn't mean anything nefarious was going on. Shitting hell, for all we knew he could have just headed back to his room, wanting to be away from it all.

I wouldn't blame him.

My mind recalled the look on his face when he'd asked me to meet him tomorrow. I'd tried to pass it off in my head as sinister or insincere, but when I wasn't breathing in his scent, I could see it for what it was. He'd been unsure to ask me— uncertain, for maybe the first time in the year I'd known him.

Something was wrong. I could sense it. Maybe it was the ghost of Halloween past, but I knew we needed to find him. My gut was sending me warning signs.

I leaned over to Leo and whispered in his ear, 'You don't think?'

I'd told him everything Ollie had said to me. Had asked him whether he thought I should meet with him or not, and Leo had convinced me to go and hear Ollie out.

'Don't think what?' he muttered.

'That he may be hurt?' I looked around the clearing. 'Or maybe hurt himself?'

'Why would you ask that?' Leo questioned, catching my eye. 'Do you know something?'

I shook my head. 'But I don't know... Something feels off about this whole thing. One year ago to the day somebody tried to drown me. Maybe it isn't a coincidence?' I'd tried not to think about it all night—tried not to replay the events of last year—but once I had thought of it, I could think of nothing else. No matter how many times Clover implicated Ollie, I just knew it wasn't him. Even knowing about his scheme to make my life hell still didn't have me believing he'd tried to murder me. 'We should at least look for him. If we find him unharmed, then whatever, at least we checked, you know?'

'Okay. You're right.' Leo's smile stopped the guilt swirling around inside me. 'Shall we go check his room?'

I nodded and mumbled, 'Please.'

Leo stood up, brushed the dirt off his trousers, and reached down his hand for me so he could help me stand. Ever the perfect gentleman these days.

'Come on then,' he said, a twinkle in his eye, and I couldn't help but swoon a little at him. 'Let's go find the prick.'

I reached into my pocket for my phone, thinking maybe Ollie had sent me a text or something. Instead of my phone, my fingers found a wrinkled piece of paper. Déjà vu hit me like a fucking truck. It had last year written all over it. I pulled it out of my pocket and it read:

Sky,
Meet me in the pool house at midnight.
I want to ring in my birthday with you. And only you.

Lost for words and breath, I handed the piece of paper to Leo. The moment he read it, he swore under his breath. He saw what I did. It was the same wording as the note I received last Halloween. The one that led me to the pool house to be nearly drowned. The note Ollie had sworn he had nothing to do with.

'What time is it?' I whispered, my fingers not listening to my brain as I fumbled around in my pocket to grab my phone.

'Quarter past,' Leo replied, bleak. 'Guess we know where to look.'

The two of us trudged back towards the school, avoiding the sloppy drunk people who were stumbling around every-where. My drink buzz was wearing off, and the cold had crept in slowly, even through my massive coat. Leo's hand firmly in mine was the only warmth.

Eventually, we came upon the school, and in the darkness it loomed in all its gothic glory. Even after so much time, the architecture of the school took my breath away any time I looked at it. It reminded me of the European gothic cathedrals. All towers and spikes. The gargoyles' beady eyes followed us as we moved at a fast pace to the pool house—all-seeing and all-knowing. It had taken us at least fifteen minutes to get to the school, and the note had said to meet thirty minutes ago. Maybe he left after ten minutes, thinking I'd rejected the invi-tation, and we were worrying about nothing. I hoped we were worrying about nothing.

He must have put the note in my pocket when we spoke away from the party. *If* he gave me the note and it wasn't another fake like last time.

The person who stabbed me still hadn't been revealed and, although I didn't mention it much because I didn't want to dwell on the negative, it plagued me every night. The face of the culprit was still unknown to me. My memories were still lost in the deep recesses of my brain.

Silence greeted us the moment we entered the pool building, and if we were in a movie, crickets would be chirping.

The pool room itself was silent, too, the gentle lapping of water the only noise. The room was dimly lit, the waves reflecting on the ceiling the exact same way they had last Halloween, with the moonlight shining through the window highlighting the pool in all its glory.

'Shit!' Leo shouted, letting go of my hand and rushing toward the edge of the pool. His terror filled me, settling in my gut, and my gaze followed his path.

There. Lying face down in the pool. *A body.*

A body dressed in a tight black T-shirt and jeans.

'Help me!' Leo shouted, wading into the pool until he reached Ollie. He gripped Ollie's collar and with excruciating slowness, he dragged him over to the edge. My legs had locked in place, and I wasn't sure I had the strength to help Leo get Ollie out of the water.

'Is he breathing?' I asked, my voice shrill and panicked in my ears.

'Just,' Leo whispered. He pushed as I pulled and with a lot of effort, we got Ollie out of the water. 'Call Griff,' he demanded, starting to administer CPR.

Being the assistant swim coach, I knew Leo had undergone real training, and I had faith in his ability.

With shaking hands, I dialled Griff, who answered on the first ring.

'Yo, Clouds. Where are you?'

'Come q-quick,' I blurted. 'It's Ollie.'

'Where are you?' he repeated, his tone urgent, picking up on my panic.

'In the pool house.'

'We'll be there in two,' he said, hanging up without a goodbye.

'Is there anything I c-can do?'

Leo didn't waste any time in responding to me, and the only thing I could do was stand there feeling like a spare part, watching as he tried to save Ollie's life. Dread sat low in my stomach. Not only did I know how Ollie was feeling, but I also knew how he must have felt when it was me lying unconscious on the tiled floor last year.

Because no matter what he did to me last year, I knew in my heart he hadn't been the one to hold me under that water. It was a gut feeling, and I had no proof, but I just knew.

Wish I knew who had held me under.

A laboured gasp left Ollie's throat, and Leo let out a nervous laugh. Ollie started to retch and I looked away when the trapped water from his lungs came up. It brought back the memories of how wretched it felt, how hard it was to take a breath, and the impaired vision. My breathing sped up.

No, Skylar. I told myself. *This isn't the time for a panic attack!*

To take my mind away from my panic, I moved to sit down beside Ollie and Leo, not caring that I'd get wet. The heavy door opened, and the sound of the hinges reverberated throughout the room.

'Fuck!' Griff called out. 'What happened?'

'He was in the water facedown when we got here,' I replied,

letting Griff hug me when he got down on the floor beside me. Clover stood awkwardly behind the group, her face pale and eyes glazed over. Maybe she was having déjà vu, too.

I rubbed my cheek, surprised to find it wet. I'd started to cry without realising it, but as soon as I knew I was crying, the tears came thick and fast.

'Sky,' Ollie groaned, and I threw myself onto him, draping myself across his chest before realising he'd just been struggling to breathe and maybe it wasn't the best idea I'd had. *Shit.*

Like he was infectious, I pulled myself back at once, chuckled, and stammered out, 'You scared the f-fuck out of us.'

A faint smile graced his lips that was more of a grimace.

'We need to get you to the hospital wing, dude,' Griff said. 'Check that you're okay.'

'No,' Ollie whispered, his breathing strained still. A faint rattle with every breath.

'P-please,' I begged, grasping his hand tightly in mine. His were cold and, for once, not giving me any comfort. 'I'll go with you.'

Leo looked at me, and I saw his slight nod. Whatever I decided to do, he'd have my back.

'No'—Ollie squeezed my hand, and I tore my gaze away from Leo's, settling back onto Ollie's face—'let's go to my room.'

'You should go to the hospital wing,' I said, but then I remembered last year it had been Leo wanting me to go there, not Ollie. Ollie hadn't wanted me to go there either but was outvoted.

'My room,' he repeated. No room for argument.

'We'll come with you,' Leo said and the two of us worked together to help Ollie into a sitting position. After he'd caught his breath a bit, we helped him to stand.

I knew the attention had to be killing him—that he hated being seen as weak. He despised having others look at him as anything less than all-powerful.

Griff took over my position, putting his arm around Ollie for support, and the three of them began to make their way out of the room, Ollie leaning on them both.

Clover and I stayed rooted to the spot, watching the three members of *The Sect* walk away in silence. I sighed and reached out to grab her hand. She startled, shocked I'd initiated contact. Fuck, I barely let the girl hug me without putting up a fight. I just wasn't the touchy-feely type.

'We should follow them,' I whispered, worried that if I raised my voice, the moment would become even more real.

'Let's,' Clo replied, giving my hand a reassuring squeeze. 'It'll be okay, Sky.'

My head hurt; my heart hurt.

One thing I knew for certain.

Halloween is cursed.

Forty

WHEN I OPENED MY EYES, it took a moment for my vision to adjust to my surroundings. The room was dark and unfamiliar at first, then the events of the previous evening hit me.

Halloween. Ollie's birthday party. The pool house. Finding Ollie facedown, lifeless.

I was in Ollie's room.

A heavy arm rested across my chest. An arm that was also attached to the hard body pressed up against my back. A constant gentle snoring in my ear. I looked around the room, making sure I didn't move enough to wake Leo—the snoring culprit.

After we'd taken Ollie back to his room, he'd instantly got into bed and fallen asleep before telling any of us anything. As a group, we decided he shouldn't be left alone, so Leo and I had volunteered to stay just in case and that was how we'd found ourselves sharing Ollie's sofa.

Not gonna lie. It was surprisingly comfy and spacious. Leo wasn't a small guy, after all, what with all those swimmer's muscles he hid under his clothes.

He looked so peaceful in sleep. Serene. I had to stop the

urge to run my fingers through his hair—something he rarely allowed me to do when he was awake—and leave him undisturbed.

Slowly, I peeled his arm from around me so I could go to the toilet. He didn't stir, so I hotfooted it to the bathroom, hoping he'd stay in the comfy position I'd left him in and that my space would still be free when I returned.

On my return from the bathroom, I heard a grumble.

'Still going to the toilet five-plus times a night?' Ollie asked. His words made me jump, and I swore under my breath.

'You know me well,' I replied, pausing in my path. For some reason, I hadn't expected him to be awake and knowing he was made going back to Leo's arms feel wrong somehow.

'How about we have that talk now?'

'I...' I tried to come up with a reason why it wasn't the best idea, but honestly, I couldn't think of an excuse that sounded plausible enough. Plus, I doubted I'd be able to fall asleep again knowing he was lying awake so close. 'Yeah, sure.'

I tiptoed to his bed and found him already sitting up, waiting for me, his back resting against the headboard. Sitting on the edge seemed like the best bet, but of course he had to ruin it.

'Get in with me,' he demanded, his voice low but firm as he lifted the duvet and shifted over to make space. 'I won't bite.'

My head swivelled to where Leo was asleep on the sofa, then nodded. After the night Ollie had, I couldn't deny him anything. Even if I knew I should.

Once I was under the cover, I positioned myself up against the headboard, making sure the two of us weren't touching.

We had too many memories together in his bed—too many instances I looked back on and doubted. Every memory was shaded with the deeds that came after. All the good, now rotten.

'Do you like him?' he asked, and without saying his name, I knew he meant Leo. Of course he did. Wasn't like I was flaunting my relationship with anybody else right in front of his face.

'You already asked that at the end of summer, remember? And I told you I did.'

'And that was a couple of months ago. I'm asking whether you like him *now*.'

'I do,' I whispered back, hoping that the dark lighting in the room meant he couldn't see the flush on my face. 'More than when you last asked.'

'Right.' In an instant, he gripped my chin between his thumb and forefinger so we were looking into one another's eyes. 'Look me in the eye and tell me you enjoy fucking him.'

'Y-yes,' I stammered, hoping he couldn't see the swirl of emotions in my eyes. I'd only slept with Leo the one time, but Ollie believed it happened often, and I didn't want him to know I'd lied, but I also didn't want to kick him while he was already down.

'Yes?' he whispered, his breath fanning my face. 'That all you have to say about it?'

'If I didn't enjoy f-fucking him, I wouldn't be with him,' I replied quietly, meaning it, but feeling bad that I did for multiple reasons. It made me sound like good sex was all I cared about in a relationship, which wasn't true, but it also wasn't completely false either. Not that I had much experience. The two guys I'd slept with both happened to be in the room.

Ollie let go of my chin, and I rubbed the spot where his fingers had been. The only bruise being the one on my mind.

He growled low in his throat, and sitting in his bed beside

him in the dark the way we were, I'd be lying if I didn't admit the situation flustered me. His growl did a thing to my insides, turning them into a big pile of jelly.

I needed to change the subject away from sex. 'W-what happened tonight?' I whispered, feeling braver once we weren't staring at each other. The darkness hid a lot.

'I went to wait for you,' he said, taking the bait. Or allowing me to change the subject, knowing it was my intention. Didn't care which.

'You gave me that note?' My nerves were climbing, and I was wringing my hands together, mostly to take my focus off him and the emotions swirling in me.

He tilted his neck to look up at the ceiling. 'Yeah. I hoped you'd see it in time and went there to wait just in case.'

'Did you get a sick thrill out of the wording?' There was an edge to my tone. Sharp as a blade. Cutting.

'I thought you'd appreciate the play on words,' he said. 'Or at least would recognise them and be curious enough to come find out what I wanted.'

'You replicated the note from last year on purpose?' I stopped fidgeting and turned to face him. 'Knowing what happened to me that night?'

'Yeah,' he said, a bite of regret lingering in that one word. 'Sounds shitty, I know, but I didn't realise just how fucked up it was until I almost drowned myself tonight.'

'Well, I didn't see the note at all until after midnight. Ophelia came screeching into the clearing, announcing you'd gone missing.'

'Having too much fun with *Leo* to notice my absence?' he spat.

'Jealousy isn't a good look on you.' I took a deep breath. Fuck being treated like shit all because Ollie had a case of the green-eyed monster. I didn't need to stay and have him snap at me. 'Griff and Clo could have stayed tonight, you know? Leo and I could have gone back to his suite and ended the night the way we'd intended to.'

Okay. I'll admit it's a low blow, but he deserves it.

'So, why did you then?' He shuffled an inch closer. 'Stay, I mean.'

'Honestly?' I looked at him, and he nodded slightly, urging me to go on. 'I couldn't leave you even if I wanted to. You never left me last year, and neither did Leo, so it only made sense we both stayed for you this time. Let's not have a repeat where we watch over Leo, ay?'

I tried to ignore the overwhelming sense of shame I felt at being so open and honest with him. I didn't owe him honesty; I didn't owe him shit.

He owed *me*. But in the dark of the night, things were different. Things you'd never say in the light come out to play.

'Let's not,' he whispered, inching closer once again. The tiny hint of light coming in through the window glinted in his eyes, shining with vulnerability. 'Why couldn't you leave?'

'You nearly died, Ollie,' I said softly. 'No matter what happens, I'll never want you dead.'

'Somebody clearly does.'

'You're not alone there,' I said. 'Somebody wants me dead, too.'

He smiled. 'Feels like I should reiterate that whoever it is, it isn't me.'

'Thanks. I'd already come to that conclusion myself, but I'm glad.' I wanted to get the conversation back on track. Back to the events of the night, so we could get to the talk he wanted us to have, and then I could go back to the sofa and fall asleep in another guy's arms. *Classy, Skylar.* Just gut the boy, why don't you? Would be quicker. 'So, you were waiting there for me?'

'Yeah.' Our gazes locked. 'I heard the door open, but I didn't look, worried I'd scare you away if I was too full-on the moment you arrived. Or maybe I was worried I'd turn to see you and Leo enter together, even though I'd asked you to come alone.'

'Go on,' I said in a breathy tone. The only other noise in my ears was my fast beating heart, and though I felt certain he could hear it, I knew he couldn't.

'Next thing I knew, somebody strong had come up behind me and dragged me over to the water. Pushed me in and held my head under.' He blinked, the memory still so fresh.

Tears formed in my eyes, unbidden. The story sounded so familiar—*too* familiar.

He continued, 'I tried to fight them off, to get out of their grip, but I couldn't. They were too strong and had a better angle than me.'

'I know what that feels like.'

'Eerily similar, right?' he asked, and I nodded, not knowing what else to say.

Wiping a tear away from under my eye, Ollie gave me a small, tentative smile.

'I hate you,' I whispered, tasting the lie the second the words formed.

'No, you don't.'

'No, I don't.' I sighed, tired of the bullshit and also just so goddamn tired of everything. Things had shifted between us after he'd saved me from Mr Hawkins' unwanted advances, and it didn't mean I forgave him for everything that came before it. Of course not. Yet having an open conversation with him made me see the times in our relationship last year that were real—or at least I thought they were. Without asking him, I could only guess.

He sighed. 'I don't hate you.'

I started. Those four words weren't what I had expected to hear. 'You d-don't?'

'No.' His light blue eyes were full of an emotion I couldn't place. 'I just wish I did.'

'Why, though?' I asked, ready for whatever answer he gave. He'd wanted to talk to me, and he had the perfect opportunity to tell me everything. Only he could decide whether he was going to take it. 'I've never done anything to you. Fuck, Ollie, you didn't even *know* me when I first started here.'

'It's complicated. What's Griff told you?'

'Griff?' My nose wrinkled, and I frowned. 'Is he meant to have told me something?'

'Has he mentioned your dad?' he asked, and it was as if a lightbulb went off inside my brain. Finally, some answers. Real answers and not just some half-arsed crap.

'Not much. Our dads were brothers, but my dad went off the grid when Griff was young,' I replied. 'That's why he didn't go live with him when his parents died.'

'Going off the grid is one way of putting it,' he said with a low chuckle that held no humour.

'Well, how would you put it, then?' I asked, trying not to let him know how much I wanted to know. How much of a burning desire I had deep down. If he knew how desperate I was for him to keep talking, he may keep it locked away, knowing I'd talk to him again to find out what he knew.

My head hit the pillow with a dull thunk, and some time during our conversation, the two of us had slid down the headboard and repositioned ourselves so we were lying side by side, facing one another. I could move back to a safer position, or I could stay put and hear whatever Ollie had to say. So I chose to get comfy, plumping the pillow, making it easier to rest on.

'Your dad stole a lot of Hawthorn money,' he said, not beating around the bush. Calm and factual. 'Then left town, never to be seen again.'

'How?' I asked, confused. 'Why?'

'Nobody knows. Just that he did and then disappeared into thin air.'

I scoffed and told him, 'Nobody can disappear into thin air. And surely somebody knows how he stole the money or at least where from.'

'True,' Ollie agreed. 'Somebody helped him.'

'Right...'

'That's not the worst of it, though. Your dad'—he paused, at a loss for words—'your dad, he'—he took a deep breath —'he had an affair with my mum.'

I squirmed under his intense gaze. *Griff definitely didn't mention that.*

'When?' I said, barely audible. 'How do you know?'

'When I was young, aged five to nine. It finished just before my mum ended her life. I only remember a little of it, but I remember the arguments between my mum and dad. Shit got bad.'

I stayed silent, hoping he'd continue if I said nothing. It was like the time he'd first spoken to me about his mum, where I could see on his face he wanted to get something off his chest but had spent so long bottling it up, he didn't know how to spit the words out.

'Dad was controlling, like I told you before, and I guess your dad was giving her something mine wasn't?' He glanced away. 'I've never asked my dad about it. Once Mum died, it became a taboo subject.'

'That makes sense,' I mumbled. I'd never even met the guy everybody was talking about. I'd only known of his existence for the last seven months, and really, he was still a figment to me. I'd never even seen a picture. 'Do you remember him?'

'Who?' His eyebrows knitted, deep in thought. 'Your dad?'

'Yeah,' I fidgeted, plumping my pillow again and trying to snuggle further under the cover. 'What was he like?'

'I don't know. In my mind, he just sort of blurs with Uncle Damien.'

'They were identical?' I asked, wracking my brain to remember if Griff had told me.

'No, but as a child, they seemed very similar. Not like Mum and Aunt Eliza.'

Without even thinking my next sentence through, I blurted out, 'Bit weird that Damien and Jacob were banging twins, right?'

When my words registered, I winced. That was our parents I was talking about. *Gross.*

Ollie's face transformed in an instant, his jaw clenched and his eyes glared a hole in my soul. Instantly, I knew I needed to take back my words to get us back to the calm, open conversation we'd been having. *Trust me to put my foot in it.*

'I'm so sorry. I have literally no idea where that came from.' I put my face into the pillow, wanting it to swallow me up. 'I didn't even think about it before I said it.'

'It's okay,' he said, reaching out to force me to face him again. Looking into his eyes, I didn't believe him—he'd closed off from me. Shut down. *Idiot me.*

'What are we doing?' I blurted out, reminding myself Leo was still in the room, asleep on the sofa. He'd been silent, except for the odd snore.

'Sky, you know we could be good together.' His blue eyes

were looking deep into mine, trying to look beyond the surface —to look into my soul. 'Deep down, you know we're meant to be together.'

'I do?' I asked, but he was sort of right. We *could* be good together. If y'know, he'd acted like less of a trash human.

'I know I've made your time here hard, and I was a total dick last year.'

I laughed. 'Last year? You were a dick last month!'

'I deserve that,' he admitted. The two of us had moved even closer together, only a couple of inches separating our bodies, and the heat emanating from him was drawing me in. 'But you can feel this.'

I could. I could feel the heat, the chemistry, and *fuck*, I wanted him.

But I also wanted the other boy in the room, the one who was sleeping through it all. Or, knowing Leo the way I did, the boy was lying awake listening but staying quiet.

'Yeah,' I whispered, 'but that doesn't always change things.'

'I know,' he whispered and gave me a light kiss on the forehead. 'I wish it did.'

'Wishing doesn't change anything,' I whispered. 'I need to get back to sleep. I'm shattered.'

'Go.' He looked at me wistfully. 'I wish I could fall asleep with you once more.'

'Well, maybe if you'd meant everything the first time around, you still would be.' With that, I slunk out of the bed and padded as silently as I could back to the sofa. Sliding under the cover, I got in while Leo made a great show of grumbling about the cold, but I could see through his phoney act.

Kissing him on the lips shut him up.

'Come here,' he said, his voice soft and alluring. He opened his arms, and I moved in between them, settling in a comfortable place, and the weight of them made me feel safe.

A small pressure on the top of my head made me smile.

'Night, baby,' he said.

'G'night, bub,' I replied, snuggling down in his arms.

'Night, Ollie,' Leo called, purposely baiting him out. I jabbed him sharply with my elbow, and he chuckled low in my ear. 'You love it.'

Shit. Maybe I do?

One thing was certain.

I was monumentally screwed.

Forty-One

A COUPLE of days after Halloween, I was in the library, working through the yearbooks from 1993 to 2000.

Flo, the librarian, had hooked me up. When I'd asked for her help, I was worried she'd tell Ms Hawthorn I was looking into the school's history, but I'd not been called into her office, so I was in the clear.

I started with the book from 1993 first, when the parents were age eleven and twelve, bright-eyed and bushy-tailed. Eager.

Flicking through to find their class photo, a chill ran down my spine, as the scent of tobacco and vanilla entered my nose.

Of course Ollie had shown up at the exact moment I was about to look at pictures of our parents.

'What you got there?' he asked, slotting himself into the seat opposite me.

'Yearbook,' I grunted, not even looking up at him. I'd found the class photo and searched the names first, so I would know where to find the parents.

My heart skipped a beat.

Shit, I was about to see a picture of my dad. The man who gave me life and then left Cora in the cold. I'd seen a picture of

Griff's dad, so I had an idea of what he could look like, but I still felt nervous. It was different.

'Are you okay?' Ollie asked, and I looked up at him. Mostly to prevent myself from looking for Jacob on the page.

I took a deep breath, gearing myself up to speak to him. 'Honestly? I don't know.'

I looked back down at the book, but my eyes weren't seeing anything. The entire page had become a bottle green blur. Funny how the uniform hadn't changed much in thirty years.

His hand reached out and covered mine on the page. 'I'm here.'

Wanting to put off looking at the page a second longer, I looked up and got trapped in Ollie's stare. He had beautiful blue eyes at the best of times, but at that moment, they looked even better. Maybe that had something to do with there not being lies between us anymore.

Reverse that.

Maybe it had something to do with there not being *as many* lies between us anymore.

He took his hand off mine and leaned forward across the desk. 'Who's that?'

'The year seven class of '93,' I told him, removing my hand so he could look at the page with me. 'Your mum and dad are in the picture.'

'I guessed they would be.' He squinted, leaning closer. His hair brushed my forehead, and I giggled at the tickling sensation. 'There's Mum.'

He pointed to a girl sitting in the front row, her smile wide and her hair in two braids. I could see the resemblance between her and Ollie; they had the same startling blue eyes.

He gave a dark chuckle and shook his head.

'Of course she's sitting next to Eliza.' He pointed again, but even if he hadn't, I would have known who he was talking about. Millie and Eliza were identical in every way. The two of them were even holding hands like some kind of shining twin shit.

'Were they always together?' I asked, partially because I was curious, but also partially because I was avoiding finding Damien and Jacob Cooper in the line-up.

'Inseparable,' he muttered. 'Or so people always say when they talk about them. I don't have too many memories of them both alive.'

My heart panged, and sympathy moved through me in waves. I'd never had a great relationship with Cora, but at least I'd *had* Cora. She may not be mum of the year, or fuck, even the decade, but at least she was still around, and it made me feel shitty that I didn't appreciate her more.

'It's shit,' I said, summing up all that I could in those two words. Like when he'd first told me about his mum, I didn't want to apologise. A sorry wouldn't help or bring his mum back.

'It is,' he whispered and coughed to hide his discomfort. 'So, guess your old man is in this picture somewhere?'

'Yep,' I said, popping the P, mostly to irritate myself. 'Assume yours is too.'

'Yep,' he said, copying me, but not in the mean way he'd mocked my stutter in the past. He pointed at the page again. 'There's Uncle Edward.'

'Where's Lottie?' I asked, not seeing her name listed.

'She's younger than the others. She'll crop up in the later books.'

That explained why she looked younger than the others, but she was the only female surviving parent, so I hadn't been sure. Also, I could never put my finger on whether she'd had a little filler to help her keep her youthful looks.

'There they are.' Ollie pointed to the back row, where two men were standing side by side, similar enough in appearance, but also, you could tell they weren't identical twins. They both had dark red hair, and when I leaned down and squinted, I could see the freckles on their noses. I could tell which one was Griff's dad. Their cheeky grins were the same, and the dimples, too, but there was something so Griff-like in Damien's features it was obvious who was who. Then I looked at *my* dad, who was a stranger to me. I guessed I could see some resemblances, maybe? Our eyes were a similar shape, and maybe we shared the same nose? I didn't feel a connection, though. I just felt sort of numb.

Ollie had noticed my despondency and chosen not to comment on it. 'Let's keep looking.'

'You joining me?' I didn't think he'd want to stick around, dredging up the past.

'I've got a spare hour to kill,' was his reply.

Over the course of the next hour, the two of us searched through the other books we had and looked for any mention of our parents, *The Sect*, and *The Set*, plus anything else we thought could be relevant.

We weren't having much luck.

In the penultimate book, Ollie stopped dead on a page that contained a collage of pictures, of students of different ages around the school grounds. 'Shit, look at this.'

I took my eyes off the sheet I was reading and looked at what he was pointing at. What the...?

'Is that my dad and your mum?' I asked, knowing that it was but wanting the confirmation.

The two of them were standing in front of one of the trees

on the outskirts of the school grounds, with my dad's arm wrapped tightly around Millie. The entire picture looked intimate, and their smiles were secretive, yet happy. 'Guess I just thought your mum was with your dad during their school years.'

Ollie shrugged and pointed to the tree behind them. 'Look there.'

I'd been too focused on the people in the picture to look at the tree, but when I did, I saw their initials JC + MH marked on the bark, in the centre of a carved out heart.

'I thought you said they had an affair when you were younger?' I asked, tracing the heart underneath my fingertip.

'They did, but maybe they were together while at school, too. Dad rarely talks about their time at the academy.' Ollie's voice was low, and I could tell he was mulling the new information over.

'Yeah, maybe...' I wondered what else we didn't know about the past. Probably quite a lot. Fuck, I hadn't even known anything about Hawthorn a year ago other than the fact it was the private school up on the hill, and back then I hadn't known the name of my sperm donor, either.

Suddenly, I had a major urge to seek out the tree from the image. If I found it, then it was real, and it actually happened. *Silly logic, I know.* Especially as that tree was carved years ago and probably didn't even exist anymore.

I got out my phone to send a message, attempting to be discreet about it.

I'M HEADING INTO THE WOODS TO SEARCH FOR A TREE. IF YOU DON'T HEAR FROM ME IN TWO HOURS, PLEASE COME LOOKING FOR ME.

Texting Leo seemed to be the safe thing to do. He was busy all day with swim team stuff, so I knew not to ask him to join me. I'd run into too many issues in the woods in the past and I wanted somebody to know where I was who could rescue me if I needed it. Yeah, I could have messaged Clo or Griff, but I didn't want to involve them until I had a bit more background.

I'VE ALWAYS GOT YOUR BACK, STUTTER.

The message warmed me. The two of us had come so far and I never wanted to lose our newfound relationship, but things were getting real, and I knew I needed to talk about it with him soon. I'd just been putting it off.

I shook myself mentally.

Snap out of it and sort yourself the fuck out.

Yep. Like it was just *that* simple.

FOR SOME FUCKING REASON, I'd allowed Ollie to convince me to let him come into the trees with me.

'I'm going into the woods to find the tree,' I told him after I'd texted Leo.

'Then I'm coming with you,' Ollie announced like it was a given. *'It involves my mum too.'*

'It could take hours.'

'Gives us more time to talk.' He sent a broad smile my way. *'Plus, they call me the tree whisperer.'*

After we'd been searching for an hour, I began to get restless.

'Ollie, don't you think we should head back?' I called. He was up ahead of me, searching every tree he passed.

'No, Sky. We will find it,' he growled out, sounding harsh, but the fact he'd used my actual name told me otherwise. He was frustrated.

'O-kay,' I said, drawing out the start of the word. It was clear to us both I was just humouring him.

'While we search, you want to tell me about what's happening with you and Leo?'

'Not really much to tell,' I grumbled. 'Nothing's changed since we last spoke about it.'

'You going to tell me anyway?' he asked, but I doubted he'd meant it as one. He wanted me to tell him the truth—well, "the truth" he believed to be real because I'd been lying to everybody for so long now I wasn't even sure what was true anymore.

Oh, who am I kidding? I'm still lying.

My thoughts may be snarky, but they were talking straight facts.

'What do you wanna know?' I asked, resigned that he'd be getting his way, but also not doing anything to stop it from happening. I was a sucker. 'There's really not much to tell.'

He looked back at me, choosing his first question carefully. 'How did you get together?'

'It's like we said. On his birthday, we met up and told one another how we felt.' I continued walking, searching the trees. 'Decided to give it a try and see how it went.'

'And how is it going?' he drawled, stopping his search for the tree to look at me.

'Truthfully'—I took a deep breath, gearing myself up to spit it out—'it's going a damn lot better than I expected. We get each other, you know? He knows me.'

His face darkened, his eyebrows furrowed, and his eyes were boring a hole into my head. I felt like I was on trial for a crime I'd never intended to commit.

'I'd be lying if I said I liked it.' He took a step closer as I took a step back. I stumbled on a twig and nearly lost my balance. 'I never thought Leo would be happy with anybody that wasn't Clover.'

I shrugged, not sure how to answer. 'Things have definitely gone differently than I expected.'

My cheeks warmed at the mention of Leo being happy with Clover. I really needed to talk to Leo.

'And you're truly happy?'

'Is that s-so hard to believe?'

'You do know he could never love you?' he asked, but for once, it didn't sound mean or like he wanted to make me miserable. It almost seemed like he hadn't wanted to say it.

'I don't know that, and neither do you. Besides, there's no way to know for sure without me asking him, and funny enough, I wasn't planning to do that anytime soon.'

Ollie started walking again, and I hoped that would be the end of our Leo conversation. Or maybe of any conversation. My wish was answered for roughly two minutes, but then he spoke once more. 'Sky, you know I really am sorry, don't you?'

'Truth?' I asked, and he tilted his head in what I assumed was a nod. 'No, I don't.'

He looked perplexed, and the pure baffled look on his face made me scoff. 'Oh.'

'Well, you've never actually apologised to me, have you?'

'I—' he started, but I cut him off.

'Not that bullshit fake-ass apology you gave at Parents' Day, but a genuine apology. One that was because you meant it and not because people expected you to. Or because Cora basically forced you into it.'

'Your mum can be very persuasive,' he said with a smile. He strode towards me, grabbing my hands in his when he was close enough and locked his gaze with mine.

'Skylar, I am so sorry.' He brushed my hair behind my ear. 'I was a complete dick to you, and I let my hatred for your dad skew my feelings for you. I'd decided before I met you I would hate you no matter what and that I would make you suffer. But when I met you, you weren't what I expected and shit got muddled.'

'What did you expect me to be like?'

He laughed. 'Honestly, Sky, I expected you to be a little money-grabbing whore. Somebody trashy who knew who her dad was and would act entitled now that she was finally at the school she should have always attended.' His whole demeanour was grave, and I could feel his seriousness and practically taste his sorrow in the air. 'As we both know, I was very, very wrong in my assumptions.'

Emotion overwhelmed me, and I had to look away. Glancing down at my feet, I watched as I shuffled them about and disrupted some debris. Anything to take my gaze off of his bright ocean-blue eyes that wanted to drown me with their newfound sweetness and sincerity.

'You get why I'm struggling to believe you?' I said, still facing the floor, so the wind carried away my voice.

'Yeah,' he mumbled but persevered, 'but I'm telling the truth this time.'

'*This time.*'

I wanted to give him a hard time. Wanted to make him squirm. But it seemed at odds with the kind of person I was. Because the fact of the matter was, he'd hurt me. No, not physically—although he most likely instructed the girls to—but mentally, and emotionally, he had.

Ollie's fingers clamped on my chin, pulling my face up to look at him. 'Skylar, I swear on your life that I am sorry and that I'm telling the truth.'

'You hurt me,' I said, going with honesty. 'More than once.'

'I know, and all I can say is that I'm a total dick.' He stepped closer to kiss me on the forehead. A loving gesture rather than a crappy, sarcastic one. 'Forgive me.'

'You can't just demand that I forgive you,' I said with a scoff. 'But I'll think about it. Let's keep searching for this tree.'

Ollie's face lit up, but when he spotted me looking, he covered it up with a scowl just as fast.

We headed off again, searching each tree for the markings, and after what felt like a very long time, Ollie called out from up ahead. 'Over here!'

I ran to where he had shouted from, being careful not to trip on the uneven ground.

'How did you find it?' I called but stopped dead when I saw Ollie—and the dead carcass at his feet. 'What the fuck is that?'

'A goat,' he said, his brows raised in a question of sorts. 'A rather dead one. There was a note attached to the tree.'

Ollie stretched out his arm, a piece of paper in his fingertips.

New Girl. The saying is like a deer caught in the headlights.
I couldn't find a deer, so this sacrificial goat is the next best thing.
After all, somebody here is the scapegoat.

Instantly, I knew the note was from the same person who'd

left the dead rabbit in my dorm room back at the start of summer.

Somebody was the scapegoat? I had no clue who that could refer to. Or why. *Bloody riddles.*

'Is that *the* tree?' I asked Ollie, not wanting to talk about the note or why it was addressed to me. His pale face told me he had no clue what the fuck was going on and he definitely didn't know about the rabbit. There was also no way he knew he was about to stumble across a dead animal.

From the smell, it hadn't been here long. It was a fresh kill, although the displaced leaves and trail of blood told me it hadn't died at the spot we'd found it. *Which, duh, Skylar?* Even I knew there were no goats living in these woods.

'I assume so.' He took the note back. 'But it looks like somebody else got here first. Something was on this tree, but it's been carved out.' He moved out of the way, so I could see what he was talking about. And sure enough, there was a gap in the trunk where somebody had taken a knife and carved off the outer layer.

'Why?' I sputtered, wondering what anybody outside of us two would want with it. We couldn't even be sure they'd carved out what we were looking for. 'Who even knew this was here?'

'Did you tell anybody we were coming out here?' he asked, raising a questioning brow at me. I shook my head violently, but then unease settled in my gut. 'Or what we were looking for?'

I took out my phone to take a picture of the tree. I needed proof of what I was seeing. Plus, I wanted to compare it to the tree in the picture in the yearbook.

Looking at my home screen, I saw that I'd received a message while we'd been searching.

Everything going okay, Stutter?

Shit. I'd forgotten to text Leo after two hours to let him know I was okay. Ollie's words repeated in my head. *Did you tell anybody?*

I had told nobody about the tree, but I *had* told Leo where I was heading. He wouldn't have had the time to do all of that, though, right?

Sure it took longer than two hours to carve out a tree and drag a dead goat. Plus, where would you even find a goat to slaughter on such short notice?

The feeling in my stomach told me I wasn't quite as sure about the answer to those questions as I'd like to be.

Forty-Two

'STUTTER!' Leo's voice called from somewhere nearby. 'Skylar!'

'Leo?' I called back. 'We're—' I paused, unsure where we were. 'Somewhere near if you can hear me.'

'I thought you said you didn't tell anybody we were out here?' Ollie said in an accusing tone.

Leo came into view up ahead and I waved, ignoring Ollie's question. 'Hey! What are you doing out here?'

'You told me to stage a rescue if I didn't hear from you in two hours.' Leo came closer and Ollie growled. 'When you didn't reply to my text, I thought I better head out here and see what was going on. I wouldn't have been so worried if I knew you were with Ollie.'

'It's cool,' I said, waving his worry off. 'We were about to head back, anyway.'

'Were we?' Ollie asked, still giving Leo an irritated glare. 'Because we just found a dead goat and a note addressed to you.'

'Want to go into a little more detail?' Leo asked Ollie, coming to stand beside me, pulling me into his body with an outstretched hand. 'What did the note say?'

Ollie thrust the note into Leo's other hand. 'Read it yourself.'

Leo read the note in silence, then looked at us both with a shuttered off expression. 'What the fuck does it even mean?'

'No clue,' I said. 'Was sort of hoping maybe you'd have a little more insight?'

'Sorry to disappoint you, Stutter, but I've not got a clue.' Leo handed the note back to me and I put it in my inside blazer pocket, so I could add it to the others when I got back to my room. I was amassing quite a collection! Lucky me.

'That's cool because neither do we,' I said with a forced smile. Not that I'd expected Leo to understand the note, but it was irritating to know he couldn't help and that we were no better off than before. 'Shall we head back? It's getting a little chilly out here and there's not much we can do. Plus, that goat *stinks*.'

'What brought you two out here, anyway?' Leo asked, looking around the patch of trees we'd stopped in. 'Seems an odd place to go in search of.'

'Just something we found in an old yearbook,' I told him. 'Means we're on the right track, though, doesn't it?'

'If you say so, Stutter.' Leo laughed at me, but I knew it wasn't meant in a nasty way. He just found it amusing how serious I was taking researching the school's history—he'd told me multiple times how cute he found it. 'Ready to head to dinner?'

'Duh!' I glanced at Ollie and the brittle smile he was faking, and saw a chance to make things a little right in the world. 'Want to join us?'

'Me?' Ollie asked, looking around as if he'd find somebody standing behind him. In the middle of the woods. Nobody around for miles. I rolled my eyes but kept my smile in his direction.

'Yes, you. Who else would I be asking? The goat?'

Ollie chuckled. 'Are you sure?'

'Yeah! The more, the merrier.' I looked over at Leo. 'Right, babe?'

Leo shrugged and gave me an assessing look. 'Right. It'll be good to have you back, mate.'

'Only if you're sure?' Ollie didn't look convinced. 'Won't Griff and Clover mind?'

'Course not,' I said, not knowing whether they would or not but also not really caring either way. 'It's always good to have a buffer from Griff's bullshit anyway.'

The three of us laughed and I could feel the ice melting, just a little.

'That's very true!' Ollie laughed. 'The boy does talk a lot of crap.'

'Proper,' Leo agreed. 'So you coming with us?'

'Yeah, I think I will. Thanks.' Ollie shook Leo's hand and all of a sudden they were mates again, no questions asked.

Boys are weird.

'No problem. Now let's get a hurry on because I'm starving!'

We headed back to school as a unit, the three of us having a stilted conversation about something and nothing, and I smiled inwardly. It felt good, ya know? Like something was once again the way it should be.

And I once again realised how far I'd come in such a short time.

'How's the research going?' Leo looked at me with care shining from his gaze and my heart about melted right there on his bedroom floor. 'Find anything else out since the woods?'

'Not yet.' I grimaced. 'But we will. I've asked Flo to help.'

The incident in the woods had happened a week ago, and yet I was no further in my mission to find out what the fuck happened and why somebody had killed a goat and left me a note.

Hey, that rhymes! I'm a poetic genius. Maybe spending all my time in the library *was* paying off.

'The ancient librarian?' He chuckled. 'Trust you to ask the oldest person here to help you.'

'Flo's a sweetheart! Plus, if she's the oldest person here, then maybe she was here when our parents were and can tell us a lot of what we don't know.'

'You're always the optimist, aren't you, Stutter?'

'Yep.' I nodded, ignoring his laugh. 'I really think Flo wants to help us.'

'Remember, she's employed by my aunt. She won't tell you more than she's allowed.'

I paused in my pacing, once again forgetting that Ms Hawthorn was his aunt. The woman was so hard and poison-faced, it was easy to forget she had a family. A family that cared, even if they acted otherwise a lot of the time. The way they'd all reacted to her being attacked on the day of the swim meet entered my mind. Their worry had been palpable and clearly they cared a little more than they let on.

'True, but a girl can hope, right?'

He nodded, and I went to sit beside him.

'Somebody left her that note,' I said, resting my hand on his thigh. 'And I want to know who.'

'Somebody or some group of people we're not meant to know about.' He lifted my hand and placed a gentle kiss on the back of it, his lips soft. Sometimes he could be so fucking endearing.

'Right,' I agreed. 'But it doesn't stop me wanting to know.'

'You are a nosey one,' he said, and I knew he meant it. I was nosey, and he'd mentioned it before, usually when I tried to earwig at the conversation taking place next to us during dinner.

'True.' I chuckled. 'But you love that about me.'

I'd been joking, but when the words left my lips, the room went quiet. I couldn't keep my hands still, waiting for Leo to speak; to break the quiet that had descended over us. He didn't need to say anything profound or even exciting. Just words to break the tension.

'I think I do,' he admitted, his voice so soft I had to strain to hear him. I stopped my pacing and went to sit beside him on the bed, the shock stopping me from being able to do anything else.

My heart was beating at an alarming rate—so fast I thought it would be visible to him, like a silly cartoon heart stretching my chest. His words, and their meaning, were something we'd been tiptoeing around, neither of us brave enough to voice the truth, and now that he'd put it out there, the full extent of my feelings came rushing to the forefront of my mind.

Shit.

'You do?' I whispered, gulping away my nerves. I'd known the moment would come—that the conversation would come

—but I still wasn't ready for it, or the repercussions that may come from it.

'Honestly, Stutter, I don't know.' Leo looked at me, a mixture of love and grief on his face. 'I think I do.'

'I thought we were just...' I looked away, unable to keep his stare. 'We started this as a revenge plot.'

'We did.'

'Didn't enact a lot of revenge, did we?' I chuckled. 'Pissed off some people, though.'

'Oh, we definitely pissed them off. Rattled some cages. But that's not what we're talking about right now.' His fingers gripped my chin. 'Look at me, Stutter.'

'I'm afraid of what I'll say,' I admitted but turned to look at him anyway. 'This may have started out as a plot and a means to an end, but it's become one of the most real things to ever happen to me.'

'It feels weird to say it, but I feel the same way,' Leo said, his tone cracking. 'What do we do?'

'You're asking me?' I laughed at the absurdity of it all. 'I was kinda hoping you'd tell me what you thought we should do.'

'If you want the truth,' he said, and I nodded. 'Then I don't want us to do anything different. I want to keep seeing where this thing is going between us.'

'Right...' My mind was turning over all the questions I wanted to ask him, wondering which one I should ask first. 'I just want to make sure we're on the same page.'

'Stutter,' he moaned. 'Do I need to talk about my feelings with you?'

'Maybe,' I said with a laugh. 'But only if you want to.'

'I wouldn't even know where to start, but there's one thing I will tell you.'

'And what's that?'

'I like you, Stutter. I more than like you. At least a little.' Leo locked eyes with me and my heart fluttered. When he turned his attention to me, it made me feel like the only girl that mattered. The only one he saw. 'And I hope you feel the same way, at least a little.'

'I'd be lying if I said I didn't,' I admitted, telling him the truth. 'But what about Clover?'

'What about her?'

'Don't be obtuse on purpose!' I punched his shoulder, with no real force behind it. 'I asked a valid question.'

'And I'll turn it back on you,' he replied. 'What about Ollie?'

'What about him?' I joked, my grin wide. 'No, but seriously'—I took a deep breath—'I'm not thinking about him right now. Or the past. Just us.'

'And that's how I feel about Clover.' Leo brushed his fingertips against my cheek. 'In the beginning, you know I was doing this all to piss her off. But then I stopped thinking about her when I was with you, alone, and as time went on, I stopped thinking about her even when she was around.'

'We're nightmares, aren't we?' Leo cracked a smile at my poor attempt at humour. Deep down, I knew it was my fault. Hadn't every film or book taught us that a fake relationship scheme *never* went the way you intended it to? Everybody always ended up falling.

And that was what was happening between me and Leo.

We were falling. *Really* falling.

To top it all off? I wasn't sure I wanted to stop.

Forty-Three

'DO you think if I were a superhero, I'd be a good one?' Griff asked the table, his tone serious.

It was another meal, and another one of Griff's incessant questions where nothing truly mattered—the question or the answer—but we were all expected to answer as seriously as we could. A game of sorts. A way to pass the time.

'What?' I sputtered, accidentally spitting out some of my soda.

'If I were a superhero,' Griff stated slowly, as if *I* was the one who was acting oddly. 'Would I be a good one?'

'How do we define good?' Ollie asked, rubbing his chin with his forefinger, taking the question a lot more seriously than Clover or me. Clo rolled her eyes behind Griff's head, when he turned to look at Ollie.

'You know, like Superman or Batman.' Griff nodded, getting into the topic, glad one of us was humouring him.

'Is Batman good?' Ollie asked, his eyes alight with interest. 'Or is he just a wealthy dickhead with a complex?'

'Hm, good point.' Griff smiled wide. 'We've met a few of them.'

'Wealthy dickheads?' Leo asked, picking up his glass to

take a sip of his water. His other hand was beneath the table, resting firmly on my thigh as he played with the hem of my skirt. 'Or specifically wealthy dickheads with a complex?'

'I mean, you're sitting next to one,' Griff said with a chuckle, and Ollie reached across the table and flicked him on the forehead.

'And you're a prick,' Ollie said.

Clo and I laughed at the three of them, and it felt like before. Actually, it felt better than before because Leo was around. The girls sat at their own table, holding court for all the kids who wanted to get close to them in the hopes they'd get special treatment.

The rest of the meal went well—surprisingly well—seeing as it was only the third time all five of us had eaten together.

'Can I walk you back to your room?' Leo asked, and I quirked my eyebrow, wondering why he had to ask. It was a given.

'Yeah...' I gave him an assessing look. 'Any particular reason?'

He laughed and leaned in to whisper in my ear, 'I just didn't want to give Ollie a chance to ask you.'

'I doubt he would've,' I replied, turning to whisper in his ear. The three others at the table gave us quizzical looks.

'Don't underestimate him, Stutter. He's apologised for real and he's realised how bad he fucked things up with you.'

'Whatever you say.'

'Me and Stutter are getting out of here,' he announced to the table. 'Enjoy the rest of your evening.'

Everybody murmured their goodbyes, then the two of us made our way back to my room.

'That dinner wasn't awful, was it?' I asked, swinging our arms in between us. 'I'd say it was a success.'

'Indeed.'

'You okay? You seem a little down.'

'I'm good, Stutter,' he said, squeezing my hand. 'Just thinking.'

'Well, don't hurt yourself.' I laughed, but he stayed quiet.

My bedroom door came into view. There was a note attached to the door by a knife. A big, sharp motherfucker with a large black grip handle.

'Don't touch that!' Leo said, reaching to stop my outstretched hand from touching the note or the knife.

A chill crept down my spine, and my mind went back to the night I'd found the dead rabbit on my bed. Every time the image entered my thoughts, nausea rose in my gut. We still didn't know who placed it there and, as much as I tried to put it to the back of my mind, it still sat there uninvited.

Not forgetting that I was stabbed with a knife. *Shit.* My hand clenched my stomach, hoping I could keep down the bile threatening to rise. 'Leo,' I whispered, my voice breaking. 'You don't think...?'

'No,' he said, knowing what I meant. 'The police have the knife that stabbed you.'

My breathing became easier. 'That's good then.'

'Let me get the note,' Leo said and I nodded, letting him snatch the note from behind the knife. Then on second thought, he took the knife, too. 'Maybe this will come in handy.'

We entered my room, moving to my bed and sitting on the edge of the mattress. Leo handed the note over and I made quick work of unfolding the piece of paper. Scrawled unfamiliar handwriting greeted me and I had to squint to understand the message.

Skylar, there is so much I wish I could tell you.
Don't trust anyone.
Take this knife for protection.
Hope to see you at the New Year's gala.

There was no name attached. No signature sign-off.

'Who do you think this is from?' I asked Leo, handing the note to him so he could read it better. 'Clearly, whoever it is, plans to go to the gala.'

Leo turned the note over, then refolded it with meticulous care. 'I've got no idea, but I don't think they're friendly.'

'What makes you think that?' I glanced at the knife in his hand. 'They've literally given me a massive knife for protection.'

'I just get a bad vibe,' he said, turning the knife around in his hand, studying it. 'There are two weeks until the gala. I'll keep an eye out for anybody and see if any of the guys know anything.' I nodded. 'It'll be okay, Stutter.'

'You promise?' It was an unfair question—he couldn't promise me that everything would be okay, but I didn't take the question back.

'I promise,' he replied, placing a kiss on my forehead. 'I'll always have your back.'

Shit, when did he become so fucking cute?

STANDING in an alcove in the admin building, Leo and I were holding on to one another tight, minding our own business in between classes, when a cough came up behind us.

'What's going on here?' Ollie walked over to where the two

of us were standing, a sly smile on his face. 'The two of you seem suspicious.'

'We're literally just standing here,' I said, and even though I knew I didn't need to, I took a step back from Leo. Ever since Ollie's apology, things between us were at least civil, and I didn't want to do anything to disrupt the truce we'd found ourselves in.

'Is there a reason why you've bothered us?' Leo drawled, not even bothering to look in Ollie's direction. 'We were having such a good time before you showed up.'

'Really?' Ollie laughed. ''Cause Sky was looking pretty bored when I walked over here.'

Before I could say something to refute Ollie's bullshit, Ms Hawthorn's voice cut across the noise in the hall.

'Son, I'll see you in my office,' she said sharply, addressing Ollie as she walked past. Her face was sour, as per usual, and her grey hair resembled a dish scrubbing brush stuck to the top of her head.

'Did you just call me son?' Ollie demanded, heat emanating off of him, and it was like standing too close to burning flames. He turned to face Ms Hawthorn, who'd halted her stride when Ollie had spoken back.

'Did you just question me?' Ms Hawthorn's glare was piercing.

I stood, frozen. Leo quirked an eyebrow but seemed otherwise unbothered. The whole scenario reeked of *odd*. She'd never called him son before. Why would she? She was his mother's sister, yeah, but that didn't mean she could call him a name he'd reserved in his mind for Millie's memory.

'I did, you bitch,' he snarled, his teeth bared.

'My apologies, Master Brandon,' she said through gritted

teeth, the apology paining her. I felt certain she would rather have eaten live bees than grovel to Ollie.

Ollie faced me, his eyes boring into mine. 'Who the fuck does she think she is?'

I didn't know how to respond. I reckoned it was a slip of the tongue and Ollie felt overly sensitive about it because of the reminders that word gave him. Also, whenever his dad called him Son, it was usually followed by something demeaning or shitty.

'Sure she meant nothing by it,' Leo said, bored of the interruption. 'She's probably losing her marbles, mate.'

'Unlike you to stick up for Winnie,' Ollie said, assessing Leo.

'Does she have children?' I asked, knowing the answer, but mostly wanting to stop the guys from arguing. The two of them hadn't acted the same around one another since Halloween, and I was too much of a coward to ask either one of them why.

'Nope,' Ollie said, his eyes hard. 'The miserable bitch found nobody that loved her enough to want to go on a date with her, let alone fuck her.'

'Oh,' I said and fell silent once more. It was clear to me that Ollie didn't think much of his aunt, but the way he'd said it was filled with so much venom I wondered if there was a history between them I hadn't heard. Leo gripped my arms, pulling me tighter to him again, no longer willing to wait for Ollie to piss off.

'No, guess I wouldn't,' I responded matter-of-factly, too tired to argue with him. And I knew how he'd meant it. I didn't understand money things—not really.

'Let's go to lunch,' Leo said, smiling at me with that tilted lip I loved the most, ignoring Ollie completely. 'You hungry?'

'Am I hungry? Pfft! It's like you don't even know me,' I said with a chuckle. I could always eat—especially if the meal contained cheese or carbs.

'I'll join you,' Ollie said, ready to follow us wherever we headed. 'Where are Griff and Clover at?'

'No idea,' Leo bit out. 'Come on then.'

The three of us headed towards the hall, Leo with his arm wrapped around my waist and Ollie walking on my other side. It was odd to spend time with both of them again, especially as it was Leo wrapped around me and not Ollie, but it also felt right. I couldn't explain it even if I wanted to.

No matter what, there was a tiny part of me still waiting for the other shoe to drop.

Forty-Four

TIME FLEW, and in no time we were all together for Christmas break at Griff's parents' estate.

Ever since Leo and I had found the note—and the knife—we'd theorised who could be behind it, but nobody we thought of made sense.

Ollie would have spoken to me about it in person. Handed the knife into my palm. After his note on Halloween went wrong, I doubted the boy would ever let a note do the talking for him ever again.

Griff also would've handed it over in person, but I also didn't believe Griff thought me to be in enough danger to even think I needed a knife for protection in the first place.

Same went for Clover.

None of it made much sense, so Leo and I had decided we'd wait until the gala and assess the situation from there.

So there we were, the five of us, sitting in the cinema room on Christmas Eve, overloading on sugar and chocolate, *The Muppets Christmas Carol* playing in the background, and Leo's arms hugging me tight to his muscled chest.

'Don't eat too much chocolate,' Clover said, looking in my direction from her position wrapped up in a blanket, sitting on

Griff's lap. 'We've got our final fittings for our dresses on the 27th.'

'Clo, I've had one hot chocolate and I'm about to have some seashells. Think I'll be okay.'

Clo shrugged, her face still uncertain. 'Well, I'm just saying.'

'And I'm saying Stutter looks good no matter what and she can eat the damn chocolates if she wants, dress be damned.' Leo's voice rumbled in my ear and a smile instantly lit up my face. 'We're paying the shop enough that if it doesn't fit, they'll fix it in time.'

Leo always knew the right words to say.

It was because of him that Clover and I even had something to wear to the upcoming gala—it wasn't like I had money lying around to go and buy an expensive dress to wear only once—and it made sense to ask for it as my Christmas present.

Leo had wanted to go all out, but I made it clear that wasn't what the holiday was about for me. Sure, gifts were great and I'd be a liar if I said I'd turn them down, but I'd much rather spend time with him.

What do you get the boy who has access to everything he wants?

Right. There wasn't an answer to that question.

So, I went with the next best thing—I got Leo nothing. Well, that was a small lie. I baked some goodies for him with the help of Clover. Okay, that was an even smaller lie. Clover made most of them and I weighed out the ingredients. Basically, I helped the way I used to help my nan. Meaning, I didn't help whatsoever.

Leo had been so thankful, bless him, and had even tried to compliment my icing of the words, *Merry Christmas*.

'Thanks, babe,' I said, turning around and placing a kiss on his stubbled cheek. 'Appreciate you sticking up for me.'

'How many times do I have to tell you I've got your back, Stutter?'

I laughed. 'Maybe I'll start believing it sometime soon.'

'Probably best if you do.'

THE CHRISTMAS TREE in the living room was the biggest one I'd seen in a home.

It was beautiful.

The white lights glittered and shone off the silver baubles. The white and red candy canes dotted around made me smile, and I couldn't take my eyes off of it all. It was a masterpiece.

It was yet another sign of what money could get you.

Back at home, Mum had bought a fake tree back in the nineties and was still bringing it out year after year, never having been able to afford a real one, or even a larger pre-lit one from the supermarket—even with my discount back when I worked there.

'Hey,' Ollie said from somewhere behind me.

'Hey,' I replied, looking at the silver-glittered star tree topper. 'You okay? Having a good Christmas so far?'

'Yeah, I'm good, thanks. It's been fun, surprisingly.' He came closer. 'I'm glad y'all invited me.'

'Didn't think it would be?'

'Spending time with you and Leo? I wasn't sure if I could cope with seeing it so close without any buffers.' He chuckled, coming up behind me. I looked over my shoulder at him, but he pushed my chin back so I was facing the tree. 'I'd rather talk to your back if you don't mind.'

'If you must,' I said, respecting his wants. 'I'm all ears.'

'Sky, I know I've said sorry already, but I feel like I need to say it again at least another hundred times. You never deserved what I did to you—what I asked others to do to you. I expected you to be so different from how you are, which is a breath of fresh air compared to the girls I'm so used to being around.'

My eyes stayed on the star. 'I don't know what to say.'

'Don't say anything,' Ollie said, taking another step closer. 'I got you a present, but I wasn't sure whether to give it to you in front of everyone.'

'Why? It isn't a dick pic, is it?' I joked, my laughter getting stuck in my throat. *Why make a joke about that, Sky?* We were still trying to navigate the new, tentative friendship we'd somehow stumbled into after his apology.

Ollie moved his hands, swept my hair off from the back of my neck, and placed a cold, thin-chained necklace on me. 'I hope you like it.'

I turned around to look at him. 'Thank you.'

Our eyes locked, and an emotion that felt a lot like love surged through me. Or maybe it was lust? Once again the thought of loving two people at once ran through my head. Leo and Ollie were such different people, but they both made me feel deeply.

'You haven't even seen it yet,' he said, his lips curling up into a smile. 'You're welcome, though.'

'Well, let's go find a mirror,' I told him, heading to the bathroom without waiting to see if he was following me. The bathroom I gravitated towards was fucking massive, the kind that belonged in a wealthy person's house. All marble, with a clawfoot tub in the centre, and it was my dream bathroom.

One wall was a floor-to-ceiling mirror, and I walked straight up to it to admire the necklace.

Fuck. It was beautiful.

It had a silver chain, with a North Star pendant hanging from the centre—a North Star made up of genuine diamonds—and shitting hell, it was the most lavish and expensive gift I'd ever received.

'I saw it and it reminded me of you and that night at the hotel in London,' Ollie said. He must have entered the room while I was observing and admiring the necklace in the mirror.

'Valentine's Day?' I asked, as I remembered that night and all the emotions that came with it. 'By the window?'

'Yeah,' he muttered, uncertain whether he should even talk about that night. 'That night...' He paused, gathering his thoughts. I was looking at him in the mirror, so it didn't feel as intimate, but it felt important. 'That was the night I doubted myself the most.'

'Doubted what?'

'Doubted my plan.' He shrugged, his eyes boring into mine. 'It was that night I realised I was falling for you, too.'

'Too?' Yeah, okay, I hadn't been subtle about how I'd felt back then, but I'd only thought I was falling at that point, and we'd never spoken about it afterward.

'I knew how you felt,' he said, low, guilt lacing his tone. 'It was the reason we knew the plan would work.'

'We?' My heart dropped, and even though I knew who he was about to mention, it didn't make it hurt less. It hurt more having it all confirmed. Things with Griff and Leo were so far away from how they were when they'd planned to make my life hell, but it didn't stop it from hurting.

'*The Sect* and *The Set*.' The way he said the group's official

names told me he was trying to shirk the full responsibility—
or soften the blow a little.

'Right,' I said.

'Sky, at first I wanted so bad to hurt you. To make you hate
the place so much you'd leave Hawthorn and never return, but
then something shifted. I got to know you, and I knew what I
was doing was twisted, but I couldn't stop it. Stop myself. Plus,
by then the train had left the station.'

'I get it, sort of.' I shrugged. 'But what I will never get is
how you could instruct the girls to beat me up.'

'I didn't,' he replied, adamant. His eyes were blazing, and
his words were clear. 'I've told you so many times that
wasn't me.'

'You d-didn't?' I asked, wanting so badly to believe.

'No. Never. I told them to intimidate you, that's all.'

I turned around to face him, touching the star around my
neck. 'Swear?'

'Skylar, I swear on your life. Things just got out of hand.' He
lowered his eyes and shuffled, moving his weight from leg to
leg, which was one of *my* nervous habits, but I guessed there
was a first time for everything.

'Super out of hand,' I said with a small laugh, trying to ease
the tension that had seeped into the room and surrounded us.

'Totally,' he said in a fake, exaggerated accent and I
laughed more.

'I forgive you, you know,' I whispered, wanting him to
know that I no longer held a grudge towards him. If I was
honest, I hadn't for a while. Everything in my life had righted
itself, and I was no longer the same girl who joined Hawthorn
with no friends and no confidence.

'I'd understand if you didn't, but I'm so fucking glad you

do.' He smiled. 'So we're friends, yeah? For real this time, no tricks or plots or schemes?'

'Sure,' I replied. 'As long as you're always honest with me. Even if my outfit is awful and my hair looks like a bee's nest. Got it?'

He chuckled. 'Got it.'

Forty-Five

THE NEW YEAR'S GALA.

Fuck, had it been an entire year since the last one?

So much had happened in the past year, and honestly, sometimes I thought about pinching myself to check I was living in the real world. And sometimes I pinched myself, just to double-check I wasn't making the same mistakes as last year but with a different guy.

Leo and I were attending as a couple, and I was more than ready to make our official debut as a couple. A *real* couple, and not just a fake one like we'd been during Parents' Day. It was hard to pinpoint the moment it'd become real to me, but I was beyond glad it had.

'Hey, babe, you ready for this?' Clo asked, dressed in a stunning, short satin red dress that suited her skin tone perfectly. Even with her hair, she looked killer. The front gave off a conservative vibe, but when she turned around, it was entirely backless until you came to a bow resting just above her bum cheeks. The skirt was a full swing skirt, making the dress fun and flirty. She looked a million dollars.

'You look banging!' I told her. 'The shop did such a good job, didn't they?'

'They've really taken it in at the right place, haven't they? I never even knew I had curves to accentuate.' Clo stood in front of our full-length mirror, assessing herself from head to toe, constantly smoothing her hands on the skirt. 'Do you think I need to thank Leo?'

'Probably best to.' My reply was muffled, a hairpin trapped between my lips. Clover had put my hair into curls, pinning the right-hand side flat to my head, reminding me of old Hollywood starlets. 'He did pay for it all.'

Leo had been super generous, paying for both Clo's and my dresses, plus any alterations we wanted. It was his Christmas gift to me, and it was so bloody thoughtful, I couldn't stop thanking him—in more ways than just with words.

I had followed my self-imposed theme of wearing princess-type dresses. I'd tried Cinderella and Belle, so for the gala I was channelling my inner Tiana. My dress was a dark emerald green, stopping at just above my knees, and it sparkled every time I moved.

I looked over at Clo and smiled. 'Right. I'm ready as I'll ever be.'

'Let's do this shit,' she said, coming forward to loop her arm in mine.

The two of us had chosen to get ready in our tiny closet room away from the boys. It wasn't that we didn't want them around, but we'd just spent the entire Christmas break with them, and it was nice to have time with Clo just the two of us —it didn't happen often these days. Most of the time I was with Leo while she was with Griff, or we were hanging around as a group of five.

Over the past year, the two of us had grown, both as people and as best friends. Yeah, we didn't have the conveniences of Leo's or Griff's enormous bathroom or the space their rooms would have given us, but I kinda liked it. Whether we liked it or not, we were the scholarship kids, and our room was a part of that journey. We didn't need a massive room with pink appliances and furniture to be happy.

We were meeting the boys in front of the hall, and as usual, I felt self-conscious walking across campus with my arm linked in Clo's. Even though I'd attended a couple of Hawthorn events, it still didn't feel natural to me yet to wear such expensive clothes, but the guys had promised me that one day soon it would.

Ollie had said, *'One day, Sky, you'll feel just at home in a formal gown as you do a summer dress.'*

I smiled at the memory. We'd been talking about how I genuinely believed I'd never fit in with the lifestyle they were all accustomed to. Since finding out I was half-Cooper, apparently, I needed to come to terms with wealth—and fast.

'Hello! Earth to Skylar!' Clo called as she waved a hand in front of my face to grab my attention. 'Where did you just go?'

'Err...' I trailed off. 'Just thinking about money, really.'

She shrugged, obviously having hoped for something a little more exciting. 'Fair enough.'

We made it to the entrance of the large auditorium and halted. Leo and Griff were standing outside the hall, waiting for us, and fuck me, Leo looked *fine*. The sight of him made me drool a little, and I attempted to subtly wipe it away without notice. Pretty certain Clo saw me in her peripheral, but she said nothing. Probably because her reaction to Griff wasn't much different.

He may be my relative, but I could accept that he also looked good! He was wearing a dark tartan suit, subtle yet loud, almost. It always amazed me how Griff could stand out and be the centre of attention while still somehow staying under a lot of peoples' radars. There was an effortlessness to him. A quality that was often overlooked.

'You two look amazing,' Griff enthused, taking me in from top to toe and then moving his gaze over to Clo. 'Babe, you are beautiful.'

A flush covered Clo's face, her cheeks going a deep red, a small smile playing on her thin lips. I had to admit, against my better judgement, that the two of them had grown on me as a couple. They seemed genuinely happy, and as long as they were happy, so was I.

It also made me happy that Leo didn't seem to care about how happy they were.

I took my eyes away from them and found myself locking onto Leo's gaze. His eyes had darkened, the way they did during sex—something we'd done more than once after we made our feelings for each other known—or when he was at his most turned on.

'You are fucking perfection,' he growled, leaning down to my ear. Pulling me close, I sighed with happiness and his warmth enveloped me. *Fuck*, falling had never felt so good.

'You scrub up pretty well,' I told him, my voice low. 'But I think I'd prefer it on the floor.'

'Well, isn't that brazen of you, Stutter.' His eyes lit up. 'I like the way you think.'

I wrapped my arms around the back of his neck, pulling his face down so it came level with mine. In my heels, the gap wasn't as big between us and I felt more in my element, more in control.

Our lips crashed together, and we shared a brief, but passionate, kiss before Clo and Griff cleared their throats. 'There'll be time for that later, lovebirds,' Griff said, waggling his eyebrows comically. We chuckled at him and broke apart.

'Oh, leave them alone, dickhead,' Clo piped up, and I cheered in response with a laugh.

'Where's Ollie?' I asked, realising he wasn't with them. 'I thought he was meeting us here.'

'So did we,' Leo said with a shrug. 'But neither of us has heard from him.'

'Strange.' I looked around at the crowd of people entering the school, hoping to spot his brown hair above the throng, but I couldn't see him anywhere. 'Maybe he's already in there?'

'Maybe,' Griff said. 'Only one way to find out. My lady.' He reached out his arm for Clo to put hers through, and Leo did the same for me.

Entering the gala on Leo's arm was a dream. One I didn't want to wake up from.

The four of us headed into the hall, all eyes turning to look as we entered. I spotted Lottie and Edward Hawthorn on the far side, meaning we had to pass everybody else to reach them. They were standing with Henry Brandon and... Ollie?

Why would he be with his dad, without us all for a buffer, if he didn't have to?

Without a word, we made our way over, and we ignored all the glares we were getting.

'Son,' Edward said, pride in his voice, reaching out to take Leo into a bear hug. 'You've scrubbed up nice as always. Skylar, dear, you look beautiful.'

'Thank you!' I reached forward and kissed both his cheeks, while Lottie was hugging Leo with even more force than Edward had. Once she let go of Leo, I kissed Lottie's cheeks, happy to be in her presence. Leo really did have great parents. 'You look stunning!'

'In this old thing?' Lottie laughed, giving me a twirl. 'Hello, Griffin. Clover.'

They murmured their greetings, and I turned to face Ollie and Henry. Ollie's eyes locked with mine and I quirked an eyebrow in his direction as if to say, *Are you feeling okay? Do you need rescuing?*

He looked away, either not understanding my telepathic question, or ignoring it completely.

I caught Griff's eye, and his face mirrored my thoughts; baffled, but keeping quiet.

'Skylar,' Henry said, noticing our presence, as his gaze travelled from my eyes down to my feet, and then travelled back up and rested on my chest. The guys coughed, and Henry once again looked at my face. 'You look absolutely stunning, as per usual. Leo is very lucky to have you.'

'Thank you,' I replied, my gut swirling, feeling uncomfortable. I gritted my teeth, making sure my smile was firm on my face. 'You're too kind.'

'Modest, too,' he said with a chortle. I glimpsed Lottie's and Edward's faces, and the two of them were wearing fake smiles too.

Guess I'm not the only person here lying.

Ollie smiled at me. 'He's not lying, Little One. You look amazing.'

A sharp intake of breath came from my side. 'Can I speak with you in private?' Leo asked Ollie through gritted teeth.

I took a step away from Leo's side to find him glaring at Ollie, super angry.

'Is it important? I'm having an *enlightening* talk with my dad.' The emphasis wasn't lost on anyone. None of it made sense.

Leo didn't let it bother him, though, and insisted, 'Come on, mate. The quicker we leave, the faster we return.'

'I've been summoned.' Ollie laughed. 'We'll be back soon.'

'Don't be too long, you two,' Lottie said. 'The meal starts soon.'

They nodded in acknowledgement and walked out of the hall, already deep in conversation. Even from across the hall, I could tell it was a heated discussion.

What the fuck is going on?

WHEN THE TWO of them came back, you wouldn't have known there had been any tension between them earlier. They were laughing and joking and seemed fine. Okay, maybe not laughing and joking, but they *were* half smiling, which was basically the same thing when it came to Leo and Ollie.

They joined us at the table and, although things were a little awkward at first, the conversation flowed once we'd eaten our starters. So many topics were covered it was hard to keep up. The food was so good I became more interested in that than whatever was being said.

So what? I love food, all right?

After the meal, the band started playing on the stage and I grabbed Clo's hand and pulled her up.

'Come fly with me,' I said with a giggle, dragging her over to the area they'd cleared for dancing.

'Only if you don't tread on my toes,' she replied, laughing.

'No promises. You know how clumsy I can be!' I smiled, so glad to be sharing the moment with her. It really felt as if Clo and I had come full circle since last New Year's. We were stronger and were entering the new year as the best of friends. *Real* friends. Somebody I'd actively choose to spend time with outside of Hawthorn and not just because we were both roped into sharing a bedroom.

We were the first two on the floor, and as soon as people saw us, they migrated our way, no longer afraid to get up and dance. The two of us were dancing away, singing along to all the songs, and just in general, thoroughly enjoying ourselves.

The music changed and became smoother. Slower.

A tall figure came up behind me, causing a shadow, and leaned down to whisper in my ear, 'Shall we dance, Stutter?'

'Didn't think slow dancing was your thing,' I replied, looking up into Leo's blue eyes.

'It's not,' he admitted. 'But I couldn't leave you looking so stunning out here without a partner. Some other guy would've snapped you up.'

'I doubt that.' I laughed. 'But thanks for the ego boost.'

'Sky'—he looked around the room, swaying from side to side—'every guy in here is jealous of me tonight, and it isn't solely because I'm the Hawthorn heir.'

'Oof, I love it when you're conceited,' I joked, looking around to see where his gaze was focused. My eyes landed on Ollie standing off to the side of the dance floor, a wide, shit-eating grin on his face. 'What did you need to talk to Ollie about earlier?'

'Nothing important.' He shrugged my words off and didn't elaborate.

'Important enough you needed to go somewhere private.' My eyes narrowed with suspicion. 'So must've been a little important.'

He let out a deep sigh. 'If you really must know.'

I waited.

'Skylar, there's something I need to tell you.' His voice was distant; his eyes shifty.

'Can I cut in?' Ollie asked, his eyes aglint with some unknown emotion. 'Please?'

'Actually—' I started, but Ollie cut me off.

'Leo won't mind, will you, mate?'

Leo's face said he minded a lot, but for some reason, instead of telling Ollie that, he said, 'Sure. But not for too long.'

Leo stepped out of my embrace, and within an instant, Ollie's body replaced him. He looked just as good as Leo in his suit, and when I'd spotted him across the hall when we arrived, I'd had to hide my natural reaction to just how good he looked. His hands came up to rest on my waist, and I locked my hands together around his neck.

We slow-danced in silence for a little while.

'Did you think this time last year we'd be here?' I asked, saying the thought that had been playing on my mind all evening. The end of a year always made people remember the past, and I couldn't help but compare everything to last year. A year ago, we'd slept together for the first time, and even though I knew it hadn't been real on his part, it still was real for me. 'So much has happened.'

He smiled. 'Who'd have thought Griff and Clover would be a legit couple at this point?'

'Not me!' I chuckled, happy the two of us were getting along without any awkward tension. 'And did you think I'd be with Leo? 'Cause I sure as hell didn't!'

Ollie stopped dancing abruptly, taking his hands off of my waist, and stepped back from me. Instantly, I was cold without his touch.

'Once again, Little One, you've been deceived.' His voice was raised, and the people nearest us stopped to look and listen.

Deceived?

'W-what?' I asked, stuttering in my confusion. I'd been doing so well, barely a stutter in weeks, yet one line from him derailed my progress completely.

I looked at him. *Really* looked at him. There was something off in his eyes. I couldn't place it and I thought I'd seen most of Ollie's emotions.

He looked back at me with equal distrust in his eyes, and the showdown after the fashion show came to mind.

The image was the same, even if the setting was different. I remembered the dark indigo of his eyes, the way they'd burned in hatred, all aimed towards me; a hatred that had been there for long before he'd ever met me.

The way they'd burned in hatred while staring at me while standing over Odette's dead body.

Fuck. What?

Was that an actual memory or my mind playing tricks on me?

I'd had wine with dinner, but I'd eaten enough that I didn't think it would've made much of an impact on me.

'Poor little Skylar. How does it feel being the last to know?'

I broke out into all-body shivers, unable to move. Unable to breathe. My whole body turned clammy at the unearthed memory. 'Being the last to know w-what?'

Surely I wasn't remembering it right? There was no way Ollie was able to get from the pool room to above Odette's dead body without some kind of teleportation.

We were both standing in the middle of the hall with nowhere to hide. Nowhere for me to run, either. All eyes were on us—the sideshow that had taken over the New Year's Gala for everybody's entertainment. I wanted to flee. Wanted to run away from the hate and the stares.

One day soon, I hoped there would be a charity function I

wasn't the main attraction at.

'It w-was *you*.' My voice left me in a whisper, not wanting to put the thought in my mind out into the universe. Vocalising it would only make it worse. 'Wasn't it?'

'It w-was?' he stuttered, a glint of menace in his eyes, the smile he'd had all night disappearing.

'You d-did it. It was you.'

'I d-did what?' His relaxed posture was at odds with the anger on his face as he mocked me—mocked my stutter. It was something I barely did anymore, yet he was able to bring it out of me as if it had never left in the first place.

My thoughts were running away from me. There was no way Ollie had drowned himself on Halloween, and there was no way he could have attacked Ms Hawthorn during the swim team meet. There was no way he had the time to leave the pool room and stab Odette upstairs in the hallway. Something didn't add up.

'You stabbed me?' I shouted, but it came out as a question because of how unsure I was. If people weren't paying attention before, they definitely were after my voice echoes throughout the hall. The band stopped playing and everything seemed to come to a halt.

'Leo can answer that question,' Ollie drawled.

'What's Leo got to do with any of this?' I looked around, hoping to find Leo in the crowd, but I couldn't see him.

Ollie opened his mouth, to explain further, determined to shatter me with his words with a sparkle in his eye.

'Get out of my way!' a deep voice shouted over the whispers, drawing everybody's gaze. 'Move!'

A figure hurtled forward, breaking through the crowd, and everybody, including me, gasped.

What on earth is going on here?

Forty-Six

MY EYES COULDN'T MAKE sense of what they were seeing.

In front of me, hatred still shining in his eyes, was Ollie. The Ollie we'd been with the entire evening, but unlike the events of the fashion show, he was no longer aiming the hatred in his eyes at me.

He aimed it at the newcomer who'd burst into the hall.

The newcomer who was the spitting image of him—another Ollie. His eyes were wild, his hair unbrushed and wayward.

What. In. The. Actual. Fuck?

'Skylar,' the unkept Ollie said, his eyes pleading with me to understand. 'I promise this isn't what it looks like! This imposter took me last night. Locked me in a room tied to a bed. I've only just been able to break free.'

'Skylar,' the Ollie who'd been at the gala all night said. His eyes, so similar to the clone standing next to him, were dark and cold. 'This guy's the imposter!'

'But who the f-fuck is he?' I asked, not knowing who to believe.

Ollie had a twin? How had I not known Ollie had a twin?

Nobody had ever said anything about it to me. Even when I'd made my jokes about my dad and Griff's dad, who were twins, banging Ollie's mum and her sister, also twins.

Because Ollie being a twin *was* the only logical explanation. The only thing in the hall at that moment that made sense. Right?

The crowd had hushed. Barely a whisper could be heard, the only noise coming from glasses being refilled and drinks being slurped. Everybody was watching the drama unfold. If I wasn't living in the centre of it, I'd have done the same.

I looked frantically around the room, trying to find Leo or Griff and Clover, but the only person who stood out from the crowd to me was Henry Brandon, who looked as shocked as I was. His face had paled, and there was a mixture of shock and fear in his eyes.

It made no sense. How had the news shocked him? Surely if anyone knew, it was him.

'I have no idea,' Ollie on the right shouted, running his hands through his hair. A gesture I always associated with a frustrated Ollie. 'Who the fuck are you?'

'I'm Ollie,' he said with a smirk, enjoying himself. 'Aren't I?'

He locked eyes with me, the question aimed at me, and I wished somebody would rescue me from the situation I'd somehow found myself in.

My eyes kept flicking between the two of them, watching a game of fucked up tennis.

Shit, was this a case of an *actual* impostor? I'd seen a movie like that once—a horror film, of course—where somebody came along and tried to steal someone else's entire life. A chill ran down my spine. Who was the real Ollie?

'I-I...' I trailed off, blindsided. 'Tell me the truth.'

'Just tell them, Son,' a voice called from the crowd, but it wasn't Henry's. The voice came from a female and everybody in the crowd gasped, turning around to find the culprit.

I could tell *whoever he was* didn't want to tell. That he was getting a kick out of this—a sick thrill—and wanted to keep up the charade for as long as possible.

Ms Hawthorn stepped into the area, breaking free of the circle of onlookers.

'Orlando, tell them,' she demanded, her voice scratchy. She'd worn an evening gown, but all I could see was a modern-day Ms Havisham of sorts. Dressed in a musty dress—decaying. Bitter.

Orlando?

What in the actual fucking fuckity fuck is happening right now?

I watched *Orlando* squirm before covering it up with a swagger. 'Fine,' he called out, addressing everybody in the room, a wide smile on his face. 'The game is up. The name's Orlando Hawthorn. Pleased to meet you.'

The room erupted. The sound of people moving and gossiping, rising, but all I could focus on were the two boys standing before me.

Leo appeared at my side, grabbing my hand tightly, an urgent whisper on his lips. 'We need to get out of here, Stutter. I don't trust this one bit.'

'Wait up!' Orlando called to us, his eyes locked on the spot where our hands met with great curiosity. 'You not gonna tell her?'

Leo shifted beside me, ready to turn and leave without giving Orlando an answer, but I was also curious and didn't want to leave without knowing.

'Tell me what?'

'Leo's been keeping secrets from you, Little One.' Orlando's smile was pure evil. 'More than a few.'

My stomach dropped, a thought entering my mind unbidden and unwelcome. Did I need to revisit every memory I had with Oliver? Did I need to doubt every interaction and worry that I'd been with Orlando instead?

Leo tugged my hand again. 'I can explain everything, just not here.'

Did Leo already know about Orlando? My heart splintered at the thought. Orlando had said while we were dancing I'd once again been deceived, and once he revealed himself, it made sense he was talking about himself. But what if he wasn't talking about himself at all?

'We can't leave without Ollie,' I said, looking across at the boy with an equally shattered heart. He was so shocked he still hadn't moved. Lost in his own head, unable to hear Griff and Clo, who were trying to get him to move, talking to him, urging him to leave with them.

'Nobody's going anywhere until we get to the bottom of this!' Edward stepped forward, brandishing a gun.

What in the actual fuck? Since when did tight-laced Edward Hawthorn own a *gun*?

'Dad?' Leo's voice wobbled, and his grip on my arm tightened. A bruise would form within hours. 'What are you doing?'

'Stay where you are!' Edward shouted, using a tone I'd never heard from him. Serious, powerful, and in charge.

I'd never seen a real-life gun before. Even growing up in a poorer area, I'd never witnessed something like this or been in close proximity to unhinged people holding deadly weapons.

The knife strapped against my leg was useless—the saying never bring a knife to a gun fight reverberating through my skull.

'Oh, *Uncle Eddy*,' Orlando mocked, moving his hand to his jacket pocket. 'I wouldn't do that if I were you.' Orlando pulled out a gun and aimed it at Edward, the two in a life-or-death stand-off.

Nobody knew what to do. Everyone was frozen in time; in disbelief.

'Don't do it,' Leo shouted, but he was no longer facing his dad. He was looking at Orlando, a plea in his gaze. 'This wasn't a part of our deal!'

My heart fully shattered, pieces scattered all over the floor, the pain indescribable. Worse than being stabbed by your ex-boyfriend's secret twin brother.

'Your d-deal?' I sputtered. 'You knew about him? About this?'

A single tear trickled down my cheek, the only indication of my broken soul. How had I put myself in the same situation twice? Did all the boys at Hawthorn lie and deceive to reach their goals? Or was that the case for every boy everywhere?

Leo glanced at me, a brief look, before he turned back to the stand-off a short distance away. 'Stutter, I can explain when there's not a gun pointed at my dad's head.'

Orlando had pointed his gun at Edward and all hell broke loose. People tried to flee, but they only ended up running into one another. A few made it to the doors, but they were closed, heavy, and nobody was thinking straight.

I was so distracted by those fleeing, I forgot the terror unfolding in front of my face.

A gunshot rang out.

A scream.

Then, silence.

Epilogue

TONIGHT WENT EXACTLY how I wanted it to. With a few minor glitches, true, but who could have guessed that he would ruin everything we had worked so hard for. I thought I'd taught him better than that.

You'd think everybody involved at Hawthorn would know they weren't going to be getting a *happily ever after*. That nonsense only ever happened in fairy tales and films.

They didn't deserve their happily ever after. Not after everything they'd done.

They disgusted me.

Every single one of them.

The boy shouldn't have ruined the plan like that. He too needed to be taught a lesson.

In the future, I couldn't trust anybody but me to enact my plans. They say if you want a job done, it's always best to do it yourself.

I wouldn't be forgetting that again.

It was a shame about the Cooper boy. I'd been quite fond of his father, after all. Shame his bitch of a mother didn't do what was right. She was a selfish cunt who deserved everything that happened to her. I only wished she'd suffered more.

It really had been a shame about her husband's death.
Now I guess you truly could say like father, like son.
Yes.
The New Year was starting exactly how I'd wanted it to.
With a bang.

To be continued and completed in *Disturbed*

Afterword

WANT MORE HAWTHORN ACADEMY WHILE YOU WAIT?

Scan the QR code below for bonus chapters.

If you would like to join my newsletter to stay up to date with my upcoming projects, then scan the QR code below.

Acknowledgements

Thank you so much to everybody who stuck by me during the journey that has been Hawthorn Academy rewrites!

The list contains, but is not limited to:

- Megan

- Cress

- Fiona

- Billie

- Els

- Jess

- Jess

- My family

I'd also like to say a special thank you to my readers and I promise that the wait for the conclusion of this series is in sight... kind of!

About Katie Lowrie

Katie Lowrie is a Brit who loves to read and write.

A list in no particular order of her greatest loves:

- Henry VIII and the Tudor era
- Her baby cat, Cress
- Musicals
- Disney
- Cheese

She loves to stalk people online (in a good way) and understands if you do too.

instagram.com/katielowrieauthor

goodreads.com/katielowrieauthor

facebook.com/katielowrieauthor

bookbub.com/authors/katie-lowrie

Also by Katie Lowrie

Hawthorn Academy Series:

Disorder

Disease

Disturbed

Rebels of Hollowdale High:

Haven at Hollowdale High

Hero of Hollowdale High

Heirs of Hollowdale High

Hated at Hollowdale High

Heartless at Hollowdale High

Re-Imagined Series:

Key of Cunning (**Dark** Billionaire Romance)

The Sleep Eternal (**Dark** Mafia Romance)